CHRISTMAS SCARF MURDER

Carlene O'Connor
Maddie Day
Peggy Ehrhart

Kensington Publishing Corp.
www.kensingtonbooks.com

KENSINGTON BOOKS are published by

Kensington Publishing Corp.
119 West 40th Street
New York, NY 10018

All Kensington titles, imprints, and distributed lines are available at special quantity discounts for bulk purchases for sales promotion, premiums, fund-raising, educational, or institutional use.

Special book excerpts or customized printings can also be created to fit specific needs. For details, write or phone the office of the Kensington Sales Manager: Attn.: Sales Department. Kensington Publishing Corp., 119 West 40th Street, New York, NY 10018. Phone: 1-800-221-2647.

The K and Teapot logo is a trademark of Kensington Publishing Corp.

First Hardcover Printing: October 2022

First Paperback Edition: October 2023
ISBN: 978-1-4967-3723-6

ISBN: 978-1-4967-3724-3 (ebook)

10 9 8 7 6 5 4 3 2 1

Printed in the United States of America

Contents

CHRISTMAS SCARF MURDER

Carlene O'Connor

This book is dedicated to my cousin, Heather Kraus. Although your journey is not going to be easy these next few years, I am with you all the way and so proud of you. Sending all my love and light to you.

Acknowledgments

Thank you to my editor, John Scognamiglio, my publicist Larissa Ackerman, my agent Evan Marshall, and all the wonderful staff at Kensington Publishing who work so hard behind the scenes on our books.

Chapter One

Siobhán O'Sullivan stood in the kitchen of her new stone farmhouse, leafing through holiday recipes and insisting yet again to her younger brother Ciarán that Santy wasn't bringing him a tractor for Christmas, when her husband opened the front door and poked his head in. She grinned. *Her husband.* Six months of marriage and it still didn't feel real. Cold air blasted in from the outside but when Siobhán caught the worried expression on Macdara's handsome face, she dropped all plans to scold him. "The Grinch paid a visit to the elder care home," he said. "The residents have all been robbed."

"You're joking me." The Kilbane Elder Care Home was small and exclusive, catering to wealthy clients. It was located outside of town in a beautiful Victorian-style house painted a cheerful yellow. They had immaculate gardens and every year the

grounds were decorated to the hilt for Christmas.
Mechanical reindeer, Santy and his sleigh, and every
tree on the property would be wrapped in colorful
lights. It was so lavish it nearly made Siobhán wish
she was old enough to move in. Siobhán had been
looking forward to visiting this year, only she was
worried her younger siblings Ann and Ciarán would
insist they decorate their new fields in the same over-
the-top fashion. Although they certainly had the
room, and Siobhán loved decorating for Christmas,
she wanted something rustic and cozy. White lights
and a gorgeous wreath for the door—maybe a candle or two in the window. And this year she wanted
them to cut down a live Christmas tree. It was their
first Christmas in their new house, and she wanted
that Christmas tree smell. Macdara's news was troubling indeed. Who would rob an elder care home a
fortnight before Christmas? "The poor pets," Siobhán said. "Is everyone alright?"

"Thank goodness no bodily harm to anyone,
but I hear some very dear items have been taken
and everyone is in quite the state."

"It's a frightening thing when you're robbed,"
Siobhán said. "They must feel so vulnerable."

Macdara nodded. "I know it's your day off, but
nearly everyone has taken their holidays."

"Say no more, Detective Sergeant," Siobhán
said. "I'll get me uniform on."

Macdara nodded. "I'll be out here, Garda
O'Sullivan." He leaned in for a kiss.

"You promised you'd stop doing that before
brekkie," Ciarán said. "I've lost me appetite. Again."

They broke apart and laughed. "You already
had two Irish breakfasts," Siobhán said.

"It's a good thing I horsed them into me before all the mushy stuff then isn't it?" Ciarán responded. Macdara clapped Ciarán on the back. Ciarán shook his head. "I deserve a tractor for this."

Siobhán wished she could bottle this moment, their first Christmas as husband and wife, as a family. The entire brood would fill the house to celebrate. Even James, Gráinne, and Eoin, Siobhán's siblings who were now independent and free, would camp out for the holidays. Her minor siblings, Ann and Ciaran, seemed to be adjusting to living at the farm house, and chuffed to the bits that they each had their own room. James, Gráinne, and Eoin were still living above the bistro, with a lot more room to spread out. Was it only seven months since they moved from above their former bistro in town to the farm house? The time had flown by. Siobhán's five siblings had lived with her ever since their parents had been killed by a drunk driver in a road accident eight years prior. There were times she wanted to keep them with her forever. Luckily, Eoin and James were building a farm-to-table restaurant on their new farm, and Grainne was chomping at the bit to help decorate it. Siobhán saw them nearly every day. Family was everything, and yet change was inevitable. But this year, they would all be together. And to top it off they had invited their friend Doctor Jeanie Brady, an esteemed state pathologist, to join them for Christmas dinner. She had let it slip that she was taking the holidays off this year and had lamented not having a big family to share it with. Siobhán was thrilled when she accepted the invitation. She handed Ciarán back his Christmas wish list. *Tractor* was the only item on it. "Better add to this," she said. "Unless you want a toy tractor."

Ciarán shook his head. "Typical."

His voice was so low now, puberty well underway. And she still wanted to squeeze his cheeks until he howled. "Isn't it enough we get to decorate our very own tractor for the parade?" Siobhán asked. Before they'd moved outside of town Siobhán was barely aware there *was* a Christmas tractor parade. James had grown close to some of the lads participating and had volunteered the rest of the O'Sullivans to decorate a tractor, most of them either a Massey Ferguson or a John Deere. They were due at Bill Casey's farm this weekend to map out a route and start decorating.

"Not unless I get to drive it home after," Ciarán said. "I could mow the field."

He said "mow the field" but she could see it now. Ciarán O'Sullivan speeding down the road in a tractor, mowing everything in his path but the grass. *Never.*

"There will be plenty to keep you busy when Eoin breaks ground on the new restaurant," she said. "You'll forget all about tractors." Their property used to contain an old dairy barn, and although it had burned down as a result of arson, Eoin was going to rebuild and open a farm-to-table restaurant. Luckily, the property was zoned for both home and business. Not that the O'Sullivans were turning into instant farmers, none of them had the experience for that, but Eoin was already making connections with local farmers to source the needed ingredients, and in the spring they were sure to at least have a vegetable garden and chickens. It was crazy how swiftly one's life could change, and although somewhat dizzying, Siobhán was finding it an absolute thrill.

"I'll never forget about tractors," Ciarán said. "I was born to ride."

"What about a hoverboard?" Macdara asked. "Santy might be able to spring for one of those."

Ciarán shook his head. "What about a Vespa?"

"No," Siobhán said.

Ciarán put his hands on his hips and lasered her with a look. He was nearly as tall as she was. "You have one."

"I'm an adult."

Ciarán threw his arms open. "Where am I going to ride a hoverboard? In the field?"

Siobhán sighed. The truth was, they were probably eventually going to have to get a tractor. But it would be the family tractor and not teenage transportation.

"You need new hobbies," Siobhán said. "Why don't you do some brainstorming to see what you fancy?"

"I'd rather do some *barnstorming*," he said. "With my new tractor."

Siobhán laughed. "No planes, tractors, motorcycles, cars, or scooters."

"Fine," Ciarán said. "I'll take the hoverboard."

Siobhán threw Macdara a look and he was smart enough to grimace. "We'll have to see what Christmas morning brings. Why don't you get out our decorations while we're gone?" She went to pat Ciarán on the head, but he ducked and she swiped air. It was starting to look like there was going to be more than one Grinch in Kilbane this year.

*   *   *

As they pulled into the lovely manicured grounds for the elder care home, Siobhán found herself wishing it was under happier circumstances. The yellow Victorian house with blue trim popped against the green fields. Lush hedges and gardens created a virtual Eden that blossomed in the spring, but during the Christmas holidays the grounds were transformed into a winter wonderland, complete with a snow machine. Everyone was hoping it would snow for real this year, although most likely it would not, and Siobhán had a feeling the snow machine would be on the ready. Lovely paths curved through gardens featuring sculptures, birdbaths, and benches. A gardener stood near a hedge with clippers, shaping the first row into large candy canes. The residents were so lucky to live in such a magical place—the thought of anyone robbing them infused her with anger. Respect for one's elders was an ironclad principle for the O'Sullivans, something the young ones of today seemed to be sorely lacking.

The house sat on a high elevation with sweeping views of hills and valleys, topped off by the curves of the Ballyhoura Mountains. Christmas decorating was full steam ahead, with large plastic bins lining the drive and in the gardens, overflowing with garland, lights, and bows. Despite the cold, residents stood outside in hefty robes and slippers clutching mugs of tea or coffee, some with winter coats, others with just hats and scarves. The minute the pair exited the vehicle they could hear the excited hum of voices. It seemed the break-in had infused the home with a bit of excitement. "The guards are here," an old man shouted, waving both his hands at them as if he was stranded on an island and they were circling above in a plane. Siobhán waved back; it was nice to feel appreciated. Soon they were surrounded by the elderly residents, all speaking at once.

"They stole Oscar's cane, it was a lovely carved wood with a golden handle."

"And Nuala's precious emeralds."

"Nuala doesn't have precious emeralds, she's messing with us!"

"I did so have emeralds and they've been stolen!"

"Maybe it was your grandson. He's always poking around."

"Wash that filthy mouth out with soap, you old grouch you, or I'll do it for ya."

"Don't forget Rory's money."

A short man with black spectacles stepped forward, brown eyes blinking rapidly. He looked like an adorable little owl. "Five hundred euro they took. All me Christmas shopping money." He held his hands palms up as he shrugged. "What am I going to do now? This may be me last Christmas and I have to buy gifts for all me grandkids."

Siobhán's heart squeezed. "I'm so sorry. We promise ye, we'll get to the bottom of this."

"Don't forget me scarf!" A plump woman in a flowered bathrobe and a bulky winter coat shoved her mobile phone at them, forcing them to look at the screen. On it was a hideous red scarf with green shamrocks.

"Beverly, Beverly, Beverly. Didn't you hear the lads warn you about that scarf?" an old man said.

His winter coat was zipped up but he was wearing pajamas and slippers. He pointed to a spot in the distance. Siobhán followed the trajectory to a bird-bath where a pair of twenty-somethings were standing, a lad and a colleen. It was nice to see young people on the grounds. He turned back to the plump woman. "That scarf is too long. You could wrap a giraffe's neck with that yoke and still have bits hanging off him. Did they not warn you about long scarf syndrome?"

"Bah humbug," Beverly said. "It was a work of passion. You can't stop knitting when you're filled with passion!"

"Excuse me," a small voice next to Siobhán piped up. She turned to find a tiny older woman clasping her hands together. She was dressed in a lovely fawn coat and had a red bow pinned in her hair. Her lips were heavily lined in a matching red. "I'm missing me Virgin Mary statue. It isn't very dear, but my mammy bought it at the very first Christmas Market in the town square, with money she'd been saving the whole year. It has great sentimental value. I can't bear the thought that it's gone."

Siobhán placed her hand on the woman's shoulders. "What's your name, luv?"

"Sinead."

"Sinead, your statue sounds most dear to me."

Sinead nodded, her eyes filling with tears. "It makes me feel connected to her. It's like a piece of her."

Siobhán nodded. She understood very well. They had items from her late parents that felt like an extension of them. "We'll treat your missing statue with the same value we do the missing emeralds." She turned to the crowd. "I promise ye, we are going to do everything we can to sort this out." They all started talking at once. "Give us a minute to speak with the director," Siobhán said. "We'll soon have a proper sit-down with each one of you." The residents stopped jabbering and stared, their faces stamped with hope. Siobhán wondered if she should warn them that it's very rare to recover items in a robbery. The thieves could be long gone by now.

As they took a step toward the house, an exuberant border collie bounded their way, a small stuffed elf in his mouth. He dropped it at Siobhán's feet and looked up expectantly.

"Aren't you a wee dote," she said.

"That's Max," the man with the black spectacles said. "He's visiting us for the holidays. Insanely intelligent that dog."

"And adorable," Siobhán said, leaning down. "Who's a good boy?" The dog, tongue hanging out, swung its head in Macdara's direction.

"Did you see that?" Macdara said. "He's smirking at me." Macdara bent down to pick up the elf. The dog snatched it and laid it at Siobhán's feet. "Cheeky dog," Macdara said. "He only wants you to throw it."

Siobhán picked up the elf. "Do you hear that, love? Me husband is jealous of a dog."

"I think we might be looking at our thief right here," Macdara said, wagging his finger at the dog.

Siobhán laughed, then tossed the elf. The dog bounded after it. Macdara gave her a look. "You're like a magical woodland creature," he said. "Beloved by all your subjects."

She punched him in the arm. "Sort yourself out, maybe you'll grow on him."

"Look at that complexion," a sweet old woman to her right said, reaching for Siobhán's face. "Like a bowlful of cream."

"And that gorgeous red hair," another cooed. "You must have all the lads after ya."

"And all the woodland creatures," Macdara repeated, ducking as Siobhán went in for another swipe.

Her hair was really auburn but it was futile correcting people. Some saw the world in a variety of shades, others couldn't be bothered. Siobhán didn't dare look at Macdara, she knew he was struggling to contain a cheeky response. She'd give it twenty-four hours before he made a "bowlful of cream" remark.

"What a handsome detective," a woman cooed at Macdara. "How can you catch criminals with that sweet face?" Siobhán rather enjoyed watching his sweet face turn red and wondered if that made her a terrible person.

"They've designated a meeting room inside for our inquiries," Macdara said, clearing his throat and trying to regain a sense of order. "But first we need to speak with the director."

"Are you going to take fingerprints?" Sinead said. "I've only seen it on *Law & Order*."

"It's highly likely that the thieves wore gloves," Macdara said politely.

"What a pity," she said, smacking her lips together. "I so wanted to see how you do it." Sinead seemed to shrink with disappointment, her little red bow dipping lower and lower.

"I'll see what I can do," Macdara said. "It never hurts to arrange a little demonstration." She grinned, stood on her tiptoes, and planted a kiss on Macdara's cheek. He turned red enough to make the lipstick marks blend in with the rest of his face.

"You can handcuff me too," she said. "I don't mind." She held up her wrists for inspection. Macdara took out his mobile and walked a few feet away to make a call. He returned moments later with a satisfied grin on his face. Before Siobhán could ask him what that was all about, a middle-aged man in a gray suit was hurrying up the path toward them, his hand extended.

"I'm Cathal Ryan. You must be DS Flannery, we spoke on the phone." He was a handsome man with salt-and-pepper hair feathered back and light blue eyes accentuated by his blue tie and pocket square.

"That would be me," Macdara said. "And this is Garda O'Sullivan. Otherwise known as me wife," he said with a wink.

Siobhán groaned. Cathal raised an eyebrow. "Six months so far," Siobhán said.

"Congratulations." He flashed perfectly straight and white teeth.

"So far?" Macdara said.

"Do tell us about the break-in," Siobhán said.

"Follow me," Cathal said. They headed up the path toward the house, and soon stepped onto the grand front porch. More bins were stacked, one on top of the other. Some had their lids off, revealing a mountain of garland and lights. A pair of lads, also in their early twenties, stood nearby, listening to opposing decorating instructions from a nearby cluster of residents.

"String them up along the roof."

"No, not the roof, are ya mad? String them along the windows."

"What about the porch rail, lads? Do you think ye can manage that?"

Max, stuffed elf in his mouth, sat happily watching the hubbub.

Cathal nodded to the younger men. "We have a small group of lads from the tractor parade helping us decorate this year."

"Grand," Siobhán said. She hated her next thought—it was cynical—but she had a job to do. Could one of them be the thief? There were four of them, a lad and a lass by the birdbath and two lads on the porch. Were they good-hearted young people giving their time to their elders at Christmas, or scheming thieves out to swindle them? It was the nature of this job that one had to explore all possibilities. Cathal pointed to the front door. It was made of oak, with a small stained-glass window and a lion knocker. Siobhán loved it. "Isn't this gorgeous," she said to Macdara, pointing out the lion. "Maybe Santy will bring me something similar."

"Maybe you should be happy with your bowlful of cream," Macdara retorted.

She gently punched his arm and he laughed. That hadn't taken long at all. Why hadn't she placed a bet with someone?

Potted holly bushes flanked the door, and a pair of gas lamps were situated on either side. She could imagine how gorgeous it looked in the evening, with the flames dancing.

"This is the main entrance," Cathal was saying. "There were no signs of a break-in per se."

"When did the robbery occur?" Macdara asked.

"Residents only discovered their items missing this morning after breakfast. But we assume it took place yesterday when most of us were on an outing."

"An outing?" Siobhán asked.

He nodded. "We helped decorate the town square for the Christmas market," he said. "It was a grand day." His grin soon faded. "Followed by a wretched morning."

"Wait," Siobhán said. "Why did you add—per se?"

"Pardon?"

"You said there were no signs of a break-in *per se.*"

Cathal nodded. "Yes. I'd rather show you once we go inside."

"Did you have any items stolen?" Macdara asked.

Cathal shook his head. "I live off-site, and nothing in my office seems to be disturbed. To be honest, I'm puzzled. Only five residents had items stolen, and coincidentally they were the five residents that remained behind."

That didn't sound at all like a coincidence to Siobhán. "Their items were nicked yesterday but you're only reporting it today?"

"I'm afraid it was chaos here last night—in a good way. There was the excitement of the residents who returned from the market showing off their wares, along with the items we shopped for the five who remained behind, and then we had carolers pay us a visit. A few residents said they had been looking for their items, but misplacing things is a common occurrence around here. It wasn't until the next morning, when they started looking in earnest and comparing stories, that we realized this was more than just misplacing their things, that they had indeed been robbed."

"Do these same residents usually stay behind?" she asked.

"As a matter of fact they do," Cathal said. "Are you saying the thief knew that? That this was an inside job?"

"Anything is possible," Macdara said. "We've a long ways to go before we make any declarations."

"Perhaps he or she was interrupted before they could steal from anyone else," Siobhán said. "But why start with the five residents who were still on the grounds?" That seemed very risky. Was this a thief who thrived on the risk of being caught?

"Downright nonsensical if you ask me," Cathal said. "The money and emeralds—if they exist—makes sense alright. But he also steals a cane, a scarf, and a Virgin Mary statue? Who does that?"

"What makes you so sure the thief is a he?" Siobhán asked.

"Pardon me, Garda," he said. "You're quite right. The thief may be a member of the fairer sex."

Inwardly she groaned at the phrase, but she wasn't here to school others on their parts of speech. "How long was the outing to the Christmas market?" Macdara asked.

"We were there for most of the day," Cathal said. "From ten a.m. to four." The town square hosted the Christmas market every year, attracting nearly the entire village. It was a grand place to find Christmas gifts, drink hot cocoa, and sample desserts. It was also where the yearly Christmas pantomime was held. Every year the pantomime was based on a fairy tale and given a comedic twist. The panto, as everyone called it, was a cherished tradition. Siobhán's own brood had starred in one a few years back, a hearty rendition of "Jack and the Beanstalk."

"All but the five residents who had items stolen attended the outing?" Siobhán asked.

"That is correct," Cathal said. "Our front office manager, Nancy Martin, remained on-site as well."

"And what about our four young volunteers?" Siobhán asked. "Where were they?"

"They accompanied us on the outing as well," Cathal said. "Although I did not have eyes on them the entire time. They're young, they come and go as they please."

"And no one saw any strangers on the property?" Macdara asked. "Or did anyone hear anything odd?"

Cathal sighed. "Unfortunately, aside from the one room in the house I need to show you, no one reported hearing or seeing a single thing out of the ordinary. It was as if we were robbed by a Christmas mouse!"

"More like a Christmas rat," Macdara said.

One of the young lads approached. He had a mop of blond curls and intense blue eyes. He wagged his finger at them. "If you wanted someone to blame, look no further than the house manager, Nancy Martin."

Chapter Two

Cathal stepped toward the young man, a look of panic stamped on his face. "Blame Nancy Martin? Whatever do you mean?"

"I was at the Christmas market but returned early," the young man said. "None of them heard a thing because Nancy was blasting Christmas songs." He glanced at Siobhán and Macdara. "Nancy is a mad one for the Christmas music." He grinned, stuck out his hand. "I'm Finn Doyle, Nuala's grandson."

Cathal leaned in. "Nuala is the resident who claims she's missing precious emeralds."

Finn's face clouded over. "If me granny says her emeralds were stolen, then her emeralds were stolen."

"Of course, of course," Cathal said. "It's just . . . none of us have ever seen these emeralds."

"I've seen them," Finn said. "We were just arranging to have them valued."

"Then why hasn't she shown them to anyone else?" Cathal asked.

"Because they're too valuable to flash around." Finn tapped his forehead with his index finger. He turned to Macdara. "That's why she kept them in her safe. And now they're gone."

Cathal turned to Siobhán and Macdara. "He's right about one thing. Nancy does like to blast her Christmas tunes."

"Who doesn't?" Siobhán said. She loved everything about Christmas.

"How many residents and staff do you have in total?" Macdara asked.

"We only have twelve residents at a time," Cathal said. "Our waiting list is very long."

Macdara leaned into Siobhán's ear. "Should we put our names in now?"

"Definitely yours," she said. His chuckle warmed her insides.

"As far as staff goes, we have myself and Nancy, the kitchen staff, and housekeeping." He began to count on his fingers. "Fifteen of us in all."

"Fifteen," Macdara said. That was a lot of suspects.

"But many are on their Christmas break," Cathal said. "Leaving three kitchen staff and three housekeepers." That certainly helped. "We're lucky to still have Nancy." He leaned in and lowered his voice. "Her husband is running for mayor of Cork in the spring. Isn't that exciting?"

Siobhán didn't get particularly excited about

politics and was trying to come up with a polite response when they were interrupted. "Don't plug it in yet!" They turned to see a red-faced old man berating a young lad with red hair and spiked fringes. He jumped at the reprimand, jostling the string of Christmas lights in his arms. He wrapped the string around his neck and mimicked hanging himself. Max barked and began tugging on the Christmas lights.

"I'm only messing, Max," the redheaded lad said. "Let go." The dog immediately let go. "Good boy." He removed a treat from his pocket and the dog snatched it up.

"Quit horsing around," the old man yelled. "Do you think this roof is going to decorate itself?"

"I'm not deaf." The young man removed the string of lights from his neck. He towered over the old man. "You don't have to shout."

"Ease up," Macdara said. The young man shot a withering look at the detective sergeant but took a step back.

Cathal, eager to move on, pointed once more to the ornate front door. "As I've mentioned, there were no signs of a break-in at our front or our back doors. They are the only two means of entry."

"Except for the roof." The comment came from another young lad stepping onto the porch. His head was shaved, but he had a baby face and fawn-brown eyes. "Down the chimney?" he added. "Santy and his sleigh?"

"Shall I introduce you to our helpers?" Cathal said.

"Makes us sound like elves," the one with the shaved head said with a laugh.

"No one would ever mistake you for an elf, Shane Boyd" Cathal said. "And that's your introduction sorted." He pointed to the redhead. "Michael Walsh." Still holding the lights, Walsh bowed. Max barked, then dipped down.

Macdara pointed at the dog. "Did he just bow?"

"He's fierce intelligent," Michael said. "Meet my wonder dog, Max."

"And I'm Bonnie Murphy." The one female of the group of young ones stepped onto the porch. She had gorgeous black hair cascading down her back in waves. She was probably six years younger than Siobhán. Bonnie flashed a million-dollar smile at Macdara and he blushed. Siobhán cocked her head, mostly surprised at the ripple of jealousy that went through her.

Macdara turned to Cathal. "Is there no security system on the grounds?" He glanced at the dog.

"He's not a guard dog," Michael said. "But I do believe he would have barked if he sensed a criminal around." He paused. "Unless they had biscuits. Then I'm afraid he would have let the Grinch himself rob everyone blind." He winked.

"Thanks for the tip," Siobhán said. She would have to buy some for Trigger, their Jack Russel terrier. He could use a little training.

"Right so," Finn said, looping his arm around Michael Walsh and nodding to Shane and Bonnie. "It's off to Casey's with us."

"Bill Casey?" Siobhán asked. He was the farmer hosting the tractor parade. Her brood would be there as well. Had they not been interrupted by this theft, she would have been there herself.

"Aye," Finn said. "The four of us are going to

have the best-dressed tractor in Kilbane." Max barked. "Make that the five of us," Finn said, ruffling the dog's head. "Isn't that right, Max?" Max barked enthusiastically and everyone laughed. The foursome bounded off the porch, whooping and singing as they headed off the grounds. Max trotted along behind them.

"To be young again," the old man on the porch said as he watched them go.

Cathal removed his pocket square and dabbed around his mouth as if trying to prevent the wrong words from coming out. "Back to the security system," he said. "Someone shut down the main panel." He gestured for them to come closer, then opened the front door and ushered them in.

The first thing that struck Siobhán when she stepped inside, was that it really did look like a proper home. The floors matched the lovely dark wood in the front door, as well as the moldings and the rails of a curved stairway just past the foyer. Parlor doors flanked the left and the right sides, and both were thrown open. A cozy sitting room was situated to their right, and a grand library with a crackling fireplace to the left. A pair of binoculars sat on a coffee table in the library room. Siobhán could imagine how lovely it would be to sit by a cozy fire and gaze out the large windows with the binoculars. She was starting to think the golden years were the ones for her. Cardboard boxes were stacked everywhere you looked. Writing in thick black marker gave away their contents: XMAS DECORATIONS.

Cathal closed the door and pointed to an electronic panel on the wall. "Yesterday morning before we left for the market, this security panel was working fine. When the thefts were reported, I ran to check it, and it was turned off. As you can see it's back on now, but the security company confirmed that it was off for twenty-four hours."

"How many people know the security code?" Macdara asked.

"All of the employees." Cathal bowed his head. "I know you'll have to investigate everyone but in my opinion, not a single one of my employees would ever be involved in something so heinous."

"What about the windows?" Macdara said, stepping into the library and approaching the panes. "Do they open from the outside?" He gave a little tug. They did not open.

"We seal them shut in the winter," Cathal said. "Otherwise it gets too drafty."

Macdara nodded. "Is it possible our thief had a key to the house?"

Siobhán wandered over to the table and picked up the binoculars. Heavy curtains obscured most of the windows so she put them down again. She turned and stared across the way at the security panel. Had this been an inside job?

Cathal chewed on his lip. "I'm afraid it is possible. We usually change the locks after a resident leaves. But it's been a very chaotic year with a lot of changeover and I've been waiting for a locksmith. Everyone is busy these days, it's taking forever."

"As soon as we're done having a nose about, I'll call a locksmith for you," Macdara said. "If you didn't need the locks changed then, you certainly do now." He stepped closer to the front door and carefully examined the edges and the lock. "No signs of distress." He turned to Cathal. "What is the usual procedure for visitors to gain entrance?"

"You ring the bell," Cathal said, stepping back onto the porch and pointing to a buzzer to the right. "One of the staff will greet you and sign you in."

"Were there any visitors during the break-in?"

"I'm afraid you'll have to check with Nancy. She keeps the visitor log."

"What about other types of visitors?" Siobhán asked. "Deliverymen and the like?"

"They're not required to sign in," Cathal said. "But we do have a security camera." He dropped his hand. "Unfortunately, it only works if the panel is powered on and I've already mentioned someone had turned it off."

"We'll need to look at your visitor log for the entire week leading up to the theft," Macdara said as they all stepped back inside.

Cathal nodded. "As I said, Nancy Martin keeps track of all that."

"Guards are on their way to dust for fingerprints," Macdara said. "Let's make sure that lovely lady with the red bow gets a demonstration."

"That's Sinead," Cathal said with a nod and a smile.

Siobhán looped her arm through Macdara's. "That is very giving of you, Santy," she whispered.

He winked. "You can thank me later, Mrs. Claus."

She gently pushed him off. "I'm way too young to be Mrs. Claus."

Cathal glanced at his watch as if wondering how long all this banter was going to take. Siobhán stepped away from Macdara and straightened her spine. "Shall I show you why I said that nothing has been disturbed *per se*?" Cathal asked.

He headed down the hall and they followed. He passed a grand kitchen filled with people in white aprons rolling out dough. The scent of sugar wafted out. "They're making Christmas biscuits," he said. "To die for." A few of the bakers waved and Siobhán waved back.

A woman pushing a cleaning cart blocked their path. Her dark hair was ensconced in a white headband, salt-and-pepper tendrils spilling out of it. "Christmas biscuits, bah humbug!" She thrust her index finger into the air. "Did you not hear me say that ever since this Christmas biscuit craze started up, I've seen ants in the residents' rooms?" she said. "Ants!"

"The residents know not to eat in their rooms, Mrs. Grady," Cathal said.

The woman shook her head. "Well, they're still doing it. I've found ants in several rooms, carrying crumbs back to their queen!"

"It is Christmas," Macdara quipped. "Even the ants are getting into the spirit." Mrs. Grady gave him a withering look. "Horrible," he said. "Ants are a horrible, horrible nuisance."

She nodded and let out a puff of air, disturbing a tendril of hair, making it fly up. "They certainly are."

"I'll have another word with the residents," Cathal said.

"You do that," she said. "I'm a housekeeper not an exterminator." She shoved the cart forward, muttering as she left.

"Here we are," Cathal said, stopping at the last room on the floor. "This is the recreational room—the main place where our residents come to relax, play games, watch telly." It was a generous room with plush sofas, a large television mounted to the wall, comfy chairs, and tables—but they were all pushed back against the walls, leaving the middle wide open. "This is why I said *per se*. When we left for the market, this room was set up as per normal—nothing was pushed against the walls. At first I thought it was Mrs. Grady, that she wanted to vacuum the center of the room—although I thought it was quite puzzling—I couldn't imagine her moving all this furniture on her own. And when I brought her to the room to show her—she was furious. She insists she didn't leave it like this and I believe her."

It was very odd indeed. What kind of thief would take time out to shove all the furniture to the back of a room?

"It's befuddling," Cathal said. "We leave for a few hours to do some Christmas shopping and the whole place goes mad!" They returned to the foyer. Cathal pointed to the formal sitting room on the right. "I'll go find Nancy. Please have a seat."

Siobhán and Macdara waited in the sitting room, listening to the sound of the cuckoo clock ticking precious minutes away. It felt like an eternity before they heard the sound of heels clacking on the floorboards. Moments later a smiling woman with chestnut hair and a flowery dress appeared. "I'm Nancy Martin," she said, extending her hand as Siobhán and Macdara stood. "Welcome to the Kilbane Elder Care Home." She was a beautiful woman with light brown eyes and a generous smile.

They shook hands and introduced themselves. Cathal Ryan popped up behind her. His hair was mussed up and there was red lipstick next to his mouth. Macdara and Siobhán exchanged a quick look, then composed themselves. Were the two having an illicit work affair? Nancy gestured for them to sit again. "Shall we?" The moment they sat a young woman in an apron and a sunny grin entered with a golden tray. On it perched two cups of tea and a generous plate of Christmas biscuits. She set them on the coffee table. Sugar cookies with colorful icing, they were in adorable shapes: trees, Santy, and reindeer.

"That's so kind of you," Siobhán said. "You shouldn't have." Macdara already had half a Santy stuffed in his gob. He finished two more before the group of five came in, insisting it would be rude not to sample one of each. Introductions were formally made: Nuala, Rory, Beverly, and Sinead. Oscar, the man who looked like an adorable owl, was the last to enter, slamming his walker down with each step.

"I. Want. My. Cane." He spit out the words, accentuating it with a *thunk* of the walker hitting the floor. "It was from my pilgrimage in Spain. It was a gorgeous dark wood with a golden head. When you find the thieves and our stolen property, I'm going to take me cane and beat them over the head with it."

"There's no need for any of you to take matters into your own hands," Nancy said. "The guards are here to sort that all out."

Cathal patted the pockets of his blazer. "My keys," he said. "Has anyone seen my keys?"

"I completely forgot," Nancy said. "The morning chef mentioned finding a set of keys in the kitchen this morning."

"I'll go speak with him."

Nancy grimaced. "I'm afraid he's gone for the day."

"What?" Cathal's voice flashed with anger. "Where did he leave my keys?"

"I can't say for sure they were yours," Nancy said. "I didn't get a good look at them."

Cathal raised an eyebrow. "Who else is missing keys?"

"You're right, of course," Nancy said. "They must be yours. Everything happened so quickly— the chef mentioned the keys and then one by one residents discovered their items missing. I completely forgot. I'm sorry."

Cathal straightened up and he seemed to be wrestling with his response. "You'll have to be a bit more organized when you're the mayor's wife," he said with a wry smile.

Nancy frowned for a moment and then laughed. "Don't tell me husband. He's a nervous wreck as it is."

"Do your missing keys include your car keys?" Siobhán said.

"Yes," Cathal said. "Why do you ask?"

Macdara nudged forward. "Where do you park your car?"

Cathal's eyes widened. "Are you saying my car might have been stolen? A getaway car?"

"Did you drive it to the market this morning?" Macdara asked.

Cathal shook his head. "No. We had a rental bus."

"Let's see if we can find the keys first," Nancy said. "Then look for your car."

"I'll check with the kitchen staff," Cathal said.

"I'll help." Nancy turned to Siobhán and Macdara. "You'll be alright on your own?"

"They've got us," Beverly said. "What do you think we're going to do? Bite them?"

Oscar eyed the dwindling plate of biscuits. "Are you sure they're here to help?" he asked.

Macdara slouched in his chair; Siobhán knew he'd been poised to go in for a fourth. Nancy and Cathal exited the room and the residents began to gab. And gab. And gab. And gab. She glanced at the clock on the wall. Nearly an hour and a half had passed, and although Siobhán and Macdara's heads were now filled with stories of their children and grandchildren, and days of yore, they were getting nowhere. She assumed Cathal had found his keys and his car, for he had completely disappeared. She felt for these folks, they were dying for a bit of company, and this was an exciting day. But she was itching to get out of here. Perhaps she wasn't quite ready for her golden years after all.

"It's been lovely chatting," Siobhán said. "But we must focus on the case now."

"Absolutely," Macdara said. The relief in his voice was palpable. He too had been having a hard time cutting them off or getting the residents to focus, and the plate of cookies had been reduced to crumbs.

"I don't know what you're doing here," Nuala said to Beverly. Siobhán recognized Beverly as the plump woman in the flowery house coat, the one who had shown them the photo of the uber-long scarf. "All you had stolen was an ugly scarf."

Beverly gasped. "It was not ugly. It was hand-made." Nuala rolled her eyes. "Obviously the thief didn't think it was ugly, now did he?"

Before Siobhán and Macdara could put a stop to it, four residents were once again yelling over top of each other. Sinead sat quietly, working her rosary beads. Suddenly, "Silent Night" blared through the room. *Ironic.*

All heads turned to Nancy, who was planted next to the stereo. When she had their attention, she turned the volume down. "Now," she said. "You're behaving like spoiled children. The guards need to file their report and they don't have all day." Apologies went around the room.

"Did you find Cathal's keys?" Siobhán ask.

Nancy nodded. "The housekeeper had them."

"And his car?" Macdara said.

"Safe and sound."

That was a relief. But Nancy and Cathel had been gone an awfully long time. Siobhán was start-ing to wonder if the missing keys was a ruse, an ex-cuse to be alone. It was risky to get romantically involved with work partners. Then again, given she and Macdara worked together, she was one to talk. However, Nancy was married. To a possible future mayor, no less. An affair wouldn't just be messy, it would be reckless. Hopefully there was nothing going on between her and Cathal. It was the nature of her job that made Siobhán suspicious of everything. She had to be careful not to jump to conclusions. "We just need each of you to write down the items that were stolen from you, and anything else you can remember from the time of the theft."

"You want us to write all of that?" Oscar held up a gnarled hand.

"We can write it for you," Siobhán said. "We'll be setting up individual interviews."

From somewhere in the room a phone rang, making them all jump. It was Nancy's. She moved into the foyer as she answered. Siobhán could still hear her talking. "Yes. Who? Oh, yes. Yes, they're still here. What? My word!" When Nancy returned to the room her face was a portrait of a woman about to panic.

"That was Bill Casey—"

Macdara stood. "From the tractor parade?"

Nancy nodded. "The tractors were on a dry run for the parade, and there's been a terrible, terrible accident!"

Chapter Three

It was not something they saw every day, an entire country road lined with tractors in all shapes, sizes, and colors at a complete standstill. A few sported the beginnings of Christmas decorations, lights, bows, and garland, but most of them had not yet been adorned. There were twenty tractors in all. The tragedy became evident when they reached the fifth tractor in line, a green and yellow John Deere. A man was lying on the road directly behind the tractor. Lying on his back, his head was tilted at an unnatural angle. A red scarf with green shamrocks was wound around his neck, the end disappearing into the wheel well. Witnesses said he had been lifted off the tractor and slammed down onto the road. The scarf must have become entangled with the wheel. The victim had spikey red hair. "It's Michael Walsh," Macdara said.

"Michael Walsh," Siobhán repeated. Sorrow

gripped her as she stared at his red fringe. No matter how many times she'd seen death, it always jarred her. Just hours ago this lad had been on the front porch of the elder care home, messing around with his friends and introducing them to his dog. Siobhán edged forward and stared at the scarf as a refrain ran through her mind. *Long scarf syndrome.* She recognized the scarf immediately. Long enough for a giraffe, as hideous in person as it was in the photo. "It's Beverly's stolen scarf," she said.

Macdara stared at the scarf, then at their victim. "Do you think he's our thief?"

"I don't know. Why would he flaunt the stolen scarf when he knows we're on the case?"

"Perhaps he liked the danger," Macdara said. "Or he had little faith in our detecting skills."

"We'll find out soon enough. At least Jeanie is in town." They'd already placed a call to Doctor Brady and she was on her way.

A burly man approached, covered in layers of flannel, sporting a tweed cap and handlebar mustache. His eyes were red, and he was still trying to wipe tears off his face with the back of his hand. When he composed himself, he wiped his hand on his trousers and stuck it out. "I'm Bill Casey."

Macdara shook hands and introduced them.

"Mr. Casey," Siobhán said. "You're the host of this year's tractor parade."

"Call me Bill. Indeed, Garda. And before you begin your investigation there's something you need to know."

"Go on," Macdara said.

"He wasn't wearing that scarf this morning, or when we started on the route."

"You mean he put it on during the ride?" Siobhán asked.

"I don't see where he would have put it," Bill said. "You can see his coat isn't that bulky."

They all looked down at his coat. He was right. It was a mere jacket. "You're sure he didn't have it tucked inside and you just didn't notice?" Macdara asked.

Bill shook his head. "I've been doing this tractor run for years. I always warn them about any loose bits of clothing, especially scarves. I definitely would have noticed."

"What are you saying?" Siobhán said. "He obviously had the scarf stashed somewhere."

Bill Casey nodded. "That's the other troubling bit to the story. We'd just begun the practice route when a blue Toyota came flying past, driving on the field. They screeched to a halt in front of yer man, here." He gestured to the victim. "The driver exited the vehicle, and others could see them head-to-head having a chat. After a minute, the driver got back into the car. It was after that yer man was wearing the scarf. The car screeched away and your one started his tractor. And then . . ." He slapped his hand over his eye. "I'm lucky I was in the front and didn't have to see it. The ones who were directly behind him are in shock. The minute he moved the tractor forward, he was yanked out of his seat, flipped into the air, and landed behind the tractor. The only saving grace is that he went quick."

Siobhán crossed herself. "Was it a man or a woman who got out of the car?"

"That's another odd thing," Mr. Casey said. "We don't know."

"Pardon?" Siobhán tilted her head.

"The person was dressed in costume. I thought it was one of the panto actors. But usually those costumes are colorful fairy-tale creatures and whatnot. This person was head to toe in a long brown robe, like a monk. His or her face was completely obscured by a brown hood."

"Tall or short?" Macdara said.

"Medium," Casey said. "Or was he short? I don't know. I didn't see him myself. The fella behind Michael just said he saw a brown hooded robe. It happened so fast."

"This person got out of the car, approached our victim, and chatted for a moment?" Siobhán asked. She was trying to picture it.

Casey nodded. "And we believe this pretend-monk placed the scarf around his neck."

Michael Walsh must have known the person. If a total stranger tried to place a long ugly scarf around her neck, she certainly wouldn't have worn it. And Michael Walsh knew all about Beverly's stolen scarf, she'd been showing pictures of it to everyone who would look. Why on earth would he flaunt it in the tractor parade?

Siobhán turned to Macdara. "Did you hear one of the residents say something this morning about long scarf syndrome?"

"I certainly did," Macdara said. "And I know you do not like coincidences."

"I do not like coincidences," Siobhán confirmed. Not a bit.

"I'm lost," Bill Casey said.

"This scarf was made by a resident of the Kilbane Elder Care Home," Macdara said. "It was reported as stolen."

"Everyone was talking about how long and dangerous it was," Siobhán said.

Bill Casey shuddered. "It's bad enough if this was a terrible accident. But if it was deliberate?" He shook his head. "Who would do such a thing? A fortnight before Christmas?"

Siobhán and Macdara remained silent. It was a question that had a depressing answer. Nearly everyone, given the right circumstances, was capable of doing such a horrible thing.

"We'll need to talk to the drivers of the tractor directly behind and in front of Michael Walsh to see exactly what they observed," Macdara said.

Casey nodded, then pointed to a cluster of folks up ahead in the field. "They're all there. Everyone is in shock."

"I'd never met Michael Walsh before this morning," Macdara said. "Was he new in town?"

"Visiting from Monaghan, I believe," Bill said. "Shane Boyd and Finn Doyle invited him."

"Were they friends?" Siobhán asked.

Bill shook his head. "I asked the group to nominate someone as our special guest this year. Every year we have a guest tractor for the parade. They read about his wonder dog, Max, in the local paper and contacted him. He seemed thrilled with the idea. And that dog is something else."

"Where is the dog?" Siobhán asked.

"He's riding in my tractor at the head of the parade," Bill said. "I have an enclosed cab; we felt it was the safest place for him." He bowed his head. "A dog that smart? He's going to know his owner is gone."

They paused for a moment of silence.

Shane and Finn. All three of them had been at the elder care home. Did this have anything to do with the theft? Were the three unwise-men in it together? Had this murder been a long time in the making? Why would they want him dead? Was he threatening to tell on the others or trying to claim a bigger share of the stolen goods?

"To tell you the truth, I should have told him he couldn't participate," Bill said. "I should have trusted my gut."

Macdara edged forward. "What did your gut say?"

"Michael took the tractor for a joy ride yesterday and ran over my neighbor's hedges. Me neighbor was livid." Bill shook his head. "He was a bit too cheeky and impulsive. I should have disqualified him."

"What is the name of this neighbor?" Macdara asked.

Casey looked startled. "I don't think he wants his name dragged into this mess."

"I'm afraid he won't have a choice in the matter," Macdara said.

"Cathal Ryan," Bill said.

"The elder home director?" Siobhán asked.

"The one and the same," Casey said.

"Odd. He didn't mention it and we were standing on the same porch with Michael."

"I'm telling ye, he was quite livid. He threatened the lad." Casey looked stricken. "I don't mean he

threatened to do anything like *this*. He just warned
him that if he did it again he'd answer for it.
Michael enjoyed trouble. You could see it in his
eyes." He stopped then shook his head. "I'm not
saying he deserved it. He was just a young lad with
a troubled past. He could have sorted himself out.
Tis a terrible, terrible day."

"A troubled past?" Macdara asked.

Bill nodded. "Apparently, he'd been released
from jail a year prior."

"Jail?" Macdara said.

"Some trouble after a breakup. A bit of stalking,
I believe," Casey said. "The type of lad that when
he becomes fixated on something or someone, he
just can't let go. At least that's what I heard."

"Hold on," Macdara said. "With that kind of
past he was allowed to volunteer at the elder care
home and be a special guest for your parade?"

"I swear to ye, I had no idea he was volunteering
at the elder care home," Bill said. "But even so—
he was supposed to have turned over a new leaf.
There was a whole article on him in the newspaper. The jail he was in paired lads with homeless
dogs, so they could rehabilitate each other, like.
Yer one's dog turned out to be brilliant. Walsh was
featured for teaching the dog over a thousand
words. Can you believe that?"

"A thousand," Siobhán said. She turned to Macdara. "How many words do you think Trigger
knows?"

Macdara gave her a look and turned his attention back to Bill Casey. "Listen," he said. "We have
to cordon off this scene. I want the tractor in front
of Michael's and behind Michael's to remain

where they are. But we'll need the other tractors to disperse. The ones in the front should continue straight ahead, and the ones in the back should turn and exit in the other direction. Even if they have to take the long way back to your farm."

"Does this mean the tractor parade is off?" Bill looked sheepish, but there was concern in his voice. "All the money we collect goes to local charities. It's been a tough year for a lot of folks and they're really counting on us."

"Let's take it one step at a time," Siobhán said.

"Such terrible business," Bill said. "I don't know how I'm going to break the news to his family. They had such high hopes that he was really turning his life around."

"We'll contact his family," Siobhán said. "But I'm sure they'll need and appreciate your support."

"And we're going to need everyone to write down their account of the car that stopped," Macdara said. "Any detail, no matter how small."

"Absolutely. We'll go back to the farm and do it."

"There are no CCTV cameras in this area," Macdara continued. "But check to see if anyone happened to be using their mobile phone during the route—maybe someone got a photo of the number plate, or even better a shot of the person who got out of the car."

"They weren't supposed to be on their phones whilst driving the tractor," Casey said.

"We all know people don't always follow direction," Siobhán said. "Let's hope that's the case with their phones."

Understanding dawned in Casey's eyes. "Right, right. George Halligan was the fella in the tractor behind Michael. I did give him my permission to keep his phone on him. He's expecting his first-born any day now. He texts with the wife nonstop."

Macdara nodded and jotted down the name. "Did everyone show up this morning for the practice run?

Casey shook his head. "All but three."

"And who were they?" Macdara asked.

Bill Casey was ready for the question. "Finn Doyle, Shane Boyd, and Bonnie Murphy," he said. "They were supposed to be on Michael's team but they never showed up."

Chapter Four

Finn Doyle, Shane Boyd, and Bonnie Murphy. Macdara's face did not show his surprise and Siobhán did her best to hide hers. At the elder care home Finn had announced he was going to the tractor-parade rehearsal and the foursome had exuberantly left together. If Michael was the only one who participated, where had the other three gone? But maybe the better, and more troubling question, was—*why?*

Macdara gave a nod to Bill Casey. "Have the lads to clear out now."

"What about Max?" Bill asked.

"Can you mind him for now?" Siobhán asked. "I'm sure Michael's family will want to take him home."

"Of course." He gave a shy smile. "He's a great dog." Casey called out instructions to the tractors and soon all but the one in the front and the back of the tractor Michael had been operating were pulling away from the scene. Garda cars had arrived, the road was being blocked off, and a cordon was set up around the body.

"Here's Doctor Brady now," Macdara said, nodding as she emerged from a guard car.

"Greetings," Jeanie Brady said. Her eyes landed on the body. "This wasn't what I had in mind when ye invited me to Kilbane for me Christmas holidays."

They all exchanged a wry smile; humor was a healthy way of dealing with the horror of murder probes. Jeanie Brady was looking fit and slim. Normally a mad one for pistachios, she had adopted a "clean eating" lifestyle and was no longer tempted by the nibbly things in life. Her curly brown hair had been cut short, accentuating her cheekbones. She may have lost several stone but she still had the same vibrant personality, and wicked determination when it came to her work. Siobhán had no idea what to buy her for Christmas, for her original plan, a lovely scarf, was now completely out of the question.

"What do we have here?" Jeanie approached the body and knelt. Siobhán and Macdara stayed at the edge of the road and remained silent. Having worked with Jeanie Brady for years they knew it was a rhetorical question. She took her time studying the scene, then shook her head and crossed herself. She gestured them over. "My exam will need to confirm it, but he appears to have broken his neck. At least his passing was relatively quick. Why on earth was he wearing a scarf this long?"

"It gets stranger," Siobhán said. She filled Jeanie in on their visit to the elder care home, the thefts, the discussion of long scarf syndrome, Bill Casey vowing that Michael was not wearing a scarf when they started the procession, and the monk-costumed stranger that pulled alongside him in a car.

"That does make for a very strange day indeed," Jeanie said. "Long scarf syndrome is no joke. The most famous case being that of Isadora Duncan."

"I'm not familiar with the case," Macdara said. "Was it one of yours?"

Jeanie Brady threw her head back and laughed. When she composed herself, she wagged her finger at Macdara. "Are you joking me?"

Macdara shifted uncomfortably. "I want to say yes. But . . . no."

"You're too young, although that's no excuse for not educating yourself." Jeanie gave him a stern look before winking at Siobhán.

Siobhán laughed along with her. Macdara poked her in the side. "An expert on Isadora Duncan, are ya?"

"Not quite an expert," Siobhán said. She turned to Jeanie. "Why don't you give us a refresher."

Macdara tapped Siobhán on the shoulder. "You could always start us off. I'm sure Doctor Brady will forgive you for being 'not quite an expert.' "

"Now," Siobhán said, "I wouldn't want to steal Jeanie's thunder."

Jeanie stepped back in. "She was an American dancer. The tragedy occurred in Paris, in September of 1927—"

"Hold on," Macdara said. "You expected me to be familiar with a case in Paris from 1927?"

"She was quite famous," Jeanie said. "Talented, and some say ahead of her time."

"Go on," Siobhán said. "I want to hear the story."

Jeanie glanced at Macdara as if to see if he had anything to add. He kept his gob shut. "She was in Nice, France, visiting a friend who was a mechanic and some say a paramour. She wore a long hand-printed silk scarf made by a Russian artist and given to her by another friend, Mary Desti. It was a cold night and just before they departed Mary tried to convince Isadora to wear a cape to keep warm. Isadora refused but said she would wear the scarf instead. Her last words were: 'Goodbye. I am off to love!' When the scarf became entangled in the axle of the motor vehicle she was traveling in, she was yanked from the car. Like our poor fella here, she broke her neck and was killed instantly."

"My word," Siobhán said, gently touching her neck. "I may never wear a scarf again."

"One does need to be careful," Jeanie said. She turned her attention back to the body. "Because of the length of this particular scarf, our victim here wouldn't have felt the tug on his neck until it was firmly ensconced in the wheel and it was too late. By then it was enough to lift him out of his seat and deposit him on the road." She shook her head. "It's a very sad day indeed." They all bowed their heads for a moment, honoring the gravity of the moment. "But we have a job to do, don't we?" Jeanie said. She looked deep into the wheel well. "I'm telling you right now, strange visitor aside, I don't see any way to prove this was anything other than a horrible accident. Even if someone admitted to handing him the scarf, it's not murder unless they also admit to depositing the end of the scarf into the wheel well of the tractor." She turned to the wheel well and peered down into it. "Although . . . given the apparent length of the scarf, it could have been done easily and quickly." She sighed. "If this was foul play, it was very clever indeed."

"A perfect murder," Siobhán said.

Jeanie nodded. "Without a witness, there's no way for me to prove it." She turned to look at the tractor behind Michael's. "How did the fella on the tractor behind him not see anything?"

"According to Bill Casey, his wife is expecting a baby and apparently, he's been glued to his phone," Macdara explained.

"You'd think if a car stops and a monk gets out, that would catch your attention," Jeanie said. "Can we speak with him now? See what he witnessed?"

"Let's do it," Macdara said. He pointed up ahead where a small cluster of people remained. "We asked him to stay behind, let's hope he listened." They headed up the road toward the group.

"I'm so sorry to interrupt your holidays," Siobhán said. She'd meant for this Christmas to be special, a celebration.

Jeanie waved her hand as if it was nothing. "Yours are interrupted too and I still have an invitation to Christmas dinner, do I not?"

"You certainly do," Macdara said.

"You'd better catch this killer then," Jeanie said. "I intend to break me diet for Christmas Day."

"But you said there's no way to prove this was anything other than an accident," Siobhán said.

Jeanie held a hand up. "I said there's no way for

my postmortem to prove it. What you need is a full confession from a killer."

"Is that all?" Siobhán said. Macdara patted her on the back.

"It's the least we can do now for the poor lad," Jeanie said. "Is he a local?"

Siobhán shook her head. "He's from Monaghan."

"He's an ex-stalker with a famous dog," Macdara added. "Max."

"Ex-stalker?" Jeanie said.

"Apologies," Macdara said. "That's not confirmed. Bill mentioned he'd been brought up on past charges for not leaving an ex alone. Rumor is he often had unhealthy fixations. Then Max came along and it gave him something productive to concentrate on. He was turning his life around."

"Max supposedly knows over a thousand words," Siobhán said. "That's a few more than me husband." She gently shoved Macdara as he laughed.

They reached the huddled group. "George Halligan?" Macdara called. The shortest man in the group turned. He was in his early thirties with a thick dark fringe feathered back.

"That's me."

"We'd like to speak with you for a moment," Macdara said.

"Can you join us back at the scene?" Jeanie added. "I'd like to do a reenactment."

"Not a bother." George headed back with them to the tractors. "I wish I could have done something. It happened so fast. I'm still in shock."

"That's understandable," Siobhán said. "Take a deep breath."

They reached the scene of the accident. The

body was now covered, but from the look on George's face, he was still reliving every bit of it.

"This is Doctor Brady, the state pathologist, and I'm Detective Sergeant Flannery, along with Garda O'Sullivan."

The man nodded. "George Halligan."

"We hear you're expecting a baby any day now," Siobhán said. "Congratulations."

"Thank you. It's our first. My wife and I are over the moon."

"Can you please take us through the events leading up to the incident?" Jeanie said.

George motioned to his tractor. "Michael seemed to be enjoying himself. Looking around with a grin on his face. I saw him on his phone a few times too, taking selfies."

"Phone," the professionals all said at once.

Jeanie knelt next to the body again. She turned to George. "You might want to turn away." He gulped and did just that. "Shall we have a look through his pockets?" Jeanie removed gloves from her pockets, slipped them on and did a quick search. She produced a wad of euro tightened by a rubber band, a key, and a receipt. "It looks as if he was staying at the Twins' Inn," Jeanie said, dangling the key. "There's no phone."

"Could it be on the tractor?" Macdara approached the John Deere. There was nothing on the seat, or the floor of the tractor. He got on the ground and looked underneath. "No phone here either."

"He definitely had one," George said. "I wanted to tell him to pay more attention, but given I was using my phone, I kept me gob shut."

Siobhán removed her notebook from her

pocket. *Phone. Selfies. Did the Monk take it?* Macdara glanced at her note and nodded.

"If there's something incriminating on that phone it could help us prove this wasn't an accident," Jeanie said.

"I wish I'd been paying more attention, but me wife texted me just as the blue Toyota pulled up."

"Can you pretend to be the person in the car?" Macdara said. He climbed onto George's tractor. "I want to see what you saw."

George nodded. He stood by the side of Michael's tractor. "The car pulled up here. Michael stopped his tractor. Lucky I was going slow or I would have crashed into him. I was on the phone, then of course I saw the car, and looked up. The person left the car running, but it must have been in park. He got out, and stood right here." George positioned himself at the back wheel of the tractor.

"That exact spot?" Macdara asked. "Are you sure?" George nodded. "My view of the wheel well is now blocked," Macdara said. "If our monk slipped the end of the scarf into the wheel well, George wouldn't have noticed."

"Did you see the monk hand Michael a scarf?"

George dropped his head. "My wife texted again—she thought she was having contractions. I was absorbed in me phone again. Next thing I know, the monk is getting back into the car, and Michael is taking off again. I noticed the scarf at the same time as Michael was airborne." He shuddered. "But I tell you one thing. That car screeched away incredibly fast. It was as if they knew what was going to happen."

"Thank you," Macdara said. "I don't suppose you got any of the number plate?"

"I wish I had. It was a blue Toyota Corolla. Looked like a newer model."

Macdara jotted that down right away. It was a common enough car, but it did help narrow down the field.

"Any sense of whether it was a man or a woman?" Siobhán asked.

George shook his head. "I figured it was a man, but the robe was oversized. It could have been a woman."

"Did you hear any of their exchange?" Siobhán asked.

"I'm afraid not. When you have twenty tractor engines running, you can't hear a thing." He frowned. "Wait," he said. "I could hear a radio. Head-banging music. Heavy metal. He or she was blasting it." He paused. "Even if the tractors weren't running I might not have been able to catch much of the conversation."

That was helpful. Which one of their suspects liked head-banging music? Or had someone chosen it with the intention of drowning out his or her voice? This was a small village; George may have been able to identify the person if he'd been able to hear the monk speak. It was likely that this one had never taken a vow of silence.

"Thank you," Macdara said. "We'll need you to come into the station to get your account down in writing."

George nodded. "I'm sorry I wasn't more helpful." He held up his mobile phone. "Do you mind if I get home now?"

"Go be with your wife," Macdara said. "Happy Christmas and all the best with the baby." They fell silent as they watched him go. Macdara turned to Jeanie. "Thoughts?"

"It would be helpful testimony," Jeanie said. "The fact that the monk screeched away and afterward there was suddenly a scarf around our victim's neck is compelling. But it's still circumstantial. I'm pretty sure the DPP would need a lot more evidence." The Director of Public Prosecutions was the governing body who decided which cases to take to trial. Understandably, they wanted rock-solid cases. "But let me see what my examination finds, and if we're lucky maybe we'll find a stray hair or DNA on the scarf."

Siobhán pointed to the key still in Jeanie's hand. "At least we know where to look next," she said. "The Twins' Inn." Inwardly, she groaned. They wouldn't need that exact key to get into Michael's room; the proprietors of the inn could give them access. But a judge would have to sign off on a warrant first. Another delay and yet another person whose Christmas holiday they had to interrupt with tragic news.

"One of the care home residents had five hundred euro in cash stolen," Macdara said, gesturing to the roll of money also in Jeanie's hand. "I'd be interested to know the amount he's got there."

"I'll process everything as quickly as possible," Jeanie said. "Do either of you have an evidence bag handy?"

Macdara retrieved one and Jeanie dumped the contents into it. Doctor Jeanie Brady nodded her thanks. "I'll get back to you as soon as I finish the postmortem."

Chapter Five

Once the body was removed and taken to the morgue at Cork University Hospital, the tech team arrived and got to work. They took extensive photos of the scene, but apart from partial tire tracks of the mysterious blue Toyota Corolla, there was very little to go on. A judge had been notified that they needed a warrant to enter the deceased's room at the Twins' Inn, and guards were assigned to interview all the tractor participants. At best they were hoping someone had caught some of the number plate off the car. By the time they received the warrant from the judge, the sun was starting to set over Kilbane. Siobhán took a moment to drink in the deep oranges and reds spreading across the sky. She took Macdara's hand in hers for a squeeze. The job was a constant reminder of how fragile and precious life was, that one needed to take time each day to appreciate the good things. And Macdara was one of the good things. He didn't even make a cheeky remark. He simply held her hand for a few minutes as they watched the sun sink into the horizon. And then it was back to work.

The Twins' Inn was run by identical twins, Emma and Eileen. They were petite and cheerful women in their thirties with curly golden hair. They rather enjoyed being twins, and often dressed alike. Today was no exception; they each sported an ugly Christmas jumper. Emma's featured a gingerbread man dancing a jig, and Eileen had Santy's legs dangling in the fireplace, as if the rest of him was stuck up the chimney. Siobhán stared at their jumpers, and couldn't help but see the long, ugly scarf. At least the jumpers weren't a death hazard. Siobhán turned back to gaze at the inn. The rooms were all arranged around a horse-shoe configuration, and if decorating for Christmas was a contest, the twins had everyone beat. Colorful lights were strung along the top of the roof, and miniature potted trees with multicolored lights had been placed in front of every door along with a fat red bow. Candles shimmered in the window of the motel office, and the twins' cottage and back garden had been decorated with more lights, and trees, and mechanical reindeer.

The twins were gobsmacked that one of their guests had died. Although Siobhán and Macdara did not use the word *murder*, the town was already speculating about long scarf syndrome, the blue car, and the mysterious costumed monk. Macdara

requested the CCTV footage from the inn for the
length of Michael Walsh's stay. "What about poor
Max?" Emma said.

"We loved Max," Eileen chimed in. "He fetched
me slippers every morning."

"And the newspaper," Emma added. "And a few
things we didn't ask him to."

"Currently Bill Casey is looking after him," Siobhán said. "It will be up to Michael's family what
happens to him."

"Took us ages to realize he'd taken our welcome
mat and dragged it to the back garden," Emma
said. "Put it right in front of the reindeer like he
was welcoming the pack!" The two laughed in unison.

"But we didn't mind. He's a wee dote!" Eileen
said.

"We'll be sure to keep you posted." Siobhán was
eager to process the room and get home for dinner and a bit of sleep.

The twins opened Michael's room and hurried
off to gather the CCTV footage. Macdara and
Siobhán suited up, including gloves and booties. It
was a possible secondary crime scene and they
wanted to err on the side of caution. The rooms were
simple and cheerful even though it was apparent
that a messy twenty-something lad and his dog had
been staying there. His luggage bag yawned open at
the foot of the bed, clothes waterfalling out of it as if
trying to escape, trousers discarded on the floor.
The end table next to the bed was equally clut-
tered: keys, a Stephen King novel, a pack of Win-
ston cigarettes, a box of vanilla dog biscuits, and

multiple packets of Solpadeine—the fizzy kind that you dissolve in water. Most of the packets were empty. Solpadeine was a popular hangover cure, but one had to be careful as they contained codeine and could be addictive. Chemists had begun paying attention to purchases, and one could not buy a pack these days without being questioned and warned of the addictive nature they posed. "We'll need to visit the chemist," Siobhán said. "See if he bought the Solpadeine here."

They did a quick search of the room, but there was nothing out of the ordinary. "I half hoped our stolen items would be here," Macdara said.

"Me too," Siobhán said. "That would have wrapped one case up with a neat little bow."

Macdara returned to the end table and studied it. "He likes his drink, but can't deal with the hangovers."

Siohban nodded. "If he was hungover, that may be the reason he wasn't paying attention to the end of the scarf," she said. Being actively drunk was dangerous enough, but often it was the next day when folks were accident-prone.

"I just can't figure out why he would let a strange man wrap a scarf around his neck," Macdara said as they stepped outside, eager to take off their suits, gloves, and booties. They tossed them in the nearest rubbish bin. The technical team was on its way, and it was a relief to get out of the room. They were having a mild start to winter so far, but Siobhán wrapped her coat around her, feeling a winter chill in her bones. "What if our killer knew that Michael was hungover and taking a massive amount of Solpadeine? Thus making him vulnerable to not paying close attention when he or she placed the scarf around his neck?"

"Especially if it was someone he trusted," Macdara said. He sighed. "It means our killer is a lot more cunning than I was giving him or her credit for."

"Are you convinced this is murder and not an accident?" Siobhán asked.

"I don't see any innocent reason why someone would disguise him- or herself as a monk, wrap a too-long scarf around the lad's neck while he's on a tractor, and screech away," Macdara said. "Do you?"

"No." Siobhán stared at the Christmas lights, trying to keep her spirits up. "But as Jeanie said, the burden is going to be on us to prove it."

Macdara put his arm around her. "The burden on us is to present the best evidence we can find. The rest will be out of our control."

Siobhán sighed. He was right. It was a maddening aspect of life that so much was out of one's control. They wandered away from the front door and gravitated toward the back garden. Siobhán continued to take comfort in all the twinkling lights and reindeer. Their mechanical heads bowed as if nibbling on grass, then lifted into the air, perhaps watching for Santy's sleigh in the distance. There was a pleasantness in the constant motion, and it calmed Siobhán as they sat in the gazebo awaiting the technical team. Moments later, Emma hurried out with a silver tray that she set on a table in front of them. On it were generous mugs of hot cocoa with little marshmallows, and delicate curled biscuits with a golden-brown sheen.

"Bless you, pet," Siobhán said. "Like a gift from the heavens."

"You're quite welcome," Emma said. "These are Irish Lace Biscuits. Baking is my favorite thing about Christmas. I have a booth at the market this year."

"After tasting these we'll be sure to stop by," Macdara said.

He was right. The Irish Lace Biscuits were light, crunchy, and heavenly, and the hot cocoa warmed Siobhán's insides. One could almost forget there was a possible murderer on the loose.

"We have the CCTV ready to review," Emma said. "Would you like to hear what we saw on the tapes?"

"Absolutely," Macdara said.

Siobhán half suspected he wanted more time with his cocoa and biscuits but given she did too, she didn't dare interrupt even to tease him.

Emma was eager to fill them in. "He had three young visitors this week. A blondie fella, a bald one, and a gorgeous young woman with black hair."

"Finn, Shane, and Bonnie," Siobhán said. "When were they here?"

"He checked in four days ago. They visited the day after his first full day. And nothing since." She handed Macdara a USB stick. "It's all on here. I've emailed you a link and password as well."

"Thanks a million," Siobhán said.

"Not a bother." Emma headed off with a smile.

"The four seem awfully close," Siobhán said. "What if we have a pack of thieves and one turned on the others?"

"That is a definite possibility," Macdara said. "And it will be to our advantage if true."

"How so?"

"It's hard enough for two people to keep a secret, let alone four."

Siobhán nodded. "And one of them is a very beautiful woman," Siobhán said. "What if Michael *didn't* let a man wrap the scarf around his neck? He allowed a beautiful woman to do it instead?"

Macdara frowned. "Interesting. But would he have recognized her dressed as a monk?"

"Not until she was right in front of him," Siobhán said. "He could have thought she was having a laugh."

"Or perhaps they were up to something, and he knew she would be in disguise," Macdara mused.

"It truly bothers me that the other three did not show up for the tractor run," Siobhán said. "We must speak with them as soon as possible."

Macdara set his empty plate and mug back on the tray with a sigh. "I agree, and I'm tempted to haul them into the station early tomorrow morning for a good grilling. But given what Doctor Brady said, that we need a full confession—I'm wondering if it's not more advantageous to proceed cautiously. Let them think we're investigating this as a terrible accident and keep an eye on what they do next."

The sound of cars pulling in lifted them from their seats, and they headed back to the front of the inn. The technical team had arrived. Macdara spoke with them then turned to Siobhán. "There's nothing more we can do here this evening. Well, wife? Shall we head home?"

Home. Such a beautiful word. *Wife* was taking longer to get used to; every time he said it there was a moment when she wondered who he was on about. "We shall, husband." They headed for the car. "Wait," Siobhán said, coming to a halt. "Did you open the press in Michael's room?"

"I completely forgot," he said. "It seemed as if all his clothes were in his luggage bag. But we should still have a look." They pivoted, and made it to the room before the team had entered. Macdara asked them to hold up as they retrieved additional gloves and booties from the team, donned them, and were soon standing in front of the press. Macdara opened it. There was only a single item hanging on the rods. A long brown robe, like that of an old-fashioned monk.

Chapter Six

The next morning, Bill Casey's farm was bustling with activity. A large working farm, he had sheep, horses, and cows out in the fields, chickens wandering near the opening to the barn, and a large section of his garden that was filled with fresh-cut Christmas trees. Siobhán was looking forward to selecting one, but given they had important work in front of them, her siblings had promised to find a good one. The tractor participants were in shock but equally determined to honor Michael's passing. They asked if after the tractor was processed they could move it to the side of the road where the incident occurred, so that they, and anyone else in town who wished to do so, could decorate it with flowers, Mass cards, and other remembrances. Their request was quickly granted, and it was determined that the tractor parade could indeed follow the original route they had planned out. This way Michael's parked tractor would be honored once again, saluted as each tractor passed it by. In addition, all the monies collected for the parade would go to an animal shelter in Michael's hometown. Michael's family would be attending the tractor parade and remembrance.

Siobhán took a moment to join her siblings at their assigned John Deere. Ciarán was holding Trigger, who was dressed in a tiny Santa outfit, and from the snarl on his face, he wasn't quite getting into the spirit of it. Ciarán's boyish looks were fading, sixteen going on seventeen. Ann, in her last year of school, was also nearly an adult, although Siobhán was having a difficult time thinking of any of them as grown and if she thought about it for too long it did her head in. Eoin was twenty-two, and Gráinne, twenty-three, and in six months Siobhán would be thirty. How did time do this? Had it sped up when she wasn't looking? Gráinne, dressed in a sequined-green top and tulle skirt, was more decorated than the tractor. She was sitting in the driver's seat, barking orders to everyone below. James, the oldest at thirty-two, was stringing lights around it and testing the battery pack that would keep the lights blazing during the parade, while Ann and Eoin were placing garland around the front.

"We need reindeer," Gráinne said. "Pulling the tractor."

"Are ye just going to sit there like the Queen of the Tractor Parade?" James asked her.

Gráinne patted her head. "That's what I need,"

she said. "A crown." She pointed to Siobhán. "What about your wedding tiara?"

"No," Siobhán and Macdara said in unison.

Siobhán turned to Ciarán, taking a moment to scratch Trigger behind the ear. "How many words do you think Trigger knows?"

"Treat, brekkie, lunch, supper," Ciarán said. Trigger licked his face. "And Trigger."

"You should work on that," Siobhán said. "See if you can teach him a few more."

"He needs a job," Grainne said. "So he can be on telly."

"Why don't you lead by example," James said, swatting her with a large plastic candy cane, "and start showing off your decorating skills?"

"I'm afraid this is where I leave you," Siobhán said as she looped an arm around Ann. "But it's a cracking tractor so far."

"It's class," Gráinne said with a grin.

"No thanks to you," James said. Eoin leapt up next to Gráinne and honked the horn, making her jump. Everyone laughed.

Ann picked up a pine garland and wrapped it around herself like a scarf. It took a moment of everyone staring at her open-mouthed before she gasped, and quickly threw it off. "I'm sorry, I'm sorry," she said. "I wasn't making fun."

Siobhán brought her sister in for a hug. "I know that, love," she said. "This is hard for all of us to process."

Siobhán kissed heads and cheeks and was about to leave when she felt a hand grip her arm. Gráinne leaned in and pointed across the field. It took Siohban a second to realize she was pointing at Finn Doyle, standing a few meters away, looking as morose as Trigger in a Santa cap.

"What can you tell me about that fella?" She had a flirtatious tone to her voice, obviously unaware of his connection to Michael Walsh.

"He's a suspect in our murder inquiry," Siobhán said.

James groaned. "Don't tell her that. She'll only want to marry him."

"You're one to talk," Gráinne said. "Your girl-friends should come with a temporary visitor's pass."

"Quit your squabbling, and the fella is off limits," Siobhán said. "Find a lad well outside of our murder probe."

"Murder?" Ann said. "Are you sure this wasn't a terrible accident?" Her siblings all stared at Siobhán, waiting for an answer.

"Please don't repeat any of this," Siobhán said. "We don't have all the answers yet. But be on the lookout for a blue Toyota, or anyone dressed as a monk."

James shook his head. "Happy Christmas," he said sarcastically.

Siobhán gave his arm a squeeze. "It will be. As long as everyone stays alert and cautious. And we really don't have any answers so it's best just to focus on trying to brighten everyone's spirits as best we can."

Gráinne fluttered her eyelashes. "Maybe I could chat him up and see what I can find out."

Ann and Eoin rolled their eyes in unison. "I

have to jet," Siobhán said. "Would the rest of ye keep Gráinne otherwise occupied?"

"Buzzkills," Gráinne said, taking Trigger out of Ciarán's arms and lifting him into the air. "Now there's two words for you, Trig. *Buzz. Kills.*"

The Kilbane Players, a local theatre group situated in the town square, was in full-throttle rehearsal for the panto when Siobhán and Macdara finally arrived. They found Cara, the costume designer, in the basement of the theatre, a clipboard in her hand and a rack of Christmas costumes in front of her. Her honey-colored hair was piled loosely on top of her head held up with a pencil, and another one was tucked behind her ear. She took one look at the brown robe, now housed in clear plastic and marked with an evidence sticker. "Yes," she said. "It's ours. Did you only find one?"

Siobhán's ears perked up. "How many are you missing?"

"Two."

That was interesting. "When were they stolen?"

"I can't say for sure. They're not part of our current production and it was only yesterday I noticed they were missing."

"When were they used last?" Macdara asked.

"I believe they were from last year's Halloween party. I had planned on cutting up the brown fabric to patch up a malfunctioning reindeer costume." The panto this year was *Rudolph*.

"I'm afraid you won't be getting this back anytime soon," Macdara said. "It's part of an ongoing inquiry."

Her eyes grew wide and she patted her head, making sure the pencil was still holding. "Does this have anything to do with that poor lad on the tractor?"

"We can't say," Macdara said. "But can you show us where the monk costumes were stored?"

She gestured to the racks of clothing. "You're looking at it." She chewed on her lip. "Most likely they were taken from the town square."

Macdara stepped forward. "What's that now?"

"I took two racks of costumes out to the square when we were rehearsing. The Christmas market was just setting up and the square was chockablock. It would have been easy for someone to slip them off the rack."

"What day was this?" Siobhán asked.

"Saturday."

The same day that the residents had their outing to the market. *Premeditated?*

"Thank you. That's helpful," Macdara said. Although it meant a possible lead, it also meant more CCTV footage to pore through.

"Why don't we go to the town square and you can show us where you placed the costume rack?" Siobhán suggested. This way they could identify the closest CCTV cameras. And maybe the Christmas market would bring them a little cheer. Despite the case, this was still their first Christmas as husband and wife, and she wanted to savor it, even if it was just with a single mug of hot cocoa and a brief search for a sprig of mistletoe.

Siobhán and Macdara were meeting with their three young suspects this afternoon, and then they would return to the retirement home to follow up on conversations they had about long scarf syndrome. Siobhán couldn't shake the feeling that there was a direct relationship between the thefts and Michael's death. They were going to be very busy indeed, and Siobhán wasn't even including her usual Christmas errands. She had yet to buy gifts, or the turkey and ham for Christmas dinner. She knew her brood would be happy to pitch in; Eoin was the chef in the family and could handle dinner with ease, but she didn't want to miss out on a single thing. Garda Aretta Dabiri, a recent addition to the garda team and a top-notch organizer, would not be on hand to help them out or join them for the celebrations, and she was sorely missed. But she was on her holidays, hopefully enjoying herself in Dublin with her family.

Cara led them to the middle of the square where the Christmas market was in full swing. A chorus of excited voices filled the background and the scent of sugar and dough infused the crisp air. Although they might not get snow, the rain was also holding off, and there was a hint of sun beneath a thin layer of gray clouds, taking the edge off the winter bite. Costumed actors rehearsed *Rudolph* on a stage near them, and Christmas music played overhead. "I placed the rack of costumes here," she said, gesturing to the spot near the panto stage. "Yesterday and the day before." Siobhán scanned the area. They were in a central location; the thief could have approached from literally anywhere. Depending on how crowded it was when the robes were nicked, it was possible they wouldn't glean much from the CCTV cameras. And it was looking like they were going to have to pull footage from nearly every camera in every shop surrounding the square. Their to-do list was growing with each passing second. Suddenly, a nearby conversation became very loud as the voices of two little girls stole all the attention.

"Mam said no more candy!"

"Don't tell or I'll tell you what Santy is bringing you this year!"

"You don't know what Santy is bringing me!"

"I do so! It's socks! That's all you're getting is socks!" A loud wail followed the pronouncement.

A mother's voice soon joined in. "Girls! I can hear every word you just said."

Siobhán and Macdara exchanged a smile. They were near King John's Castle, a tower house with a passageway underneath which sat at the entrance to the town square. Most of the locals knew that when you stood at a certain spot in the passageway, your voice would amplify and everyone around would be able to hear you, even if you were whispering. It was nearly a right of passage that young ones found this out, sometimes in the most embarrassing of ways. The mother hurried out from beneath the passageway, holding two little hands as one continued to plead for confirmation that Santy was bringing her something more exciting this year than socks.

"Do you have children of your own?" Cara suddenly asked, interrupting the moment.

"No," Siobhán and Macdara said in stereo. From the look on Cara's face, perhaps they had sounded a bit too emphatic.

"We're newlyweds," Siobhán said. "And I have five siblings."

"That's child-minding sorted then isn't it?" Cara said. "Now."

"Have you had anyone from outside of your cast approach you lately?" Siobhán asked, avoiding the talk of all-things-babies. "Anyone from the elder care home or the tractor parade?"

"No," Cara said. "I've been completely absorbed with the production."

A pair of missing brown robes. It bolstered the theory that they were most likely looking at a pair of thieves. They thanked the costume designer and moved out of earshot. Macdara called in the request to pull CCTV from the shops surrounding the square. A live band was starting to set up near the bookshop Turn the Page, located at the corner of the square. The owners, Oran and Padraig, stood outside in thick wooly sweaters, clutching mugs and watching the hustle and bustle of the market. Books would make lovely Christmas gifts and Siobhán tucked the thought away for the near future.

"What do you say we get something delicious to eat and a mug of hot cocoa?" Siobhán said. "And then pay a visit to Bonnie's tent." There was another reason they found themselves in the town square today: They had learned that Bonnie Murphy would be working at one of the tents. It was the perfect opportunity to have an informal chat with her.

Macdara took her hand, and planted a kiss on it. "That's the best idea I've heard all day."

The tent for hot cocoa with or without Irish cream had an enormous line. But luckily it was run by Declan O'Rourke, a previous neighbor of the O'Sullivans, and Maria, one of Siobhán's best friends.

She was a petite girl with a large personality. Her dark hair was streaked with red and green for the holidays and she wore a Santa cap with bells that jingled every time she moved her head. Maria caught Siobhán's eye in the crowd and gestured for her to cut the line. "Let the guards through," she commanded. "They're on duty. If anyone whinges about it, you won't be getting any cocoa from me!"

Declan, a hearty man with an even heartier disposition, threw his head back and roared with laughter. Siobhán and Macdara, slightly embarrassed, nodded and waved to the kind people who parted and let them move to the front of the line.

"If it isn't Herself and Himself," Declan said with a wink. "Happy Christmas."

"Happy Christmas," they echoed.

"Is it true?" Maria whispered when handing Siobhán her hot cocoa. "The lad on the tractor was murdered?"

"We're investigating all possibilities," Siobhán said.

Marie leaned even closer. "That's why I gave you a nip of Irish cream. Just a touch."

Siobhán laughed. "Macdara too?"

Maria shook her head. "Let him drive," she said with a wink.

By the time they made it to Bonnie's tent, featuring hand-painted ornaments of the Irish countryside, there was a lad manning the booth all by himself. Siobhán particularly liked an ornament featuring their ruined abbey covered in a blanket of snow. The abbey wasn't just her favorite spot in town, it was where they'd held their wedding reception. She had to have it. Macdara saw her eyeing it and leaned in. "Don't go buying anything until you see what Santy brings," he whispered.

She laughed. "Subtle, Mr. Detective. Shall I close my eyes so you can buy it now?"

"There's no fun in that, now," he said. "I'll wait until Christmas Eve like I always do."

"Do that and you might find I bought new locks for Christmas."

He chuckled and then they turned their attention back to the matter at hand. "We were told Bonnie Murphy would be working this tent today," Macdara said.

The lad nodded. "She took the morning off," he said. "We're expecting her after the lunch hour."

Macdara scribbled his mobile number on the back of his calling card and handed it to the lad. "Text me the minute she arrives."

"Yes, DS Flannery," the kid said.

Siobhán gave Macdara a playful shove as they walked away. "See that?" she said. "You're infamous."

"I think you mean famous," Macdara said, standing straighter.

"Infamous," Siobhán repeated with a gentle shove. All of their other appointments were for late this afternoon and early this evening, and Jeanie Brady had yet to finish her postmortem, so they took time to enjoy the market. They bought shepherd's pie from a stall and Macdara insisted they finish it off with a brownie with vanilla ice cream. "We'll have to come back when we're off duty and get our cocoa with Irish cream," Macdara said longingly.

"Absolutely," Siobhán said. "It's not like Maria already gave me a nip in mine."

Macdara's mouth dropped open. "She did not."

Siobhán shrugged. "I suppose we'll never know."

"Keep this up and you'll be on Santy's naughty list," Macdara said.

Siobhán didn't reply; she was drawn into a tent that made adorable wooden statues. Some were religious in nature, others featured Santa, nutcrackers, and even Christmas trees. They reminded her of Sinead's Virgin Mary statue, although she had a feeling these were much more ornate. They were painted with glorious colors. Siobhán remembered these from years past, and if she wasn't mistaken they had a secret little compartment on the bottom. "Do you have a statue of the Virgin Mary?"

"She's right here," the woman said, picking one up. Although less adorned than some, it had exquisite detailing.

"We have a friend whose mother bought one of these at the very first Christmas market."

The woman nodded. "That would be my greatgranny. I've been keeping the tradition alive."

"I know it won't replace the one she's missing, but maybe it will cheer her up some," Siobhán said. "I'll take it."

The woman nodded and began to wrap it up in lovely red and green tissue paper. She stopped. "And you know all about the secret, don't you?"

"Do you mean the secret little compartment?" Siobhán grinned. "I remember. But show it to me again, it's delightful."

The woman nodded, then unwrapped the statue. She turned it over. "There's a little compartment underneath." She pushed in on the center and a little secret door opened up. "She's hollow. You can't fit much in there, maybe a secret note or some money that you don't want anyone else to nick."

"It's a brilliant idea," Siobhán said. "Have they always had that component?"

"Right from the very beginning. Did your friend's statue have something inside?"

Did it? "I have no idea. I don't even know if she knew about the compartment." Was it possible Sinead was so determined to get her statue back because of something that was hidden inside of it? Macdara came up behind her and placed his hands on her waist, making her jump. After swatting him, she showed him the statue and the secret compartment.

"I sincerely hope that sweet old woman hasn't been lying to us," he said. "Or I really will have to handcuff her."

Chapter Seven

Siobhán felt a tiny glow of satisfaction as she took her Virgin Mary statue and headed for Bonnie's tent with Macdara. One Christmas present sorted, even if it was for someone who wasn't on her list. *Progress.* Macdara's mobile phone dinged with a text. "Bonnie is here," he said. "But she's been moved to a new tent. Let's see if I can follow these directions."

They wound around the square, taking in toys, and jewelry, and food. They jostled their way through a sea of winter coats and gloves, hands full with bags and boxes. "This should be the lane," Macdara said as they turned down another path. "Down here on the right." It might have been difficult to pick out Bonnie Murphy from all the other young, beautiful women at the market, but they had been told that she had taken to wearing a red and green knitted flower in her hair, compliments of Beverly. It took a while to spot her, but they finally spied the knitted flower in the far corner, at a candle stall.

"Candles!" Siobhán exclaimed as they neared the tent. "I can buy some for our windows."

"Make sure you get the glass covers," Macdara said. "I don't ever want to worry about you and fire again."

There had been an incident shortly before they were married where Siobhán and Maria, along with their third bestie, Aisling, were trapped in the dairy barn on their property, which an arsonist had set on fire. They managed to escape relatively unharmed, but Macdara still had nightmares. "I will absolutely buy the hurricane covers," she said, picking up a pair of long creamy candlesticks. "And I can wrap the bottom in garland." She pointed to the decorative garland next to the glass covers.

"Happy Christmas," Bonnie said when there was finally a moment for her to speak. When she tucked a strand of black hair behind her ear, Siobhán noticed her hand was trembling. "Happy Christmas," Siobhán and Macdara echoed back.

"I made these myself," Bonnie said, gesturing to the candles.

"You did?" Siobhán was quite impressed. "Well played. That's amazing." She meant it. They were gorgeous. For a second Siobhán lamented all the talents she didn't possess. She wasn't craftsy, she wasn't an artist, or a chef, or a musician. She used to be able to whittle, but it seemed her special talent had been reduced to sussing out murderers. It wasn't something she'd ever dreamed of as a little girl, but on the other hand there was nothing more satisfying than getting a killer off the streets, and bringing justice to victims. Still. Had she more time, perhaps she would be a fantastic candle-maker.

"Thank you." Bonnie clasped her hands below her chin, her eyes alert and friendly. "I know you're not here to buy the candles. I'm sorry I wasn't at the ornament tent this morning. Michael's death has just been such a shock."

"We understand," Macdara said. "We wouldn't blame you if you decided not to have a tent this year at all."

Bonnie chewed on a chipped green-painted fingernail. "I thought about that. But what good is being sad all on my lonesome going to do? I'd rather be out here keeping my mind occupied."

"I'm definitely buying some candles," Siobhán said. "But first we need to ask you a few questions."

"Of course," Bonnie said. "I'm horrified about what happened to Michael. Are you investigating for insurance purposes?"

"Pardon?" Siobhán said.

"It was just a terrible, terrible accident, wasn't it? I suppose you have to write up a report, or what-ever, and I don't mean to be dense, but I don't quite understand what you're investigating."

"We have loose ends to tie up," Macdara said. "Including identifying someone who pulled up alongside Michael's tractor in a blue Toyota Corolla."

"Right," Bonnie said. "I heard something about that. I wasn't sure whether it really happened or it was just a rumor."

"The person was dressed in a brown robe with a hood," Macdara said.

"How odd." Her eyes darted around as if she was looking for the nearest means of escape.

Siobhán picked out four yellow tapered candles, four covers, and four decorative garlands. "We just moved into a new house," she said as Bonnie began to wrap them up. "I can't wait to put them in the windows."

"They'll be stunning," Bonnie said. "And if you're looking for a wreath for the door, you'll want to see Oscar at the elder care home," Bonnie said.

"Oh?" Siobhán said. She was definitely in the market for a wreath.

"He makes them," she said. "And they're exquisite."

"He should sell them here," Siobhán said.

"He was supposed to." Bonnie shook her head in dismay. "He hasn't gone anywhere since his cane was stolen. To tell you the truth, I think it was more like an emotional support cane."

"Emotional support cane?" Macdara said, lifting an eyebrow.

"He was so attached to it. I think it meant as much to him as a family pet."

Family pet. Siobhán needed to get their Jack Russell, Trigger, a present for Christmas too. Beverly had seemed rather attached to her scarf as well. Did the thief take some items to cause a distraction? Creating an emotional disturbance to keep everyone off balance?

"Where were you, Finn Doyle, and Shane Boyd yesterday?" Macdara asked. "Mr. Casey said you didn't show up to the tractor rehearsal."

Bonnie dropped her fingernail and chewed on her bottom lip this time. Siobhán was tempted to buy her some beef jerky. "I'm to blame." Bonnie looked at them as if waiting to see if they would interrupt. They kept silent. "I heard of a shop in Cork that sold canes. I wanted to see if we could get one for Oscar. We tried to get Michael to come with us, but he was eager to drive the tractor."

"I find it odd that the three of you signed up to participate in the tractor parade and then missed the first outing," Macdara pressed.

"I'm glad we did," Bonnie said. "It may have saved our lives."

"Why do you think that?" Siobhán said. "You just pointed out that you think it was an accident."

Bonnie bit her lip. "Yes," she said slowly. "I did." Siobhán cocked her head and stared at her. Bonnie threw her arms open. "If it was me on that tractor, who's to say I wouldn't have had something similar happen to me?" She folded her arms. "I'm very accident-prone."

"What time did you leave for Cork?" Macdara asked. "What time did you get there, how long were you there, and when did you return?"

Bonnie chewed her lip and stared at the ground. "I said we were *going* to drive to Cork. I never said we made it there."

That got their attention. "Didn't make it there? Why not?" Siobhán asked.

Bonnie crossed her arms and let out a puff of air, sending her fringe flying. "It's Finn and Shane you need to question. They drove into town, stopped near the Christmas market, and chucked me out of the car!"

"Did they say why?" Siobhán said.

"Shane wanted to go to a pub where his mate was bartending. Said he was going to give them free drinks."

That seemed like it would have appealed to Michael as well, Siobhán thought. "Do you know if they told Michael about it?"

Bonnie shrugged. "I don't think so. Michael was mad for the drink, he certainly would have gone with them." Bonnie handed Siobhán her candles all wrapped up. "You don't think . . . you don't think someone *wanted* Michael dead, do you?"

"We're still conducting our inquiries," Macdara said politely.

"He definitely wasn't wearing that scarf at the start of the tractor practice," Bonnie said.

"That's the theory we're working on, but how do you know for sure?" Siobhán asked.

Bonne reached into her coat pocket and pulled out her mobile phone. "He sent this to me fifteen minutes after we dropped him off." She swiped through it and turned the screen toward them. On it was a picture of Michael atop the tractor, flashing two fingers and sticking his tongue out. The road was visible in the background. A scarf was nowhere to be seen.

"I'm going to need you to email that to me," Macdara said, taking out his calling card and handing it to her. "Do you have any other photos from that practice run?"

"It's the only one he sent me," Bonnie said. "Shall I send it now?"

Macdara nodded. "Please."

Bonnie seemed pleased to be useful. She nattered on as she brought up her email. "Why do you think Beverly made such a long scarf? It was more like a Rapunzel rope."

"Perhaps she enjoyed making it and didn't know when to stop," Siobhán said.

"Or she knew exactly what she was doing," Bonnie said. "And where that scarf would end up."

Siobhán stepped forward. "You're saying that Beverly wanted Michael Walsh dead?"

"I don't have any proof, mind you," Bonnie said. "But she didn't like him. I know that much."

That was news. "Why is that?"

Bonnie poked at her screen and soon a whooshing sound could be heard. "Done!" she said. She stuck her phone in her pocket. "I don't mean to speak ill of the dead, but Michael knew how to get under people's skin. He rather enjoyed pushing buttons."

"And what buttons did he push with Beverly?" Macdara asked.

"She overhead him talking to us, making fun of that scarf," Bonnie said. "She heard every word."

"Can you give us those words?" Siobhán said.

Bonnie gulped. "He said . . . he said the scarf was so ugly he wouldn't be caught dead wearing it."

Chapter Eight

They returned to the Casey farm when there was only a half hour of decorating time left in the day. Siobhán's siblings saw her coming and blocked her from seeing their progress. "It's a surprise," Ann said, wagging her finger. The youngest girl, she was getting so grown-up. She had chopped her blond hair over the summer, but it was starting to grow in now. She was beautiful either way, a spirited and athletic girl.

"Not even a peek?" Siobhán said.

"Not even a peek," her siblings echoed. Siobhán ruffled some heads, and had a gander at the other tractors. They were delightful to behold adorned with colorful lights, garland, and illuminated signs reading HAPPY CHRISTMAS. She could imagine the procession now, lights twinkling through the darkness and giving the illusion of moving through space. She couldn't wait. In the meantime, there was work yet to do. Bill Casey invited them into his farmhouse and gestured to the kitchen table. A feast was laid out before them, coffee, tea, and a full Irish breakfast.

"Breakfast for supper!" Macdara exclaimed, eagerly pulling out a chair. "That's class."

Casey shrugged. "Me wife passed on years ago. At first I did it because it was the only meal I knew how to make. Now I just like it. I eat breakfast all day long."

"You shouldn't have," Siobhán said. Macdara was already planted in front of a full plate. Siobhán stuck with tea, toast, and an egg. Macdara hummed as he ate. When they were finished they exited the house and stood near the line of tractors in the drive.

"They would have been on their way home now, but everyone knows to wait until you speak with them."

"Good man," Macdara said. They gave Bill Casey another nod of thanks and readied their notebooks. They approached Finn Doyle first. He seemed jittery, his thin legs bounced as he tried to stand in one place, and his eyes were rimmed in red. Every few seconds as they tried to talk to him, he wiped his nose with the back of his sleeve. Siobhán was having a hard time concentrating, she was so fixated on wanting to hand him a tissue. But she wasn't his mammy and they would get more answers out of him if they gave him some autonomy.

"I never suspected," he said. "I swear."

"Suspected what?" Macdara asked.

"That Michael was the thief." He pawed the

ground with his boot. "I suppose I should have, given his background." He looked up at them. "Did you know he was recently in jail?"

"We haven't determined that he was the thief," Siobhán said.

Finn shook his head as if something was stuck in there and he was trying to jostle it out. "But he had Beverly's ugly scarf."

"Do yourself a favor, lad, and just call it a scarf," Macdara said. "You wouldn't want that getting back to her and hurting her feelings, would you now?"

"You're right, you're right," he said. "My bad."

"I'm sure you've heard that a blue Toyota Corolla pulled up next to his tractor, an unidentified person in a brown hooded robe exited the vehicle and spoke with Michael for a moment?" Siobhán said.

Finn nodded. "He gave Michael the scarf too, didn't he?"

"We're making that assumption," Macdara said. "Did you see a scarf on him that day?"

Finn shook his head. "He must have known the person, don't you think? Why else would he wear it?"

Siobhán noted that he had yet to volunteer the fact that he had skipped the tractor rehearsal. Guilty conscience? "You were supposed to be on the tractor route," Siobhán said. "Mr. Casey told us you didn't show up." They weren't going to divulge that they had already spoken to Bonnie Murphy. They needed to see if their stories would match up.

"Yet you left the elder care home with Michael at the exact same time," Macdara added. "Along with Bonnie Murphy and Shane Boyd. But Michael was the only one who participated in the tractor route."

"Right, right," Finn said. "Bonnie wanted to go into Cork City to buy Oscar a new cane. We dropped Michael off." He stopped as if that was the end of the story.

"The three of you drove to Cork then, is that what you're telling us?" Macdara asked.

Finn shook his head. "Bonnie changed her mind as soon as we dropped off Michael. She got a text—I don't know who from—and asked if we would drop her off in the town square instead. And she was really the one who wanted to buy Oscar a new cane. I mean Shane and I were willing to tag along, but I don't know what kind of cane he'd like. Shane said he wanted to have a pint so I dropped him off in town and then I decided to go the chemist to sort out my Aunt Nuala's medications."

Interesting. Was Finn lying or was Bonnie? Would Shane back one of them up or add a third version to the story? By *chemist* did Finn mean *pub* and by *medication*, did he mean a *pint*? Siobhán took the next question. "What chemist did you visit?"

Finn looked away. "I didn't ask for his name or anything."

"Was it the chemist in town?" Macdara probed.

"No. I went for a drive. It was pretty far out."

Siobhán knew Macdara was getting frustrated, so she stepped in. "What town?"

Finn shrugged. "I couldn't tell ye that now."

Siobhán wondered if Santy would forgive her a little slap but she managed to control herself.

"Do you think we're daft?" Macdara said. "You can't walk into any chemist and get prescription meds."

"Ah, I see. I see," Finn said. "They weren't prescription. Me granny likes her Solpadeine. They give you the side-eye if you come in too many times to the same chemist to buy them, so whenever I'm near a new chemist I stop in for a pack."

Solpadeine. Just like the packs they had found in Michael's room. Not that there was anything unusual about that. You'd find a pack in many Irish homes. Especially if there were any drinkers in the household. But what if Michael hadn't purchased them himself? Had he been snooping around Nuala's room, searching for jewels? Did he come away with Solpadeine instead? And assuming he stole them, perhaps it wasn't a far leap to believe Michael Walsh was the thief after all. But if that were the case—where were the rest of the missing items? And more to the point—who killed him? Was the killer a vigilante furious that Michael had stolen from the elderly a fortnight before Christmas?

"Do you have the receipt from this chemist?" Macdara asked.

"Nah," he said. "I never keep receipts."

Macdara was not going to let up that easy. "What direction did you travel? What did you pass, and were there any landmarks near the chemist you can remember?"

Finn swallowed hard and the twitching amped up. "Are you like . . . asking for my alibi?"

"I'd say you should be eager to provide it," Macdara said. "Given you left with Michael and are a frequent visitor to the elder care home."

"If you're looking for answers, look no further than the mystery man in the brown robe," Finn said. He frowned. "That's odd," he said to himself.

"What's odd?" Siobhán nudged forward.

Finn shook his head. "It's probably nothing."

"Go on, then," Macdara said. "Give us your nothing."

"I could have sworn I heard Cathal Ryan saying something to Nancy Martin about someone running around the grounds of the care home early in the mornings. Someone dressed in a brown hooded robe."

Nuala was seated in a rocking chair in her room, next to a window, her fingers deftly working her knitting needles. The view was sublime; from here she could see the front of the grounds with the mountains in the background. The Christmas decorations were done and dusted, and the gardens were glowing with lights and cheer. It was somewhat mesmerizing to watch Nuala rock as she knitted. "I'm making a replacement scarf for Beverly to give to her daughter," she said. "But I assure you this one is going to be very short."

"That's very kind of you," Siobhán said.

Nuala frowned. "Let's hope Beverly sees it that way."

"We overheard someone mention long scarf syndrome the other day," Macdara said. "But we can't remember who introduced the topic of conversation."

"And who else was around," Siobhán said.

"It was that Bonnie lass," Nuala said. "I've been hoping she and my grandson would have a little spark, but I think she had her eye on that Michael Walsh. May he rest in peace."

Siobhán and Macdara exchanged a quick look. Bonnie hadn't mentioned having a crush on Michael Walsh, but next time they spoke with her they would have to venture into that territory.

"Did you have any interactions with Michael Walsh?" Macdara asked.

"He and my grandson got on like a house on fire. But to tell you the truth, I thought he was a bad influence." She stopped rocking. "Maybe even the thief."

"We've processed his room at the Twins' Inn and there wasn't a trace of the stolen items," Siobhán said. "But we did find a heap of Solpadeine on his end table."

"I'm afraid that's my fault," Nuala said. "I was going through my products and had a load of it from my days where I liked to have a martini or four before bed. Those days are long gone." She grinned. "I have a strict two-martini policy now."

If she was telling the truth, and why wouldn't she be, that meant her grandson Finn had been lying. She didn't need more Solpadeine if she no longer had hangovers. Finn *hadn't* been driving to a chemist. Where had he gone instead? Was Finn the murderer?

"Did Michael Walsh steal the packets from you?" Macdara asked.

"Heavens, no," Nuala said. "And if he had, I wouldn't have cared. It's me emeralds I want back."

"Was there any particular reason Michael needed all that Solpadeine?" Siobhán asked.

"He was moaning about needing the hair of the dog," Nuala said. "You know how the young ones are."

Siobhán's gaze fell to the grounds outside the window. "Have you ever seen anyone walking around here in brown robes?" she asked.

"Are you on about Rory and Oscar?" Nuala said.

Macdara stepped forward. "Rory and Oscar?"

Nuala nodded. "They nicked a couple of robes from the panto costume rack at the Christmas market, then ran around here like a couple of children. When they went to take them back, one was missing."

"Why are you just telling us this now?" Siobhán said. "You know we're looking for a mysterious person in a brown robe, do you not?"

Nuala shrugged. "Oscar and Rory were here the entire time and I figured if you wanted to know more you'd ask, and here you are asking, and here I am, answering."

"Now," Siobhán said. *That's that.* She and Macdara exchanged a look. If the robe was stolen from the grounds, it brought them right back to their four young suspects. As Nuala pointed out, all the residents were home when the brown-hooded figure made his or her approach.

"It has come to our attention that you have a safe where you kept your emeralds," Macdara said. There was no safe visible in the room, but the rest was lovely. A four-poster bed, evergreen wall-paper adorned with golden leaves, a dresser, the rocking chair and a cedar chest. There was one closet door, and of course a small safe could be under the bed, in the dresser, or in the cedar chest. Nuala didn't respond, she simply kept rocking. Why was she keeping her lips sealed about this safe? Did it not exist? Suddenly the door swung open and Nancy Martin stepped in.

"Pardon the interruption," she said. "Nuala has a doctor's appointment and her transportation is waiting downstairs."

"Of course," Siobhán said. She turned to Nuala. "If you tell us where to find the safe and give us the combination, we might be able to make some headway on the disappearance of your emeralds."

"How? The safe is empty now," Nuala said.

"We're going to make a round to the charity shops, in case someone tried to sell them for cash," Macdara added. "But we would still like to see your safe."

Nuala eyed Macdara. "You can see it but I won't be able to open it for you."

Macdara kept a patient smile on his face. "Why not?"

Nuala dropped her knitting into a nearby basket with a sigh. "Someone has gone and changed my combination!"

"Is there any chance you've simply forgotten it?" Nancy asked gently.

"Bah humbug," Nuala said. "It's me birthday. Are you telling me I've forgotten me own birthday?"

Nancy exchanged looks with Macdara and Siobhán. "I've encouraged her to change it. But it can be difficult to remember new combinations."

You can't teach an old dog new tricks. The thought popped in Siobhán's mind before she could stop it. It sparked another thought. Max was a young dog. And he knew plenty of tricks. She had no idea why her mind was torturing her with that right now—safecracking probably wasn't one of the dog's many talents.

"You're definitely going to have to change the combination now," Siobhán said.

"I told you, someone else has already changed it." Nuala rose from her chair. "Besides, the emeralds are gone. I don't need a safe now, do I?" She was certainly defensive. Was she worried it was her grandson who'd changed the combination?

"Why don't you show us the safe when you're back," Macdara tried again.

"If I make it back," Nuala said. "After all, there's a murderer making the rounds, a Christmas angel of death."

Chapter Nine

They found Beverly in the kitchen, on cookie duty. The air was filled with the smell of fresh baked chocolate chips and all things sugar and dough. When Macdara and Siobhán stepped into the room Beverly gasped. "Are you here to arrest me?"

"Arrest you?" Macdara said.

She brought her hands up to her face. "Is it true? Did me scarf kill that poor lad?"

"You mustn't blame yourself," Siobhán said. Unless, of course, she was the killer. In that case, she *should* blame herself but probably didn't. In fact, if Beverly was the killer, it was quite clever. Make the murder weapon with your own two hands, then pretend it was stolen a day before the murder. But given she was in the sitting room with them when the murder occurred, she was probably in the clear.

"Everyone kept warning me about the length. But it wasn't supposed to be worn by a lad on a tractor!"

"Of course not," Siobhán said. "How were you to know?"

Macdara shook his head. "If only we had all learned our lesson from the great Isadora Duncan."

"Someone is doing this to get at me," Beverly said. "Someone wants to torment me." She thwacked the rolling pin on the counter, then set upon a ball of dough, rolling it out and pounding it with gusto.

"We heard that Michael was making fun of the scarf before it was stolen," Macdara said. "Can you tell us about that?"

Beverly's eyes narrowed as she thunked the rolling pin on the table. "Who told you that?"

"We're not at liberty to say," Siobhán said. "But we'd like to hear your version of what happened."

"I don't quite remember everything these days," Beverly said. "But he said it was ugly and that he wouldn't be caught dead wearing it."

"Where was everyone when this occurred and who all was there?" Macdara asked.

Beverly sunk a cookie cutter into the dough. "We were outside in the gardens. I asked Michael if I could wrap it around him to check out the length. I suppose I should have asked someone more agreeable." She lifted the cookie cutter and sunk it down in a new section. "The foursome was there. I don't know why Bonnie was hanging around those lads—attention I suppose. And then myself, Rory, and Oscar."

"By the foursome you mean Bonnie, Shane, Finn, and Michael?" Macdara asked.

"Yes. Rory and Oscar call them the Four Horsemen but I just call them the foursome."

"The Four Horsemen?" Siobhán asked. It was rather a grim nickname.

Beverly waved it off. "Rory and Oscar are jealous of their youth," Beverly said. "Some people grow old gracefully, others claw and hiss all the way to the grave." She took a spatula and carved around the cookie. "Now," she said. "Isn't this a lovely snowman?"

"I'm sure he will be," Siobhán said politely. "Once you give him a head."

Speaking to the residents one-on-one had proven to be a bit frustrating. The residents all went on tangents, or blamed someone else. They decided it might be advantageous to give it one more go as a group. They gathered in the library around the cozy fire. Cookies and hot cocoa were served. Christmas music still played overhead, but Nancy turned it down so that they could easily talk over it.

Macdara waited until everyone had taken their seats and had a mug of hot cocoa and a helping of cookies. "Let's go over the day of the thefts one more time as a group," he said.

Nuala bit the antlers off a reindeer cookie. "It was a dark and stormy night," she said.

"No, it wasn't," Oscar said. He snapped the leg off a snowman. "It was morning and the sun was shining—we were all in exercise class." He leaned in. "That's what they call it but it's really just old folks standing in a circle passing wind."

"Oscar!" Nuala shook her finger at him.

Oscar chuckled. "Ah, now. It is. You know it is."

"Ever since they stole his cane he's been as prickly as a briar patch," Beverly said.

A tear came to Oscar's eye. "That was from me pilgrimage. You can't replace it." He looked at the guards once again. "But you are going to try, aren't you?"

"Of course we are," Siobhán said. "In the meantime, we're still trying to figure out how the thieves entered the house without being seen."

Rory squirmed in his seat, then lifted his hand in the air. "No need to raise your hand," Macdara said.

Rory extended his arm, pointing at Beverly. "This one's been leaving the back door ajar trying to woo a wee fox."

"Trying to what a what?" Macdara asked.

"He's a lovely red fox, so he is," Beverly said. "I've named him Rudolph."

"He's a wild animal," Rory said. "You're asking for trouble."

Beverly gasped. "That's the same thing you said about me scarf."

Rory threw his hands up. "I was right, wasn't I?"

Beverly dropped her head and moaned.

"It's alright, luv," Siobhán said. "Rory isn't blaming you. It's the killer who's responsible for where that scarf ended up, and no one else."

"She's right of course," Rory said. "I'm sorry, Beverly. I didn't mean to imply you had anything to do with that poor lad's death. I just don't think you should be inviting a wee red fox into the house."

"It is best to leave wild animals alone," Macdara said. "Did you leave the back door ajar that morning?"

Beverly lifted a Christmas tree cookie in front of her face as if she was hoping to hide behind it. "Will I be arrested if I did?"

"Throw the book at her!" Nuala said. "I'll sue. We should all sue!" Heads turned to stare at Nuala. She stared back and then finally broke it off with a laugh. "I'm only messing. I'm just back from the doctor and he's given me terrible news."

Everyone leaned forward, concern stamped on their faces. "What's wrong, pet?" Beverly cooed.

"He said I'm perfectly healthy and going to live a long, long life." Nuala kept her face still as those around her took ages to catch on to the joke.

"That's a terrible, terrible thing to say to people of our age," Beverly said. "Shame on you, Nuala."

Nuala shook her head. "You'd think at this age we'd have learned to have a bit of craic."

"There's a killer running loose," Oscar said.

"And a thief," Rory added.

"Who cares about the thefts when there's a killer?" Oscar said.

Rory shook his head. "That's easy for you to say. All you lost was a cane. I lost five hundred euro and it was me Christmas shopping money!"

Siobhán's heart gave a squeeze. She still wanted to replace all their stolen items as soon as possible.

"Go on, lads, have a row," Nuala said. "That will be some craic. Do you want to put on your brown robes and settle it like men?"

All chatter came to screeching halt. Oscar froze with the rest of his snowman cookie halfway to his gob.

Rory placed his hot chocolate on the table with a *thunk*. "I suppose that's us outed," he said. "Oscar and I did borrow a pair of brown robes from the Christmas market. As Nuala said—just for a bit of craic." He seared Nuala with a look. "You seem fond of the craic, yet won't let us have a bit of our own, heh?"

Nuala pursed her lips and shrugged.

"Wait," Siobhán said. "You weren't at the Christmas market that morning. You said you were here in exercise class."

"Max scared the fox off anyway," Beverly said as if there wasn't an entirely new conversation taking place. "Came tearing out the back door barking. The fox took off. And that was a good ending to the story. As soon as I realized that Max and the fox might get into a row, I stopped encouraging the fox to come around."

Macdara nodded. "Well played, Beverly." He turned back to Oscar and Rory. "Were the two of you at the Christmas market?"

"No," Oscar said. "A little friend of ours brought the robes back for us. I'd been telling her all about the monks from days of yore. She thought we'd get a laugh at it."

She. Bonnie. Had she stolen the robes for herself and a partner-in-crime? When Oscar and Rory noticed them did she switch tracks and pretend they were for them?

"And she works at the market, so she was going

to return them the next day. Only when we went to give them back, they were missing!" Rory added.

"It's obvious what happened," Oscar said. "The robes we borrowed were stolen!"

"You stole them first," Beverly pointed out.

Oscar frowned, then shrugged and started over. "I hung it on a hook right next to the bedside table where I used to have me cane."

"Why didn't you tell us about this immediately?" Macdara said.

"You were only just here," Rory said. "Now you're back. In our world, this is as immediate as you get."

"Sorry I'm late," a little voice popped up. They turned around to find Sinead in the doorway.

"Hello, luv," Macdara said. "How was the finger-print demonstration?"

Sinead clasped her hands together. "It was wonderful. They did a fine job, I'm telling ye."

"Did they lift any prints?" Oscar asked.

"They lifted mine," Sinead said. "I put me hands all over the doorknob and they showed me how it's done."

"Were all of the items stolen out of your rooms?" Siobhán asked.

Heads nodded. "And the rooms are all on the second floor?" Once again heads nodded. "Is there a lift?" Siobhán said.

"There is," Rory said. "But we've also got a me-chanical chair that goes up the stairs, and a few of us can still walk it."

"He means him," Nuala said. "He can still walk it."

"And were you all in the same location doing your exercises?" Siobhán asked.

"We were all outside for exercise class," Beverly said. "It was a grand fresh day and we had a walk about the gardens."

Siobhán turned to Oscar. "Isn't that an activity where you would normally have your cane?"

Oscar shook his head. "That's my going-out-on-the-town cane. I wouldn't want it in the muck."

Beverly joined in. "Me scarf was on the table near my bed."

"My Virgin Mary statue was on my bedside table too," Sinead said.

Interesting.

Everyone looked at Nuala. Would she say something about her safe? She took her time before speaking. "Why are you paying attention to our things when you have a killer to catch?"

"We believe there may be a link between the thefts and the murder," Siobhán said.

All five of the residents leaned in. "I'm afraid there's nothing more to say at this point," Siobhán said. "But given our victim was wearing one of the stolen items, it's obvious there might be a link."

Sinead bit into a cookie and grimaced. "These aren't nearly as good as the vanilla biscuits Nancy's been leaving on me beside table."

"Vanilla biscuits on your bedside table?" Everyone turned as Nancy Martin piped up. Siobhán hadn't even noticed her in the room. Perhaps she would make a fine politician's wife, always there but never drawing attention to herself unless it was absolutely necessary. It sounded like a dreadful life to Siobhán, hiding in the shadows. "I haven't been leaving vanilla biscuits on your beside table," Nancy continued.

"Then where have they been coming from?" Sinead said. "Santy's elves?"

"I've been getting them too," Nuala said.

"And me," Rory added.

Oscar raised his hand. "Me too."

"It sounds as if our ant problem has been solved," Nancy said, shaking her head. "Our housekeeper has been very cross about the whole business."

Beverly bobbed her head. "I gave one to the fox. I'm sorry. I won't be doing that anymore." She reached into the pocket of her house dress. "I have a few more in here. Where are they?" She pulled out a pair of glasses and a handkerchief and set them on the coffee table. She kept digging until she pulled out two biscuits. She held them up. "See?" She offered one to Macdara and he wasted no time sticking it into his pie hole.

Siobhán edged closer. "Those look like the dog biscuits we found in Michael's room."

Macdara lunged for a napkin as if he was think-ing of spitting it out, then paused as if considering it, shrugged, and swallowed. "They aren't bad, but if I start barking you can put me outside at night." He winked at Siobhán.

"Dog biscuits?" Rory sputtered. "Someone's been feeding us dog biscuits?"

A whir of black and white fur shot through the room. Max was suddenly sitting up straight in front of Beverly, tongue out, whining.

"I thought Max was at Bill Casey's farm," Siob-hán said.

"We missed him terribly," Beverly said, patting him on the head. "We're all over the moon about him."

"Bill dropped him off for a little visit," Nancy said.

"Have a biscuit," Beverly said, pointing to the one on the table. Max leaned in. "Wait," she said, holding up her finger. "Wait until I say you can have it." Max eyed the biscuit but remained still.

"He's so well trained," Beverly said.

"Hold on a minute." Siobhán approached the coffee table and pointed to Beverly's glasses. "Are these very dear?"

Beverly shook her head. "Cheap ones from the chemist, luv. Why?"

"I'd like to try something. I promise I will buy you a new pair."

Beverly shrugged. "Be my guest."

Siobhán moved the eyeglasses right next to the Christmas biscuit. Without hesitation, Max ignored the cookie, snatched the pair of eyeglasses, and ran out of the room.

"What just happened?" Nancy Martin said.

"We've just learned we've all been eating dog biscuits," Rory said.

"And we just caught our thief," Macdara added.

Siobhán headed after Max. "He was trained to steal any item that was situated right next to a biscuit. Let's see where he goes." Everyone scrambled up and headed after Siobhán.

"Woof," Beverly said as she trailed behind. "I didn't see this coming."

Chapter Ten

Max was quick. He was down the hallway and whining at the back door by the time they caught up. "This door was propped open when all the items were stolen," Siobhán said. "Beverly had been forgetting to close it after looking for the fox."

"Let's see where Max takes the glasses," Macdara said. He opened the back door and Max zoomed off, morphing into a black and white blob as he streaked across the grounds. They hurried after him.

"He is super fast," Siobhán said.

"It explains how he managed to steal all the items while everyone was exercising out front," Macdara said. "Good on you for putting it together."

"Lucky for us Beverly had that biscuit in her pocket." They jogged after Max; he knew exactly where he was going. The grounds ended at a road. Max sat at the edge of the road, the glasses in his mouth.

Siobhán and Macdara stopped. "It's like he's expecting someone to be here," Siobhán said.

"A car," Macdara said. "Max brought the goods to a waiting car."

Max dropped the eyeglasses. Siobhán swooped in and grabbed them. "Unharmed," she said. Max turned and looked at them. Siobhán patted him on the head. "Little thief," she said. She turned to find the residents making their way toward them. She handed Beverly her eyeglasses.

"They have slobber all over them," she bemoaned.

"We'll still buy you a new pair," Siobhán said.

"Why is he just sitting there?" Rory said. "Where did he take our things?"

Macdara turned to face the group. "We're sorry to report we think our thieves had been waiting here in a car. Your items could be anywhere by now."

"But why?" Oscar said. "A cane? A Virgin Mary statue? A scarf? That doesn't make any sense."

"I think it was part of the training," Siobhán said. "The game. What they were really after were the emeralds. It's the only thing that makes any sense."

"You believe me now, do ye?" Nuala said.

"Yes," Siobhán said.

Nuala thrust her chin up. "I told youse I had emeralds. They've been in me family for ages."

"Don't be ridiculous," Beverly said. "A dog

couldn't open a safe and carry emeralds out in his mouth."

"You're right there," Siobhán said. "I believe the emeralds were in Sinead's Virgin Mary statue."

Sinead gasped. "Whatever do you mean?"

"When we were at the Christmas market we found similar statues. Made by the same family for generations. Were you aware the statue was hollow and there's a little compartment inside?"

"I was," Sinead said. "I never used it."

"I'm afraid that Michael must have known about it. He hid the emeralds in the statue and trained his dog to take the items. I think he wanted to throw us off by stealing items that seemed to have very little value."

"How did anyone get my emeralds?" Nuala said.

"Does your grandson have the combination to the safe?" Siobhán asked. It was delicate territory.

Nuala's face hardened and she wagged her finger at them. "Are you calling my grandson a thief?"

Siobhán stayed calm. "I'm only asking if he had the combination."

She pursed her lips. "I trust him with me life."

"Perhaps he showed someone the emeralds. Perhaps he didn't realize how good that person was at reading combinations," Siobhán said. She started walking toward the house. "Follow me." She led them back inside to the library. She pointed to the binoculars on the table. "I don't have any gloves." She pulled her sleeves over her hands, picked them up, and looked through them. "I can see the security panel from here," she said. "I think our thief used these binoculars to steal that code. Perhaps the same was done with Nuala's safe."

"We need to speak with Finn, Bonnie, and Shane," Macdara said. "One of them was in on it with Michael. I have a feeling whoever was in the mysterious blue car might be Michael's devious sidekick." He glanced at Nuala. "I think we're going to need a look at that safe now."

Everyone gathered in Nuala's room as she opened her closet. On the back shelf sat a small safe. She gestured to it. "How could anyone have used binoculars to see this combination?"

She was right. It was hidden by Nuala's wardrobe, mostly long, dark dresses. "Had you taken them out of the safe for any reason?" Macdara asked. "Maybe to polish them or show them to anyone?"

Nuala frowned. "I didn't. But my grandson is sweet on that Bonnie girl. Only she liked Michael. I'm worried he may have decided to impress her. He must have opened the safe to show them to her and she was sneaky enough to watch him do it."

"Do you have any paperwork or photos of the emeralds? Any insurance on them?" Siobhán asked.

"We'd like to get any documentation we can on them," Macdara said. "Including any valuations."

"If they were the reason that young man is dead, I don't want anything more to do with them," Nuala said. "A life is way more precious than a few emeralds."

"Of course," Siobhán said. "But we'll still need that paperwork for our inquiry. And everyone has been very generous in giving to Michael's favorite causes."

"Finn has all my paperwork," she said. "And his friend Shane has been such a big help."

"What do you mean?" Siobhán asked feeling a tingle at the base of her spine. "A big help in what way?"

"He appraises precious gems," Nuala said. "Finn hired him to get an appraisal on me emeralds."

"You mean they removed the emeralds to appraise them?" Macdara asked.

"No," Nuala said. "They were stolen before an appraisal could be done."

There was something very odd about that. Neither Finn nor Shane had stepped forward with this information. Macdara and Siobhán gravitated toward the window on the far side of the room so they could have a private chat.

"Bonnie and Shane," Macdara said. "Or should we call them Bonnie and Clyde?"

"What do you make of this appraisal business?" Siobhán said. "Not one of them has mentioned it."

"They're definitely being squirrely," Macdara said. "But we still need hard evidence of a crime."

Siobhán sighed. "Unless we find the stolen items, we can't even prove my theory that the emeralds are in the statue," Siobhán said.

"The good news is that Michael's partner or partners in crime, whoever they may be, haven't had enough time to do anything with the stolen objects." Macdara gave a wave to Nuala, who seemed keen on overhearing their conversation. Nuala quickly looked away.

"I wouldn't be so sure about that," Siobhán said.

"A small statue is very easy to ship. And with so many packages being mailed out at Christmas, it's not like the post office would have been suspicious."

"We could, however, find out if any of our suspects have been to the post office since the theft," Macdara said. "It wouldn't be proof but it might help us narrow down the suspect pool."

"Sounds like we have a ton of CCTV footage to go through. Shall we make popcorn?"

"Sounds delicious."

"Not to eat," Siobhán said. "To string and to make into decorative balls. For Christmas."

Macdara scrunched his face. "Popcorn on a string? In balls?"

"Gráinne saw it in a magazine. I think it would be lovely."

"I'm making a batch just to eat," Macdara said. "If you want to string yours up, be my guest."

"And, we should pop by the market for some hot cocoa. And maybe a nip of Irish cream."

"Now *that's* the woman I married," Macdara said, slinging his arm around her. "But next year, instead of hours and hours worth of CCTV footage, let's watch *It's A Wonderful Life* instead."

Bellies full of popcorn later, and no balls or strings to show for it, Siobhán and Macdara had gleaned nothing of value from the CCTV tapes. They had one more to go. Macdara held up the USB stick. "This little piggy went to the market," he said. They watched as another camera angle opened on the Christmas market. At first it just looked like a sea of townsfolk doing their pre-Christmas shopping and eating. Macdara yawned, his eyes drooping. Siobhán caught movement in the corner of the screen. She zoomed in on what looked like a couple arguing. It took her a moment to realize it was Nancy Martin and Cathal Ryan. She looked at the date on the tape. It was from the trip that most of the residents had taken, leaving the five behind who were exercising in the yard. Siobhán elbowed Macdara. He jerked awake and rubbed his eyes. "Sorry."

"Look at this." She pointed to Nancy and Cathal on the screen. "Didn't Nancy say she stayed at the grounds with the five who remained?"

"She did," Macdara said. "Why would she lie?" He peered closer. "Is it just me or does that look like a lovers' quarrel?"

"And remember when Cathal looked all mussed-up and was tucking his shirt in on our first visit to the home?"

"They were making up," Macdara said. "From whatever this is."

"I'd nearly forgotten about what Mr. Casey said," Siobhán said. "How Michael Walsh ran over part of his garden with his tractor."

"Looks like we need to confront Mr. Ryan with a few things," Macdara said.

Siobhán stopped the tape and stood. "He wasn't at the care home earlier, so it must be his day off."

"Let's pay the man a visit." He looked at his watch. "I think it's best if we call it a day and surprise him in the morning before he goes to work."

Macdara's mobile rang, startling both of them. "It's Doctor Brady," he said. "Our plans are going to have to wait."

Jeanie met them at O'Rourke's Pub. They exchanged pleasantries with Declan and took a cozy booth by the fire. "Thank you lads for meeting me here," Jeanie said. "I'm so hungry I could eat a small horse." She winked. "Or shall I get with the season and say 'eat a small reindeer'?"

Siobhán was too full on popcorn to join her but Macdara ordered a ham and cheese toastie and crisps while Jeanie ordered bacon and cabbage. They all had a pint of the black stuff, and soon it was on to business.

"There are only a couple of findings that I thought might be of interest to you. The rest is as I surmised. He died quickly, at least there was that." She removed a roll of cash in an evidence bag and placed it on the table. "Five hundred euro," she said. "Belonging to a man named Rory."

"How do you know it belongs to Rory?" Macdara asked.

Jeanie nudged the cash forward. "He's written 'Rory' on every bill."

Siobhán laughed. "I'm so thankful we can return it to him soon." She and Macdara leaned in and waited, knowing Doctor Jeanie Brady liked to build up a bit of suspense.

"Did Michael Walsh have a girlfriend?" Jeanie tilted her head as she awaited the answer.

"There's one lass we know of who had a crush on him," Macdara said. "Bonnie."

"Have you found his mobile phone yet?" Jeanie asked.

"No," Siobhán and Macdara said in unison.

"I'm thinking he might have sent someone, perhaps this Bonnie, a little photo just before he was murdered." She made a clucking noise. "Young ones these days. They do that sort of thing, don't they? Send photos of all their bits to each other." She looked forlorn. "I suppose nothing shocks me anymore, but I do wish they had a bit more restraint."

"You think he sent someone a photo?" Macdara said. "How could a postmortem tell you that?"

"His neck," Jeanie said. "He had a giant hickey." She removed a print-out of a photo and slid it across the table. It was a close-up of Michael Walsh's neck and indeed there was a big red spot prominently featured. "I'm speculating of course, but I'm wondering if whoever handed him the scarf wanted to make sure it was covered up."

"Wait," Macdara said. He turned to Siobhán. "Bonnie showed us a selfie Michael had sent her." He dug in his pocket and brought out his mobile, then swiped through his phone. "Here." He showed them the photo. Michael had taken it from a peculiar angle, and as he was holding up two fingers. The view and his arm blocked the mark on his neck.

"The love bite wasn't from Bonnie," Siobhán said. "Or if it was—he didn't want her to see it."

"We need his mobile phone records *yesterday*," Macdara said. "I'll nudge headquarters. If your theory is correct, then whoever received the last photo from him, and rushed to bring him a scarf, could possibly be his killer."

"And the reason why his mobile phone is missing," Siobhán said. "Maybe this person realized the photo exchange could lead to his or her identity."

Jeanie Brady sighed. "Love possibly kills once again," she said. "On days like this I miss me pistachios."

Cathal Ryan's gardens were extraordinary. He seemed to have taken a page from the elder care home gardens. His front hedges had all been trimmed to look like giant candy canes. Except for the left side—what should have been three candy canes were now hacked-off. Tractor marks were still visible in the dirt. "I can see why this irked him," Siobhán said. "But we'll need more than this to connect him to a murder."

Just then a petite woman came out of the house, dressed in a fancy winter coat, carrying a handbag. "May I help you?" she said, stopping at the end of the walk.

Macdara introduced them. She cocked her head. "I'm Cindy Ryan," she said. "We didn't expect you to follow through with this," she said, gesturing to the destroyed hedges. "After all, the perpetrator is dead and there's possibly a murderer running around."

"Is your husband home?" Siobhán said. She had a sinking feeling. If one's marriage was at stake, that could be a clear motive for murder. But why kill Michael Walsh? He had been hanging around the elder care home. What if he had copped on to the affair between Nancy and Cathal and had been blackmailing him? Maybe mowing down his hedges was a warning . . .

"My husband is at work," Cindy said. "He said he needed to get a word in with Nancy."

Siobhán and Macdara exchanged a glance.

"Were you here when Michael ran down the hedges?" Macdara asked.

"I was in the house," she said. "When I heard my husband getting worked up I came out to see what on earth was going on."

"Did you hear any exchanges between them or speak with Michael?" Siobhán said.

"Why is that of interest?" Cindy asked.

"We don't have much to go on," Macdara said. "Any little thing Michael said might be a clue. I know it sounds impossible but we've broken many a case with the slightest overheard conversation."

He was exaggerating but at least Cindy Ryan seemed satisfied. She relaxed as she nodded her head. "Let's see. My husband was asking if he'd been drinking—Michael apologized and said he'd been reading a text and not paying attention to where he was going." She stopped and gasped. "I bet you'd like to know who that text was from!"

"If you think of anything else, please give us a call," Macdara said.

Cindy nodded. "Brilliant. Happy Christmas."

"Happy Christmas," they echoed, with slightly forced enthusiasm. Cindy Ryan got in her car and drove off. They stood for a moment and watched it disappear down the road.

"It looks like Mrs. Ryan has no idea her husband is having an affair," Siobhán said. It wasn't the type of news Siobhán wanted to break to anyone, let alone at Christmas. But if it turned out to be part of their case, they weren't going to have a choice.

"Bonnie and Michael, and Nancy and Cathal," Macdara mused. "Are we down to suspecting lovers?"

"Nancy is a married woman as well," Siobhán said. "Didn't she say her husband is running for mayor?"

Macdara nodded. "Indeed, she did. But if Cindy Ryan doesn't have a clue, it's likely Mr. Maybe-Mayor doesn't either." He reached into his pocket and took out his mobile. "I'm going to call the station, see if nudging headquarters about Michael's mobile has paid off." If they could get his mobile records it wouldn't include photos, but they were hoping to glean something from the texts and calls. Siobhán studied the mutilated candy-cane hedges as he spoke. Something wasn't quite adding up with this case. It felt jumbled. Like a jigsaw puzzle where they had all the pieces, just not in the right places. "Great news," Macdara said. "I've managed to charm them." He grinned. "The records have arrived."

"To the station then, Mr. Charming," Siobhán said.

Macdara sighed. "It's starting to look like there's quite a few folks on Santa's naughty list this year."

Siobhán removed a sprig of mistletoe from her pocket and held it over her head. "If you can't beat 'em, join 'em."

Macdara grinned and came in for a kiss. "What did I tell ya? Charm."

"You're full of it alright," Siobhán replied.

Chapter Eleven

Siobhán and Macdara hurried to the Kilbane Garda Station. A giant wreath greeted them from the door, Christmas music played softly overhead, and the counter had been decorated with a string of multicolored lights. They grabbed some coffee from the break room and took the mobile phone report to Macdara's office. Michael Walsh had sent three texts during the practice. The first was to Bonnie:

Why don't you dump that loser and date me?

The second text was to Finn:

You won't get away with this

The last text was to Shane:

I wish I had never met you

There was one more text, sent forty minutes before Michael died, to a number that turned out to be a burner phone. There was a notation explaining the text as an image and Macdara would need to file a request to retrieve it. There was no time, they were working against the clock. Macdara called the number. "It's dead," he said.

"Maddening," Siobhán said. "I bet the photo is of the love bite on his neck and whoever received it has to be our killer."

"Agreed," Macdara said. "An affair so illicit they needed burner phones."

"If Bonnie is dating someone else, would that be reason enough for her to murder Michael?" Siobhán mused.

Macdara rubbed his chin. "It might be reason enough for her to take him the scarf. Perhaps it was meant as a joke—one that had horrible consequences."

"I suppose we should focus on the clues we do have." She went back to the texts. "The one to Finn is intriguing. 'You won't get away with this.' Get away with what? Michael could be referring to the robberies, but it's clear he was a major part of them, if not the leader, given Max's participation."

"Maybe Finn double-crossed him. Took the emeralds for himself?"

"The emeralds already belonged to his granny," Siobhán said. "And given the two seem close, I don't think she's cut him out of the will. Finn wouldn't have needed Michael's help to steal them."

"Perhaps he needs the money from the emeralds now," Macdara said. "But his granny was saving them for later? There may be some drama unfolding in his life that requires it."

Siobhán focused on the text to Bonnie.

Why don't you dump that loser and date me?

"What loser is Bonnie dating?" she pondered aloud. "Does that mean she and Michael *weren't* intimately involved?"

"I guess you don't have to be dating to give someone a hickey," Macdara said. "I say it's high time we bring those three into the station for questioning."

"What about speaking with Cathal Ryan and Nancy Martin?"

"Let's get our three unwise men in here first," Macdara said. "If we can't get anywhere with the emeralds, let's see if we can shake some gold out of them."

Finn Doyle and Shane Boyd were set in interrogation rooms 1 and 2 while Bonnie Murphy waited on deck in the reception room. They were just about to question Shane first, when Nuala barged into the station.

"I hear you've taken my grandson into custody and I demand you release him." Her volume startled nearly every clerk within earshot.

"We're conducting interviews, love," Siobhán said. "No one has been charged with anything."

"This entire murder is somehow related to the theft of my emeralds," Nuala said. "Is that right?"

"We're looking into all possibilities," Macdara said.

Nuala scoffed. "Are you guards or are you politicians?"

"You should walk around the market while you wait," Siobhán said. "It's much cheerier than waiting in here."

Nuala waved a document. "Finn wouldn't steal my emeralds, because they were already his."

"What's that?" Macdara edged forward and Nuala handed him the documents.

"I'd already signed the emeralds over to Finn," Nuala said. "He was the one refusing to take them—he said he wanted to make sure we had a safety net—insisted I could live another twenty years." She glared at Siobhán and Macdara until they wholeheartedly agreed with the prediction.

Macdara glanced the certificate. "Why did it take you so long to bring this paperwork forth?"

Nuala dropped her chin. "I truly didn't think it was anyone's business. I wasn't going to divulge anything unless it was absolutely necessary."

"Why didn't Finn tell us this himself?" Siobhán asked.

"Because Finn wouldn't even imagine that you'd suspect him of murder. He's very naïve in a lot of ways. But he's the best grandson ever."

"Thank you for this. If you prefer to wait here I can bring you a cup of tea," Siobhán said.

"You're still going to question him? Even after what I've told you?"

"Why are you so afraid of us asking him questions?" Macdara said.

Nuala's eyes moved ever so slightly to the left. *Bonnie Murphy.* Siobhán thought of Michael's text: *Why don't you dump that loser . . .* Was Finn the loser? What if Michael had stolen Finn's inheritance, and was going after his girl next? If that wasn't a double motive for murder, Siobhán didn't know what was. Nuala had come here to help her grandson, but she'd just placed a big bull's-eye on his chest.

* * *

"Yes, the emeralds were mine. But it's still not what you think," Finn said. "Is it possible to bring Shane and Bonnie in?" He seemed uncomfortable in the interrogation room, which is exactly what the rooms were designed to do.

"No," Macdara said. "We'll be interviewing you all individually."

"I can only hope they tell the truth," Finn grumbled. "You have to promise me that you won't tell my granny what I'm about to say."

"That's not how this works," Macdara said.

Finn sighed. "I invited Shane here to help me."

"Help you?" Siobhán asked.

Finn nodded. "My granny was so excited about leaving the emeralds to me in her will. She wanted to have them valuated again—she was hoping the value had gone up since they'd last been appraised, which had been when my da was around." He sighed. "I needed Shane to fake the appraisal. I told my granny that's what he did for a living. The truth is—he's just great with graphic design and was able to fake the appraisal and certificate."

This was unexpected. Macdara straightened up. "Faked? Why on earth did the appraisal need to be faked?"

"Because they're fake." Finn crossed his arms and waited.

"Explain," Macdara said.

Finn's head drooped. "My granny talked about those emeralds her entire life. How her mother had inherited them. It was her big nest egg, one she was proud to leave to her family—to me. I got some money when my da passed on. I used it to pay for

Granny's place at the elder care home. Granny only agreed to it because she thought I'd be paid back when she died and I inherited the emeralds. When this last bill came due, she said she was bequeathing them to me now. What she didn't know was that when my da had had the emeralds appraised a long time ago he learned they were fake. My granny and her ma had been swindled. My father didn't want her to know. And once he passed, I didn't want her to know. They're worth nothing—except to her. And to her—they're worth everything."

Siobhán was momentarily stunned. If he was telling the truth it was a touching thing to do. Finn looked at them with a pleading expression. Macdara frowned. "Are you saying that Michael and someone else planned the robberies because they didn't realize the emeralds were worthless?"

"No. It was about protecting Granny. Those emeralds were the world to her, her nest egg. I couldn't have her finding out they were worthless. I came up with the plan to have them 'stolen' and I was going to give her the rest of me savings, telling her the insurance had paid out on them. Shane had just read an article about Max—how Michael would tell him to go fetch his dolly or whatnot, and as long as there was a biscuit next to it, Max would fetch it. Sinead had just shown me the secret compartment in her Virgin Mary statue. I wanted to practice and see if Max would actually do it. He was only supposed to nick the cane and the Virgin Mary statue with the emeralds hidden inside. I thought it would look too suspicious if only the emeralds were stolen. I did not plan on stealing Rory's money. I have a sneaking suspicion

Michael stole Rory's five hundred euro. We were going to return the cane, and statue. And, of course, if Michael didn't confess to taking the money I was going to replace that too. I was gob-smacked that it worked. Max actually took the items. We were waiting for him in me car by the back gardens. It was an absolutely eejit thing to do and I deeply regret it. But I swear to you. I had nothing to do with Michael's accident. I didn't hand him that scarf."

Macdara slid the report forward with Michael's text to Finn highlighted.

You won't get away with this

Finn sighed. "It was the last thing he ever said to me. It looks menacing but it just supports what I've just told you. When you two arrived he realized it was going to be seriously investigated. That's what he meant by me not getting away with it."

"Wait," Siobhán said. "If Shane was going to fake the appraisal, why did you need to pretend the emeralds had been stolen?"

"Because my granny was insisting on using her own appraiser. Any day now she was going to find out her emeralds were a fake. It doesn't seem too dire in the light of what happened to Michael, but at the time I thought I couldn't let that happen." Finn was starting to sweat. "I swear to you I was going to return all the items. Even the five hundred euro—although I had nothing to do with that."

"Where did you go when you dropped Michael off at the tractor parade and Bonnie off at the Christmas market?"

Finn grew animated. "I went to collect the items. They were all going to make a magical reap-

pearance on the front porch on Christmas Eve."
He paused. "There is one odd thing, and I know I
should have said something when it ended up on
Michael . . ."

"Go on," Macdara said gruffly.

"That scarf," Finn said. "We didn't take the scarf."

"But wasn't there a biscuit found in Beverly's
room?"

Finn nodded. "I'm not saying Max didn't take
the scarf, but he didn't bring it to us with the rest
of the items."

And what about the fake emeralds?" Macdara said.
"Were they going to make a magical reappearance?"

Finn shook his head. "I was going to tell my
granny that the insurance money would pay out instead." He stared forlornly at the tabletop. "That's
why we split up. One of us had to retrieve the
items. But Michael thought it would look suspicious if only one of us was missing from the tractor
rehearsal. We decided to divide and conquer. Michael would take the tractor practice, Bonnie
would go to the Christmas market, and Shane
would wait it out at a pub, while I collected the
stolen items from my flat. Michael was really on
edge that day. He was terrified you were going to
cop on to the scheme, his involvement would be
reported, and all his fancy publicity with Max
would be soured."

Parts of the puzzle were shifting now, forming a different picture. *Publicity.* Michael grinning, snapping a
photo of his hickey and sending it someone . . .

Finn was still talking. "That dog would have been
worth a fortune if Michael had been able to attract
sponsors. Worth way more than any emeralds . . ."

Finn stopped talking for a moment and tilted his head, as if just now realizing something. "Max," he said, to himself. "Would have been worth a fortune." He stared at Macdara and Siobhán. Beverly's words the other day came roaring back to Siobhán, and she couldn't help but repeat them. "Woof."

Once Finn was released, Siobhán turned to Macdara. "We don't have time to interview Bonnie or Shane. I believe Finn about the robberies. It was a terrible thing to do to the residents and they may have to face charges for the scheme—but they're not the killers."

"None of them?" Macdara asked. "Are you sure about Bonnie and Shane?"

Siobhán nodded. "We need to ask Cathal Ryan a direct question, and depending on his answer—I believe we'll have our killer."

"Does it have something to do with Max?" Macdara said. "All those fancy sponsors?"

"No."

"Then what on earth are you talking about?" Macdara said.

Siobhán gestured for Macdara to follow her outside. She held up a finger as she found a private spot. The hustle and bustle of the market was dim enough for them to make the call, and loud enough so that they could be on speaker and no one else would overhear.

Cathal Ryan answered on the first ring. "I don't have time for a lot of explaining," Siobhán said quickly. "I have to ask you a question and you must answer honestly."

"I'm always honest, Garda."

"When we first visited the care home, and you returned to the sitting room with Nancy Martin, you seemed a bit . . . out of breath. You had red lipstick on you."

"And you were tucking in your shirt," Macdara added.

"Oh," Cathal said. "And you thought Nancy and I?" He chuckled. "I see, I see. Hopefully you haven't floated that theory to Nancy's husband. He'd kill me."

"We assure you, we kept our theory to ourselves," Siobhán said.

"I had been accosted by Sinead. She was over the moon she was going to get to watch guards take her fingerprints and she ambushed me with a kiss to the cheek. I was out of breath because I was late to the sitting room so I ran. I'm madly in love with me wife. I would never cheat on her."

"Good man," Macdara said.

"There's something I forgot to tell you," Cathal said. "I found out why all the furniture in the recreation room was pushed against the walls. The staff was making room for the Christmas tree."

Another piece of the puzzle sorted. "Also on that visit you were missing your car keys, were you not?" Siobhán asked.

"I was," he said. "The housekeeper found them. I must have dropped them out of me pocket. I'm always on the go, I should be more careful where I put my keys."

"Do you drive a blue Toyota Corolla?"

There was a long pause. "I do."

"When you returned to your car that day—was

there anything odd? Seat placement? Scents? Any-thing?"

"As a matter of fact—the radio station had changed. Horrible, horrible noise."

"We saw you on CCTV with Nancy Martin at the underpass," Macdara said. "It was the same day as the thefts. You appeared to be arguing."

"We were just upset," Cathal said. "The robberies had just occurred so she came to collect me."

"Thank you." Siobhán hung up before Cathal started asking them questions.

"Well?" Macdara asked.

"Nancy and Cathal were not romantically in-volved. Whoever was involved with Michael was willing to kill to keep the affair a secret." She waited as Macdara frowned. "Do you not think the future Mrs. Mayor might have wanted it kept under wraps?"

"Nancy Martin?" Macdara said. "And Michael Walsh?"

"I'd bet me life on it. She had access to every-thing. The brown robe. Cathal's car. Remember how his keys went missing? Don't tell me that's a coincidence. We know Michael could fixate on people. My guess is what started out as a little romp turned more serious for him. Maybe he wanted Rory's five hundred euro to splurge on her. She was in and out of Beverly's room; she could have easily taken the scarf right after the thefts. The residents had just been talking about long scarf syndrome. And then there was the loud music playing in the car—heavy metal. Prior to that she'd been blasting Christmas music in the house. Everyone commented on it. She wanted people to notice it. This way no one would associate her with someone else's car blasting heavy metal. And that way no one could hear her voice as she got out of the car and spoke with Michael."

"He must have sent her a picture of his hickey so she brought him a scarf to cover it up," Macdara said.

"That's probably what Michael thought. That's why he allowed her to put the scarf around his neck. A little joke between secret lovers. But she was around for all that long scarf talk. I think she knew exactly what she was doing." Siobhán sighed. "That doesn't mean I can prove it."

"But she was at the care home when Michael was killed," Macdara said.

"She must have snuck out. Remember—she brought all the folks who'd had items stolen into the sitting room to have a chat with us. But Nancy and Cathal took ages, remember?"

"How could I forget."

"Nancy had enough time to take Cathal's keys, then drive to her lover and back, and return the keys before we even knew she was gone."

"Doctor Jeanie Brady was right all along," Macdara said. "We need a confession. We need a Christmas miracle."

"Then let's help one along, like Santa's elves," Siobhán said. "I have a plan."

Chapter Twelve

Siobhán and Macdara stood in the underpass to King John's Castle, waiting for their opportunity. They had set up an additional tent and parked it at the end of a row just a few meters away. The tent would be set up to collect donations for animal shelters in honor of Michael Walsh. Nancy Martin had taken the bait and would be working the first shift. The tent was located in a unique position. Siobhán and Macdara could stand at the edge of the underpass and pretend to have a private conversation, but given the special acoustics in that spot, and where Nancy's tent was located, she would be able to hear every word. When Nancy arrived, they would launch into their "private" discussion and hoped it would do the trick. It took nearly an hour for Nancy to arrive, at which point they were tired of practicing their faux-discussion and the smells and sounds of the Christmas market made them long to be a part of it. But finally, it happened. Nancy was alone and in place at the tent. They were ready.

"We've got a breakthrough," Macdara said. "Can you believe the future mayor's wife is involved in something like this?" Although they could not see Nancy from this vantage point, another guard was catching it all on film and the feed was going directly into Macdara's mobile. They watched Nancy freeze as she caught the sound of her own name.

"Nancy Martin," Siobhán said. "I still can't believe she was having an affair with Michael Walsh. Do you think she intended on murdering him?"

"I do," Macdara said. "And the Technical Bureau was finally able to access Michael's photos. Thank goodness for the cloud. We didn't even need his mobile! Let's pay a visit to her husband while she's occupied here."

Nancy was on the move. She exited the tent, and broke into a run.

"That didn't take long," Siobhán said.

"She must be headed for her car," Macdara said. "Lucky for us we have primo parking." They hurried to the car park at the back of the garda station and hopped in. It was a little over fifteen minutes to Nancy's house right along the tractor route. Siobhán and Macdara had already arranged for a tow truck to block the road in the exact spot where Michael had died. Hopefully this would heighten her distress, and weaken her lips. Unless they received a full confession, this was all for nothing. But the one thing they had in their favor was human nature. Secrets were difficult to keep inside. People tended to have a clawing need to let them out.

Their Santy outfits were awaiting them in the garda car. Siobhán changed into hers first while Macdara drove. Once they reached Michael's tractor, now adorned with flowers and wreaths and cards, another guard hopped out of the tow truck and backed up to allow their car past. They would park it behind the giant tow truck and Nancy would be none the wiser. Macdara changed into his Santa outfit and they were ready. He turned to Siobhán and grinned. "You make a great Mrs. Claus."

She laughed. "And if you keep eating the way you have been lately, you'll grow right into that Santa tummy." That was the end of their playful banter. Nancy Martin screeched up in a red car. She frowned at the pair of Santas and then laid on her horn. Siobhán put her white-gloved hand out and gestured for her to roll down the window.

"I have to get home," Nancy said. "I have a family emergency."

"I'm afraid you'll have to turn around and take another approach," Siobhán said. "We've just been called in to move this tractor."

Nancy's gaze pivoted to the tractor. "I thought it was supposed to stay as a memorial for the tractor parade."

Macdara hopped down from the tow truck. "We just do as we're told," he said. "But between us, it seems there's new evidence they think they can glean from the tractor."

"Really?" Nancy said, her chin quivering. "I don't believe it."

Siobhán leaned forward. "A stray hair," she said. "Clinging to the wheel well."

Nancy's eyes widened.

"It's amazing what they can do these days, isn't it?" Macdara said.

"The hair of the dog," Siobhán said. "Or in this case . . . the killer."

"Killer?" Nancy said. "Surely it was a horrible, horrible accident."

"Not what I heard, but what do I know," Macdara said.

"If it was an accident, why would the fella have to disguise himself?" Siobhán said.

Nancy frowned. "I assumed it was an actor in the panto," she said.

"We shouldn't have told you about the hair," Macdara said. "Do you mind keeping this to yourself?"

"Of course," Nancy said. Her voice wavered. "If you let me pass?"

Macdara grinned. "No can do. We need to tow this baby. Do you mind turning around and finding another way home?"

"I can't do that. Do you know who my husband is?" Not even mayor yet and she was already putting herself above them.

Siobhán pointed to Macdara. "My husband is Santa Claus. Can you beat that?"

Nancy let out a roar of frustration, turned off her car, and exited with her mobile phone glued to her ear. Siobhán and Macdara exchanged a glance. Neither of them had any idea how to tow away a tractor, so they hoped this would work. "Darling," they heard Nancy say. "Are you at home?

I need you to go to Charlesville. The butcher has a turkey and ham waiting for us—and they've had a run on them so if we don't pick it up today, we'll miss out on our Christmas dinner. I know. I know. I know. I can't—there's an emergency at the care home. Just do it. Just do it. Bye. Bye. Bye-bye-bye." She hung up, then approached the tractor.

"Did you know the victim?" Siobhán asked as Nancy got as close as she dared, eyeing it as if trying to figure out where that pesky little hair could be.

"I know I'm not the mayor's wife *yet*," Nancy said, ignoring the question. "But it would really help me if you'd let me pass, and maybe when my husband is the mayor, there's something he can do for you? Better pay, shorter hours?"

"We're actually not locals," Macdara said. "Just called in to do a job."

"I see." Nancy looked around as if trying to make sure no one was in earshot. "Then perhaps you could do me a favor that's in your wheel-house."

"What's that?" Siobhán said.

"It's so embarrassing, but I wonder if you could look at my back tire. I think it's flat, but I'm not an expert."

Macdara and Siobhán exchanged a look. What was she up to? They had learned in this business to never underestimate a killer. Especially when she was desperate.

"Have a look," Macdara said to Siobhán.

"Not a bother," Siobhán said. She strolled toward the back of Nancy's car, wondering what the possible-future Mrs. Mayor had in mind. Luckily, she had an inkling what Nancy was up to and had already formulated an idea of her own. Once she arrived at the boot, sure enough, Siobhán heard a beep and the boot yawned open. Nancy was controlling it with a remote. Next, Siobhán felt a shove from behind and her front half toppled into the boot. As she pretended to struggle to get up, Nancy grabbed her feet to maneuver her all the way in. Siobhán waited a few seconds, allowing her entire body to be shoved inside. Then, she yelled for Macdara. He was there in a flash, grabbing Nancy as she tried to make a run for it.

"She just fell in," Nancy said, once she stopped trying to squirm out of Macdara's grasp. "I opened it to see if there was a spare tire."

"She pushed me all the way in," Siobhán said. "She thought you would come running to help me out of the boot and she could make a run for it."

"I did come running," Macdara said. "Too bad yer one wasn't fast enough."

Nancy stopped struggling and her shoulders slumped. Just then Siobhán spotted something in the corner of the boot, grabbed it, and held it up. "And then there's this." It was a piece of red yarn, presumably from Beverly's scarf.

Nancy seemed to shrink before their very eyes. "You're not really tow truck workers, are you?"

"We're not Santa either," Macdara said, ripping off his beard. "Detective Sergeant Flannery, and you know Garda O'Sullivan."

Siobhán dangled the yarn. "Belongs to Beverly's scarf, doesn't it, Nancy?"

"You can't prove a thing," Nancy said.

"But we can book you on kidnapping charges, and hold you in custody until enough evidence comes in to charge you with Michael's murder," Siobhán said.

"Kidnapping?" Nancy said.

Siobhán smiled. "You shoved me in the boot against my will."

"I saw the whole thing," Macdara said. "Kidnapping charges is spot-on."

"You two think you're so clever don't you?" She shook her head. "Fine. I gave Michael the scarf. Good luck proving it was anything other than an innocent gesture."

"You're forgetting about the affair," Siobhán said. "And the love bite."

"DNA on the neck," Macdara said. "Amazing what science can do these days, isn't it?"

"And that burner phone you tried to get rid of," Siobhán said. "I'm afraid we have that as well."

"Please," Nancy said. "My husband is running for mayor. He'll never forgive me."

"Michael Walsh was a young lad with his entire life ahead of him," Macdara said. "Shame on you."

Nancy's eyes flashed with anger. "Shame on me? He was the one who wouldn't let it go. What did he think? I was going to leave my husband? It was just a little fling."

"Did he threaten to tell your husband?" Siobhán asked. "Was he stalking you?"

Nancy was crumbling, Siobhán knew the look. "He sent me a picture of the mark on his neck and said he was going to send it to my husband." Nancy thrust her chin up. "I suppose you think I'm a joke. Having an affair with a man half my age."

She was talking and Siobhán wanted to keep it that way. "I don't think you're a joke. I'm sure you never imagined you'd have to do something like this."

"I did it for my husband. It would have ruined his chance at becoming mayor. For what? A little fling? It meant nothing."

"But Michael wasn't the type of lad to let things go," Macdara said. "Was he?"

"Being middle-aged and around all those elderly folks does something to a person," Nancy said. "Don't get me wrong. I love them to bits. But it's a stark reminder of what's coming. Michael was into me. When will that ever happen to me again? One's husband running for mayor isn't as glamorous as it sounds. He's never home. He certainly never shows me any attention anymore. Michael was different. He was so full of energy. I thought for sure he'd understand that it was never going to be more than a brief affair." She gazed at the tractor with a sad expression. "And then Cathal told me Michael had a criminal past. A *stalker*. I saw it then. My life becoming a nightmare. And then I turned around, and there was Beverly's scarf tucked under the chair in the library. It hadn't been stolen after all."

"We're going to need you to come to the station," Macdara said.

"Can I call my husband?" she said. "He'll straighten this out." He didn't have *that* kind of power, but Nancy Martin would find that out in due time.

"You'll get a phone call," Siobhán said. "I promise."

"What about my car?" Nancy said as they guided

her into the guard car. Just then the tow truck started up.

"He'll sort that out," Macdara said, with a nod to the driver. Siobhán turned on the radio and "Silent Night" came on. She increased the volume. After all, Nancy was a mad one for the Christmas tunes. They rode the rest of the way with the music on high.

Folks lined both sides of the winding road as the sky turned a fiery orange before morphing into a bluish-black. Christmas Eve was here at last. A low hum filled the air as the tractors passed by, lights moving through the darkness. How gorgeous they all were. Some had mechanical reindeer and candy canes, others bows, and bells. Even the wheels were decorated, making it seem as if the lights themselves were moving through time and space. Siobhán was wondering which tractor belonged to her brood when she saw an enormous heart made from red lights featured prominently on the bonnet of a tractor. Inside the heart, lights spelled out: *Our 1st Xmas.* Tears came to Siobhán's eyes, and just when she was starting to wonder why Macdara wasn't teasing her for the waterworks, she turned to find his were brimming as well. She slipped her hand into his and squeezed it. James and Ciarán yelled out "Happy Christmas!" as Eoin, Ann, and Gráinne, dressed as elves, tossed candy canes out to the people lining the road. Eoin had Trigger under an arm and he was sporting a little red bow. Max was in the parade too, riding with Bill Casey, and sitting up proud as he took in the crowd. Gráinne flung something at Siobhán. It whacked her in the forehead and dropped into the palm of her hand. She looked down to find a sprig of mistletoe.

"You're welcome," Gráinne yelled.

"Well," Macdara said, turning to her. "When in Ireland."

Siobhán laughed and held the mistletoe over their heads. "Happy first Christmas, wife," Macdara said.

"Happy first Christmas, husband." They kissed as bells and cheers rang out.

After the parade, Siobhán, Macdara, and her five siblings stood in front of their stone house, taking in the beauty. Jeanie Brady would arrive on Christmas Day, but the eve was just for family. A brand-new lion's-head knocker gleamed from the door. Macdara said it must be a gift from Santa. Eoin and James had brought in a Christmas tree the day before and everyone planned on decorating it all through the night. Siobhán had squeezed in the last few hours at the Christmas market and this year each of them would have a new ornament to commemorate their new home. Candles flickered in the window, and a bespoke wreath with white lights and a red bow winked from the door. Bonnie had been spot-on, Oscar's wreath was class.

Thanks to the prodding of Nancy Martin's husband, who very well might make a great mayor, she had made a full confession to the murder. Given the stolen items had all been returned, and the three young folks had agreed to do community service, they were not charged with any crimes. Mostly they were spared due to the pleading of the folks at the elder care home who did not wish to see them charged. Max had gone home after the tractor parade with Michael's family. Siobhán and Macdara planned on paying the elder care home a visit tomorrow, this time with her brood in tow. Cathal Ryan would be busy looking for a new house manager, and everyone was rallying around to support the effort.

Gráinne turned to them, a grin planted on her face. "We have another surprise."

"I don't know if I can take anymore," Siobhán said.

"Sort yourself out," Gráinne said. "Hit it, Eoin."

Eoin revealed a small remote hidden in his pocket and pressed a button. Soon, a word and a heart symbol lit up above their doorway: HOME. Tears filled Siobhán's eyes as she forced everyone to smash in for a group hug.

"*Nollaig shona daoibh,*" Macdara said. *Happy Christmas to you.*

"*Nollaig shona daoibh,*" they all responded.

"As long as we're all together," Siobhán said, "we'll always and forever be home."

I met Noel McMeel, an award-winning Irish chef, at a book event in Chicago a few years ago. He said I was welcome to use his recipes in my books. Here is one from his book Irish Pantry. *(I highly recommend the book.) The photo shows lacy curled-up biscuits that he notes are "eaten with the eyes first." And if the dog happens to snap one up, he or she will love it too.*

Irish Lace Biscuits

Reprinted from *Irish Pantry* by Noel McMeel and Lynne Marie Hulsman—*Shared with oral permission*

Makes about 3 dozen biscuits

Ingredients

12 ounces unsalted butter at room temperature
    (Kerry's Irish butter a great choice—my comment)
2¾ cups light brown sugar
2 tablespoons all-purpose flour
2 tablespoons milk
2 tablespoons vanilla extract
1¼ cup old-fashioned rolled oats

Directions

Preheat the oven to 350 degrees

Grease 2 baking sheets with vegetable oil or line with parchment paper. Set in oven while it is heating up.

Using an electric mixer on high speed, cream the butter and brown sugar together until smooth.

Beat in the flour, milk, and vanilla. Fold in the oats. Place teaspoonfuls of dough 3-inches apart on the hot pans. Bake for 10 to 12 minutes, keeping a close eye on them so you can remove them from the oven as soon as they are fully spread and turn light golden brown.

When the cookies are done, let them cool on the pans for 1 minute or until they are just firm enough to be removed with a metal spatula. If you like them rolled into tubes, turn the cookies upside down on the pans, and working quickly with your hands, roll them into cylinders on the pans. (If the cookies become too firm to roll, return them to the oven for a few seconds and allow them to soften.) Transfer the cookies to a cooling rack and let them cool completely, then serve them at room temperature or store in airtight container for up to a month.

Follow this link for a great article on Noel:

https://www.forbes.com/sites/margiegold-smith/2019/03/18/top-chef-noel-mcmeel-king-of-modern-irish-cuisine/?sh=3830811013f9

SCARFED DOWN

Maddie Day

Chapter One

I kept learning about new ways to murder people. Was it bad karma or something more random? Either way, I wished I could instruct the universe, "That's quite enough, thank you very much."

"More coffee?" I—Robbie Jordan—asked the knitting club members that mid-December Tuesday morning.

"No, thanks, hon." Vicky Chakrabarti clicked away at a green scarf. Her hands and fingers were reddened. The knitting looked like it might be painful, but she kept on. "I surely do love what you've done with your decorations."

It did look festive in Pans 'N Pancakes, my country store and restaurant. My staff and I had gone to work more than two weeks ago stringing garlands and fairy lights, hanging wreaths and red ribbons, and trimming the store's Douglas fir, which my husband Abe O'Neill and I had cut at Greasy Hollow Christmas Tree Farm. My customers seemed to enjoy the decor, even people who might not celebrate Christmas themselves.

"Thank you." I held up the carafe. "Anybody?"

"I'll take a hit, if you don't mind." Eva Kenney set down the four needles enmeshed in the multi-hued yarn she was using to knit a sock and held up her mug. Eva, a few inches taller than my height of five foot three, had a soft figure indicating she might like a rib-eye more than running, would choose cheesecake over calisthenics, and generally preferred eating over exercise.

I certainly wasn't judging Eva for her choices. I loved cake as much as the next girl, and my hips showed it. It was only my bicycling habit and my hundred sit-ups every morning that kept my waist in line. That, and running my tush off as chief chef of my own eating establishment.

"Me, too, please." Cole Brewster pointed at his mug with his chin, his hands being full of needles and yarn. The tall, austere-looking real estate agent was knitting something red that was starting to look like a hat.

"I do love your aunt's yarn," Vicky said. "Why, it's softer than a talcum-dusted baby's bottom after its bath." Despite her last name, her speech held the same Hoosier twang as many of the locals. Vicky had told me she was born in Bloomington, the university town to the west of us, where both of her Indian immigrant parents had been professors. She was a handsome woman, slender with only a bit of silver shooting through her dark hair.

I poured. "I'll tell her you said so. Aunt Adele

takes a lot of pride in her wool." My late mom's sister, Adele Jordan, raised sheep on the outskirts of South Lick here in southern Indiana and dyed the wool herself. I made a note to ask her to bring in more. For sale in the retail area of my store, it was a popular purchase at the holidays, and I was nearly out.

"It don't make my skin itch, neither, not like some wools." Eva gazed up at me with light brown eyes bordering on green.

I was so not a crafter and couldn't imagine focusing on tiny stitches—itchy or otherwise—over and over for hours. But when these three sixty-somethings from surrounding towns had asked if I minded whether they stayed on after their mid-morning breakfast twice a week to knit and schmooze, I had readily welcomed them. It was our lull time in the restaurant, when my assistants and I took breaks, grabbed a bite to eat, and got going on the lunch menu. We rarely had a line of hungry diners waiting for a table between ten and eleven-thirty on a weekday unless a tour bus rolled in.

Speaking of the lunch menu, it was smelling pretty good right now in a space already redolent with the alluring aromas of bacon and biscuits. I headed back to the kitchen area and pulled open the oven door.

"How's the Partridge in a Pear Tree looking?" Danna Beedle, one of my two employees, asked from the grill.

"If by partridge you mean boneless chicken breasts baking with sliced pears, it's looking great."

Turner Rao, my other employee, walked up with a load of dishes in his arms. "And smelling even better. But what are we going to do when we get to Twelve Lords a-Leaping?"

I wrinkled my nose. "Riffing on the 'Twelve Days of Christmas' for our daily specials seemed like a good idea yesterday."

"Nine Ladies Dancing is going to be tough, too," Danna chimed in.

"We could do a dessert with ladyfingers." Turner cocked his head.

"Brilliant. We'll figure out each day as we go along." I glanced over at the knitters.

Was Cole clandestinely rubbing Eva's foot under the table? I'd never seen those two act like a couple, and their expressions looked perfectly normal for friends knitting and chatting. *Oh, well.* Definitely not my business. None of the three wore wedding rings. Even if they did, I still didn't care what they did in their personal lives. My mission here was to provide delicious breakfasts and lunches, make customers feel comfortable and welcome, and keep the finances in the black. So far, my business had been a rousing success on all fronts for over four years.

The cow bell on the front door jangled. Adele pushed through, with a giant—and stuffed-full—cloth tote bag in each hand. I hurried over to relieve my mid-seventies aunt of her burdens. Over her slate-gray pageboy, she wore one of her own creations, a knitted red-and-green striped hat with a puffball at its pointed top.

I kissed her cheek. "Some hat."

"You like it? It's my newest design." She dragged it off her head.

"I do."

"Brung you a new load of yarn." Adele pointed at the totes now in my hands.

"Perfect. I was about to call you to say we're nearly out. Did you price them?"

"Yup, just like usual."

"And, as usual, you don't have an invoice for me."

"Nah," she scoffed. "If I can't trust my own niece, who can I trust? Just keep track and pay me for what sells. That's all I ask."

"I promise. Do you want something to eat while you're here?"

"Sure thing, kiddo. Who can't use a second breakfast? I'd take me a plate of biscuits and gravy any old day."

"It's yours." I smiled. She and I shared a love of eating, and we both worked hard enough to earn the calories. "Hey, do you know the people knitting at that table? They all love your yarn."

"Well, butter my butt and call me a biscuit."

I was amused by her colorful language, but that particular phrase was over the top.

"I might have seen them folks around town," she went on. "Yes, I do believe I have. Welp, no time like the present to renew our acquaintance. Thanks, sugar." Adele sauntered over to the knitters' table.

My aunt was one of those people who had never met a stranger she couldn't instantly turn into a friend. A friend for life, usually. Today was no exception. I headed back to the kitchen to plate her morning snack as she pulled up a chair and started yarning about yarn.

Chapter Two

I was about to lock up behind Danna and Turner at three that afternoon when my stepson, Sean, rode up and jumped off his bike. I greeted him, then wrapped my arms around myself. So far, we hadn't had any snow, but it was already frigid out. My winter uniform of long-sleeved blue T-shirt and jeans wasn't anywhere near warm enough for standing outside. I waited to hear why he was here.

"Hey, Robbie." His fifteen-year-old voice had stopped cracking and had settled into a nice baritone like Abe's. "I need help with something."

Maybe it was a math assignment for school. I could dust off my former high school math-team chops and help with that. "Come on in." I stood back and held the door open for him.

He carried the bike up onto the wide covered porch and left it. It wasn't a fancy bike and should be safe out here.

Inside I thought about what I could offer him to eat. "The grill is off and clean, but I can make you a ham and cheese on rye."

"Thanks, Robbie." He slid out of his jacket and took off his gloves, his cheeks still pink from the cold. He was already taller than Abe's five nine and was still growing. "I'm starving."

"When are you not?" I smiled at him. Sean's teenage appetite was as legendary as our local police lieutenant's. I'd never seen anyone eat as much as Buck Bird—until I met Sean. I busied myself with sandwich makings. "Grab yourself a glass of milk, sweetie."

I had slowly, cautiously, ventured into using endearments with him. The poor kid had lost his mother to a murderer last spring, and I knew I couldn't take her place. But I was quite fond of him and hoped he knew it. He'd never pulled back from my affection, for which I was grateful. He and Abe and I had been sharing a home since I'd married Abe at the end of May.

I set down the plate, plus two brownies, on the table nearest the kitchen area. "Talk to me while I do breakfast prep for tomorrow, okay?"

"Sure, and thanks."

For tomorrow's breakfast special, we were reprising an easy spinach–red pepper egg bake we'd done during a previous Christmas season, with the reds and greens reflecting the season. I brought out red peppers, butter, and milk from the walk-in, scrubbed my hands and the peppers, and began seeding and dicing.

Sean made quick work of the sandwich. He opened his backpack.

I glanced over. And stared. He had pulled out two skeins of yarn, one red and one green, and a set of knitting needles with a project already underway.

"You know how to knit?" I asked.

"Sort of." He swiped and thumbed his phone. "I mean, I'm, like, learning. I have an app, but I'm kind of screwed up right now." He frowned, holding up the needles and a few inches of loose uneven knitting.

"Is that what you wanted my help with?"

"Can you?" His hopeful tone matched his expression.

"Sorry, dude. I have never knitted and have no desire to learn." I smiled to soften my answer. "Math homework? That I can help with."

"Except I don't need help with math. But I don't know what to do with this mess. I wanted to make something nice for Maeve." He blushed as he said her name.

"Sean, honey, you need Aunt Adele. Is that her yarn?"

"Uh-huh." He nodded.

"She'll be super happy to help you. Text her. I'll bet she'll come right down, or maybe visit at the house tonight."

He brightened, his thumbs already flying with the text. He finished and took a bite of brownie.

"Is Maeve the girl from math club?" I asked.

"Yeah. We've been, like, hanging out a lot this fall."

"That's cool to want to give her something homemade. You can invite her home for dinner sometime if you want." I covered my container of prepped peppers and set it aside. We had seen a girl who was part of a group Sean spent time with, and I thought it had been a friend from math club. Until now he hadn't mentioned that Maeve was more than a friend, but it sure looked like it. "We'd love to get to know her."

He stopped short of rolling his eyes. "Maybe." He stashed the knitting back in his bag. "Hey, Robbie?"

"Yes?" I measured out flour for tomorrow's biscuit dough.

"Yesterday after school, before you and Dad got home, this guy came to the door." Sean frowned.

"What did he want?" I added baking powder and salt and stirred.

"He wanted to know if we wanted to sell the house."

"Really? Unsolicited?"

"Yeah. I told him no way. I forgot to tell you guys last night." He pulled a crumpled business card out of his jacket pocket. "Here." He extended it toward me.

I dusted off my hands and stepped over to the table, keeping my arms bent and my hands near my shoulders. "Lay it down so I can see it. I need to keep my hands clean."

I leaned over the table where Sean placed the card. "Cole Brewster?" I straightened. "Was he a tall, serious-looking man? Kind of bony?"

"Yep. Why, you know him?"

"He's part of the Tuesday-Thursday knitting club that comes in here. He sat right over there a few hours ago." I gestured with my chin. "He didn't say anything about the house."

"Maybe he doesn't know you live with us now. You lived back there for a long time." Sean pointed to the door at the back that led to the apartment where, in fact, I had resided since I'd bought the country store, thanks to my inheritance after my mom's untimely death. Until I married Abe, that is.

"True," I said. "What he did just seems strange. Did he knock on other doors on the street?"

Sean lifted a shoulder. "I don't know. I went back to my room. We have an essay due on Friday."

"On what?"

"Yuck. *The Old Man and the Sea.* Talk about picking apart a story until it dies a slow death. If I'd found it and read it for fun, I might have liked it. Now I never want to read another word by that Hemingway dude."

I laughed and resumed prepping biscuit dough. "You know, you don't have to answer the door when someone knocks or rings the bell. It might be safer not to."

"Robbie." He gave me a look.

Sheesh. Did teenagers practice The Look?

"I'm not a little kid," he went on. "I mean, look at me."

"You're right. I'm sorry."

He was totally right. Low voice, on his way to six feet tall, hairy. Obviously—I hoped—Cole Brewster was harmless. Still, Abe and I were responsible for this young person for years to come. I'd hate to see him threatened or hurt by some random stranger.

"Be careful, okay?" I cut a two-pound block of butter into cubes.

"I will."

"And don't ever let anybody in you don't know."

This time he did roll his eyes. His phone dinged and his expression brightened. "Adele's meeting me at the house in fifteen for a knitting lesson." He jumped up and shrugged into his warm outerwear and his pack. He grabbed his dishes, setting them in the sink before rushing a kiss onto my cheek. "Thanks, Robbie. See you at dinner."

"See you then. Have fun with Adele." I followed him over and locked the door after him. Before I began cutting the butter into the flour mixture, I again peered at Cole's card, which Sean had left on the table.

" 'Residential, business, and vacation real estate,' " I read aloud. The address was in Nashville—Indiana, of course—which made sense. The county seat five miles away was a much larger town than South Lick. Next time the knitting club came in, I was definitely asking Cole about scoping out our house. Something seemed fishy about it. But what?

Chapter Three

When I walked into our cottage at four-thirty, Adele was still there. She and Sean both glanced up from their side-by-side perches on the sofa. They weren't genetically related, and their ages were separated by six decades, but their grins were identical. Cocoa, Sean's two-year-old chocolate Labrador, sat in a relaxed Sphinx pose, watching them. He cocked his head to check me out, then resumed guarding his human.

"Looks like things are working out." I plucked off my maroon knitted cap and slipped out of parka and mittens.

"Hard to believe this kiddo thought he could learn to knit from some fool program on his phone." Adele winked at Sean. "The youth of today. Heaven help us."

"Hey, Aunt Adele, most apps are, like, super useful," Sean protested.

I loved that he called her "Aunt." We were a blended family, but a family, nonetheless.

"I s'pose that's true. Anyhoo, I think the boy picked up a couple few tips. Show her, hon."

Sean smoothed out ten inches of red-and-green scarf on his lap. The piece was even, the stitches regular, and the knitting tight.

"It looks beautiful," I said. "You got a mini-apprenticeship. That's really the only way to learn something you do with your hands."

"She's a good teacher. Thank you, Aunt Adele." Sean picked up his phone and muttered what might have been a mild swear word under his breath. "I promised Dad I would put in the roast beef."

"Do you need help?" I asked him.

"No, I know how. Stick some garlic in, add a bunch of salt and pepper, and pop her in a hot oven." He stood and bussed Adele's cheek, then stashed his project in a cloth Bloomingfoods bag, which he held up. "Cool, right? I went to the food co-op in Bloomington last week with Maeve."

"Very."

"Aunt Adele, want to stay for dinner?" he asked. "We'll have plenty. I'm roasting potatoes and vegetables, too."

"Thanks, sugar, but I can't." She beamed at Sean. "Next time."

"Come on, Cocoa. Want to go outside?" Sean patted his thigh.

I watched teen and dog disappear into the kitchen.

"He's a good boy," Adele murmured.

"I'll say. Want a glass of wine or anything?" I asked Adele. "Four Roses?"

"Thought you'd never ask. Samuel's picking me up at five, so I have time for some of my favorite bourbon with my favorite niece."

Samuel MacDonald was Adele's eighty-something sweetheart, an arrangement I approved of.

"Ice?" I asked. "Or mixed with some sweet vermouth for a quick Manhattan?" Manhattans always seemed like a cold-weather drink to me.

"That sounds yummy."

"Coming right up." In the kitchen I filled a couple of glasses with ice, alcohol, and a dash of bitters. The oven was preheating but Sean seemed to be elsewhere.

I handed Adele her drink and took Sean's place on the sofa. My kitty, Birdy, wandered in and sprang up to nestle next to me, purring louder than a ceiling fan in summer. He'd adjusted perfectly well to his new home after only a couple of days. My aunt and I clinked glasses.

I sipped and let out a contented breath. "That totally hits the spot."

She tasted her own, agreeing. Sounds from the kitchen indicated Sean had gotten back to the task at hand.

"You know Cole Brewster." I sank into the soft seat. I'd been up since five. Finally sitting down and sipping an adult beverage was exactly what the doctor ordered.

"Real estate man? Course I do, hon. The fellow in the knitting club, with Vicky Chakra-whosit and old Eva Kenney."

"Yes, exactly. Sean said Cole was in the neighborhood yesterday cold-calling at houses asking if they wanted to sell. Why would he do something like that?"

"I'd hate to think the man's hard up for money. I thought he was purt successful in his work." She sipped her drink. "But I don't know. Maybe he isn't. What I did hear is that he's sweet on Eva."

"I might have picked up on that this morning. It was just a little thing, but that was what I thought."

"Vicky used to go out with him, but she dropped him one day like he was hotter than a potato baked the other side of Hades and blessed by Lucifer himself."

The senior dating scene around here was more active than I'd suspected.

"How do you know all those people?" I asked her.

"Oh, heck, Robbie. You know I'm acquainted with plum anybody south of Indy, it seems like. And when I had that little chat at their table this morning, it all came back to me."

With a burst of cold air, Abe pushed through the door. "Whew, it's getting colder by the minute. Hey, Adele." He gave me a cold-lipped kiss, and leaned over to kiss Adele's cheek, too. He sniffed. "Smells like Sean got dinner underway."

"He's a good boy you got there, Abe." Adele drained her glass.

"Thank you." Abe shed his coat and hat and stuffed his gloves in his pockets. "We try."

My aunt stood. "Samuel's going to be waiting for me. Thanks for the drink, hon."

I rose, too. "Of course. Thanks for helping Sean."

"You and Samuel are joining us for Christmas Eve dinner, right, Adele?" Abe asked.

We'd decided to host both sides of the family for a feast here, since it was my first Christmas in the house.

"Wouldn't miss it for nothing. Can we bring Phil, too? His parents are going away somewheres."

"Of course," Abe said. "And if he wants to include his girlfriend, let him know that's fine." Phil MacDonald, my friend and dessert baker, was Samuel's grandson.

Adele suited up and made her way out. Abe wrapped his arms around me for a long embrace.

"How did I get so lucky to find you?" he murmured into my hair.

I pushed back and laughed. "I was about to say that myself. Sit down and I'll get you a beer."

"Gladly."

A minute later I was nestled next to him telling him about Sean's encounter with Cole.

"Sean didn't let him into the house, did he?" Abe frowned.

"No, and he says he knows he shouldn't. I find it odd, though, what Cole was doing. Sean didn't know if he knocked only here or on other doors on the street."

"I'll see what I can find out."

We sat keeping quiet company, sipping our drinks. I mused on a possibly suspicious person. And on our little town having been blessedly free of suspicious goings-on for nearly half a year. May it stay so.

Chapter Four

By seven-thirty the next morning, Pans 'N Pancakes was hopping. Nearly all the tables were full. We'd already gone through one pan of hot biscuits, and the breakfast special was proving popular. Danna poured and flipped at the grill as fast as she could, while I poured coffee and took orders at a similar pace. Turner would report for work at eight, which was a good thing.

Buck ambled in a few minutes later, all lanky six-foot-six of him. I pointed to his preferred two-top at the back. The weather continued frigid, especially with the sun not rising until eight at this darkest time of the year, and the coat rack already overflowed with puffy jackets and wool coats. The lieutenant kept his uniform winter jacket on, not shedding it until he sat. I made my way over, coffee carafe in hand, and greeted him.

"Boy, howdy, Robbie, it's colder than a bullfrog's hind leg out there, and darker than a pocket."

I smiled as I poured his coffee. "But there's peace in South Lick, I hope."

"So far, and that's the way we like it. Now, though, I got a hole in my stomach as big as two Grand Canyons." He squinted at the Specials board. "I don't need no green stuff in my breakfast. Can I get me the—" His phone made a sound. He held up a finger and jabbed at it. "Yes. You what, now?"

"I'll bring you your usual," I murmured.

He glanced up and nodded, his expression pivoting into ultra-serious.

I poured coffee on my way back to the kitchen area and scribbled an order for Buck on my pad— pancakes, biscuits with sausage gravy, two sunny-side-up, ham, and hash browns. It was a lot of food, and he would get through every single bite. I hoped his call wasn't a colleague reporting a bad accident or something worse. Except I hadn't heard any sirens.

We were so busy it was ten minutes before Danna signaled Buck's order was ready.

"Here's his blowout patches, heart attack on a rack, two sunnies with Noah's boy, and hash browns."

I loved her diner lingo. "Thanks. I think Buck might have gotten some serious news. Let me see if he'll tell me, then I can swap in at the grill, if you want."

"Cool." She folded over a Kitchen Sink omelet and flipped four whole-wheat banana-walnut pancakes before transferring three rashers of bacon to a plate waiting under the warming lights.

I set Buck's breakfast on the table, where he was staring at his phone but not holding it to his ear.

"Is everything okay?" I asked.

"What?" He shook himself. "Oh, thanks, Robbie. No, everything's not okay, not by a heck of a long shot."

I waited, even though I didn't really have time to.

"Seems an older lady died over in Beanblossom, and it weren't a natural death, neither."

"You mean homicide." I kept my voice low, but it was so noisy in here, I doubted the diners at even the adjacent tables could hear me.

"Yup. Her friend found the victim in her apartment."

"In the victim's?"

"Yeperoo."

"Beanblossom is an unincorporated county town, so that means the county sheriff's office will handle the investigation, right?"

"You got it, and Cousin Wanda's on the case. That was her on the phone."

Buck's cousin, Wanda Bird, had started out with the South Lick police. She and I clashed a bit early on. After she transferred into the county sheriff's office in Nashville, she found romance and improved health in her life, losing a bunch of weight and marrying a state police detective only a few months ago. She also became more easygoing.

"Good. Buck, I have to get back to work. Can you tell me the name of the woman who was killed?"

"I don't see why not. Knowing you, you'll start

poking around, anyway. She was Victoria Chaka something or other. Went by Vicky."

No. My breath rushed in. "Vicky Chakrabarti?"

Buck pointed at me. "That's it. Why, you knowed her?" He forked in a too-large bite of pancakes.

"She comes in here with a knitting group. They were here only yesterday. That's awful she was killed. How did she die?"

"Don't rightly know yet. All I can say is, the county coroner thought it looked suspicious. And the death was definitely unattended. You know the drill by now, Robbie. They gots to investigate."

"Was the friend named Eva Kenney?" I whispered.

'That's exactly who it was."

Suddenly the world wanted me. A man waved his empty coffee mug. Danna hit the Ready bell three times. Two women pointed at their empty plates and signaled for the check.

"Enjoy your breakfast, if you're able," I said. "And will you pass along news as you get it?"

He swallowed before he spoke. "I'll do what I can."

I hurried back to the present, but my thoughts were on Vicky, murdered in Beanblossom.

Chapter Five

I was still stunned by the news of Vicky's homicide, but a busy restaurant waits for no one. Who knew a mid-December Wednesday would lure seemingly everyone in the county to eat breakfast out? And not just out, but here. The breakfast special was gone, and we'd baked additional pans of biscuits too many times to count. Buck had left the minute he finished eating without us speaking again of the death. Even with Turner on hand, he and Danna and I didn't have a moment's break until ten-thirty.

Danna made a mad dash for the restroom, and I planned to follow her path the minute she emerged.

"Do we have a lunch special?" Turner asked, neatly flipping two eggs for one of the remaining customers.

"Phil was supposed to bring a load of turtle cookies. That's it."

Turner grinned. "For 'Two Turtle Doves'?"

"Exactly."

"What is a turtle dove, anyway?" he asked.

"You know, I haven't the slightest idea." I whipped out my search device, also known as my phone. "According to Wikipedia—not always the best research tool, but a good starting point—there is a European turtle dove. The name *turtle* has nothing to do with the reptile but comes from the Latin word *turtur*, which comes from the sound the bird makes." I glanced up at him. "Live and learn."

"I guess. My next question is, what are turtle cookies?"

"No clue. Maybe sugar cookies shaped like turtles and dusted with green sugars?"

He laughed. "Not that real turtles are green."

"No, they aren't, are they? We'll find out when Phil shows up."

Danna headed toward us looking much relieved.

"Back in a flash." I headed for my own quick break.

When I came out, Danna was helping Phil carry in trays of cookies.

"Awesome." At the stainless-steel counter, I peered at the cookies, which looked like a chocolate thumbprint cookie rolled in chopped pecans, filled with caramel, and drizzled with dark chocolate. "Thanks, Phil. Is that caramel in the middle?"

"You got it." Phil bobbed his head. "I tried to approximate the candy, but in a cookie. Try them, guys."

I popped one in my mouth, chewing and savoring. "Phil, you've outdone yourself." I should have eaten something more substantial than a sweet for my snack, but I couldn't resist.

He beamed.

Danna nodded her agreement, swallowing before she spoke. "O. M. G., dude. To die for."

Turner gave Phil a high five, pulled off his apron, and headed for the restroom.

"Speaking of dying, Robbie." Phil's smile slipped away. "I heard Ms. Chakrabarti was killed in her apartment."

"She was. You knew her?" I asked.

"Sure," he said. "Who didn't? She was the best English teacher at South Lick High. It's incredibly sad that she's gone."

"I didn't know her." Danna finished tying a clean apron around her waist.

Turner returned and did the same.

"She retired at the end of the year I graduated." Phil gazed from Danna to Turner, then raised both palms. "Sure, you can cut to the jokes about how I wore her out. Not true." He shrugged. "Well, maybe a little. I asked more questions than anyone else in AP. With a name like Philostrate, how could I not love Shakespeare?"

When I'd first met Phil, the budding opera singer had told me his full name came from *A Midsummer Night's Dream*, where Philostrate was the Master of Revels.

"But Ms. Chakrabarti was awesome and responded to every single question," Phil continued. "Often, instead of giving me the answer, she would

ask me what I thought, or she would tell me to go
look it up. Now I realize she was the best kind of
teacher, ever."

"That's quite a testimony," I said.

"She deserves it."

"Phil, where did you hear of her death?" Turner
asked.

"A guy who was in my class works for the county
sheriff," Phil said. "He sent around a message to a
few of us who were in Literary Club. She was our
advisor."

"Buck told me when he was in here eating. He
said Wanda has the case." I thought. "Phil, the
name Chakrabarti sounds like it fits her heritage.
Was she married when she taught?"

"She had been." Phil bobbed his head. "She was
actually getting divorced during my senior year.
That's gotta be hard, and she was still an awesome
teacher."

"Who was she married to?" I asked.

"A Mr. Kenney."

Kenney as in Eva? Interesting. Maybe he was
Eva's brother.

"She never talked about him in class, but one
time in Lit Club we were reading *Pride and Preju-
dice*," Phil continued. "It's set during an era where
women were basically their husbands' property.
Ms. Chakrabarti talked about why she never
changed her name when she got married."

"Can you even think of a more arcane thing to
do?" Danna asked.

Turner chimed in. "Don't shoot me. I know I'm
a guy. But my mom told me she changed her name
from Turner to Rao to kind of unify the family.

She's not Indian like Dad, but she said it was a way to show her love for him, and to give everybody in the family the same name."

"Then why doesn't the man change his name?" Danna snorted.

"You didn't become O'Neill last summer, Robbie," Phil said.

"And Abe didn't change his name to Jordan, either," I pointed out. "When—if—we have kids, we can hyphenate or choose one of our names for them, or even make up a new one for all of us. To unify the family, as you said, Turner." At this point, having abandoned birth control for the last four months with nothing to show for it, I wasn't all that confident a pregnancy would happen, anyway. The disappointment tugged at my heart when I didn't shut it away deep inside.

A diner at a four-top raised her index finger as if wanting her group's check. Phil said he had to run. The bell on the door jangled, and a half dozen ladies streamed in, chattering and admiring the cookware. A full two dozen additional women poured through the door after them.

"Looks like it's tour-bus time," I said. "Thanks for the cookies, Phil. Person your stations, gang." I didn't have a quiet moment to contemplate the murder of the world's best English teacher for another couple of hours.

Chapter Six

No sooner had the ladies from Cincinnati left than the lunch rush began. That one turtle cookie, no matter how delicious, had not been the substantial snack I should have eaten, and my five-thirty scarfed-down breakfast was a distant memory. I finally grabbed a hot dog rejected for being over-charred, wrapped it in a piece of whole wheat bread, and ate it standing up.

By one o'clock, a few tables were open, and my co-chefs had been able to snatch a bite on the run, too. With the lull, thoughts of a murdered Vicky flooded back in. Buck was right. I was eager to start poking around. Except I didn't have any reason to, other than having met and served the victim. I hoped her soul was resting in peace, wherever that might be.

Eva Kenney pushed through the door a few

minutes later, followed by a thickset man of about Abe's height. I hurried over to greet them.

"Eva, I heard about Vicky," I said. "I'm so sorry"

The man's nostrils flared. He pressed his lips together and looked away. What was that about? He had remained standing with Eva, so he was obviously with her and hadn't simply followed her in. In fact, his eyes were the same light brownish-green as hers. It looked like they were related.

"I know you and Vicky were friends," I went on, speaking to her.

"We were." Eva's eyes welled. She sniffed and gave a swipe at the tears. "Thank you, Robbie."

"It must have been so hard to discover her." I had come across a homicide victim or three in the last few years. I knew what a horrible shock it was to encounter a corpse who had not died of natural causes. But none of them had been my friends. That had to be much worse.

Eva could only nod.

I glanced at the man. "I'm Robbie Jordan, proprietor."

"Adam Kenney. Brother." He gestured at Eva with his thumb.

"I apologize," Eva rushed to say. "I should have introduced you to my baby brother."

"No worries, Eva," I said. "Nice to meet you, Adam. Are you both here to eat lunch?"

"Yes, please," Eva murmured. "I'm sorry for, for this." She waved her hand in front of her face.

"You don't have to apologize. Please follow me." I led the way to an open and cleaned two-top. "Coffee?"

"Only water for me," Eva said.

"Do you have beer?" Adam asked.

"Sorry." I shook my head. "Customers can bring their own, but I need to open and serve it."

He pulled his mouth to the side. "I didn't bring any, so I'll have a Pepsi, please."

"Is Coke all right?" I asked.

"Of course." He lifted a shoulder and dropped it. "I prefer Pepsi, but you must get that a lot."

"We do." We didn't, actually, but the customer was always right. "I'll bring your drinks over in a minute and take your order when you're ready."

Eva thanked me. He stared at the menu on the placemat. I headed over to our drinks cooler, wondering if their parents were fundamentalist Christians to name their children after God's first couple. Giving siblings the names of people who went on to procreate together was kind of bizarre, when you really thought about it.

I set down their glasses. "What can I get you to eat today?"

"You wouldn't think I would have an appetite." Eva slid her cat's-eye reading glasses onto her nose to inspect the menu. "But I can always eat. I'd like a grilled cheese and ham on rye, with tomato, please."

I looked at Adam.

"Give me a double cheeseburger with onions, no lettuce, and a side of biscuits and gravy." As an afterthought, he added, "Please."

"Coming right up," I said.

Eva glanced at the Specials board. "Those turtle cookies are bound to be good. Can we get a couple, please?" she asked.

"Of course." I headed back to the grill. Adam wasn't a tall beanpole like Sean or Buck, but he'd put in a similar order. His was the kind of thickset build that looked like he had formerly been muscular, but it had mostly turned to fat with age. He didn't seem to be doing much to comfort his sister as she grieved. She'd said he was her baby brother. Maybe him comforting her wasn't part of the roles they'd played for decades. She might be the nurturer of the two. And if he was Vicky's ex, that could explain the reaction when I'd mentioned her name.

I gave Danna their order.

"You got it, boss." She glanced over at Eva. "Who's the dude?"

"Adam Kenney. He's Eva's brother."

"Brother and sister are named Adam and Eve? That's gross."

A laugh rolled out of me. "I had the same thought." My stomach gurgled at the heavenly smell of beef patties and onions frying on the grill. My stomach would have to wait.

I busied myself delivering checks, collecting money, and busing tables while Danna cooked and Turner worked the sink. When I passed near Eva's table, she and her brother seemed to be arguing. They kept their voices low, but it was clearly a dispute. About what, I had no idea. I took a surreptitious glance. Adam sat back, arms folded across his chest, shaking his head, glowering. Eva leaned forward, as if pleading. As I watched, her expression morphed, with the edges of her mouth drawing down, her eyes narrowing in anger. She began to stand. He grabbed her arm like he wanted to persuade her to sit. She sat.

Danna hit the Ready bell twice. The cow bell on the door jangled, admitting four young hunters in camouflage gear. A woman signaled for more coffee. I couldn't stand here and spy on customers. I had work to do.

By the time I delivered their lunch, the Kenney siblings seemed to be getting along again. I set down their plates. "Can I get you anything else?"

"No, thank you." Adam lifted the top bun and squirted ketchup onto the loaded burger.

Eva, having already taken a bite of her sandwich, shook her head.

Wanda Bird strode through the door. Eva's eyes widened. She brought her hand over her mouth. Wanda, wearing a black blazer and dark trousers, stood holding her elbows out from her sides, hands dangling, scanning the restaurant. Eva swallowed.

"She's the cop who questioned me for hours this morning," she whispered. "I hope she's not looking for me."

"I doubt it," I said without any basis in fact for my opinion. "I'll go see what she wants." I hurried toward the detective. The person who reported the body was always looked at with extra interest. In Eva's case, she also knew Vicky and was friends with her. Of course the police would begin by focusing on Eva.

"Hey, Wanda," I said. "Here for lunch?"

"I do have me a hunger, Robbie. But I'm obliged to do a piece of work before I eat."

"Eva Kenney says you already questioned her. I hope you're not here to interrupt her lunch."

"Nah. She can eat in peace."

"Have you learned yet how Vicky died?" I kept my voice low.

"We are not entirely certain, but it appears to have been a contact toxin in that green yarn she was knitting with."

"A toxin in the yarn? Not Adele's yarn." *No.* It couldn't be.

"In fact, it was hers." Wanda swallowed, shifting from foot to foot and looking uncomfortable. "Which is why I'm here to confiscate all the skeins you have for sale in your store. And any other products made with your aunt's wool."

"What?" I screeched. I clapped my hand over my mouth and glanced around, but nobody seemed to have noticed. "Adele *made* all that yarn. You can't possibly believe wool from sheep she raised and sheared, wool she dyed herself, has something wrong with it."

"I sure to high heaven hope not, hon, but we gots to play it safe."

"You can't just take it all," I protested. Two years ago the state police detective had confiscated all the special Mexican hot chocolate packets I'd made for sale, suspecting they'd been poisoned. That had been bad enough. Taking Adele's lovingly created skeins was a step too far. "Please don't."

"People in hell want ice water, too. By that I mean, we actually can take it. Come on, Robbie. You don't want nobody else to keel over while knitting a Christmas scarf, do you?"

"Of course not, but . . ." I let my voice trail off. What was going on? How could Vicky—"Wait. Vicky was in here only yesterday morning knitting. She seemed fine. Do you mean someone poisoned the yarn last night or something?"

"Look, alls I can tell you is that I got a guy coming right behind me to load up his bags. And you're not to restock until we give you the old go-ahead."

Sure enough, a man in the two-toned brown uniform of the county sheriff's office was next through the door, toting two big bags. But the first thing he pulled out was a white papery-looking garment.

My horrified breath rushed in. "He can't put on a hazmat suit right here in my store."

"He sure enough can. In fact, he's obliged to."

"Wanda, please wait until I close." I grabbed her arm, begging. "Seriously. I'll block off the yarn shelves. I'll lock the door to newcomers right now. Let the diners in here eat without thinking my entire store is toxic." But what if it was? *Ugh.*

She gave it one second of thought. "Joe, hang on a little minute." She headed over to the officer.

Whew. I scanned the diners. Eva and Adam appeared to be the only ones watching the action. Danna and Turner were, as well. Nothing slipped by them.

Chapter Seven

I locked the door behind the last customer at two o'clock and put up the sign I'd lettered earlier. CLOSING EARLY TO GO FISHING. SEE YOU TOMORROW! Fishing, we weren't, but folks didn't need to know that. Wanda was fishing, for sure. I could only hope she wouldn't hook anything in the rest of Adele's yarn.

I turned to the detective and her deputy pal, who had enjoyed lunch on the house while they begrudgingly waited for the rest of my diners to finish up.

"Go for it," I told them.

The dude pulled on the hazmat suit, plus gloves and a mask. Wanda stood with hands clasped behind her back, looking like a civvies-clad guard. Within minutes the two were out the door with their bags full of yarn, mittens, and hats. Adele's display shelves sat empty, forlorn, abandoned. I would need to rearrange all the retail stuff so the gaping hole wasn't obvious, but not right now. My shoulders sagged as I faced my crew.

"So much for Christmas sales to crafters," I muttered, making my way over to Danna and Turner. He scrubbed the grill while she washed pots in the sink. And so much for Christmas spirit, to be honest.

"What was that all about, Robbie?" Danna asked. "Wanda and her sheriff buddy taking Adele's yarn and knitted stuff."

I hadn't had a chance to tell them what Wanda had said earlier.

"Don't you guys want to sit down?" I asked. "I have beers in the back."

"Thanks, but I have volleyball practice at four," Danna said.

"Rain check for me, too." Turner gave rueful smile. "Talk about holiday retail. I have to work in the maple shop the minute I get home."

His parents ran a maple tree farm as a sideline, and their little shop amid the trees was a popular destination for gift-seekers at this time of year.

"Be that way." I softened it with a laugh. "Well, here's the deal. As you know, Vicky Chakrabarti was murdered. Apparently it was by handling poisoned yarn."

Danna made a horrified face. Turner's frown lines went deep.

"Wanda said Vicky was knitting with Adele's yarn," I added. "So they took it all. I assume out of an abundance of caution. No way did Adele use some kind of contact toxin on her lovely wool."

"Of course she didn't." Danna nearly stomped with outrage.

"Contact toxin." Turner looked thoughtful. "I think that means if it touches your skin, it poisons you."

"That's what it sounds like," I said. "I don't know what it could be, though, or where it can be found."

"Do you think Adele knows anything about this?" Danna asked.

At that very moment, my phone rang—and the ID said Adele. "This is her." I held up a finger.

"Robbie, they're hauling me in for questioning," my aunt said with no preamble.

"You're kidding."

"I am not. The whole shebang is ludicrous, but what can you do? Can you come out here in an hour and check on the girls? I don't have no idea when I'll be back."

"Of course." Could I take the time to see to her sheep before dark? I absolutely could.

"Thanks, sugar. And feed Sloopy and Chloe, please. Samuel's busy."

"Of course. Do you need me to call a lawyer for you?"

"Done."

"Text me if you need me," I said. "And when you get home."

"Gotta run, child."

My "love you" was cut short by her disconnecting the call. I sat staring at my phone for a moment, then glanced up at my team.

"They took Adele in for questioning." I let an expletive slip. "Sorry."

Danna dried her hands and sank into the chair

next to mine. "Robbie, we all know she's innocent.
I'm sure they only want to find out if she knows the
evil person who did that to the yarn."

Turner joined us. "You know what? We closed
early. I think I have time for a beer, after all."

"Me, too" Danna said. "So I don't play my best
game. Who cares?" She held out her palm. "Give
me the key to the apartment. I'll get the brew-
skies."

My throat tightened as I handed her my keys.
"You guys are the best."

Two minutes later we had toasted Adele's inno-
cence and a speedy resolution to the case. The
cool beer went down just right.

Now I did have a VGR—a Very Good Reason—
to investigate how Vicky ended up dead. I'd listened to a podcast not long ago featuring a
cozy-mystery author who had talked about the need
for an amateur sleuth to have a VGR. I seemed to
have become a bit of an amateur sleuth myself,
oddly enough. If having your favorite living rela-
tive be a person of interest in a homicide investigation wasn't a VGR, I didn't know what was.

Turner worked his phone. He looked up.
"There are a number of contact poisons."

"Ick," Danna said. "I hope they're super hard to
find."

"Clearly not impossible, though." I squared my
shoulders. We weren't going to solve this today.
"Murder aside, Three French Hens is up tomorrow. Ideas for specials, you brilliant people? Me,
I'm not feeling a bit inspired."

"Chicken stew and call it coq au vin?" Danna
suggested.

"Ooh. I like that," I said. "Chicken, mushrooms, and red wine. We have the first two, plus onions, and I can pick up a few big bottles of burgundy or pinot noir when I go check on Adele's sheep."

"Don't forget the lardons," Turner said. "You can substitute bacon for that. We have plenty."

"We could do French baked eggs for a breakfast special," Danna said. "You know, because hens."

"How do you make those?" Turner asked.

"I've made them before," I piped up. "It's basically eggs poached in the oven but fancied up. You break one into each cup of a greased muffin tin, add a little cream on top, a little Parmesan, and a sprinkle of herbs. They're done in under ten minutes."

"Oo-la-la, I want a couple right now." Turner faked a French accent as he twirled the end of a nonexistent mustache.

Danna laughed and elbowed him. Our mood lightened. My crew was the best. They weren't that much younger than me. But as the business owner, I felt older than I really was. Still, they were good friends. Today they'd seen I needed some comfort and had rearranged their priorities to provide it.

Chapter Eight

I pedaled, head down, up the last hill to Adele's farm at four o'clock. Cycling the up-and-down roads of Brown County was my exercise and my mental health all in one vigorous package. It was tempting, after a hard day at work, to stretch out on the sofa at home and fall asleep. I felt much better if I fit in a workout on my bike first. I could think through problems or not think at all. I'd chosen the latter on this leg of the trip out to make sure Adele's animals were fed and safe.

The wind and the temperature chilled my cheeks, but otherwise I was covered in wicking layers. My muscles were well-warmed by the time I leaned the bike against the side of Adele's cottage. Abe and I had held our wedding here half a year ago, outside on a sunny day when all was right with the world. I'd almost never been at the farm when my aunt wasn't, and the place seemed bereft with-

out her old red pickup truck in the drive. At least
Wanda had let Adele drive herself to the station and
hadn't hauled her away in the back seat of a cruiser.

Inside, I gave Adele's sweet white cat, Chloe,
half of a small can of food and made sure she had
plenty of dry food and fresh water. She glanced
up, asking to be petted while she ate. I obliged, of
course, gazing around the warm kitchen with its
broad table where I had both grieved and celebrated with Adele over the years. I'd also eaten
loads of baked goods here, yeasted bread and butter, sweet cakes and pies, and indulged in more
than one nip of Four Roses. This was a place of
comfort for me, for so many reasons.

Right now it was decorated for Christmas, which
made it even more homey. On the door to the
basement hung a quilted wall hanging featuring
none other than the Twelve Days of Christmas. I
raised my eyebrows and moved closer to examine
it. For Seven Swans a-Swimming, six little cygnets
wore red and green caps, and the mother swan in
front had a wreath around her neck. My eyes
perked up at the square depicting Twelve Lords
a-Leaping. The crown-wearing lords were puffy
baked fellows with green belts and red buttons. We
could do that in the restaurant with biscuit dough,
or get Phil to create them out of cookie dough. I
made a note to tell Danna and Turner tomorrow.

I shouldn't get too comfortable here. If I didn't
finish my errand promptly, it would be dark before
I arrived home. I had lights on my cycle and my
helmet, but the temperature would drop even
more, and I preferred to ride while the sun still
shone. It was a lot safer when cars could easily see

me, too. Speaking of light, I left the kitchen over-head light on to welcome Adele home, whenever she got here, and flipped on the outdoor light while I was at it.

I fed border collie Sloopy, who had followed me in, and made sure he had fresh water. I shot Abe a text about where I was and that I was heading for my store soon to do prep for tomorrow. I knew I couldn't relax until we were ready for the morning rush. He wrote back almost instantly.

I'll meet you there with dinner plus hands ready to help.

A smile split my face. What a guy.

You're on. And thank you!

I would be sweaty from the ride, though, and hadn't thought to bring a change of clothes on the ride. I sometimes kept a few extras in my old apart-ment, but I didn't think I had anything warm back there.

Bring my black leggings and UCSB fleece?

I'd picked up a sweatshirt from the local Univer-sity of California campus almost two years ago when I'd been back in Santa Barbara for my high school reunion, even though my own alma mater was the San Luis Obispo campus. Abe texted back, including a winking emoji.

Gotcha.

On my way out, I glanced into the front room, where Adele had her loom. She sold her knitted products, mostly hats and mittens, but she saved her weavings for loved ones. I hated the thought of my aunt—strong and kind, fierce and fearless, com-petent and caring—being questioned by the police, even though I knew she could stick up for herself.

Who would have wanted to kill Vicky Chakra-barti by poisoning the strands that ran through her fingers? Adele sent her wool out to be carded and spun, but she dyed it herself. She wound the skeins and added her custom paper label. Did Vicky's murderer also hold a grudge against Adele? Had the killer wanted to redirect blame away from themself and cast it on Adele?

Sloopy kept me company as I forked fresh hay into the wire rack in the barnyard. The fenced-in space connected to the barn with a low door so the sheep could scoot inside to shelter from cold and rain if they wanted. I broke the ice in their water trough and added fresh water from the hose that ran from inside the barn. I counted the beasts, happy that all fourteen were present and accounted for. The herd grew in the summer with the year's new lambs, but Adele had always said two dozen plus a couple was a manageable size for her.

I gave Sloopy's head a scritch and locked the door to the cottage, since he had a dog door that let him go in and out at will. Gazing around the property after I clipped my shoes into the pedals of my metal steed, I took my memories back to Abe's and my beautiful wedding right here on the farm at the end of May. After the ceremony, facing all our loved ones—and with the sheep also ob-serving from the other side of the fence—my heart had nearly burst. Eating roast pig under a tent and dancing in the barn, scrubbed down for the occasion, had provided a proverbial cherry on the top.

Now I began my trip homeward, sort of, with a detour planned to the market in downtown South

Lick where I could pick up wine for tomorrow's stew.

As I rode back down Beanblossom Road through the dark and slanting shadows of a December afternoon, I thought again about Cole Brewster. Adele had said he'd dated Vicky, but that she'd dropped him. Surely he wouldn't murder her over a relationship that hadn't worked out—would he? Phil had mentioned Vicky was divorced from a Mr. Kenney. If her husband had been Adam Kenney, would he harbor long-standing resentments and now, after at least a decade, kill her? That seemed like a stretch, too.

When my front wheel hit a rut, I was almost wrenched from the bike. I kept my balance at the last minute and cycled more slowly. The daylight was already dimming into the gloaming. *Gloaming* was a word I'd loved since I'd first read it, possibly because it conjured an image of a gloomy, mysterious twilight. Which was all fine in a work of fiction. In real life while riding a bicycle? Not so desirable.

My mind didn't slow along with my wheels. Eva had been tearful about her friend's death. What if she'd faked her grief? I didn't know anything about the two women's relationship. Maybe Eva had hated Vicky and was only biding her time before seizing the right moment to kill her. Or maybe I didn't have a snowflake's chance in Phoenix of figuring out this mystery with such scant information.

Back on a more recently paved stretch of the road, I sped up again. Hard exercise automatically quieted a speeding brain. It had no choice but to focus on the job at hand.

Chapter Nine

By six o'clock I was in my comfy warm clothes, including dry socks and Uggs, both of which I needed but had forgotten to ask Abe to bring. It was no fun clacking around in bike shoes. Abe, bless his sweet heart, had included fleece socks and the furry slipper-boots with my clothes. *Tosca* played on the speakers, a loaded roast beef sandwich on toasted sourdough bread and a drinking glass half full of cabernet sauvignon sat in front of me, while a handsome husband faced me across the table. I'd picked up a bottle of wine for our dinner while grabbing the big bottles for the coq.

"I'm worried about Adele." I had to trust that Wanda was only soliciting information about Adele's yarn and would believe what my aunt told her, but it wasn't easy.

"Everything's going to be fine, darlin'," Abe

said. "I'm sure Adele will be released and home soon."

"I hope so." I took a big bite, savoring the horse-radish, smear of avocado mayonnaise, and thin slices of cucumber Abe had added. "Mmm, thank you." I covered my mouth as I spoke.

"Any time. What will we be prepping, besides the usual breakfast?" he asked.

I told him about our Twelve Days of Christmas project. "So it's chicken stew for Three French Hens."

"Fun. Don't know what you're going to do when you get to Lords a-Leaping, though."

"I had been worried about that, but over at Adele's I saw a quilted wall hanging depicting the song. It had ten puffy lords who looked like the Pillsbury Doughboy wearing crowns and green belts." I shrugged. "We'll figure something out."

"You could have Phil make leaping gingerbread men."

"That's brilliant. Better that than trying to shape biscuit dough. And he could do toy drum cookies for the twelfth day. I should see if I can find a cookie cutter in that shape."

Abe swallowed a bite. "I did some checking around today about Cole Brewster."

"And?"

"He doesn't seem to be the most popular real estate broker in town, for sure. A few customers weren't happy with deals he struck—or failed to—and found themselves a new agent. I didn't hear that he'd attempted anything fraudulent, at least not that I could find, but Brewster might not be doing as well financially as he'd like."

"Hmm." I sipped the wine. "So, he could be trying to drum up business door-to-door. It still seems like a strange thing to do."

"I agree." He popped in his last bite about the same time I did. "Why don't I chop and do the *mise en place* for the stew? I know you have your biscuit and pancake recipes in your head, and that way you won't have to write them down for me."

"Sounds good."

Abe stood and cleared our dishes. "Just tell me what to do, boss."

"You bet." I headed for the walk-in to grab mushrooms, onions, chicken, butter, eggs, and whatever else we needed. My phone dinged with a text from Adele before I got there. I stopped to read the message.

Am home. Thx for doing beasts. Catch you in AM.

Good. They hadn't kept her overly long, but that was a terse message, at least for Adele. She must be exhausted.

Glad they let you go. Anything you need?

No, doll. Samuel will be here by and by.

Samuel keeping her company sounded like a good idea. Adele had been questioned in a case some time ago, so this hadn't been her first go-around. Still, being grilled in an interview room wasn't a fun experience, and my beloved aunt wasn't getting any younger. I tapped out a quick reply.

Love you.

She responded with a winking emoji, which was possibly not the way she was feeling. I didn't care.

I emerged from the walk-in with my plastic mesh carrying-basket full of food. As I unloaded it on the counter, I glanced at Abe. He frowned at his phone.

"What's up?" I extracted a half dozen pounds of mushrooms and set them on the counter.

"Mom's been in an accident."

Freddy. My breath rushed in. "Is she okay?" I hurried to his side and laid my hand on his shoulder.

"I think so." He swiped through the message again. "Dad said her car was sideswiped as she was leaving Nashville after some Christmas shopping. Her air bags went off and such, but she might have a broken leg. She's in an ambulance on the way to Columbus Regional Hospital. Dad is heading there now."

"Of course." Taking her to Columbus—Indiana—to the west made sense. From Nashville, it was about equidistant from the IU hospital in Bloomington to the east. "I'm so sorry, sweetheart. What can I do?"

He glanced up from the phone, worry written all over his face. "I have to go, but Seanie has school tomorrow. Could you—"

I held up a hand. "Abe. I've got him. I can get Turner to fill in for me tomorrow early to make sure Sean gets off to class okay." I thought for a split second. "But he's fifteen, and you know how close he is to your mom. Why don't you ask him what he wants to do? He might feel terrible not going to the hospital with you."

Abe looked at me. "You are so wise. Of course that's what I should do." He gave me a quick hug and a quicker kiss. "I don't care if he skips a day of classes tomorrow, come to think about it." He turned away and spoke to Sean briefly, then faced me. "I'll let you know what happens, sugar. I'm sorry to leave you with all this."

"Go. I'll get it done. Do give your mom my love, all right? And text me how she's doing."

"I will. I'm sure we'll be super late getting home." He kissed me again, grabbed his coat and hat.

"Wait," I said. "Let me grab my bike from your car. If I don't, I'll be walking home." He'd loaded it into the car when he'd arrived, knowing we'd be going home together in the dark.

"Good thought. But be careful, Robbie. Are you sure you want to ride home? You could get a ride-share."

"I'll be fine on the bike, sweetheart. It isn't a long ride." Getting a ride-share in South Lick was always an iffy proposition. It wasn't exactly the big city. Only a couple of drivers worked around here, and they were often busy or AWOL.

A minute later I stood on the front porch holding my bike as I watched him drive off. I sent healing intentions for Freddy out into the universe and crossed my fingers for good measure. Clouds had blown in, so I couldn't wish on a star for her. I adored Abe's petite, quirky mother as much as she adored Christmas. She was going to be madder than a hopping frog missing a leg, as Buck would say, to be laid up during the holidays. I would do what I could to make it up to her.

For now? I wheeled in my bike, locked the door, and got going on my tasks for tomorrow.

Chapter Ten

I glanced around the store at eight-thirty that evening. Breakfast and lunch prep was as done as it was going to get. The usuals were ready to go, and the easy version of coq au vin was cooling in our biggest pot in the walk-in. If we started running short tomorrow during lunch, we could easily augment the stew. We always had chicken stock at hand, and it was easy to quick-sauté chicken, onions, and mushrooms, plus throw in some chopped parsley.

My phone pinged with a calendar reminder. I glanced at it, grateful for the notification. I'd nearly forgotten Monday afternoon at three was my volunteer stint at Cornerstone Connections. Last summer, I'd met a few of the cognitively delayed adults who were served by the day program. I'd enjoyed being around them. One young man had a relentlessly cheerful approach to life that was contagious. A girl I'd interacted with was intense and ruthlessly truthful. When the woman running the organization mentioned they had a need for volunteers, I'd signed up for a weekly spot on my day off.

Speaking of volunteers, I really hoped Freddy would recover easily. My mother-in-law, a volunteer at several worthy service agencies, was only in her early sixties. The older I got, the more I had a perspective on how young sixty really was. Heck, Buck's grandmother was still alive and well at a hundred. Adele and Mom's parents were deceased, but my Italian *nonna* still made her way through life, although her dementia was worsening. I hadn't been able to communicate with her very well when I visited a couple of years ago. Still, she'd recognized my similarity to Roberto, my father, and had given me fond, almost mischievous looks, plus lots of hugs and hand squeezes.

Keeping the twinkly fairy lights lit, I switched off the store's main lights. I clipped on my bike helmet, loaded my biking togs into my pack, and zipped up my jacket. Home was only two miles away. I wouldn't bother changing into bike shoes for the ride, even though Uggs, while warm, weren't exactly athletic footwear. Door locked, bike lights and headlamp switched on, I mounted my bike.

Instead of pedaling, though, I stood with one foot on the ground. My skin crawled. My neck prickled, and I hugged my shoulders to my ears. I whipped my head left and right. I couldn't spy a threat. So why did I feel as if someone or something malicious was out there? I hadn't done a lick of investigating—yet. But if someone was watching me, it could only be Vicky's killer. A killer so far without a name.

The cold night air didn't hold a hint of scent to tell me who was watching. Sniffing, I picked up only a whiff of woodsmoke from a fireplace or wood stove. I inhaled again, detecting the metallic smell of impending snow. But the goose bumps on my arm did not retreat. I kept feeling every hair follicle on my head.

I squared my shoulders. I'd been in danger before. I'd always survived. I pulled out my phone. Texting Abe was no good. He was absorbed with his mother's health, and rightly so, at a hospital an hour away. But I did want to let someone know where I was and where I was headed. I quickly mulled over Danna, Buck, or Adele, discarding each for different reasons, and settled on Wanda. It was her homicide case, and if I was at risk of attack, she should know.

Wanda, FYI, am riding my bike from store to home. Having Spidey sense of a threat. Will text when I arrive home and am inside with doors locked. Hope it's a false alarm.

I sent the message. I seriously didn't care if the detective thought I was being silly or crying wolf. I looked around. No strange car lurked. There was no hint of cigarette smoke wafting from around the corner of a building. It didn't matter. I sensed danger.

Then I pedaled for home. I'd never ridden with such determination. I wanted to speed, but I had to watch out for potholes, patches of ice, and other obstacles barely visible in the dim light from my headlamp. I knew my bike's strong front light and red flashing rear light made me visible to motorists, but the roadway itself wasn't as well illuminated. I cycled past the bank through a mostly darkened downtown. I passed the bike shop and South Lick's artisanal bakery. Both were closed up tight for the night. Strom and Pete's—otherwise known as South Lick Stromboli and Pizza—was still open, but I could see Pete through the plate-glass window wiping down empty tables, getting ready to lock the door at nine.

Few cars were out on this dark Wednesday night. I should have been glad. I'd been nearly run off the road in the past. But I still felt a deep unease as I swung onto Bow Street a half mile from Abe's cottage. It didn't help that my sock was sliding off my heel into the Ugg, nor that my earlobes were freezing because I hadn't pulled on a watch cap under my helmet. No way was I stopping now.

I coasted for a moment, listening. I couldn't hear an engine. *Good.* Except . . . out of the void, a vehicle clunked through a pit in the pavement. My blood turned as icy as my fingertips.

I chanced a glance behind me. About a block back, a dark car crept along in silence, keeping pace with me. Its headlights were on, but it wasn't making a sound. An electric car, or a hybrid? It didn't matter. Somebody was following me. Were they planning to wait until I reached the house and attack me as I unlocked the front door?

Now I was sweating inside my fleece and my puffy winter jacket—and not from my exertions. I wasn't about to lead this person to my one safe haven. Where could I go? I thought frantically, desperately. A side street was ahead. I could circle around and make a beeline for the police station. I wanted to switch off my back light, which signaled my location with every flash, but stopping would make me too stupid to live.

I swung a sharp right. Bad choice. This street had fewer streetlights than ours. My tail followed. And sped up. I'd never be able to outrun whoever it was. Ahead on my side of the street was a well-lit house, illumination from all the downstairs windows a welcome wagon pushing into the darkness. I made a split-second decision, veering into their driveway. Surely the inhabitants would take me in. I dismounted, intending to let the bike fall as I raced to the door. Except my Ugg caught on the back wheel. Bike and I crashed to the pavement in one ugly yard sale of a heap.

The dark car pulled to a stop. As my throat thickened, I let loose a few choice swears. I struggled to extricate myself from the tangle, knowing I was so very screwed if I didn't. And even if I did.

"Robbie?" Wanda called through the passenger window, her voice a clarion call of rescue for my panic zone to stand down. "What in hog's heck was you up to?"

Chapter Eleven

I was dragging the next morning. Abe had called at nine-thirty last night, telling me Freddy had, in fact, broken her leg, but had been lucky to escape with only that injury. Sean was going home with his grandfather, but Abe was going to wait with his mom until she was admitted to a room. He didn't arrive back from the hospital until two o'clock, after I'd been asleep for several hours. I'd woken up to talk with him for a few minutes and then hadn't been able to get back to sleep for almost an hour.

I'd kept musing about my ride home and whether I'd imagined the danger I'd sensed—or not. Yes, the car following me had been Wanda, making sure I got home okay. But I didn't think I'd made up my sensing a threat. Maybe Wanda's presence had scared away whoever it was. When I'd told her I thought I was being pursued, she laughed but

followed me the rest of the way home, nevertheless, and watched until I was safely inside and
flashed the porch light to signal she could go.

Now, despite my fatigue, Danna and I managed
to open the restaurant on time. By seven she'd already baked two pans of French eggs and had
more prepped. She lettered *Three French Hens* at
the top of the Specials board as I unlocked the
front door and turned the sign to OPEN.

"'Mornin', Robbie." Buck removed his hat.

"Come on in, Buck." Beyond him stood a dozen
customers, none of whom I recognized. "Welcome
to Pans 'N Pancakes, everyone. I'm Robbie Jordan, proprietor. Please come in and sit anywhere
you'd like."

Buck ambled to his favorite table. I was almost
physically itching to find out what he knew, if
there were any developments in learning who had
killed Vicky, but that conversation would need to
be back-burnered for now.

"Your place looks so dang cute all decorated,
hon," a plump woman said, her bouffant white
hair a puffball. "Don't it, Gladys?" she asked the
angular woman who had come in with her.

"You bet." Gladys's hair, more of a sheet-metal
gray, was pulled back in a bun. "We approve."

"We came to eat," the first one said to me. "But
we're also fixing to pick up some of that pretty
yarn you sell."

Ugh. "I'm sorry, but we're all out right now. If
you give me your number, I'm happy to let you
know when my supplier has more ready."

"Well now, that's a crying shame." Bouffant

shook her head. "We're down from Fort Wayne for the day. It's quite a piece of driving, isn't it, Gladys?"

"Yep."

The heck with the police. "Tell you what," I began. "The person who makes the yarn lives on the outskirts of town. I'll give you her card. Call Adele. I'd say she probably has some ready and simply hasn't brought it in yet."

"Thanks, hon," Bouffant said.

"From me, too," Gladys said.

I hurried over to my desk and came back with one of the cards I'd had to remove from the display area after the sheriff's deputy had confiscated the yarn.

Gladys took it. "Jordan. Didn't you say that was your last name?"

"It is." I smiled. "Adele is actually my aunt." I glanced at the grill, empty because Danna was out pouring coffee and taking orders, doing what I should have been busy doing. "Please grab a table and enjoy your breakfast. Right now you'll have to excuse me." I waded into my job, my livelihood. Wanda didn't have to know what I'd just done.

I thanked Danna and took over coffee and order duty. As expected, Buck wanted nothing to do with French eggs. By the time I delivered his massive order, Wanda had joined him at the two-top.

"Here you go, Buck. Good morning, Wanda. Coffee?"

"I'd love some, thanks."

"Thanks for, um, looking out for me last night."

"Just doing my job," she said.

Buck's eyebrows went up.

"I'll tell you later, Cuz," Wanda told him. "Your knee okay, Robbie?"

"Yes, thanks." Even though I didn't really have time to stop and talk, I asked, keeping my voice low, "Any news about Vicky?"

She held up her left hand, her three-month-new gold wedding band gleaming on her ring finger. "Gimme a little minute, okay? In the meantime, I'd like two French eggs, a slice of ham, and a bowl of fruit, if you please."

"You got it." I wove my way back to the kitchen, crossing my fingers for Wanda to tell me something after she ate her low-carb breakfast. I gave her order to Danna and took a moment to start another pot of coffee before wading back into the fray with the full carafe.

Every time I looked Wanda's way, she and Buck were either deep in conversation or working their phones. When I delivered Wanda's order, she barely glanced up as she thanked me. It wasn't until Turner arrived at eight that I had a free minute, and by then both Wanda and Buck were on their feet donning their jackets.

I swore under my breath before intercepting them at the door. "Wanda, do you have any, I mean, can you tell me—"

"No. I don't, and I can't. Gotta run, Robbie. Left my money on the table." She jammed her official hat on her head and set her hand on the door handle.

Sheesh. Nothing like eat and run. She'd shared the bit about the contact toxin yesterday. Why clam up today?

"Well, can Adele at least restock her yarn here?" I asked.

"Not yet. I will inform her when she can." Wanda leaned toward me. "Robbie, stay out of this for once, would you? We got ourselves a real-live murderer out there. We don't want no more homicides around here. Leastwise not before Christmas." The detective, now a much-reduced version of her former well-padded self, slid out the door.

"Nothing, Buck?" I flipped open my hands and faced him with what I was pretty sure was a look of entreaty. "Can't you tell me something? Anything?"

"I might if we had something, but goldang it, we don't, Robbie, and that's a fact. I admit to the case being a frustrating one." He tilted his head toward the door. "Which is why old Wanda was a tiny little bit short with you. It's her case, and it's the holidays."

"I can understand that. But . . . she hasn't learned if Vicky had any enemies? Or how the poison got into the yarn?"

If Buck had worn glasses, the look he gave me would have been from over the top of them.

"Okay, okay," I said. "The answer is obviously a no."

"You would be correct. And now I'm later than a—" He seemed to catch himself. "Later than the old White Rabbit for a dee-partmental meeting." He rolled his eyes. "Just another piece of buffalo patty the chief insists on."

"Good luck, Buck." I held thumb and pinky to my ear. "Call me when there's a development?"

"Sure thing." He turned toward the door, then

pivoted back, looking concerned. "I meant to ask how your mother-in-law is doing. I heared about the accident."

"Thanks for asking. She has a broken leg but otherwise is apparently okay. She's in Columbus Health."

"God bless Fredericka. I'll be praying for her."

I watched the big-hearted officer trot down the steps. I hoped God blessed Freddy, or whatever part of the universe was watching over her. Meanwhile, back here in earthly South Lick, I had people to feed.

Chapter Twelve

W e continued busy through the next hour. The rush kept the three of us, if not on our toes, then certainly scurrying here and there to provide breakfasts and smiles, not to mention tables that were clean and set. When previous homicides had occurred in South Lick and surrounds, the death often became the topic of the day among my diners. Not so this morning. Fine with me.

I continued to ponder, when I had the rare minute, why I'd thought someone was after me last night. Had it been my imagination at work? Maybe. If not, who could it have been? Had I already been obviously questioning likely persons of interest in Vicky's murder? I didn't think so. I'd been thinking about the case, for sure.

"Robbie, I'm going to erase French eggs from the board," Danna said. "Keeping them warm after we take them out of the oven makes them overcook, and not that many people have ordered them, anyway."

"Sounds good," I said.

From the grill, Turner nodded his approval, his backwards red IU ball cap not budging.

"By the way, I made a simple coq au vin last night," I told them. "We're set for the lunch special. In fact, I think I'll get the pot out now to take the chill off the stew before we start warming it."

"I'm already hungry." Turner grinned as he flipped pancakes and shoved around peppers and onions sautéing on the grill.

Before I could arrive at the walk-in, Eva Kenney and Cole Brewster made their way through the door. Was it a knitting club day? I supposed it was, but eight-thirty was two hours earlier than they usually met. Plus, neither carried a bag full of yarn, needles, and whatever project they'd been working on. It didn't matter. I went to greet them and tried not to stare at Eva's arm tucked through Cole's.

"You're here earlier than usual." I smiled.

"We aren't knitting today," Cole said. "We only want breakfast."

Eva, with eyes no longer tear-reddened, gazed up at Cole with a look that was unmistakably adoring. This was new. In all the times the knitting club had eaten and crafted here, I'd never seen a hint of a romance between the two, other than when I'd spied Cole and Eva playing literal footsie. *Whatever.* They had every right to enjoy each other's company.

I surveyed the restaurant, which had every table

filled. "It'll be a few minutes until a table opens up. I'll seat you when one does."

"Not a problem, hon," Eva said. "We can do a little shopping for stocking stuffers."

"Sounds good." I had an entire endcap devoted to Christmas ornaments, which included tiny kitchen implements on red strings. Mini box graters, little whisks, and tiny mixing bowls, plus an array of miniature black frying pans three inches long, each painted with Pans 'N Pancakes in store blue on the back. The smallest jars of Mennonite honey and the mini bottles of maple syrup from Turner's family farm were good stocking stuffers, as were the vinyl Brown County stickers depicting a covered bridge and fall leaves. Normally we would also have Adele's knitted hats and hand warmers in all colors of the rainbow, but those were likely locked in whatever county sheriff's evidence room Wanda had stashed them in.

By the time I emerged from the walk-in, carrying the heavy stew pot in two hands, our waiting area had filled with a dozen more customers. People dusted snow off their shoulders and shook it off hats. At least the storm had held off until now. If I'd had to ride like the wind in fresh falling snow last night, only twelve hours ago, I would have ended up in even more trouble. Not that I had been imperiled in the end, but my knee still ached from when I'd tangled with my steel steed.

That fall had been from nerves, not weather conditions or an attacker coming at me. The evening could have turned out much, much worse. In the light of day, I again wondered if I had imagined being followed, made up the sense of being watched. It was worth some thought, but not right now.

I carried the stew to the kitchen area. From the grill, Turner shot me a pair of raised eyebrows.

"Yes, we're busy," I said. "All good, right?"

He gave a single nod as he rescued a couple of nearly burnt pancakes. I returned to greet the newcomers.

We stayed busy. I found Eva and Cole a table, but I couldn't pay any extra attention to them. I also didn't have a free minute to see what the weather was doing. The rush was subsiding by nine-thirty, and no one was waiting to be seated by the time Adele and Samuel hurried in. I headed in their direction as they shook snow off their colorful Knitted-by-Adele hats.

"Good morning, you two," I said. "How's the storm?"

"It's picking up." Adele leaned in for a kiss. "You got yourself a warm cheek there, hon."

Hers was chilled and pink.

"How are you, Samuel?" My cheek got a cold kiss from him, too.

"I am well, thank the good Lord. And happy to have my lady love nearby." He squeezed Adele's hand.

"He means nearby as opposed to in the clink." Adele gave a snort and tossed her head.

"We all are, Adele." I lowered my voice. "They didn't really think you had poisoned your own yarn, did they?"

"I ain't in the business of figuring out what folks in uniforms are thinking, sugar. I surely made it clear to them that I had not and would never dream of doing such a terrible thing. Now then, I got me a hunger worse than an itch in a place that don't lend itself to scratching."

I laughed. "Please sit anywhere that's open."

Adele squinted at the restaurant area. "Why, is that Eva Kenney setting there with old Cole Brewster?"

"It is. They've been having a leisurely breakfast."

"I reckon I'll go say hello. You coming, Mr. Mac-Donald?"

"Of course, my dear." Samuel winked at me and murmured, "Do I have a choice?"

I watched him trail in Adele's wake to where Eva and Cole sat. When Adele arrived at their table, Eva glanced up. Even from here I could see her glare, although I couldn't hear what they were saying. Eva folded her arms and shook her head, hard, as Adele spoke to her. Adele shrugged, hooked her arm through Samuel's, and turned away.

Something was up between them. I just didn't know what.

Chapter Thirteen

By ten-fifteen things were quiet enough for me to slip a slice of cheese and a crispy rasher of bacon inside a biscuit. I pulled up a chair at Adele and Samuel's table. Eva and Cole had left shortly after Eva's encounter with Adele, and I was itching to find out what had gone on.

Samuel sat with his chair pushed back, turning the pages of the *Brown County Democrat*. Adele poked at her phone with her index finger but laid the device on the table as I sat.

"I s'pose you want to know what in heck old Eva was so het up about," my aunt began in a soft voice.

"I do." I matched her tone.

Samuel glanced over his readers at us and went straight back to his article. I'd been acquainted with him long enough to know that he rarely butted into Adele's business or even asked about it.

"Seems Eva's buying into the thought that I applied that there toxic substance to my own yarn. That's why she and Brewster weren't knitting this morning. The only yarn they got is mine, and neither wants to touch it."

I wrinkled my nose. "That's crazy, Adele." I took a bite of my snack.

"Sure it is. But what can you do? Thing is, the yarn Wanda and crew showed me wasn't the exact same green as I use. Sure, it had my label on the skein and all such like that. But that green was a bluer shade."

"That's strange, isn't it?" I asked.

"I told em which end was up, so to speak, and one of those cops had the audacity to suggest my eyesight's going. Why, I've been using that same shade of green dye for nigh on twenty years, Robbie. You'd think I'd know when my yarn's been tampered with."

"Nothing wrong with my girl's eyes, I can attest to that." Samuel beamed at his "girl" of seventy-four.

I had to agree. But was it the toxin that made Adele's green yarn look more blue? It had to be.

"I told Eva I wadn't under arrest or nothing," Adele continued. "I said the detective doesn't have a chicken-picking thing to charge me with. Eva didn't appear to care."

"Did Wanda give you any sense of what the toxin was?" I asked. "The one in the yarn Vicky was knitting with, I mean. How it got there?"

"She suspects it was something agricultural or whatnot. They were still waiting on some lab results." Adele shook her head. "It's a frustration, Robbie. No two ways about it."

I narrowed my eyes. "Something agricultural." I'd learned about a lethal herbicide in California when I was out there and had explored whether it had been the cause of my mom's sudden death. "Like an herbicide or a pesticide?"

"Might could be." Adele drained her coffee.

"So, the question is, who has access to agricultural poisons and also wanted Vicky out of the way?"

"That would be the question, all righty."

I thought for a moment. "Cole sells real estate. He could have found something lethal in a client's shed."

"Didn't he sell a farm a while back?" Adele asked. "I'll have to check. Too, he and Vicky were a number for a bit. He could still be holding a grudge against her."

"What does Eva do for work?" I asked.

"Let's see. I do believe she worked for IFCC before she retired."

Around us a few tables of customers ate. Danna cooked. Turner cleared and took orders. The cow bell on the door jangled, admitting a handful of midmorning diners. I stared at Adele.

"What's IFCC?" I asked after she didn't elaborate.

She opened her blue eyes wide. "Indiana Farm Chemical Corporation. She had a position of some power, as I recall."

"Seriously?"

"Yup. And guess what else?"

I waited.

"Her brother Adam owns a soybean farm.

Shoo-ee, the chemicals they put on them fields would kill anybody."

My jaw dropped. When she seemed to be about to tell me the flies would get in, I shut my mouth. The three people I knew of who had connections to Vicky, also had access to agricultural toxins. That was stunning news. I sat there, thinking. Did Eva have any reason to wish harm to her friend? Maybe her loyalty had been stronger to her brother than to her knitting buddy.

Samuel folded his paper and cleared his throat. "Adele, we need to be moving along." He laid a twenty-dollar bill on the table, more than enough for their meals. "No need for any change, now, Robbie."

"Thank you, Samuel," I said. "We're not going to solve this here and now, anyway." The cow bell jangled again, admitting a dozen more people of all ages looking glad to get in out of the snow. I stood. "And I need to get back to work."

"Say, I heared poor Freddy O'Neill got hit," Adele said. "Is your mom-in-law going to be all right?"

"She is." *But, ugh.* I'd been too busy to look at my phone. Now I pulled it out and swiped into my messages. "Abe says they want to keep her in the hospital one more night."

"Too bad. Well, I'll take and bring a meal by the house tomorrow for them."

"You're the best." I said goodbye to both of them and gathered up the dishes. After I deposited them in the sink, I returned to my livelihood even as my brain exploded with questions about toxins and motives and so much more.

Chapter Fourteen

Three French Hens, in the form of coq au vin, proved a popular lunch special. By twelve-thirty, Danna was already in the process of augmenting it. Buck was demolishing a hamburger alone at his usual table, and I was on greeting-and-clearing duty when Abe pushed through the door. I gave a table a last swipe and hurried over to greet him.

"Too bad your mom has to stay in the hospital," I said after a quick hug, during which my shirt was adorned by rapidly melting snow.

"I know. She really wants to be home. But she's been running a low-grade fever, and the doc wants to get rid of that before she'll release her." He glanced back at the door. "This snow isn't helping anything."

"I haven't even been out." I peered through the glass in the front door. "Abe O'Neill, did you shovel the front steps and walk?"

"Of course I did. I don't want my wife sued by somebody who slips in six inches of snow."

"You're the best. Thank you." I squeezed his arm. "Did Sean go to school?"

He shook his head. "Snow day. He's with Dad."

"Is it forecast to keep snowing?"

"I haven't had time to check. Man, it smells good in here."

I sniffed the air. It did, with the usual bouquet of fresh biscuits and frying meats, plus the background scent of coffee. "Are you hungry?" I asked him.

"I'll say."

"The coq turned out great."

"That sounds perfect. Can I have an extra-big bowl?"

"For you, anything." I turned to survey the place, which had every table occupied and six people waiting. "Go eat with Buck. He won't mind."

Abe gave me a thumbs-up and headed over. I stole another glance at the swirling white stuff outside. With any luck, the storm would keep moving and be over soon. Half the time, it seemed, the temperature warmed in the afternoon. Some of the mess melted, and then overnight the melted snow froze, so the next day all walkways were sheets of ice. I'd never lived in or even visited farther north places like Minnesota, Maine, or Manitoba, but I'd heard there the snow stayed snow until March or later.

I waded back into the fray of a busy lunchtime. Whenever I glanced over, Abe and Buck were both staring at their phones. I personally dished up

Abe's bowl of thick fragrant stew, adding a biscuit
on the side, a bowl of fruit salad, and a glass of
chocolate milk.

"Your lunch, husband." I set down the array of
dishes.

"Thank you, darling wife." He gave me one of
his signature beams before slicing the biscuit and
applying two pats of butter. He worked hard physically and seemed to burn up every gram of fat he
took in.

I gazed at Buck, who really needed to wipe his
mouth with his napkin. But I wasn't his mother,
and his eating habits were his own business. Homicide, on the other hand, I had an interest in.

"Buck," I began.

"Before you up and ask, Robbie, just hang on a
little minute." Buck held up a hand.

"What are you, a mind reader?" I cocked my
head at him. "Did you think I was about to ask you
for any new developments?" Any developments at
all, actually. But the thought of asking was theoret-
ical. I usually figured if he had something to share
he would.

"I do have a small bit we've learned that I'm willing to tell you."

Ooh. My eyebrows went up.

"Do I have to cover my ears?" Abe asked.

"Shoot, no, O'Neill. She's going to tell you, anyhoo." Buck pushed away his plate. "So it seems
somebody soaked a bundle of Adele's yarn in a
contact toxin."

A bundle being a skein, but so what? I didn't
correct him.

Buck scrunched up his nose. "The victim had

open sores on her hands, which made it easy for the poison to get into her bloodstream, although touching it even with unbroken skin woulda done the trick sooner or later."

"I noticed her red hands," I said.

"The substance is worse than the Devil's own cocktail," Buck added.

"What kind of poison was it?" I asked, even though Adele had said it was of agricultural origin.

Abe looked back and forth between us as he ate. I was pretty sure he sensed I already knew something about the means of murder.

"It seems to be a herbicide called paraquat dichloride. Kills weeds and that type of thing. It also kills humans who touch it with bare, broken skin. The whole business is a crying shame, no two ways about it."

"A crying shame and also a horrific crime," Abe murmured.

"That, too, O'Neill." Buck gave a definitive nod. "You got that right."

"Adele told me Eva worked for a farm chemical company," I said. "I assume you know about that?"

"IFCC," Buck said. "And old Adam has himself a soybean farm. Guess what kind of plants they apply that paraquat around?"

"Soybeans?" I asked.

"Yeperoo."

"Adele thought Cole Brewster had been the selling agent for a farm not too long ago," I said. "He might have had access to the herbicide, too."

"I think I heard about that sale," Abe chimed in. "It was a soybean farm on the way down to Madison."

"Seems old Wanda should oughta check that out," Buck said. "Thanks for the intel, kids."

Yes, she should, and ought to, too. Now we knew what the poison was. Who had applied it to the yarn and made sure Vicky received it was still a wide-open question.

Chapter Fifteen

"Tomorrow is Four Calling Birds," I said to Danna and Turner after the last customer left. "What are we going to do about that?"

Danna shook her head, dreadlocks swinging under her purple scarf. "Cookies shaped like old-fashioned telephones?"

"How about four tiny turkey sliders, or four turkey meatballs for a lunch special?" Turner swiped at a table. "Turkeys are birds, right?"

"I like that, dude," Danna said. "What do you think, Robbie?"

"Great idea. I'm pretty sure we have a load of frozen ground turkey." I cast around for a serving idea. "How about this? We could line up four in a hoagie roll. If you squint, the roll looks like an old telephone receiver or one of those clunky early cell phones."

"Serve them in tomato sauce like a meatball sub?" Turner asked.

"That sounds good, with cheese," I said.

"Whew. I'm glad we've settled tomorrow's lunch special, but what are we going to do for Five Golden Rings?" Danna scrubbed at a stubborn spot on the grill. "I'm not sure we totally thought through this twelve-days-of-specials deal."

"I hear you," I said.

"Pour pancake batter in rings?" Turner asked.

"They would puff up and look like bagels," Danna said. "How about onion rings, five at a time?"

"But we don't have a deep fryer," Turner said.

That was by design. I'd picked up a used fryer when the restaurant opened, but it had soon malfunctioned. I hadn't replaced it. I hadn't wanted the mess and danger of hot oil, not to mention how to dispose of old oil. The perfection of our menu was marred only by the lack of deep-fried food, and that was fine with me.

"Maybe we could batter and flash bake slices of onions," Danna offered. "In fact, I think that's a brilliant suggestion. I'll look up the best method."

"Baked sounds good," I said. "I'm sure we'll figure it out. In the meantime, I'll get out the turkey meat from the freezer." I headed for our chest freezer next to the walk-in. I extracted all the three-pound packages of ground turkey and set them on the back of the stainless-steel counter to defrost in room temperature until I left for the day. The meat would finish thawing overnight in the walk-in, and we could roll meatballs midmorning tomorrow. I might even have a few unfrozen pounds in the walk-in that I could assemble after I finished breakfast prep.

Turner frowned at his phone. "Robbie?"

"Yeah?"

"My aunt heard something about Vicky," he said. "Auntie Meena—my dad's oldest sister—is so tied in with the Southeast Asian community, you wouldn't believe it. She hears everything. And what doesn't cross her path, she digs up."

"She's the gossip-in-chief?" Danna asked.

"Pretty much. Meena means well—most of the time—but if you want the scoop, she's the lady to see. She never married or had children, so gossip is a big part of her life."

"Does she live with your family?" I asked.

"Yes and no." Turner tilted his head one way and then the other. "She has her own apartment above the garage. But she usually eats with us. Heck, half the time she cooks for us. Anyway, I know her pretty well. She came to the US about ten years ago. She was living with my grandmother in Indy and working as an engineer, but after Dadiji passed on to the next life, Meena retired early and moved in with us."

Turner's paternal grandmother had taught him to cook and had left him her Indian recipes. She was a big reason he loved making food and why he wanted to become a chef in his own right. Still, I wanted to know what scoop Meena, single snoop that she was, had uncovered. I hadn't met her a couple of years ago when Turner's father had been suspected of murder, but she must have still been living in Indianapolis with her mother at the time.

"And?" I pressed.

"And Auntie Meena thinks Adam Kenney was trying to get back with Vicky, even though they were divorced," Turner said. "Like, you know, sending her flowers and chocolates and stuff."

Adam. Vicky's ex-husband. Soybean farmer. Brother of Eva.

"I wonder what she thought about that." I loaded up a few last plates and pushed the Start button on the dishwasher.

"Meena said Vicky's cousin's wife told her Vicky was, like, furious about it. That she'd considered reporting Mr. Kenney to the police for stalking."

"Wow," Danna said. "Remember last Christmas when that reporter guy wouldn't stop taking pictures of my brother and me at the town tree lighting? I wanted to get a restraining order against him."

Turner snorted. "And instead you grabbed his camera and ended up hurting your newly found bro. Reporter Whatshisname could have turned right around and reported you for assault."

"Yeah, well." Danna lifted a shoulder. She made one last wipe of the grill before throwing the cloth in the laundry box. "Not my proudest moment."

Especially not at the holidays. Things had worked out in the end, though.

"Turner, has Meena ever been in here to eat?" I asked.

"No, I don't think so."

"You could invite her in sometime," I said. "I'd love to meet your aunt." And pick her brain about Vicky while I was at it.

"She's holding down the fort in the gift shop every day in this season." He headed over to grab the floor sweeper. "Plus, she'd probably want to take over the cooking and throw all the beef in the trash. You don't know my auntie, Robbie. She's a force of nature."

I laughed. Maybe I could get out to the maple farm to have a little chat with her after prep for tomorrow was done. If the snow stopped, that is.

Chapter Sixteen

After my staff left at three o'clock, I switched on a playlist of Christmas songs—sung in Italian—and hummed along as I set to work on breakfast prep. We'd decided to reprise another red-and-green breakfast special from a prior holiday season: cranberry-mint muffins. I whipped up four dozen of them, plus dry ingredients for more that we could assemble tomorrow.

As always, having my hands busy set my mind free. What had Buck said that herbicide was called? Panko. No, that was flaky breadcrumbs. It had been pan-something, or maybe para-something. I got an image in my brain of an inch-long oblong-shaped orange citrus fruit I'd eaten as a child in Santa Barbara, one where the skin was sweet, but the flesh was too tart to taste. *Got it.* The chemical was paraquat, which was why I'd thought of the kumquat citrus.

As the muffins baked, I mixed baking powder, brown sugar, and salt into whole wheat flour for the pancake mix. My expression turned as sour as a kumquat's insides. Siblings Adam and Eva both had access to paraquat dichloride. Had they killed Vicky together? Eva had seemed genuinely sad at her friend's death, but she could have been putting on an act.

I moved on to biscuit dough, even though my fingers were itching to do research into the toxin and into Cole's real estate sales history. My hand holding the big pastry cutter slowed. Of course we—that is, Wanda—needed to figure out who killed Vicky. But maybe it was more important to understand how poison had been applied to Adele's yarn after it had left her farm and before Vicky began knitting with it.

Had the skein been purchased here in my store or elsewhere? Had Vicky bought it? Maybe someone gave it to her as a gift, knowing her love for knitting. My brow was the thing being knit right now. Turner's aunt Meena told him Adam was courting Vicky, apparently in vain.

I stopped cutting butter into the biscuit mix. Meena had said Adam was sending Vicky gifts. Including yarn? Possibly. I hastily wiped my hands on a towel and extracted my phone. Buck and Wanda needed to know what Auntie Meena had said.

Turner's aunt, Meena Rao, told him Adam Kenney was trying to woo Vicky back, sending her flowers and candy and "stuff." Maybe poisoned yarn? Meena lives with the Raos.

I sent the text to both Buck and his detective cousin. Because Meena hadn't married, I assumed her last name would be the same as Turner's father's—or hoped it was. I'd been about to urge my message recipients to check out her veracity and sources but had stopped at the last minute. That was their job.

The biscuit dough finished, I swathed it in plastic wrap. In the walk-in, I exchanged it for the three unfrozen turkey packages I found. Now, what would be a good turkey meatball recipe? Should I go Italian seasonings or head in the Thanksgiving route? Sage and poultry seasonings might fit better with Christmas, but we were going to serve the meatballs in tomato sauce. Italian, it was.

To three pounds of ground turkey, I measured out and added breadcrumbs, finely grated Parmesan cheese, a healthy dose of dried oregano and basil, and three eggs. I added salt and pepper and scrubbed my hands anew before starting to smoosh the mixture between my fingers.

It was a good thing I did. My hands were heading toward the mixing bowl when my phone vibrated with a call. Buck or Wanda calling back, maybe? I connected without paying attention to the number.

"Robbie, you need to know something," Abe's mom said without preamble.

"Freddy! How are you feeling? I was going to call you as soon as I was done with prep in the restaurant."

"I'm fine, hon. It's a blasted nuisance, of course, that idiot running into me and my leg. I could . . . well, I won't go there. It's the holidays, after all."

"How are they treating you?" I wandered over to

the door and peered out as we spoke. By some miracle, the snow had stopped falling and a weak sun was trying to assert itself through the clouds toward the west.

"Everyone here is a gem. It's just that they wake you up every couple hours at night, and the dang leg wakes me up every other hour."

"What can I bring you?"

"I don't need a thing, Robbie. They're supposed to spring me tomorrow. If they don't, I'm going to order that son of mine to take me home, anyway. Run an intervention."

"Are you sure I can't bring you a book, or a couple of muffins? Or would you like a visit sans gifts?"

"Nah, you stay put. Roads can't be too great for driving right now, anyway. Only thing I'd like is a tumbler of Scotch whiskey, and I'd bet my cello these . . . kind nurses wouldn't allow me to drink it." Freddy snorted, then whispered, "One just walked in."

"Fine. But Abe and I will make some food and bring it by tomorrow after you're settled." And maybe we'd add a bottle of Scotch to our offering.

"Sure, that'd be great. But listen, Robbie. I've picked up a little scuttlebutt about the recent incident, if you know what I mean, to share with you."

"I'm listening." She had to mean the incident of Vicky's murder. Or I hoped she did.

"Cole is in the Indianapolis Symphony with me," Freddy continued. "He plays viola. You know he also sells real estate?"

"Yes, although I didn't know about his musical abilities."

"Why would you? He's reasonably talented, but

of course the Indy Symphony doesn't pay any of us a living wage. We only get a token payment and do it for the love of music, mostly. Anyway, Cole fought hard to get the contract to sell that farm down on the road to Madison."

"Fought hard against whom?" I asked.

"Nobody you'd know. Another agent. Thing is, my cousin's neighbor's brother caught Cole leaving the barn with something under his coat. Sounds suspicious, wouldn't you say?"

"If he was removing a piece of property he didn't own, I'd say it sounds very suspicious. Do you know how big this thing was?"

"Nope. But I can—" Her voice broke off, then she mumbled something away from the phone. "I'll have to call you back, Robbie. Doc's here."

She disconnected before I could even say good-bye. I stared at the phone. I still had so many questions. What was the name of the cousin's neighbor's brother? If Cole had concealed an object under his coat, it could have been a container of herbicide. Except it seemed like a stretch for him to murder a woman simply because she hadn't wanted to continue dating him, especially when he now seemed enthralled with Eva.

I hoped Freddy would call me back after she talked to the doctor. If she didn't, Abe might know who the unknown brother was, and I could ask the man myself. And if not the neighbor's brother, Abe could at least put me in touch with his mother's cousin.

Either way, I decided to be a good doobie and pass along what Freddy had said. Both Buck and Wanda were so tuned into the local populace, one of them might be able to trace the convoluted connection without even having a name. Or they might simply go interview Cole and ask him.

I tapped out a text and sent it along.

Meanwhile, those turkey meatballs weren't going to roll themselves. I plunged my hands in and squeezed the eggs into the meat, crumbs, and cheese. It smelled divine. As long as my phone didn't ring again, I could be out of here by five.

Chapter Seventeen

I sat in my car at five-fifteen. I'd finished all the prep I could do and had shoveled the porch, front steps, and walkway again. I considered visiting Meena at the Rao Maple Farm, but I didn't want to get entangled in her gossip machine. Instead, I could drive out to Adam Kenney's soybean farm. I did a quick search on my phone and found Kenney Farm on Gatesville Road, which ran between Beanblossom and Taggart to the east but was still part of Brown County.

A truck fronted by a yellow triangular snowplow attachment rumbled by, maybe one of the contractors the town hired to clear the roads. Main Street, on which my store was situated at nearly the edge of town, looked entirely drivable. I doubted Gatesville Road would be as cleared, running through a much more rural section of the county as it did. From here, it would take me at least twenty minutes to make my way to the farm, and the sun would have set by the time I got there.

Most important, I had no reason in the universe to pay a visit to a soybean farmer on a cold, snowy afternoon. A farmer who might be a murderer. That would definitely slot me into the Too Stupid to Live category. They gave out Darwin Awards for lesser acts.

I thought. Did I have any excuse to call Adam? I drummed the steering wheel. And snapped my fingers. *Duh.* I could always invent a reason. I took a deep breath and made the call.

"Kenney Farm."

"Is this Adam?" I asked.

"In the flesh. How can I help you?"

"This is Robbie Jordan in South Lick. We met recently when you came into my restaurant with Eva."

"Oh." He cleared his throat. "I suppose you want to talk about my late ex-wife."

"Not really, no." Of course I did, but I didn't want to start with that. "I was actually wondering about soybean waste."

"Soybean waste." He sounded incredulous.

I didn't blame him for not believing me, but I forged on. "The thing is, my aunt has a sheep farm, and she's thinking about adding pigs. I told her I'd check around on food sources for them. Do you compost whatever you don't sell, or would you consider giving some away, as long as we pick it up?"

Adele would be surprised to hear she was considering adding porcines to her ovine mix, but Adam didn't need to know that.

"You do know it's December, Miss Jordan."

"Naturally. I was only thinking ahead for next year." I didn't bother asking him to call me Ms. Jordan, or better, Robbie. If he wanted to go all old-school on me, let him. I shut up and waited.

He finally spoke. "I could consider that. Have your aunt contact me in the spring. What's her name?"

"Adele Jordan. Her farm is in South Lick but it's out on Beanblossom Road."

"Heck, I know Adele. She's good people."

Maybe he knew Adele well enough to buy yarn from her and then poison it.

"Well, I'd better let you go," he added.

And I'd better give her a heads-up about my lie, stat. But . . . first things first.

"I am so sorry about Vicky's passing," I said. "I know you were no longer married, but I wondered if there were any funeral arrangements yet. I'd like to pay my respects."

"Not yet." He didn't elaborate.

"Do you know if they've found the awful person who ended her life?"

Again I was met with silence. Again I waited. It was getting cold in here, but I didn't want to start the car and add any distracting background noises.

"I've heard you're all buddy-buddy with the police," he growled. "Why are you asking me about who killed Vicky?"

I smiled, not that he could see me, but I knew it altered a person's voice quality. "I do know a couple of officers who come into my restaurant to eat, but they don't tell me a thing."

"They sure as heck don't tell me."

I thought I heard a voice in the background. His voice came through muffled, as if he held a hand over the phone, but I could have sworn he said "Eva." His sister must be visiting.

"Sorry about that," he said, his voice clear again. "Anyway, Miss Jordan, you might not believe me, but I loved my wife even after she left me. She didn't deserve to be murdered." His voice broke and the last words came out almost as a sob.

Was that sorrow real or an act? I waited a moment to let him compose himself and to be sure he was done talking.

"Of course, she didn't," I said in a soft tone. "Listen, I don't want to keep you. I'll let Adele know you're willing to talk with her about food for the pigs. Take care now."

He disconnected almost before I stopped speaking.

Me, I fired up the hybrid and headed for the warm solace of home, hearth, and husband.

Chapter Eighteen

A fire crackled in the wood stove at seven. Abe and I sat side by side on the couch, both with a bellyful of the yummy lasagna he'd baked, each with our own choice of reading material. His was a book he needed to read for a course he'd be starting in January.

Abe had decided to change careers, saying working as an electrical lineman was too dangerous for a husband and father. He was going back to school to earn a certificate in wildlife education. He loved the woods and was at home in wild spaces, so retraining in that field made perfect sense. I'd told him he had my full support.

My book was a new mystery by an author named Becky Clark, which featured a crossword-puzzle designer solving crimes. That one was right down my alley.

We had set up our fresh-cut Christmas tree on

Sunday in the front windows, across the room from the stove. The tree's small white and colored lights glowed with the season, and the fir's aroma filled the air.

Sean had disappeared out the door for a library study session with his math club buddy—that is, his girlfriend, Maeve. The house was quiet. Birdy nestled happily between us. Sean's half-completed green scarf peeked out of his cloth tote knitting bag. My sheepskin-clad feet on the coffee table were snug and warm. But I couldn't concentrate on the story.

"I talked with your mom this afternoon," I began. "I'm glad she can go home tomorrow."

"Did she tell you if they don't spring her, we're doing what she calls a 'liberation intervention' in the morning?" He laid his book facedown on his lap.

"She implied that, yes."

"Do I sense a 'but' coming along?" He twisted to gaze at me.

"You do. Not about facilitating her release, not at all. That's perfect. But she mentioned her cousin's neighbor's brother seeing Cole Brewster smuggle something out of the barn at a farm he was selling."

"And this is important why?" Abe tilted his head.

I scrunched up my nose. "I haven't had a chance to fill you in on a few pieces of information. Buck said the toxin that got into Vicky's blood via her hands—that is, the substance that killed her—was an agricultural herbicide used on soybean farms. The farm we were talking about, the one Cole was the selling agent for, was a soybean farm like Adam Kenney's."

"So Brewster might have been in possession of the poison. Why would he want to kill Vicky Chakrabarti?"

"That's the question, isn't it? I really have no idea." I stroked Birdy's long, soft fur. "This cousin intrigues me. Do you know who your mom was talking about?"

"Not really. I'll see if I can find out more tomorrow." He squeezed my hand. "And if I don't get this book read before January second, I won't have much of a place in my class."

"Go for it." I squeezed his hand in return. It wasn't fair of me to drag him into every question I had about the latest homicide investigation. Adele seemed, for now, to be in the clear, but I still had an intense interest in the case.

I sat thinking. Adam had seemed suspicious about my asking questions. He'd also sounded broken up about Vicky's death. But had he been, really? Eva had looked like a grieving friend on the first day. She'd gotten over it fast enough, cuddling with Cole in public the following day. If she believed Cole still pined for Vicky's affections, would Eva want to get her friend out of competition in the most final of ways? I couldn't come up with a reason for Cole to kill Vicky. But he could have helped someone else do it by purloining poison—unless he'd stolen something else. That would still be a crime, just not a homicide-related one. Alternatively, Eva could have helped Adam or vice versa.

What a tangle of yarn it all was. I idly poked

around the Internet on my phone, looking for more information on any of the three. Adam seemed the most likely, his sob and reports of his trying to win Vicky back notwithstanding. Maybe he was paying alimony to her and was sick of it. Maybe he didn't like seeing her thrive without him. Some men would take that as a slight.

Then we had Eva, who had worked for a chemical company. Eva—with her comfortable body and purple reading glasses on a beaded chain, with her knitting bag and homey accent—didn't look like a murderer. Except, if I'd learned anything in the last few years, it was that killers come in all shapes and sizes. I dug into IFCC, pairing it with her name.

My eyes widened. She had held a position in senior management in the company. In fact, she'd been the chief financial officer. On the surface, Eva didn't look like what one thought of as a CFO, either. More proof of the old books-and-covers adage.

What was making me stare at the article from five years ago was that she'd apparently been asked to step down, to leave the company. The news was couched in careful wording about Ms. Kenney deciding to leave in pursuit of other opportunities. I was pretty sure that was code for the company asking her to resign. That is, firing her.

I found another source saying there had been financial irregularities at the time Eva left IFCC. The mention of missing inventory really caught my attention. I kept searching but couldn't unearth any criminal charges associated with it. The board of directors must have found out what she was up to but kept it quiet as long as she went without a fuss.

I sat back. Did she still have that missing inventory in her garage? In her barn or storage unit? I was horrified to think she'd used it on Adele's yarn, a skein she knew Vicky would knit with. I wondered if I should pass along the news articles to Wanda but decided not to. Researching persons of interest would be one of the first things she and her team would do. Eva finding the body, as well as being Vicky's friend, should have automatically made her a person of high interest.

At the sound of a soft snore, I glanced over at Abe and smiled to myself. He'd leaned his head back on the cushion to read, except the book now lay collapsed against his chest. Between us, Birdy purred, knowing a kindred napper when he heard one.

I focused on my novel again, where all murders were fictional. I felt safe here, and I couldn't do anything about this tonight, anyway.

Chapter Nineteen

After I parked behind my store at six o'clock the next morning, I stretched my arms high. It was so very dark at this time of year and so cold. We hadn't gotten any more snow overnight. Instead, the clear skies let the temperature plummet. My boots crunched on the plowed snow in the driveway. I paid a plow guy to clear it, but I'd asked him not to get down to the gravel or it would all end up in the pile. Instead I had a packed inch of snow left, which made it drivable and easy enough to walk on unless it thawed and refroze, always a possibility in this neck of the woods.

A yawn overtook me. But the show must go on, or, in my case, the restaurant must open. I slid off one glove to insert the key in the lock of the service door at the side of the building. I pulled open the automatically locking door and stuck my hip in the opening so I could remove the key. My eyes narrowed at a sound somewhere behind me.

An arm wrapped around my neck. "Inside," a woman's voice ordered.

Eva. My breath rushed in. I didn't want to be alone with her in my store. She pushed at me. I dug my feet in, bracing myself with my strong cyclist's thighs.

"I have a container of something rather lethal," she threatened in a low, gravely voice. "Do you want me to pour it on you out here and leave you to freeze to death?"

I thought frantically. Fight to stay out here where the fresh air would help dissipate any fumes? No. Better to be indoors where I knew the space and had kitchen tools I could defend myself with. And maybe call for help, too. I moved forward, leaving the key in the lock. When Danna got here in half an hour, maybe she'd know something was wrong. Would she spy Eva's car, wherever she'd left it? I didn't have time to dwell on it.

The door clicked shut behind Eva. She kept her arm firmly around my neck. She pressed on my throat. Her soft torso pushed at me, but her forearm was an iron bar under her wool coat.

"Please let go, Eva." My voice croaked.

"As if. Here. Turn on the lights." She nudged me toward the switch plate.

I flipped on all the store lights. "You're hurting my throat." At least she wasn't pressing hard enough for me to black out, but that could change in a flash.

"Listen to me, Robbie Jordan, and listen up good," Eva snarled. "I know you're about to turn in the two people in my life I actually love."

"What are you talking about?" How could I turn the tables on her? I had to escape and call for help. My thoughts raced. "Do you mean Adam and Cole?"

"Brother and lover. You think one of them killed Vicky." She pushed me into the kitchen area.

"Not at all." I was now certain Eva had. "I can't figure out why anyone would murder her." Just in time, I stopped myself from saying, "any of you," which would not go over well at this particular moment.

She snorted. The pressure of her arm lessened. Not much, but a little.

"Who wouldn't want to get that smug woman out of the way?" Eva scoffed. "She always pretended to be so self-sufficient, divorcing my brother, dropping poor Cole. Even talking about what great friends she and I were. You wouldn't believe how she looked down her nose that I hadn't kept my figure like she did. And what did she ever do for me? She wasn't much of a friend when the company I started kicked me out the back door like I was garbage."

Delusional much? "They did?" I pretended to be shocked. "That's terrible."

Her grip softened even more as she ranted.

I shot a glance at the wall clock. Ten after six. I sent out a prayer to the universe that today Danna would find herself awake and alert early and I'd see her walk through the door any minute now. Except I couldn't rely on wishful thinking. My life was up to me.

Me, who had both hands free. *Doh.* My initial terror had made me stupid. Why wasn't Eva gripping my hands behind me, or holding on to my arm with her free hand? Because she had a vial of poison in the other hand. She'd said as much. I had to free myself and get far away from her. As fast as I could. I was sweating inside my coat even though my feet and hands were cold and numb from fear.

I zipped through my options. She had pushed me up against the under-counter drawer that held a set of sharp skewers. I'd never be able to push back, open the drawer, grab one, and wield it before she counterattacked. My cell was in my turquoise cross bag, not in my coat pocket. Eva was at least two inches taller than I and heftier, but I was a lot fitter and faster.

A click came from the service door. Eva's grip slipped. I dashed toward the front door.

"Hey! Get back here," Eva shouted at me.

At the door, I whirled to see Danna appear in the service door opening. She held up my keys, looking quizzical until she spied Eva.

"What's—?" Danna started to ask.

"Get out, Danna!" I screamed. "She has poison. Run!"

I rammed myself against the fire bar, making it onto the porch. I scrabbled for my phone, even as I raced down the steps and around the side. Danna

had to have made it out. She had to have. I jabbed
the emergency button.

"Murderer attacking in Pans 'N Pancakes," I said
to the dispatcher. "Nineteen Main Street, South Lick.
Eva Kenney has a vial of poison. Hurry!"

Chapter Twenty

I'd never been happier to see Danna jogging toward me under the street light. "Is Eva following you?" I grabbed her arm.

She shook her head, hard. "What's going on, Robbie?"

"Come on." I kept hold of her arm and glanced behind us. "Tell you in a minute after we're across the street."

I checked both ways for cars, waiting for a sedan to speed by, its driver apparently oblivious to the drama inside my store. Danna and I rushed to the other side of the road and huddled in the dark next to the now-abandoned antique store.

"Eva Kenney surprised me as I was unlocking the service door." I panted as I spoke.

"Thus these." Danna extended my keys.

"Yes, and thanks." I pocketed them. "She forced me inside, saying she had a vial of poison. She ranted about Vicky, listing all the reasons anyone would want to murder her." I shuddered.

Eyes wide, Danna brought her hand to her mouth. "That's terrible."

"Of course it is. When you showed up, her grip on me slipped, out of surprise, I think. You know the rest." I kept a close watch on both the front door and the driveway, but Eva didn't appear.

"Why didn't she come after us?" Danna's breath made little clouds in the frigid air.

"Maybe she spilled the toxin on herself? I don't know."

When the lights and sirens roared up, I stepped forward and waved. Buck jumped out of one of the SLPD cruisers, hurrying across to us. Officers piled out. The ones who emerged from the Brown County Sheriff's SUV wore SWAT gear. Wanda directed the officers, some to the front door, some to the side.

"You girls all right?" Buck asked when he reached us.

"Yes." Girls, we weren't, but I knew he, unlike some men, meant no belittling by the term.

"Gimme the high-speed version," he said.

"Eva Kenney surprised me when I was opening the side door." The words rushed out of my mouth. "She said she had a vial of 'something lethal' ready to spill on me. She pushed me inside and accused me of being ready to turn in both Adam and Cole for Vicky's murder. Danna arrived, and it startled Eva. Danna and I got away out of separate doors. We ran over here. Haven't seen Eva appear."

"Got it."

"Wait. You'll need these." I pulled out the keys

and isolated one before handing over the bunch. "This is the front door. The one with the red thing on it is the side door."

"Thanks. Stay right here." Buck loped back across the road.

"Be careful," I called.

He gave me a thumbs-up without looking back. He quickly conferred with Wanda. They crept up the front stairs. Buck crouched to unlock the door, then handed the keys to Wanda. She ran with surprising speed for a woman her size around the side and disappeared. A moment later, the SWAT personnel burst into the front door shouting, "Police!" and other warnings. I assumed they'd done the same at the side. Eva didn't have a chance. Still, I crossed my fingers that no one would be hurt.

Chapter Twenty-one

"Sorry about all this, Danna." I shivered as my adrenaline ebbed. I hugged my arms around me.

"Hey, no worries. I hope she doesn't try to spill whatever she claimed to have on the cops."

I quickly thought back. "Did you see her holding a vial or a container? She was behind me the whole time until you came in, and then I was focused on warning you and escaping. I didn't get a good look."

Danna stared at the lit windows. "Yeah, no. I didn't, either."

"Maybe she was bluffing. Somehow I don't think so."

We stood waiting together in the cold air. The homey smell of woodsmoke and pine needles jarred with reality.

I tried to peer into the store, but the porch overhang made it impossible to see more than vague shapes moving about. Had Eva crouched behind a counter and surprised them? Maybe she'd tripped trying to reach Danna or me and spilled the poison on herself. With any luck it wouldn't have landed on broken skin but on her winter clothing. She needed to be able to stand trial, that much I knew.

An ambulance sped up and braked to a stop, lights flashing but no siren. I brought my gloved hand to my mouth. Could that mean Eva was dead? I shook myself. No. Surely it was because she needed medical help but not urgently. Or maybe an officer was hurt with nonlife-threatening injuries, as the news always put it.

A thought hit me. I swore out loud. Danna glanced over with a skeptical look.

"You don't usually talk like that. Dish, Robbie. What's going on?"

"It occurred to me that we're not going to be able to open the restaurant today." I wrinkled my nose. "I think."

"Why not?"

"They'll say the whole store is a crime scene."

"Is it?" Danna asked.

"I'm not sure. Forced entry, sure, and assault? Maybe it depends on if Eva hurt herself or not."

"Hey, worse things have happened than staying closed for a morning or even a day."

"You're right." I kept my gaze on the lit windows of my livelihood, made garish by the addition of strobing red and blue lights. "I made the muffins yesterday, but they'll keep."

"Everything will keep for a day, boss."

"You're right. Of course it will."

Danna was nearly a decade younger than I was, but she often seemed older than her years. I appreciated her even-keeled approach to life, especially at times like these, when mine felt bumpier.

I pointed when the front door opened. An officer gripped Eva, whose wrists were handcuffed behind her back, by the elbow. Wanda followed close behind as Eva was escorted to the back seat of the sheriff's department vehicle. The officer protected Eva's head as she slid in. The door clicked shut behind her. Eva didn't appear harmed, and she was docile as she went, not rebellious.

Wanda looked across the street at us. "You done good, Robbie. Catch you later."

I raised a hand in reply. Wanda climbed into the front seat. Without siren blaring or emergency lights flashing, the SUV drove off. A quiet ambulance followed. Buck peered across the road from the store's front porch.

"Come on back over." He gestured to us.

We made our way across. It had to be nearly seven by now, but the sky was still dark. The weak pre-solstice sun wouldn't rise for at least another hour to start one of the season's shortest days.

Adele's pickup pulled up, which surprised me not one bit. She loved monitoring the police radio she'd never relinquished after her last term as South Lick's mayor. If she heard of something happening that involved her only niece, she was all over it. I was a bit surprised it had taken her this long to get here.

Danna and I made it to Buck before my aunt.

"What happened in there?" I asked.

"Hang on a little minute," he said. "I might as well wait for Adele. You know as sure as the Pope's Catholic she's going to want to know all about it."

Adele climbed down from the Ford.

"What on God's green earth is going on around here?" She peered at me. "You girls all right?"

"We're fine," I said. "Can we go inside, Buck?"

"That'd be a negative."

I blew out a breath. Despite agreeing with Danna that everything would keep, I hated when Pans 'N Pancakes had to be shuttered, even if only temporarily.

An officer strode around from the side carrying a roll of wide yellow tape.

"Jimbo here's about to string up the crime-scene tape," Buck said. "He's got to establish a perimeter."

No. "Do you have to?" I grabbed Buck's sleeve. "I promise not to go inside. I'd much, much rather keep the door locked and put up a sign saying something about being closed due to circumstances beyond our control. Please?"

Buck regarded me with cocked head. "You don't want folks thinking somebody was killed in there or nothing, am I right?"

"Yes, exactly."

He thought for another moment. "All righty, then. Hold off there, Jimbo. We can make the single point of entry the side door."

The officer shrugged and headed back around the side.

"Listen up, y'all," Adele said. "It's colder than a miner's lunch pail in Antarctica out here. I got me an idea."

Chapter Twenty-two

Ten minutes later I sat around the table in my apartment kitchen with Buck, Danna, and Adele. Buck had agreed we could sit in the apartment as long as we entered by the back door.

Besides the beer and wine I kept in the fridge in here, I also had coffee makings and a small drip machine. Adele had had a notebook and tape in her truck, so I'd lettered another Gone Fishing–type of sign for the front door. I'd also texted Abe.

Had police activity at PnP. Danna and I are fine. Eva Kenney in custody. Won't be opening today. Home after a bit. XXOO

While I was texting, Danna had conveyed the news to Turner, telling him we were fine but that the store was closed, and he should stay home.

"Okay, Buck," I began after we four sat with our coffee. We all kept our coats on. I heated this space only enough so the pipes didn't freeze. "I'm ready."

"Welp." He slid sideways in his chair and stretched his legs out nearly to the door. "You girls saw the way we went inside, full SWAT and vests and all. Old Eva was just setting on the floor, arms around her knees, like she was cowering or some such. Wadn't no need for all our fuss, but, 'course, we don't know that before we head on in."

"So she lost her nerve after we escaped and the sirens showed up," I said. "Did she have poison with her?"

He bobbed his head once. "It appears she did, in a test tube kind of a thingy. But it was stoppered up in her coat pocket. Sure didn't look to have been opened."

"Eva must have had her other hand on it while her arm was around my neck," I said. "I wondered why she left my hands free. But she would have needed two hands to open it."

"Isn't that kind of a serious flaw in her plan?" Danna asked.

"Nobody ever said murderers were brilliant," Adele said with a snort.

"How long are we going to have to stay closed, Buck?" I cradled my hands around the warm mug.

"That'll depend on the team, when they get here and what they find. Seeing as how nobody ended up hurt at all, it might could be tomorrow or even as early as today lunchtime." He picked up his cup but set it down before drinking. "You gave me the quick summary out there, Robbie. Did Eva confess to anything in there? This ain't the official interview, you know. My cousin will be conducting that. But I'd sure as shooting like to know, and I'd bet a year's worth of nickels Adele would, too."

Adele's eyes lit up as she bobbed her head with way too much enthusiasm.

I told them how Eva had forced me inside. "She said she knew I was about to turn in Cole or Adam for the murder, then she listed all the reasons why she hated Vicky."

"She stopped short of admitting she poisoned the yarn?" Buck asked.

"I'm afraid so."

"Last night I found something pretty interesting," Adele began. "Y'all know Robbie sells my yarn in the store, but folks also come to the farm to buy it. I started going through my receipts. I'd plum forgotten that Eva had bought a dozen skeins from me way back in May. I was so busy getting ready for the wedding, it must have skipped my mind."

"Were they of green yarn?" I asked.

Adele pointed at me. "On the nose. But what I don't get is why the shade of the poisoned yarn was different from my green dye."

"I know why," Buck said. "That paraquat stuff is dyed blue. You soak green yarn in it, and it's bound to alter the color."

"That's gotta be it." Adele pointed at him.

"Turner's aunt told him Adam was trying to get Vicky back," Danna said.

"Right," I agreed. "Eva was obviously jealous of Vicky in all kinds of ways. She probably poisoned the skein, put it in a bag, and pretended to be supporting her brother by suggesting it would be a perfect gift for Vicky."

"That's exactly what happened," Buck added. "Last night one of Wanda's team finished going through the victim's trash. She found a note from Adam offering the yarn as a gift, saying he felt bad they had been arguing. But get this. It wadn't in his handwriting."

Adele whistled. I shook my head.

"They'll get a handwriting sample from Eva," Buck continued. "If she hasn't confessed already, she will, mark my words."

"Dumber than a box of rocks, as my mom says." Danna cast her gaze toward the ceiling.

"By the way, Adele, obviously you're off the hook for the crime," Buck said. "I expect Wanda'll be returning the yarn and whatnot she confiscated."

"I told you what Freddy said about Cole and the thing he took from the barn on the property he sold," I said. "What about that?"

Buck made a tsking noise. "We up and asked him. The idiot found a antique gallon jar in the barn that reminded him of his granny. Taking it was surely a stupid thing to do, but it wasn't no homicidal act."

"I sure as heck am glad this affair is over," Adele said. "It needed solved before Christmas, and you and Wanda got the job done. With Robbie's help, natch." My aunt smiled as she patted my hand.

I returned the smile. "I'll tell you, Buck. If I never learn a new way to kill someone, I'll be a happy woman."

Chapter Twenty-three

Abe had gotten his mom, cast and all, nestled into a corner of our couch by five o'clock on Christmas Eve. We'd rearranged the furniture so the couch faced the room. Anyone sitting there had a sightline all the way back to the kitchen, where three generations of O'Neill men currently toiled away. The carved Italian figures in the nativity scene my father had sent me last year clustered around the manger on a bookshelf, and the lights on the tree sparkled, although only unbreakable ornaments were hung on the lower third of branches. This was Birdy's fourth Christmas, but he still loved to bat at anything hanging from a string. The base of the tree was loaded with presents wrapped in either newspaper or cloth, as we'd requested, our small gift to the environment

I handed my mother-in-law a glass of spiked egg-nog.

"It's too bad Donnie and Georgia couldn't be here," Freddy said.

"I don't know." I smiled and sat in the nearest chair. "Christmas combined with a honeymoon in Puerto Rico doesn't sound too bad." Abe's older brother Don and his sweetheart had gotten married last week in a simple ceremony. It was a second marriage for both of them, and they'd decided to celebrate far from home.

Freddy took a sip. "My, my, this is very nice, and it sure packs a wallop, too. Good thing I'm off the pain meds." She chuckled.

I tasted my own small glass. "Whoa. Somebody got carried away with the bourbon." My father-in-law, most likely. I set down the glass. I'd have to pace myself or I'd be under the table before dessert.

"You got everything solved on that murder, right?" Freddy asked. "I was in a bit of a fog at the time, what with the painkillers."

"Wanda and Buck did, for sure. Did you hear what the thing was that Cole took from that barn?"

"No, I didn't."

"He stole an antique jar," I said. "An empty jar. That's all it was."

"The idiot. What kind of a real estate agent goes around lifting antiques from a property he's trying to sell?" She snorted. "Seriously."

"Agree."

"And, in the end, Eva Kenney was the murderer." Freddy shuddered. "Poisoning yarn with some-thing that gets into the skin is just cruel, don't you think?"

All I could do was nod my agreement.

The front door opened to admit Adele, Samuel, and Phil with a burst of cold air. My aunt knew she didn't have to ring the bell or knock, at least not when a festive evening was in store. Samuel carried a wide cloth-covered basket fragrant with fresh-baked something. Phil toted a cardboard box, his eyes sparkling. In one hand, Adele held the handles of a maroon cloth carrier with wine bottle tops peeking out of the top. With her other she set down a quilted bag stuffed with soft things.

"Merry Christmas!" Adele beamed.

"And to you." Abe emerged from the kitchen, his green apron with red elves cavorting across it a perfect accessory to his red silk shirt. "Are those the rolls?" Abe took the basket from Samuel.

"As requested," Samuel said. "But baked by herself, not me."

I stood to greet the newcomers. "What are you all tickled about, Phil?" I tried to peek into his box.

"Hey!" He turned away. "All will be revealed in due time."

Birdy trotted in. He wound around Phil's ankles, then jumped up to nestle next to Freddy and survey his kingdom.

"Where's Cocoa?" Adele asked.

"I think Sean let him out into the backyard a little while ago," I said. "He's way too excited to be in here."

"Sean's actually out walking the pup," Abe said. "Trying to wear him out before dinner."

"Good idea." Adele handed the wine bag to Abe and began shedding hat, coat, and gloves.

"Let me take your wraps." I held out my arms and hung everything in the coat closet.

Abe delivered glasses of eggnog to Adele, now sitting at Freddy's feet, and Samuel, who'd settled into an armchair. Phil was laying a slender tube wrapped in red and green foil at each place on the already-set dining table.

"What are those?" I called to him.

"You don't know?" Samuel asked.

"They're crackers," Phil said.

"They don't look like any crackers I've ever seen." I scrunched up my nose.

Phil just grinned. "You'll see. It's a British tradition my mum brought here from Jamaica."

Like Samuel, Phil's father was an American Black, but I'd forgotten Phil's mom was born in Jamaica.

Three hours later we were all stuffed, sated, and a bit soused, back in the living room in various relaxed poses. Our heads were adorned with crowns from the crackers, which had turned out to be little noisemaker pull-apart packages. Each had contained a paper crown, a tiny toy, and a wrapped piece of ribbon candy.

Sean now stretched out on the floor with his head on a cushion. Beside him, Birdy was curled up next to Cocoa, all three apparently snoozing, although the cat's ears were on alert. When Adele rose to fetch her cloth bag, Birdy perked up.

"Heads up, folks." She grinned. "I took and made a Christmas Eve present for all y'all."

She started handing out red or green knitted scarves tied with a ribbon to each of us. I untied mine and spread it on my lap where I sat, Abe's back against my legs.

"Adele, I love it." She had knitted a pattern of little red skillets into the green yarn.

Freddy held up hers. She had green cellos amid red yarn. Sean's featured dogs. Phil's oven mitts, and so on. Last, Adele wrapped a thin red and green striped strip around Cocoa's neck and tied it in a bow.

"And this one might not last long." She held up a knitted orb smaller than a tennis ball. "I tucked some catnip in with the jingle bells." She threw it down the hall.

I laughed, watching Birdy race after his gift. "Thank you, Adele." I reached out my arms and gave her a big hug.

" 'We wish you a merry Christmas,' " Abe began singing in his melodic baritone.

Everyone else joined in. When the song switched to "Silent Night," I stopped singing and just listened as my eyes welled up. The murder was solved. All my most cherished people—and animals—were right here in this room, and my heart was full. I hoped the peace of the season would extend indefinitely, at least in South Lick, in our tiny corner of the world.

Recipes

Roasted Chicken and Pears

The chicken, fruit, and vegetables in this dish all roast together in the oven, and they come out golden and caramelized. It's exactly the kind of crowd-pleasing dish for Robbie to serve during the holiday season as a nod to a Partridge in a Pear Tree.

Ingredients

2 large carrots, peeled and cut into 1-inch chunks
2 small red onions, cut into inch-wide wedges
2 tablespoons red wine vinegar
2 tablespoons olive oil
1 teaspoon dried thyme
Coarse salt and ground pepper
2 tablespoons chopped fresh parsley
4 boneless chicken breasts and 4 boneless thighs
   (about 2 pounds total)
1 tablespoon honey
3 firm, ripe Bosc pears (about 1½pounds total),
   halved, cored, and cut into ½-inch-thick wedges

Directions

Preheat oven to 375 degrees. On a large rimmed baking sheet (or two small ones), toss carrots and onions with vinegar, 1 tablespoon oil, and ½ teaspoon thyme. Season with salt and pepper.

In a small bowl, combine parsley and remaining ½ teaspoon thyme. Season with salt and pepper. Carefully slide fingers under chicken skin to loosen. Spread parsley mixture under and on top of skin. (If you have skinless chicken, pat the mixture into the meat.) Push vegetables to edges of baking sheet; place chicken pieces in center, and roast 30 minutes.

Meanwhile, in a small bowl, combine honey and remaining tablespoon oil. Remove baking sheet from oven. Add pears and toss with vegetables to combine. Brush top of chicken pieces with honey mixture. Roast 30 minutes more or until a thermometer inserted in thickest part of thigh registers 175 degrees. Serve immediately.

Turtle Cookies

Phil makes these, mimicking turtle candies, for dessert on the Two Turtle Doves day.

Makes about thirty.

Ingredients

For the cookies:
1 cup all-purpose flour
⅓ cup unsweetened cocoa powder
¼ teaspoon salt
½ cup butter (1 stick) at room temperature
⅔ cup granulated sugar
1 large egg, separated
2 tablespoons milk
1 teaspoon vanilla extract
1 cup pecans, finely chopped

For the caramel:
⅔ cup caramel chips or regular caramels (about 15)
½ teaspoon water
½ cup semisweet chocolate chips

Directions

Combine flour, cocoa and salt. In a separate bowl, cream together butter and sugar until light and fluffy. Mix in the egg yolk, milk and vanilla. Stir in flour mixture until just combined. Chill dough in the refrigerator for one hour.

Preheat oven to 350 degrees Fahrenheit.

Whisk egg white in a shallow bowl until frothy. Place chopped pecans in another shallow bowl.

Remove dough from fridge. For each cookie, scoop out less than a tablespoon and roll into a small ball.

Roll each ball in the frothy egg whites, and then roll and press in the chopped pecans. Place on a greased baking sheet.

Use the back of a small round measuring or soup spoon to make an indentation in the center of each dough ball or use your thumb.

Bake for about 10–12 minutes, or just until set. Don't overbake, as cookies will harden as they cool.

As the cookies come out of the oven, gently re-press the indentations with a small round spoon.

In a microwavable bowl mix the caramel bits and water. Microwave at 30-second intervals, stirring after each interval, until caramel is melted (1–2 minutes). Pour small spoonfuls of caramel into the indented cookies. Let cool.

Melt chocolate and drizzle lines over cookies.

Dear Readers:

I'm delighted to bring you another Christmas novella in the Country Store Mysteries series. *Scarfed Down* takes place in Robbie Jordan's fourth year as proprietor of Pans 'N Pancakes, her country store restaurant in fictional South Lick, Indiana.

The story follows *No Grater Crime*, which ends with Robbie's May wedding to Abe O'Neill, and *Batter Off Dead*, in which Robbie investigates not only the murder of a senior citizen during summer fireworks but also a similar homicide from decades earlier. The next book to release will be *Four Leaf Cleaver*, a book set at Saint Patrick's Day and number eleven in the series. *Scarfed Down* slots right into the seasons.

Every book and novella includes recipes, because . . . of course! Robbie is always thinking about innovative ways to feed her hungry customers. I hope you enjoy Robbie and crew's angst at following through with their Twelve Days of Christmas theme. It mirrored my own when I started writing it. Then I found my mother's quilted Christmas wall hanging, which I gave to Adele, and that sparked ideas for specials, especially for Ten Lords a-Leaping.

I'm always interested, as we crime writers are, in new ways of killing someone on the page. For my part of *Christmas Scarf Murder*, I knew I didn't want to strangle the victim with a scarf. When I learned about contact poisons, I realized paraquat dichloride was going to be perfect. The facts that the poison is dyed blue *and* used on soybean farms, which abound in the Midwest, were extra bonuses.

Thanks so much to brilliant author—and sheep farmer—Sarah Stewart Taylor for help with details about Adele's animals. My Wicked Authors blog-mate Barbara Ross came up with the term VGR, because an amateur sleuth always needs that Very Good Reason to investigate a crime. Apologies to the Indianapolis Symphony for my fictional version of their pay scale.

I hope you'll find my talented author pals and me over at wickedauthors.com and mysterylovers kitchen.com, where we talk books, food, and mystery. I also write as Edith Maxwell, and you can read about all my books and short fiction under both names at edithmaxwell.com. Happy reading, and very happy and delicious holidays to you.

DEATH BY
CHRISTMAS SCARF

Peggy Ehrhart

Acknowledgments

Abundant thanks to my agent, Evan Marshall, and to my editor at Kensington Books, John Scognamiglio.

Chapter One

A lively conversation was already in progress when Pamela Paterson took a seat on Roland DeCamp's low-slung turquoise sofa and extracted her knitting from her knitting bag.

"Such a terrible shame!" Holly Perkins had just exclaimed. "And so close to the holidays!" Absent her usual cheer, Holly barely resembled herself, despite the bright green streak in her luxuriant dark hair and her festive candy-cane earrings.

"And so unlike Arborville!" Next to her, Karen Dowling shuddered. "Dave and I and our little Lily have always felt so safe here."

"Just a few steps from the shops on Arborville Avenue . . ." Bettina Fraser shook her head. "Who would imagine a killer could be so brazen? And to think I take a shortcut through that passageway all the time."

"Not so brazen. It was snowing hard and it was

dark," Roland cut in. As was often the case, his intense expression and his tone implied that his was the voice of reason. "People were undoubtedly rushing up and down Arborville Avenue trying to get their errands done and get home. The killer probably didn't think the body would be discovered until the next morning. And he probably thought the snow would cover his footprints."

"He didn't count on Laurel Lewis working late." Bettina looked up from her knitting to focus on Roland across the room. He occupied a sleek chair that matched the sofa. "How shocking for the poor woman to stumble over a corpse on her way to her car!"

"At least she didn't have to deal with it all alone," Holly commented. "So that's something."

"Yes," Bettina said. "Here's poor Mort Quigley leaving the library after a long day and all of a sudden a desperate voice screams that there's a body in the passageway."

"Convenient that the police station is so near the library," Holly said. "Mort was able to summon an officer right away—though Carys Walnutt was obviously beyond help at that point."

Pamela had read the article about the murder in the *County Register* that morning. She hadn't really known Carys Walnutt, but in the photo accompanying the article she recognized a dour-looking woman she occasionally saw around town.

A curious sound like a cross between a moan and growl emanated from the most comfortable seat in the DeCamps' elegant living room: an armchair always reserved for the knitting group's most senior member, Nell Bascomb.

Nell regarded the assembled knitters with a baleful stare, focusing her faded eyes on each in turn. "This tragic event is not gossip fodder," she said firmly. "We all know what happened last night, thanks to Marcy Brewer's report in this morning's *Register*. Now I suggest we tend to our knitting and let the Arborville police tend to the issue of who strangled Carys Walnutt and why."

The sofa trembled as Bettina, who was sitting next to Pamela, thrust her knitting aside and flung her head back in distress. Pamela turned to see her staring at the ceiling.

"I don't think I can keep working on this scarf," Bettina moaned, fingering her in-progress knitting project but speaking as if to the ceiling. "Every time I look at it now I picture it being wrapped around someone's neck and pulled tighter and tighter, just like what happened to Carys Walnutt. I wish I'd finished it in time and was starting some whole new thing tonight."

Pamela, in fact, *was* starting some whole new thing, as were the other four members of Knit and Nibble. For most of December the group had been focused on producing woolly scarves to donate for a silent auction to benefit the Arborville Public Library. Five scarves had been completed and donated, and the silent auction had taken place the previous Saturday in connection with the town's annual tree-lighting ceremony. But Bettina had fallen behind and her scarf was still in progress. "I'll give it to them next year," she had said. "No problem."

Holly, who was sitting next to Bettina on the other side, set down her own knitting—the bare beginnings of perhaps a sleeve—and seized Bettina's free hand. "You could tuck it away," she whispered, "and get it out again next December. There really was no reason for Marcy Brewer to be so specific about how the strangling was accomplished."

"No, there wasn't." Nell's voice reached them from across the room. "And I can see why Bettina is upset. But busy fingers soothe a troubled mind." She turned her gaze from Holly to Bettina. "Tuck that half-finished scarf back in your knitting bag and come over here and sit by me. The Haversack women's shelter can always use more teddy bears for the children."

Ever the gentleman, Roland leapt from his seat, startling the lustrous black cat he had been sharing it with. He hurried across the hall to the dining room and returned with a wooden chair that he positioned right next to Nell.

A few minutes later Bettina and Nell sat side by side, leaning toward each other until Bettina's scarlet tresses nearly mingled with Nell's halo of white hair. Nell had pulled an extra pair of needles from her knitting bag, as well as a ball of turquoise yarn. She had declared the yarn to be just enough for a teddy bear and was watching as Bettina followed her instructions to cast on fifteen stitches. Nell never worried about verisimilitude in the colors of the knitted animals she turned out in such profusion.

Pamela was happy to concentrate on her own work, murmuring "knit two, purl two" as she created the ribbing that would edge the bottom of her new project, a sweater.

Bettina's departure from the sofa had left a gap

between Pamela and Holly, but Pamela could hear Holly and Karen exchanging quiet confidences relating to Karen's daughter Lily and the ongoing home-improvement projects that occupied both young women and their husbands. Holly and Karen were the youngest members of the Knit and Nibble group, as unalike in appearance and personality as any two young women could be, but drawn together by a shared interest in renovating the century-old wood-frame houses that were typical of Arborville's housing stock.

Roland, as always, was content to knit in silence, looking up only when the front door opened and Melanie DeCamp entered, leading the DeCamps' dachshund, Ramona.

"We had a lovely walk," Melanie announced as Roland's greeting was echoed by the other knitters. "People have been out all day shoveling, so the sidewalks are quite clear. Good thing too, because Ramona was longing for some fresh air and exercise."

Melanie was bundled up in a sheepskin coat, caramel suede with the pale furry inside turned back to form a wide collar, and Ramona was wearing a chic doggy sweater made for her by Roland. Melanie and Ramona continued down the hall, Ramona's toenails clicking on the wooden floor.

After several minutes, Melanie returned, minus Ramona and minus the coat. Her simple black leggings flattered her long, slim legs, and the creamy tones of her slouchy turtleneck suited her blond elegance.

"What wonderful projects are you all working on?" she inquired. She surveyed the room and

headed first for the armchair where Nell sat.
Crouching at Nell's side, she smiled as Nell displayed the oval of pale yellow yarn hanging from
her needles and explained that it was to form the
body of a teddy bear destined for the Haversack
women's shelter.

"The children have little enough," Nell said.
"But the knitted animals are theirs to keep when
they leave with their mothers."

"So you keep pretty busy." Melanie's smile grew
wider.

"Sadly, yes," Nell responded. "The shelter doesn't
lack clients."

Melanie crept closer to Bettina. "And it looks
like you're the student tonight," she observed.

"It's going to be a teddy bear too," Bettina said.
She'd reached the end of a row and held up a needle
with half an inch of knitting already completed.
The three women chatted for a few minutes about
the shelter and about the variety of knitted animals Nell had produced over the years.

On the other side of the room, Roland was beginning to stir. He pushed back his immaculately
starched shirt cuff to consult his impressive watch,
set his knitting atop the briefcase he used in place
of a knitting bag, and gently disengaged himself
from the cat stretched along his thigh.

Apparently sensing that her husband was on the
move, Melanie rose. "Do you need help with anything, sweetie?" she inquired.

"Completely under control." He raised both
hands in a gesture suggesting she should remain
where she was. "I've got this," he added and
headed for the kitchen, followed by the black cat.

"He so enjoys serving the refreshments when it's his turn to host the group," Melanie said as she perched on the edge of the chair Roland had vacated.

She directed her smile toward the sofa and its three occupants. "Such beautiful colors of yarn you've all chosen," she said. "Pale pink, magenta, and tawny brown. Someday I'll get ambitious and become a knitter myself, but in the meantime, tell me about your projects. Something for your dear little Lily, Karen?"

Karen held up a page torn from a knitting magazine. It showed a winsome blond toddler modeling a pale pink cardigan. "And I'm using the same pale pink for my own little blond sweetheart," she explained. After the appropriate murmurs of approval, Melanie shifted her gaze to Holly.

"I couldn't resist this amazing yarn," Holly said. A prolonged knitting session in the company of her fellow Knit and Nibblers had restored her to her cheerful, dimply self. She lifted her skein of yarn in one hand and her in-progress work in the other so that the strand of yarn connecting them could be seen more clearly.

"It's like a long, long strip of eyelashes," she exclaimed, "and it looks like shaggy fur when it's knit. I've just done a little bit so far, but you can see."

She extended her needles to display the fur-like texture—though not quite the color of any known fur-bearing animal—of the several rows she'd completed.

"And your pattern?" Melanie inquired.

"Oh—I'm just inventing it," Holly responded

with a flash of her perfect teeth. "It's going to be like a short jacket, sort of flared, with no collar or buttons or anything, and the sleeves are going to be flared too."

Pamela reached for the knitting magazine at her side to show what the end result of her industry would be: a simple crew-neck pullover with the fun detail of a large black cat on the front. But Melanie's attention was suddenly diverted.

It was clear that refreshments were in the offing. The tantalizing aroma of coffee had begun to drift in from the direction of the DeCamps' kitchen. Also from the kitchen came the sound of cupboard doors opening and closing in rapid succession, accompanied by explosive mutters. After a brief lull, a single word replaced the mutters: *"Melanie!"*

Suppressing a laugh, Melanie rose and hurried to the kitchen. After a few moments she darted back out, ducked into the dining room, emerged with a large oval platter, and returned to the kitchen.

Coffee and tea were served first, Melanie standing by and Roland insisting that he could handle the task himself. The coffee made its appearance, five steaming cups on an elegant pewter tray, which also held two empty cup-and-saucer sets for the tea drinkers. Next came a second pewter tray bearing the tea in a pale porcelain teapot that matched the cups, a cream and sugar set, and spoons and small napkins.

Roland made sure the trays were arranged on the coffee table in such a way that a wide space remained between them, and then he returned to the kitchen.

"He's so pleased with himself," Melanie whispered, as Roland reappeared with the platter Melanie had fetched held proudly aloft. He lowered it to the coffee table and stood back, smiling a closed-mouthed smile.

Holly was the first to speak. "Roland!" she exclaimed, clapping her hands. "These are absolutely amazing!"

Arranged in careful rows on the platter were snowmen, each constructed from three round cookies in graduated sizes. Shredded coconut made them convincingly snowy and silver dragées provided their eyes.

"I agree!" Bettina rose from her chair and stepped forward for a closer look.

"Help yourselves," Roland urged, gesturing toward the platter of cookies. "And"—he whirled around—"Nell! Let me pour you some tea."

He tipped the teapot over one of the empty cups and the bright liquid swirled golden brown against the delicate porcelain. While Roland ministered to Nell, delivering tea, cream and sugar, and a spoon to the small table beside the armchair, Melanie slipped into the kitchen. She returned with a stack of porcelain dessert plates, which she set next to the cookie platter. Roland added two snowmen on a plate to the small table at Nell's elbow, though she protested that one would be plenty of sugar for one night, Christmas notwithstanding.

A pleasant bustle ensued, with people bobbing up and down as they provided themselves with drinkables, sugared and creamed them to their satisfaction, and settled back into their places with steaming cups and snowmen ready to hand.

Roland's snowmen were sugar cookies with a sweet buttercream icing beneath the coconut, and they complemented the coffee—Pamela preferred hers black—to perfection.

Roland was happy to accept the compliments praising the tender butteriness of the underlying cookie, the convincing effect of the coconut, and the cleverness of the production process he described. He'd rolled balls of dough in three sizes and then arranged them on his cookie sheet in sets of small, medium, and large, near each other but not touching. The balls had flattened and spread as they baked, fusing together to form snowmen.

Melanie had been out walking Ramona when the topic of the body in the passageway was raised, and so she had missed Nell's admonition that gossiping about the tragic event was unseemly, as well as Bettina's anguished renunciation of her still-in-progress silent-auction scarf. And so when Melanie remarked that it was a shame the holiday cheer surrounding the silent auction and the tree-lighting ceremony had dissipated so quickly and sadly with that morning's news, she was startled by the shocked faces that confronted her.

"Did I say something wrong?" she exclaimed, raising a pretty hand to her mouth.

"It's just—" Pamela hesitated, unsure how to complete the thought.

But Nell cut in. "There's no question that a murder, on Arborville Avenue at that, is out of keeping with the spirit of the season. But rehashing the details does no one, except the police, any good."

"Oh, I didn't mean—" Melanie's chagrin was genuine. Roland's lovely wife seemed to have been born with a gift for comporting herself well in social situations. This had been a rare faux pas.

"Has anyone heard how much the silent auction made?" Holly, in her own ebullient way, was also socially adept, and she was skilled at rescuing conversations steered into stormy waters by the more opinionated Knit and Nibblers.

"I'm sure the library will send out a press release." Bettina, in the act of reaching for a second snowman cookie, looked up. "And people can read all about the auction results when the *Advocate* comes out on Friday."

The *Advocate* was Arborville's weekly newspaper. It was described by both admirers and detractors as containing "all the news that fits," and Bettina was its chief reporter.

"It's a shame that libraries have to depend on charity to supplement their funding," Nell remarked, "though I was certainly happy to donate my knitting efforts to the cause."

"I'd rather charity funded libraries than have my taxes raised to pay for services I never get a chance to weigh in on." Roland spoke from the wooden chair he had now pulled close to the coffee table, having yielded the sleek turquoise chair to Melanie.

"Roland!" Nell's expression was fearsome. "You certainly use and appreciate services other people's taxes support, people who might be just as happy if their money went for something else. Roads, for example?"

"Who doesn't like roads?" Roland seemed genuinely puzzled.

"We don't all drive the same number of miles on the roads. Why should the same proportion of our taxes go toward the roads?"

"Toll roads!" Roland looked as pleased with himself as when he'd accepted compliments on his snowman cookies. "That's the fair way to do it!"

"Should Arborville Avenue be a toll road then?" Bettina had been following the discussion and now she jumped in. She gestured with a hand that held half a snowman cookie, causing the snowman to shed a bit of coconut.

Roland hesitated. "Well . . . that—"

"Would be ridiculous." Bettina finished the sentence for him.

"In the case of local streets, yes, perhaps," Roland conceded. "But when it comes to the library, if people choose not to work hard for themselves and therefore have to freeload off the taxpayers for their entertainment, it's not my job to look after them."

"We are not all as smart and hard-working as you, Roland." Holly's flirtatious smile neutralized any implication of sarcasm.

"I choose to work hard."

"Are you sure it's a choice?" Nell inquired, her gaze penetrating. "Maybe it's genetic. Like the grasshopper and the ant. And you're the ant."

"I don't really think . . ." Roland shifted in his chair and tipped his head forward to survey his torso, his legs, and then his feet, as if genuinely concerned that some metamorphosis was underway. Seemingly satisfied that his luxurious cashmere pullover, nicely creased wool slacks, and gleaming loafers still clothed a human body, he reached for his coffee.

"Charity certainly has its place," Nell conceded. "With the budget shortfall this year, I'm sure the library will be grateful for the extra money. And I think I will have just one more of those tasty snowmen."

Soon the knitters returned to their knitting, and general conversation was replaced by quiet murmurs as Nell tutored Bettina in the finer points of teddy bear creation and Holly and Karen compared notes on the joys and sorrows of their old houses. Half an hour passed in this manner, at which point Roland checked his watch, transferred his briefcase from the floor to his lap, and carefully stowed his yarn and his knitting.

Taking the hint, the other knitters speedily finished in-progress rows and gathered their own projects into their knitting bags, Nell assuring Bettina that she would do fine continuing the teddy bear body on her own and that they could tackle the head the following week.

"How did you get here?" Bettina asked Pamela as they headed down the DeCamps' front walk. The walk was bordered by tall ridges of shoveled snow, and beyond the ridges smooth snow glistened in the light from the streetlamp. "I don't see your car," Bettina went on, "and I know how much you like to walk. But who knows when the passageway stalker might strike again?"

"The passageway stalker?" Pamela laughed and

a puff of steam escaped into the chilly air. "Is that what they're calling him?"

"No." Bettina halted and turned to Pamela. "But that's what I think he was. Unless the killer was stalking Carys, how would he have known she'd be conveniently hidden from sight in the passageway right then, and he'd be able to strike?"

"That's a good point," Pamela agreed. "I hope the police have some leads."

They had reached the street. "How *did* you get here?" Bettina repeated the question. "I'm sorry we couldn't ride together like we usually do, but I was with the grandchildren all afternoon and up through dinnertime."

"Penny brought me," Pamela said. "She's at her friend Lorie's, and I didn't want her to be walking around in the dark, so she's got my car."

"Hard to believe she's a senior in college already." Bettina steered Pamela toward where her faithful Toyota waited at the curb.

"Yes." Pamela nodded. "Yes, it is. She'll be off on her own soon, but I hope she'll always come home for Christmas."

Ten minutes later, Bettina was turning onto Orchard Street where she and her husband, Wilfred, lived directly across the street from Pamela.

"Do you mind walking from my driveway?" Bettina asked. "Or shall I pull into yours?"

"I'll be okay crossing the street," Pamela said. "I really will."

She'd be entering a house empty but for three cats. Pamela had raised her daughter alone after her husband was killed in a tragic accident on the site of an architecture project he was managing. The house, a hundred years old, with clapboard siding and a wide front porch, was a fixer-upper project that they had fixed up and cherished, and Pamela still felt her beloved husband's presence when she was within its walls. Now it welcomed her with lights glowing softly in the front windows.

"I'll be over in the morning," Bettina remarked as Pamela set out across the street. "After I meet with Detective Clayborn."

Chapter Two

The visitor was unmistakably Bettina. Through the lace that curtained the oval window in her front door, Pamela recognized her friend's pumpkin-colored coat, vivid against the black and white scheme of the wintry landscape. But when Pamela opened the door, the Bettina who stepped over the threshold was a far cry from her usual cheerful self.

She flung her arms wide with fingers extended, as if to emphasize the emptiness of her hands. Startled by the gesture, a lustrous black cat who was napping in a spot of sun looked up.

"After I talked to Clayborn, I was too upset to even stop at the Co-Op," she wailed as she slipped out of her coat. "So I don't know what we'll eat with our coffee." She had dressed for her meeting with Arborville's chief (and only) detective with her usual stylish flair, but now the bright yellow sheath that hugged her ample curves seemed ill-suited to the role of tragic heroine that her creased forehead and downturned mouth implied.

"What on earth has happened?" Pamela slipped an arm around Bettina's shoulders and drew her toward the kitchen, where Bettina slumped into one of the two chairs that flanked the small wooden table.

Pamela took the other chair and watched as Bettina swallowed and blinked a few times before starting to speak. "The murder scarf was hand knit," she said, her voice trembling. "And he knows I'm in the knitting club and all, so he took me into the room where they store evidence and asked me if I had any ideas about who might have made it."

"It could have come from anywhere," Pamela said. "Maybe Carys is a knitter herself and was wearing a scarf she had knit and the killer simply used the weapon that came to hand."

"No." Bettina's grief had bowed her head, and the whispered syllable emanated from behind a tousled mass of scarlet curls.

"Or someone made the scarf for her, or she bought it at a craft shop, or it was a scarf the killer's mother—whatever—made for *him* and he set out with it, planning all the time to strangle his victim, or—"

Bettina reached out and grabbed Pamela's hands, which were resting on the table.

"It was the scarf Holly made for the auction," she moaned. "That pretty aqua scarf with the pattern of white snowflakes worked in. And I had to tell him." Bettina looked up. "Poor Holly will be so sad—to think her beautiful scarf was a murder weapon."

"Oh, dear." Pamela sighed and squeezed Bettina's hands. "So at least Detective Clayborn doesn't think that Holly is a suspect."

"No, of course not." Bettina looked marginally more cheerful. "Someone had the winning bid for the scarf at the auction and that person ended up with the scarf."

"So," Pamela said, "the next question is, who was that person? Carys? Or the killer?"

Bettina nodded. "That *is* the next question for Clayborn. The next question for *me* is"—she gazed toward the counter, focusing on the carafe in which Pamela made her coffee—"do you have a bit of coffee left?"

Pamela rose. "Better than that. I'll make a fresh batch. Penny hasn't been down yet and she'll want coffee too."

As Pamela set the kettle to boil and measured beans into her coffee grinder, Bettina transferred the cut-glass sugar bowl from the counter to the table and poured a dollop of heavy cream into the matching cut-glass cream pitcher.

"I suppose you've already had your toast . . ." Bettina commented as she moved about the little kitchen, letting the statement trail off in a suggestive way.

Pamela pressed on the lid of the coffee grinder, and the beans whirled and clattered. She waited to respond until, with a whining growl, the grinder finished its work.

"You can certainly have toast," she said with a

fond smile. "And I think I still have some of that Tupelo honey you and Wilfred gave me."

"That was ages ago!"

"I only get it out when you're here," Pamela explained.

"And that's why you're thin and I'm not."

Pamela *was* thin, and tall, and her simple wardrobe of jeans and casual tops mystified her fashionable friend, who could never understand why Pamela eschewed the fashion-forward looks her lanky frame might have displayed to such advantage.

The kettle's whistle interrupted the conversation then, but Bettina knew her way around Pamela's kitchen nearly as well as Pamela did. She fetched the honey from the cupboard where it shared a shelf with various vinegars, cooking oils, and jars of herbs and spices. And then, while the boiling water from the kettle dripped through the freshly ground beans in the carafe's filter cone, she slipped two slices of whole-grain bread into Pamela's toaster.

A few minutes later, the two friends took their places across from each other at the little wooden table. The simple meal was elevated by the rose-garlanded china on which it was served. Pamela saw no point in having nice things that came out only on special occasions, so she used her wedding china every day—and anyway, most of her other "nice things" were treasures unearthed at thrift stores and tag sales.

In a ritual with which Pamela had become very

familiar over the years, Bettina first spooned sugar into her coffee and then added dribbles of cream until the contents of the cup reached the perfect shade of pale mocha that she preferred. After a sip that evoked a smile and a contented purr, Bettina set about spreading honey on the toast she had buttered when it emerged from the toaster. That task completed, she lifted half a slice to her mouth.

It was at that moment that Penny Paterson appeared in the kitchen doorway. She was wearing pajamas and a robe and carrying Bettina's stylish maroon-leather handbag.

"It's making a noise," she said. "I heard it from the bottom of the stairs. I think it's your phone."

Bettina returned the slice of toast with honey oozing off the edges to her plate, accepted the handbag, and with sticky fingers plucked her phone from its depths.

"Clayborn," she murmured after glancing at its screen. "What could he want now?" Her words trailed after her as she stepped toward the entry to take the call.

Pamela's daughter hadn't inherited her mother's height, and it was hard for Pamela to accept the fact that this small pajama-clad person with face still softened by sleep would soon be out of college and ready to take on the world. At the counter Penny filled a wedding-china cup with coffee and slipped a slice of whole-grain bread into the toaster.

"I see there's cream," she said, glancing at the table, "and honey. And I'd better grab a chair from the dining room."

But at that moment, Bettina returned. "You can have my chair," she said. "And my toast. And even my coffee, if you don't mind that I already took a sip." She stepped across the floor and gave Penny a quick hug. "We'll have to catch up later, Miss Penny. Clayborn wants me over at the police station ASAP."

Pamela had remained seated, but once Bettina identified the caller as Detective Clayborn, interest in her toast and coffee had been superseded by curiosity about the nature of the call. Now she spoke.

"Did he say what—"

"No." Bettina tightened her lips. A furrow appeared between her carefully shaped brows. "But he sounded . . . excited. And . . . oh, dear . . ." She sighed a trembling sigh. "It's about the scarf, I'm sure."

Her hands were shaking as she lifted her handbag from the table.

"I'll come with you," Pamela announced, hopping up from her chair. "We can go in my car. I'll drive."

An hour had passed, and Pamela and Bettina were standing just outside the door of the Arborville police station. The day was bright, all the brighter for the sunlight reflecting off the brittle ice that crusted the snow in the field beyond the parking lot's asphalt expanse.

Bettina looked around. Apparently satisfied that no one was listening (in fact they were the only people in the parking lot), she said, "It was all off the record, but I know you won't tell anyone."

"Of course not." Pamela was very much in Nell's camp when it came to eschewing town gossip.

"He wanted to know if I knew who 'S. Claws' was."

"Santa Claus?" Pamela laughed. "Why, everyone knows who Santa Claus is."

"Not *that* S. Claus!" Bettina grabbed Pamela's arm. "C-L-A-W-S, like *claws*." She relinquished Pamela's arm and shaped the fingers of her gloved hand as if to mime a paw with claws extended.

"*Do* you know?"

"I'm afraid so." Bettina nodded mournfully. "And I had to tell him. S. Claws is Laurel Lewis."

"I'm impressed," Pamela said. "But how did you know that? And how did Detective Clayborn know that you would know? And why on earth did he want to know?"

"Which question do you want me to answer first?"

"Why he wanted to know. I suppose it has something to do with . . . the murder."

Bettina nodded. "You're right. But let's get in your car. I'm freezing." Despite her pumpkin-colored down coat, the olive-green beret that hid all but a scarlet fringe of bangs, and matching fur-trimmed booties, Bettina's teeth were chattering and her cheeks were pale.

Once they were settled in Pamela's car—no warmer than outside but at least sheltered from the wind, Bettina explained. After the early morning conversation in which she had identified the murder scarf as the one that Knit and Nibble member Holly Perkins had made for the silent auction, Detective Clayborn had asked an auction volunteer at the library to retrieve the auction bid sheets. The bid sheet for the aqua scarf with snowflakes indicated that the winning bid had been made by one "S. Claws."

"Obviously not a real person's name," Bettina concluded.

"Obviously, and I can certainly see why he'd want to know who S. Claws is in real life. But why did he think you'd know—though you obviously did?"

The car windows had begun to steam up as the moisture exhaled by the breathing and talking occupants condensed on the chilly glass.

"He did an internet search," Bettina said. "And an article I wrote last year for the *Advocate* came up. It was about a fundraising drive for the Haversack animal shelter and I mentioned that a cat-loving donor identifying herself as 'S. Claws' had given a thousand dollars." Bettina shrugged. "I knew S. Claws was Laurel Lewis's charitable alter ego because the shelter people knew, but I couldn't put her name in the article because she wanted to remain anonymous."

Bettina turned away and focused on the fogged-up window for a moment, though nothing was visible on the other side. "But I had to tell Clayborn because now it has to do with a murder."

"Laurel Lewis found the body." Pamela stared at the window too.

"*Claimed to.*" Bettina corrected her. "Now it appears she could be the murderer."

Pamela arrived back home to find a note from Penny in the entry saying she and her friend Lorie had gone to the mall. She stepped into the living room and inspected the Christmas tree, looking for signs of cat damage, but all was well. She and Penny had brought the tree home the previous Friday and spent the afternoon decorating it with their favorite ornaments chosen from among the vast collection Pamela had assembled from tag sales and thrift stores. Now a rainbow of glittery balls interspersed with antique Santas, angels, fanciful animals, candy canes, and snowflakes dangled from the tree's fragrant boughs, and its perfume filled the entire house.

Near the arch between the living room and the dining room, Precious, the elegant Siamese cat who was Pamela's most recent feline adoptee, lounged on the top platform of the cat climber.

The morning's adventure and the revelations accompanying it had distracted Pamela from the fact that lunchtime was approaching. But now, back in her own house, she was aware that her body had exhausted the nutritive possibilities of that morning's toast and coffee and was demanding more.

In the kitchen, she peered into the refrigerator. The previous night's dinner had been meatloaf sandwiches, eaten in haste before she and Penny hurried out, she to Knit and Nibble and Penny to Lorie's. There was enough meatloaf left for another sandwich, and soon Pamela was feeling nourished and ready to go to work.

To reach her office, Pamela had only to climb the stairs. As associate editor of *Fiber Craft* magazine, she was responsible for evaluating submissions, copyediting articles chosen for publication, and—occasionally—reviewing books on topics relevant to the magazine's focus. Before Penny went off to college, Pamela had been particularly glad that all of those things could be done from home and that her job required only the occasional trip into the magazine's headquarters in Manhattan.

That morning, before she descended the stairs for breakfast, Pamela had checked her email and found a message from her boss with three articles attached. Strung across the top of the message were the abbreviated titles, each identified as a digital file by the Word logo next to it. The abbreviations were "Sericulture," "Prayer Rugs," and "Spy-Craft." She was to evaluate them and respond with recommendations for or against publication by the following Friday evening.

Sericulture, she knew, had to do with silk, and she opened that file first. The article's full title was "Sericulture in the Cévennes: When Silkworms Had Royal Patrons." The article told the fascinating story of how a remote region in Southern France became the hub of the French silk industry. Fed up with the expense of imported silk, Henry VI offered financial incentives and perks of all sorts to the communes whose livelihood depended on cultivating silkworms and harvesting the thread they produced.

A few photos taken by the author documented what was left of the monumental stone structures that had housed extended families and their silkworms until disease and religious strife led to the industry's decline.

Pamela wrote an enthusiastic recommendation that the article be published, and looked up from her computer screen to realize that the room in

which she sat had become totally dark but for the
glow of the screen and a desk lamp angled toward
her keyboard. When she opened her office door,
the sound of Penny's voice reached her. The one-
sided nature of the conversation suggested that
Penny's words were directed at one or more of the
cats. Pamela saved her document, closed her file
and Word, and descended the stairs to greet her
daughter.

Chapter Three

At the moment, Pamela had only one feline sleeping companion, Catrina, adopted as a woebegone stray, but now plump and contented. Catrina's daughter Ginger, named for her coloration, had taken to Penny right away and preferred Penny's bed when Penny was in residence.

On Thursday morning Pamela opened her eyes to find the sun bright behind her bedroom's white eyelet curtains. A pair of amber eyes in a furry heart-shaped face returned her gaze.

"Breakfast?" she inquired as she sat up against her bed's brass headboard. Dislodged from her chest, the cat leapt to the floor.

Having added slippers and a robe to her ensemble, Pamela headed for the stairs with Catrina leading the way. At the bottom of the stairs they were joined by Precious, who preferred to spend the night in the living room. Once they reached

the kitchen, Pamela took a can of crab and liver
medley from the cupboard, opened it, and scooped
generous portions into two bowls. She set water to
boil on the stove and headed outside to fetch the
Register.

She had slept well, slumbers undisturbed by
concern about the murder case. A few hours spent
reading about silkworm culture in Southern
France, followed by a pleasant evening with Penny,
had dimmed her recollection of Bettina's visit and
the trip to the police station. But back inside, slip-
ping the newspaper from its flimsy plastic sleeve,
she recalled with a jolt that the previous day's developments had certainly brought the issue of
Carys Walnutt's murder closer to home.

The boldface headline, revealed once the paper
was unfolded, amplified that jolt. And the kettle's
jarring hoot seemed an appropriate soundtrack.
Arrest Made in Arborville Passageway Murder,
the headline screamed. Smaller print below added,
"Laurel Lewis, who said she 'found' the body, taken
into custody." The byline credited Marcy Brewer
with the article.

Pamela shuddered. Marcy Brewer was known
for her aggressive reporting, and she didn't shy
away from ferreting out the most sensational aspects of the stories assigned to her. Pamela re-
folded the paper and set it aside. Coffee and toast
would be necessary fortifications before reading
any further.

Five minutes later, enveloped by the comforting
aromas of fresh-brewed coffee and toasted whole-
grain bread, and with the coffee and toast at hand,
Pamela once again unfolded the *Register.*

Who would think that a pretty aqua mohair scarf with a white snowflake design could be a cruel instrument of death? she read. *Yet that was the murder weapon chosen by the killer responsible for the death of Arborville resident Carys Walnutt last Monday night between 8:00 and 9:00 p.m. As this paper reported previously, Walnutt's body was found in the narrow passageway that connects Arborville's small shopping district along Arborville Avenue with the parking lot that serves the library, the police station, and a park.*

The article was illustrated with a photo of the Arborville Avenue entrance to the passageway. Businesses that bordered the passageway were also visible: Hyler's Luncheonette on the right and one of Arborville's three hair salons on the left. Several strips of yellow crime-scene tape were stretched across the passageway's mouth.

The article went on to say that Carys Walnutt lived in a garden apartment farther north on Arborville Avenue and across from St. Willibrod's Church. Neighbors were reluctant to talk about her (curious, Pamela thought to herself, given that Marcy Brewer could be very persistent). *"She was an unusual person,"* a neighbor who didn't want to be named was quoted as saying. *"That's as far as I'll go. It's the season of good cheer after all."*

The Lifestyle section of the *Register* offered a welcome diversion, and Pamela was enjoying her second cup of coffee as she read an article about decorating one's garden with suet and birdseed "ornaments" to give the birds a Christmas treat. As she was studying a particularly charming "ornament" that featured fresh cranberries, the doorbell's chime summoned her to the entry.

Bettina swept in on a draft of chilly air.

"I suppose you saw the *Register*," she said as she began to unbutton her coat. Without waiting for a response, she went on. "So they've arrested Laurel Lewis, poor thing. And Marcy Brewer is an absolute menace. Holly called me first thing this morning. Not only did Marcy describe Holly's scarf—so everyone who knows which scarf Holly donated now knows that Holly's scarf was the murder weapon—but now she wants to *interview* Holly."

Pamela reached for the coat, but Bettina didn't remove it. "I can't stay," she said. "I'm on my way to meet with Clayborn. It's late to get something in tomorrow's *Advocate*, but I'll see what I can do. This coat is just very warm." She fanned her face with a gloved hand. "Holly called me to ask if you have to say yes if a reporter requests an interview. I told her of course not. Marcy Brewer isn't the police."

"I hope she doesn't track Holly down at the salon," Pamela said. Holly and her husband, Desmond, owned a hair salon in the neighboring town of Meadowside.

"I do too. I'm just so angry, I had to unburden myself to someone—and Wilfred has driven out to Newfield to buy a honey-roasted ham for Christmas Day." Bettina tightened her lips, glossy with lipstick in a fetching shade of pumpkin-orange that matched her coat, and shook her head until her scarlet bangs vibrated. "And that photo! Crime-scene tape on Arborville Avenue four days before Christmas! It's bad enough that people have to see it in person, but to put it on the front page of the *Register*—" She stopped, and then completed the sentence with a disgusted snort.

"There's a little coffee left," Pamela suggested, striving for a comforting gesture.

"I can't stay, really." Bettina fumbled with the top button of her coat. "But I'll drop back in after I finish with Clayborn. Or—let's have lunch together in Timberley. My treat. I have some last-minute shopping to do, and the shops there are so interesting, and I just can't face the idea of eating at Hyler's with that crime-scene tape right next door. And we can talk about the menu for my Christmas Eve party."

She continued with her buttoning task, commenting half to herself, "I'll know more too, after I've talked to Clayborn, like is there other evidence pointing to Laurel Lewis besides the fact that she won the scarf at the auction?"

A nimble ginger-colored cat darted between Pamela and Bettina and headed for the kitchen doorway. Bettina watched it vanish then shifted her gaze to the stairway. Pamela turned to look in the same direction and saw Penny standing on the bottom step.

"Good morning, Miss Penny!" Bettina brightened.

Penny, however, didn't respond in kind. Silently, her glance traveled from Pamela to Bettina and then back to Pamela. "I know what you two are up to," she said at last. "And you know how much I worry when you think you can do better than the police at solving murders."

Arborville, New Jersey, was a small, safe town, the sort of place where police spend more time responding to complaints that someone has put their tree trimmings out too far in advance of the pickup day than solving murders. Yet over the years there had been murders, not committed by strangers intent on mayhem, but rather by friends or even family members. And curiously—despite the acknowledged expertise of Arborville's sole police detective, Lucas Clayborn, Pamela and Bettina had frequently been responsible for the crucial insight that allowed the police to finger the evildoer.

With a hug, Bettina assured Penny that she had no intention of trying to usurp Detective Clayborn's investigative role and that her sole interest in the case derived from her responsibility to readers of the *Advocate*. She was on her way then, ushered out on another draft of chilly air.

Left alone in the entry, Pamela and Penny regarded each other, Penny's expression still tinged with suspicion.

"That's really the only reason we were talking about it," Pamela said. "Bettina takes her job very seriously."

Without commenting, Penny headed for the kitchen and Pamela followed. They found Ginger waiting patiently in the corner where the cats had become accustomed to taking their meals, and Penny handled the feeding chore while Pamela set water boiling for her daughter's coffee.

Some minutes later, Penny sat at the kitchen table sipping coffee sweetened with sugar and much diluted with heavy cream, and nibbling whole-grain toast liberally spread with honey. Pamela busied herself at the counter measuring out poppy seeds for the special poppy-seed cakes she made every year at Christmas.

She poured the seeds—dark, fragrant, and so tiny that static caused some to cling to the interior of the measuring cup—into a small pot, added a cup of milk, and set the pot over a low flame. As soon as delicate bubbles began to form around the edges of the liquid, she turned the flame off and covered the pot. The seeds and milk would sit for an hour before they were ready to use. Meanwhile, though, sticks of butter could be cut into chunks and allowed to soften, flour and sugar could be measured, eggs could be separated and the whites beaten, and loaf pans could be buttered and floured.

Penny seemed content to read the *Register* without comment. Pamela was happy to work in silence, and the next half hour or so passed pleasantly enough. Penny finished her breakfast and went back upstairs, saying something about texting Lorie. Pamela launched the creaming and blending and beating and mixing that would turn her assembled ingredients into batter. When the batter had been created, she divided it between two buttered and floured loaf pans.

Once the poppy-seed cakes were in the oven, she repaired to her office, where she opened the Word file labeled "Prayer Rugs" and immersed herself in "Totemic Animal Motifs in Traditional Prayer-Rug Design."

"Heavenly!" Bettina exclaimed, closing her eyes and inhaling deeply.

"I just took them out of the oven and I'm ready

to go," Pamela said, "so your timing is perfect." She stepped to the closet to fetch her coat. It was a down coat too, though not as colorful as Bettina's, and it had been a Christmas gift from Penny a few years earlier.

"Christmas Eve isn't going to be a potluck," Bettina explained as they headed out the door, "but I hope you'll bring one of your poppy-seed cakes."

"Of course!" Pamela pulled the door closed behind her and inserted her key in the lock. "And anything else you'd like me to make as well. I'm going to the Co-Op later."

"Just the poppy-seed cake is plenty," Bettina said. "There will be other desserts too. Wilfred is buzzing with ideas about what else to serve— though with so many people coming, it's not going to be a sit-down meal, so things have to be easy to manage."

Chatting about the party plans, they made their way across the street to where Bettina's faithful Toyota shared a wide driveway with Wilfred's ancient but lovingly cared-for Mercedes. They were soon cruising north on County Road, on their way to the charming restaurants and shops of Timberley, which was larger and more affluent than Arborville—though the residents of Arborville considered their town quite as nice a town as anyone could want.

It wasn't until later that the conversation between the two friends took a darker turn. Pamela and Bettina were seated at a small table in one of the two French restaurants along Timberley's main shopping street. The plates that had held wedges of quiche Lorraine and salads of baby lettuce dressed with oil and vinegar had been cleared, and orders had been placed for chocolate mousse and coffee.

Above the wisp of country lace that curtained its lower panes, the window offered a view of bundled-up people scurrying here and there, as well as storefronts sporting swags of Christmas greenery made festive with red ribbons and twinkling lights.

"Were you able to get something to the *Advocate* in time for tomorrow's issue?" Pamela asked.

Bettina closed her eyes and shook her head slowly from side to side.

"They couldn't hold the presses for such an important story?" Pamela leaned forward.

"There wasn't anything important," Bettina said sadly. "Nothing new at all—not beyond what the *Register* already reported, at least that Clayborn was willing to reveal." Her lips tightened into a disgusted knot.

"But what about other evidence, evidence significant enough to make them arrest Laurel? Besides just the fact that she won the scarf?"

Bettina continued to shake her head.

"They interviewed people who know Laurel, lots of people. Apparently they think they've uncovered a motive, but he wouldn't tell what it is. He did say, though, that she had opportunity."

"She *was* in the area," Pamela agreed. "That's how she came to find the body."

Bettina looked up to greet the server, who was approaching with a tray bearing two cups of coffee and two servings of chocolate mousse in parfait glasses.

When the coffee and mousse had been delivered and the server had departed, Bettina spoke. "Laurel's accounting office is above one of the shops near the passageway, and her window faces the parking lot. If Carys was coming from the parking lot and heading toward Arborville Avenue, Laurel could have seen her approaching the passageway from the parking lot end and hurried down to enter from the Arborville Avenue end. That's what Clayborn thinks anyway."

The mousse was a tempting sight, deep chocolate-brown and garnished with a puff of whipped cream. As if the motion had been purposely synchronized, Pamela picked up her spoon just as Bettina did, and each conveyed a sample to her mouth. The flavor—rich and sweet—and texture—creamy and cool—didn't disappoint, and the blissful expression on Bettina's face indicated that her reaction was positive.

Bettina took another bite and closed her eyes as she savored the dessert. At one point the tip of her tongue peeked between her lips in a motion that seemed almost catlike. But when she opened her eyes, it was clear that her brain had been occupied with more than the felicitous combination of sugar, cream, and cacao beans.

"I just can't believe someone like Laurel would do a thing like that," she declared. "With her charitable giving and her devotion to cats."

Pamela set down her cup and shrugged. She had been alternating sips of coffee and spoonfuls of mousse, enjoying the way the black coffee echoed on a more intense level the faint bitterness still lurking in the much-sweetened chocolate.

"Marcy Brewer couldn't get anyone to say anything specifically bad about Carys," she pointed out, "but she couldn't get anyone to say anything specifically good either. So maybe there are other people, maybe lots of people, who wanted Carys dead."

Pamela took another sip of coffee, caffeine seeming more appropriate than mousse to the investigative turn the conversation had taken. "There's the scarf though," she said. "Laurel won the scarf at the auction."

As if to signal that she had no wish to prolong the discussion, Bettina remained silent and tackled her mousse with renewed enthusiasm.

The lunch had been prelude to a shopping expedition, and after they had finished eating and settled their bill, Pamela and Bettina set out past storefronts whose tasteful window displays offered everything from poinsettias and amaryllis (florist), candy-bedecked gingerbread cottages (bakery), hampers overflowing with gourmet treats (cheese shop), and much, much more.

Bettina's first destination was a shop that featured crafts made by local artisans. There she picked out a string of handmade glass beads for her Arborville daughter-in-law and, after much indecision, a simple silver necklace for her Boston daughter-in-law.

"Greta has such plain taste in clothes," Bettina complained. "Even worse than you, and then there's my sweet little Morgan . . ." She sighed. "Warren and Greta are wonderful parents, I'm sure, but wouldn't a little girl want to wear pink every once in a while?"

Pamela steeled herself for the lament that she

knew was coming. Bettina's son Warren and his wife Greta were both professors, and when their daughter Morgan was born they declared they were raising an ungendered child. Bettina had been forbidden to lavish on her only female grandchild the girly clothes and toys she had been looking forward to purchasing.

Bettina continued to browse as she rehearsed the themes Pamela had come to know so well, starting with her disappointment a few years earlier that the pink granny-square baby blanket she had labored over would not be a welcome gift. Pamela followed in her wake, pausing to examine a display of earrings that resembled delicate golden leaves and then noticing a card explaining that they had been cast from molds made from actual leaves. She already had several gifts for Penny— she collected gifts for family and friends all year and stored them on a special closet shelf. But the leaf earrings were so lovely that she picked up a pair.

When she caught up with Bettina, her friend was gazing longingly at a row of handmade dolls. Their bodies were cloth, like old-fashioned dolls, their hair was yarn, and their faces were embroidered. But no two were alike. One wore a puffed-sleeve dress in a flowery print, another wore leggings and an oversize sweater, a third was bundled up in a plaid wool coat with a knitted hat pulled down to her eyebrows.

"Aren't these just too too cute!" Bettina sighed, fingering the skirt of the puffed-sleeve dress. She turned away. "I can't though! They wouldn't let her keep it and they'd be mad at me besides." She mustered a smile. "Are you ready?"

Pamela held up the earrings. "For Penny," she said, and Bettina gave an approving nod.

When they reached the counter, which was staffed by an artistic-looking woman with a long dark braid and a striking patchwork jacket featuring silky fabrics in random colors and shapes, Bettina motioned for Pamela to go first.

Pamela set the earrings down and took out her credit card, aware that Bettina had left her side and darted away. By the time her transaction was complete, Bettina had returned, carrying the doll in the puffed-sleeve dress.

"It's for Lily, Karen's daughter," she explained before Pamela could say anything. "And look"— she rotated the doll so its back was facing Pamela— "the dress comes off. See all the little buttons! So she can have other clothes, clothes that I can knit." Bettina was fairly vibrating with happiness. "Ohh! Lily and I are going to have so much fun!"

Chapter Four

Pamela wanted to be dropped off at the Co-Op
Grocery, so instead of returning to Arborville
via County Road, Bettina cut over to Arborville Avenue after they crossed the Arborville-Timberley
border. They headed into Arborville's shopping
district from the north, cruising past houses set in
snowy yards and decked with wreaths and greenery.

Soon St. Willibrod's Church came into sight,
and across from it the garden apartments where
Carys Walnutt had lived. They were two-story brick
buildings—or actually one long building, with doors
opening off small porches arranged at intervals
along its façade. Concrete paths leading from the
doors converged into a longer path that led to the
sidewalk. Despite the chilly weather, one of the doors
was open, perhaps related to the fact that a U-Haul
truck was parked in the street.

Bettina slowed down and veered toward the curb in front of St. Willibrod's.

"Seems awfully soon," she murmured to herself.

"Soon for what?" Pamela leaned forward and peered around Bettina, looking for whatever had provoked Bettina's comment.

"The moving truck," Bettina said, as a pleasant-looking woman, quite buxom and with curly gray hair, emerged from the open door carrying a large cardboard box. With a click, Bettina opened her car door. "There might be a story here," she said, lowering a fur-trimmed bootie onto the asphalt.

Pamela followed her across the street, but Bettina could move fast when she wanted to. By the time Pamela caught up with her, she was already chatting with the woman who had emerged carrying the box, and the box had been added to the boxes already in the back of the U-Haul.

"Sure," the woman was saying. "No reason to wait, if you ask me. Her lease is up at the end of the year and the landlord will be just as happy to rent the apartment to someone else, the sooner the better. But he wants to repaint first."

"Just as happy?" Bettina assumed a teasing expression—a half smile, a raised eyebrow, and a sideways glance beneath a delicately shadowed eyelid—that implied a bit of gossip wouldn't be amiss.

"I think we'll all be glad to have someone else in there." The woman nodded toward the apartment with the open door. "Basically Carys was just a sour person." She paused and pushed the box closer to the others. "Not that I want to speak ill of the dead."

"Of course not." Bettina offered a sympathetic wink. "When you say *sour* . . ."

"Ill-tempered, grumpy, complaining about everything, any little bit of noise—snowblowers, leaf blowers, contractors' radios, St. Willibrod's chimes, the kid who played the drums in the apartment next door, even Christmas carolers. if you can imagine. A real Ms. Scrooge."

"Hey, Fran!" came a voice. The woman, apparently responding to her name, swiveled around. Advancing toward them was another woman, middle-aged but younger than Fran, carrying a bulging plastic garbage bag in each hand.

"Marlyn!" Fran darted forward. "Let me help."

"Getting it done," the woman, now identified as Marlyn, said. "Little by little, but there's still all that furniture to deal with." Noticing Pamela and Bettina, she added, "I'm Marlyn Walnutt . . ." The slight lift at the end of the statement, as well as the raised brows, hinted that she hoped to elicit self-introductions in return.

Pamela and Bettina complied, then glanced at each other as the import of Marlyn's last name became clear.

"You must be—" Pamela began but was cut off by Bettina's "Oh, you poor dear! Carys Walnutt must have been—"

Marlyn nodded. "My sister."

"I'm so sorry for your loss!" Bettina's mobile features expressed genuine concern.

"Yes," Pamela murmured. "What a shock!" She might have made the connection even without the last name if she'd studied Marlyn a bit more closely. The woman standing before her had a sweet, eager-to-please manner, but physically she resembled her dour sister, though softer, rounder, and younger.

"It *was* a shock," Marlyn said in a matter-of-fact way. "And now I've got this whole apartment to clear out within the next few days, as if Christmas wasn't already busy enough." Noticing that Fran was still standing there, she added, "I'm forgetting my manners. This is Fran Calvert, my neighbor. She's been helping me."

Bettina peered into the back of the U-Haul truck. "You've both been busy," she said.

"Most of this is being donated." Marlyn gestured toward the truck. "Kitchen stuff, knick-knacks, linens, clothes . . . nothing very special. But some of her furniture was nice, and it's up for grabs. My kids don't want it and Carys didn't have kids." She turned and advanced a few steps on the path that connected the apartments to the sidewalk. "Come on in!" she said over her shoulder.

Bettina glanced at Pamela and shrugged and they fell in line behind Marlyn. Fran brought up the rear.

The apartment was large and airy, with cream-colored walls and a wide window looking out on the street. A rolled-up carpet and several cardboard boxes occupied the middle of the floor, which was pale hardwood. Another box with its flaps folded back and lumpy objects wrapped in crumpled newspaper visible sat on a glass-topped coffee table. Curtains were draped over the back of the sofa, which was cream-colored like the walls.

"Take off your coats, look around, and help yourselves," Marlyn offered with a wave of the hand. "There's a small table and some chairs in the kitchen and a bureau and some other things in the bedroom. Also a bookshelf."

Fran busied herself sealing up the box on the coffee table.

Pamela had furnished much of her house with thrift store and estate-sale finds, and she still loved to discover pre-owned treasures—all the better if they were free. But she had no more need for major pieces of furniture, and looking around, she surmised that the smaller things among which she might have found a curious bowl or vase or knick-knack had already been packed away.

Bettina had strayed into the bedroom. Now she emerged smiling like a surprised shopper who, while not in search of anything in particular, has stumbled upon a lucky find.

"That trunk," she said, addressing Marlyn. "Are you really giving it away?" Marlyn nodded. Bettina clapped her hands and went on. "My son and his wife would love it."

"Take it," Marlyn said.

"I will, but I think it's too big for my car." She beckoned for Pamela to join her in the bedroom doorway and gestured toward a painted wooden trunk about the size and shape of large hassock. The ornate latch, the peony motif in the decoration, and rich reds, greens, and golds gave it an Asian look.

"Definitely worth rescuing," Pamela agreed. "It could be used as a coffee table or . . . just as a trunk to store blankets in the summer . . ."

Bettina took a quick photo of the trunk with her phone, then darted back out into the living room.

Pamela heard her arranging with Marlyn to return with a larger car and a husband or son within the next few days.

"No problem," Marlyn said. "I live here too—in this same complex, I mean. Number twelve. So I can let you in anytime."

"And I'm right next door in number eleven," Fran added. "So if she's not home I can let you in."

After a last, admiring look at the trunk, Pamela returned to the living room. At that same moment, a phone lying on the coffee table emitted a shrill ring. Marlyn scooped it up and stepped to the edge of the room to take the call. After saying "Hello," she listened for a few minutes, said "Okay," and ended the call.

"I have to collect some paperwork from the Realtor who manages the complex," she said. "He's coming to me, which is thoughtful, swinging by in his car."

She pulled on a down jacket that had been tossed over an armchair, added a stocking cap and gloves, and headed for the door. Before opening it, she turned. "Keep looking around if you want— or I'll see you when you come back for the trunk." She added, "Nice to meet you both."

The sound of pots and pans rattling in the kitchen suggested that Fran had been at work there. Now she emerged carrying a teetering pile composed of baking sheets, muffin tins, a frying pan, saucepans in graduated sizes—with their lids, and balanced on top, a flour sifter.

"Running out of boxes," she commented before transferring her precarious burden to the armchair.

Bettina gave her a flirtatious smile and Pamela braced herself. Often such smiles were a prelude to questions that, in Pamela's view, Bettina had no business asking.

"Do you think she's sorry that her sister has been murdered?" Bettina inquired. "She doesn't seem terribly sad to me."

Pamela expected Fran to respond that she had no way of knowing such an intimate thing, and/or that Bettina had no business even asking. But instead, she frowned slightly, stretched her lips into a half smile, and tilted her head. The flour sifter that topped the pile of kitchenware in the armchair threatened to tumble onto the floor and she reached out to steady it.

"Carys cost Marlyn her marriage," she said.

"What?" Bettina took a step back and opened her eyes so wide that the white around her irises was visible. She did tend to overdramatize her reactions, but even Pamela felt a jolt and sensed that her own expression reflected her own surprise.

"Not the way you think." Fran waved a hand in a soothing gesture. "Carys convinced Marlyn to divorce the poor guy." In a sing-song voice she went on: "*He doesn't treat you well, the children are grown, you deserve your own life, take back your own name.* But if you ask me, Carys was just jealous that Marlyn had a husband and family and she didn't. But anyway, she convinced Marlyn to squirrel away household money for an escape fund and then make her break. So finally Marlyn did."

Fran leaned close and whispered, though no one but her intended audience was near. "Marlyn is very suggestible. And then when Marlyn leaves her husband she moves here, practically next door to her sister!"

"Maybe she's happier now," Bettina ventured. "Not every husband is as ideal as my Wilfred."

Fran shook her head. "A few months later, Marlyn had second thoughts and begged hubby to come back. But he wouldn't. Now she misses him."

"And he's off sailing, and I'm still here," came a fake-cheery voice from the doorway, accompanied by a gust of chilly air. "Midlife Crisis: His Turn." Marlyn had returned. She smiled a stiff smile.

Fran suddenly became very interested in the stability of the flour sifter, and Pamela, who rarely blushed, felt her cheeks grow warm. But Bettina stepped forward and reached out to hug Marlyn, who—surprisingly—accepted the hug and even hugged back.

"You poor thing," Bettina murmured in the same tones she used when comforting Woofus, the troubled dog she had adopted from the Haversack animal shelter. "You've really been having a tough time, haven't you?"

Marlyn dropped the unconvincing bravado with which she had greeted them and nodded dolefully. Putting an arm around her, Bettina led her to the sofa, where the two women perched at the end not occupied by the curtains.

"I loved my sister," Marlyn said, "in spite of everything. Carys was just born that way. She always had to be in charge. She thought people wouldn't respect her otherwise—like it wasn't enough to just be an ordinary person."

"Bossy, if you ask me," Fran whispered to Pamela.

Marlyn's voice quavered. "And I knew she was jealous of me. I *was* lucky, and she seemed so lonely." She sniffled and Bettina pulled a tissue from her handbag. "It's all just been *hard*, and my husband won't come back, and it didn't help that the police treated me like a suspect, at first—before they figured out where that scarf came from."

Bettina's eyes grew wide again. "No!" she breathed. "They actually thought *you* might have killed your own sister."

"They always interview the family members," Fran declared with a toss of her gray curls. "Anybody who watches mystery shows on TV knows that."

"You're right." Marlyn nodded meekly. "Of course. Detective Clayborn was nice about it, but he did ask me where I was between eight and nine Monday night."

"Where were you?" It was Pamela who spoke, the question popping out independently of any volition on her part.

"Home. Where else?"

"She was," Fran cut in. "We were both shoveling snow—getting a head start on it. We have to keep our own porches and walks clear, but the complex takes care of the rest. I heard the chimes so I know just when it was."

She stepped closer to the sofa and reached out a hand toward Marlyn. "It's time to get back to work," she said. "No point in sitting around moping when you've got plenty to keep you busy."

"Okay." Marlyn stood up.

"And what are you thinking about for dinner?"

"Hamburgers?" Marlyn's tone implied doubt.

"We ate hamburgers last night," Fran said firmly. "I'll order a pizza."

Bettina climbed to her feet. "I'll be back for the trunk," she told Marlyn, adding a quick hug. "You take care of yourself."

"She does seem suggestible," Bettina noted after they had returned to her car and settled into their seats, "though it's kind of amazing that she actually let her sister talk her into getting a divorce."

"Maybe the husband was horrible," Pamela suggested. "Maybe she just needed that little nudge—and to know that her sister would be there for her afterwards."

"She wanted him back though, so he can't have been all that horrible. But now he's gone off sailing, and her sister's to blame."

It felt colder in the car than outside, where the bright sun at least created the illusion of warmth. Pamela folded one gloved hand around the other and massaged her fingers as she spoke. "So—motive then, for sure."

"But she apparently has an alibi that convinced Clayborn, and Laurel turned up as the likelier suspect anyway." Bettina twisted her key in the ignition and the car's engine grumbled for a moment and then caught. "I just don't think it could be Laurel though"—she swiveled her head and gave Pamela a significant look—"or at least I don't want it to be." She pulled away from the curb and into the flow of traffic heading south on Arborville Avenue.

"Other people could have wanted Carys dead," Pamela commented after a minute or two. "People she complained about, like the kid who played the drums in the apartment next door, or the Christmas carolers . . ."

Bettina laughed. "Killer Christmas carolers? That's like something out of a horror movie."

Pamela laughed too. "And I doubt a kid who just wanted to play his drums loud would murder someone. Besides, he probably got complaints from a lot of other neighbors too."

They had reached Arborville's main intersection, with most of the shopping district behind them and the Co-Op on the corner across the way. Bettina waited for the light to change, navigated the intersection, and eased to the curb in front of Borough Hall.

"You're sure you don't want me to wait and give you a ride home?" she asked.

"I'm fine walking." Pamela clicked her door open and started to climb out.

"Here's something to think about," Bettina said in parting. "Maybe the ex-husband resented Carys for destroying his marriage. How do we know he's really 'off sailing'?"

Inside the market, Pamela pushed her cart along the narrow aisles, collecting the ingredients for the chicken with dumplings she planned to make that night, as well as half a pound of the Co-

Op's special Vermont cheddar, a fresh loaf of whole-grain bread, and tomatoes and cucumbers for salad.

Penny was out when she got home, with a note left behind that she was at Lorie's but would be back by dinnertime. Up in her office, Pamela removed Catrina from her computer keyboard and returned to her evaluation of "Totemic Animal Motifs in Traditional Prayer-Rug Design."

Chapter Five

The next morning Pamela was back at work in her office. The article on prayer rugs, like the one on sericulture, had been excellent, and she'd given it an enthusiastic thumbs-up. Now she was tackling "Spy-Craft," whose full title proved to be "Spy-Craft: The Knitting Spies of World War II." The premise was fascinating, and the utility of knitting as a tool of espionage seemed obvious once the author pointed it out.

The knit stitch and the purl stitch could be used like the dots and dashes of Morse code, and any message at all could be encoded that way. Who would suspect, for example, that elderly Belgian women whose parlor windows looked out on train tracks were recording the times and frequency of German troop trains in the swathes of knitting that hung from their needles?

Unfortunately, though, the author's tendency

to mangle the English language distracted mightily from the article's value—though there was no hint that her native tongue was anything other than English. "It would be splinting hairs," she had written, "to question motives," and elsewhere rumors were "viscous," danger reared its ugly visage, and nearly every paragraph included at least one misspelling, a malapropism, or a metaphor garbled into unintelligibility.

Pamela closed her eyes, but the image of the bright computer monitor lingered. The article wasn't to be copyedited, only read, with a thumbs-up or thumbs-down evaluation returned to her boss. Yet even just reading it was painful. She was relieved, then, to be distracted by the telephone's ring.

She swiveled around and picked up the handset.

"Are you busy?" asked a familiar voice.

Pamela responded with a grateful "Hi, Bettina."

"*Are* you busy?" Bettina repeated. "Laurel Lewis is out on bail."

"That's good news," Pamela said. "I wonder how she's doing?"

"We could know." Bettina's enthusiasm carried over the phone lines. "I think it would be useful if I talked to her, in my capacity as a reporter for the *Advocate*, of course."

"And you're inviting me to come along?" Pamela had swiveled back to her normal position, facing the computer monitor—and a paragraph in which an intrepid knitter-spy evaded death despite its being "hot on her heals." She groaned.

"Are you okay?" Bettina asked.

"Fine!" Pamela said. "And if you're inviting me, yes. I'll come."

She thought for a minute. Penny was downstairs, she knew, because she had heard her daughter talking to one or more of the cats.

"Don't come here," she said. "If we're going out together, Penny will suspect it has something to do with the murder. She has kind of a sixth sense. I'll come to you."

Happy to escape from "Spy-Craft," at least for a while, Pamela closed the file, exited Word, and shut down her computer.

Penny was sitting at the kitchen table, still in her pajamas and robe, sipping coffee with Ginger on her lap. "Going out?" she asked as Pamela picked up her purse from the counter.

"Post office," Pamela said. "I realized I have more cards to send and I'm out of Christmas stamps. It's a nice day for a walk, so . . ."

"*Mo-om!*" Penny's forehead puckered. "It's freezing out. The paper says high of twenty degrees and that's this afternoon."

"Nice and bright though. That makes a difference." With a wave, Pamela headed for the entry, where she collected her warmest coat, the down one Penny had given her.

Laurel lived in a townhouse development at the southern edge of Arborville. The land had once been occupied by a very grand house, built at the beginning of the previous century when families were much larger. No buyers had come forward when the most recent owners died, but a conve-

nient rezoning made the property attractive to de-
velopers. The crumbling mansion had been replaced by twelve attractive townhouses whose
wood-frame construction made them blend in well
with Arborville's typical housing stock.

In spring, summer, and fall, meticulous land-
scaping added to the development's appeal. Now a
brittle crust of snow covered the lawn, and the
leafless shrubs were spiky skeletons of themselves.
A carefully shoveled sidewalk led from the parking
area to the complex, where glittering icicles hung
from the gutters that edged the roofline.

After walking several yards, Pamela and Bettina
stopped to scan the first cluster of units for the address they were seeking. A door in one of the units
opened and a woman emerged, dressed for the
chill in a spotted fur that was obviously fake, a
bright red beret and matching scarf, and sturdy
lace-up boots with thick soles. She headed toward
them, apparently on her way to the parking area,
and nodded pleasantly as she got closer.

She passed, and Pamela and Bettina continued
on their way as well. Laurel's unit hadn't yet come
into view. But after a moment, a voice behind
them called Bettina's name. They turned.

"It's you, isn't it?" the woman in the spotted fur
said. "Bettina Fraser from the *Advocate*? I recognize
you from the senior center—you cover so many of
our events."

"Why, yes!" Bettina responded with a wide smile,
enhanced by the lipstick that matched her pumpkin-
colored coat. She took a few steps toward the woman
and offered a gloved hand. "And you're . . . ?"

"Suzanne Turner." The woman offered her hand

in return, then said, "I suppose you're here because of poor Laurel."

Bettina nodded.

"I don't think she did it," the woman declared. "Laurel is a lovely person and even if she wasn't, nobody who has such a soft spot for cats could be a murderer. I was happy to take care of them while she was in jail, but they missed their mommy." She interjected an emphatic nod and then went on, her breath condensing into wisps of steam as she spoke. "I hope the police figure out who really did it—though I can't say I'll actually miss Carys."

"Really? Did you know her?" The questions were asked in an offhand way, but Pamela could tell by the way Bettina's eyes narrowed that the encounter with Suzanne was now more than an impromptu chat.

"I was in a writers' group with Carys"—Suzanne added a half smile and shrug that implied she hadn't taken the experience too seriously—"for a while at least. I'm retired now, trying new things."

"You're not writing anymore?" Bettina inquired.

"It wasn't really me," Suzanne said. "I prefer to be out and about, not sitting at a desk for hours all by myself. And I wasn't very good either, at least according to Carys. Laurel, though . . . Laurel was—"

"In the group too?" Bettina interjected. Pamela could tell from her voice that she was excited.

Suzanne nodded. "She was really good. *I* thought she was good. Carys didn't think she was good. In fact Laurel gave up on a novel she was writing because Carys convinced her that it had no chance of ever being published, and Laurel was so demoralized she dropped out of the group. I don't know if there's anybody left in it now." She laughed. "Carys might have driven them all away—and now she's gone too." She raised a hand to her mouth and added, "Ooops! I shouldn't laugh."

Suzanne went on her way toward the parking area, but Pamela and Bettina didn't move for a moment.

"Interesting," Bettina commented.

"Yes, interesting," Pamela agreed.

They continued along the sidewalk, past the first cluster of townhouses and then the second, until they reached the address they were looking for. Laurel's front door sported a cheery wreath, undoubtedly hung there in earlier, happier times—sprays of balsam intertwined with gold ribbon and studded with red berries. A few steps led up to a small porch. They climbed the steps and rang the bell.

"Hello?" Bettina spoke into the narrow gap that opened between door and doorframe. "It's Bettina Fraser. I know you from the Haversack animal shelter, and I'm so sorry about what's happened. I was wondering if you need anything—like cat food? Or something for yourself?"

The door swung back to reveal a tall woman almost as tall as Pamela, and with shoulder-length dark hair like Pamela's. She hadn't yet dressed for the day, but was wearing a long fleecy robe, pale green. Two cats peeked out from beneath its hem.

"No, I don't . . ." Her eyes roved from Bettina to Pamela and back. "But . . ." She backed up, leaving the cats exposed. "Come on in. It's cold out there."

One of the cats, a pretty calico, ventured forward. Bettina removed her gloves, bent down, and offered a finger. The cat responded with a sniff and then lowered its head for a scratch. The other cat, a Persian with a drift of pure white fur, stood aside and watched.

"Sweet baby," Bettina murmured to the calico. She straightened up and focused on Laurel. "But how are *you* doing?"

"So-so." Laurel shrugged. "It all just seems unreal." She looked around. "We can sit down, I guess, if you want to stay. It cheers me up to have company, but I really don't have the energy to make coffee or anything."

"Of course not, you poor dear." Bettina's sympathetic head-tilt, contracted brows, and sad half-smile emphasized her concern.

Laurel meanwhile had flopped into a peach-colored armchair, and the cats that had accompanied her to the door were now in her lap. They were joined by a third cat and then a fourth, also calicos. The room was charmingly decorated with a Victorian-style sofa, peach-colored like the chair, and a few pieces of ornate wooden furniture that looked very old. Several paintings of flowers rendered in an impressionistic style enlivened the pale walls.

Pamela and Bettina loosened their coats and perched on the edge of the sofa.

Laurel devoted herself to cuddling her cats for a few moments, then she looked toward Bettina. "I guess you know Detective Clayborn pretty well," she said, "because of the *Advocate*."

Bettina nodded.

"He doesn't actually listen, does he?"

Bettina made a noncommittal sound. Pamela

suspected that the detective's willingness to cooperate with Bettina's reporting depended on his confidence in her discretion.

But Laurel didn't need an answer to go on. "I never actually got the scarf," she announced, leaning forward despite the lapful of cats. "And I told him that, several times." Her eyes, which were large and a startling shade of blue, lent her a guileless air that had evidently been lost on Detective Clayborn.

"You never got the scarf!" Pamela had so far been content to let Bettina take the lead, but this information was so startling that she'd been provoked to speech.

"Never," Laurel said with a tight-lipped headshake. "It was already claimed when I went to pick it up after the auction."

"How can that be?" Pamela and Bettina both spoke at once.

Laurel shrugged. "Everyone was crowding around the table where they were collecting the money from the winning bidders, and just thrusting cash at the auction volunteers. And when it got to be my turn, they said someone had already claimed the scarf. I knew I had the winning bid because I checked the bid sheet right before the auction deadline, but I guess the volunteers expected people to be honest and so they didn't ask for ID or anything."

Bettina frowned. "I can't believe Clayborn didn't follow up! If the whole case against you relies on the idea that the murder weapon belonged to you, well—" As if words failed, she concluded with a disgusted snort.

"But I had . . . I guess they call it 'opportunity' too." Laurel's expression was bleak. "My office is so close to where it happened, and then . . . who's to say—except me, of course—that I didn't just pretend to have found Carys's body, to allay suspicion, after I had killed her?"

"That seems far-fetched." Bettina laughed—though Pamela recalled that Bettina herself had raised that very point.

"Of course it is. And it assumes I'm quite the actress, which I'm not. It was dark in that passageway, and I almost tripped over her, and I tried to talk to her but she didn't answer, and I stumbled to the other end and called out to Mort Quigley—though at first I didn't recognize him because he was facing the other direction and he was so bundled up and it was snowing. And then when he turned around, he was as shocked as I was."

The fluffy white Persian had been reposing on the arm of the chair, apparently napping. Now it raised its head and twisted its neck around to glance at its mistress. Laurel reached out and began to stroke its back, her fingers disappearing into its luxuriant fur.

"Luckily I have these sweeties to comfort me," she said, and bent over until she was almost nose to nose with the cat, adding, "Mommy had to cancel her Christmas trip, didn't she?" She looked up. "A condition of being out on bail—how odd it sounds to say that!—is that I can't leave Arborville. I was going to spend the holiday with my sister and her family in Philadelphia."

"Come to my house!" Bettina exclaimed. "No

one should be alone on Christmas, and there's always room for one more at my dining room table."

"Oh, no. No, no, no." Laurel smiled sadly. "You're so kind, but I can't impose like that. I wouldn't be good company. My kitties and I will get along okay on our own."

The fluffy white cat had resumed its slumber, but one of the calicos had ventured from its mistress's lap and was investigating Bettina's fur-trimmed bootie. Laurel continued talking, as if to herself, staring ahead at nothing in particular. "I've got work to take my mind off things, the audit of the library budget and some estimated tax figures for an antiques dealer in Timberley and then there's that caterer . . ." Her voice trailed off, but after a moment she added, "Plenty of nice distracting work."

"You're sure?" Bettina leaned forward, staring as intently as a parent might stare at a child suspected of stretching the truth.

"Really sure!" Laurel tried to muster a smile that wasn't tinged with sadness. "The library thing is due right after the holiday, so I *do* have to work."

"Okay . . ." Bettina drew the word out as she rose to her feet. "If you're sure, but I'm going to leave my number so you can call me if you change your mind and want some company." She carefully disengaged her foot from the calico's explorations.

"One step forward and one step back, I'd say," Pamela remarked as they neared the parking area. They were passing a huge holly bush that offered a welcome flash of color—deep green with red berries—against the dark asphalt and ridges of piled snow that was no longer all that white.

Bettina signaled assent with a humming sound. After a moment she spoke. "If she never even claimed the scarf, how could she have used it to strangle Carys?"

"That's the step forward," Pamela said, "assuming she's telling the truth about not claiming the scarf. We only have her word for it."

"What's the step back?"

"The writers' group."

"Ohhh!" Bettina moaned. "That's right. She has a motive now—but would somebody really kill a person who told them they were a bad writer? I don't mind it when the editor of the *Advocate* asks me to do more research or talk to more people for a story."

"But he doesn't tell you to forget about being a reporter because you're hopelessly bad."

"That's true." Bettina nodded.

"Suzanne said she thought Laurel was really good—and it sounds like Laurel was serious about her writing . . . with a novel in progress. And then she just abandoned it. If you had invested your whole self in a project like that and somebody demolished it, maybe you'd want to demolish that person."

They had reached Bettina's car. She pulled her keys from her handbag and a few minutes later they were cruising along the road that served the townhouse development. Bettina was silent until she had made the turn onto Arborville Avenue and driven a few blocks.

When she spoke, it was to say, "Clayborn must have checked with Mort Quigley or one of the other auction volunteers about who claimed the scarf. That just seems like basic police work to me."

The houses along Arborville Avenue south of Orchard Street were quite grand, many constructed of brick in a classic center-hall colonial style, and set well back from the road. This time of year, the imposing façades had been made festive with miniature Christmas trees flanking impressive doorways, oversize wreaths decking ornate doors, and garlands of Christmas greenery spiraling around columns.

Pamela had been enjoying the scenery, but Bettina's comment roused her from her reverie. "I would think so," she agreed. "I wonder what Mort Quigley or whoever he talked to told him."

Bettina stopped at a crosswalk where a woman pushing a stroller was waiting to cross. She turned to Pamela. "Obviously not that somebody else claimed the scarf."

"Maybe the person just said they didn't know—that it was crowded and confusing."

Bettina, still turned toward Pamela, nodded vigorously. "So Clayborn is just going on the fact that Laurel—or S. Claws—had the winning bid, and he thinks Laurel's statement that the scarf was already gone when she tried to claim it is an attempt to establish that she's innocent."

From behind them came an irritated honk. The woman pushing the stroller was long gone and the way was clear to proceed.

"I don't know why people have to be so impatient," Bettina muttered as she accelerated.

A few moments later they were speeding past the stately brick apartment building that marked the corner of Arborville Avenue and Orchard Street.

"Where are you going?" Pamela asked. "That was our turn."

"To the library to talk to Mort Quigley," Bettina said, her eyes focused on the road.

Chapter Six

"To what do I owe the pleasure of your visit?" Mort Quigley directed the question at Bettina, with a nod toward Pamela as well. He'd been summoned from his office by the young woman stationed at the circulation counter, which was decorated for the season with a potted poinsettia. On the wall behind the counter, foil letters spelling out HAPPY HOLIDAYS hung from a string stretched taut like a clothesline.

Bettina smiled coquettishly. The *Advocate* had given lavish coverage to library events over the years and Mort Quigley had more reason to woo her than the reverse, but Bettina had charm to spare.

"It's that time again," she said. "The new year is right around the corner, and I was wondering if you have a list of the library events you've planned so far. That way I can get a sense of what I'm going to be reporting on. And the *Advocate* will post notices well in advance, of course, so people know what's coming up."

"Good thinking!" Mort exclaimed. "Step into my parlor, said the spider to the fly." Energetic despite his bulk, he hopped to the end of the counter, pushed open a hinged gate, and beckoned them to enter. He was taller than Bettina but not as tall as Pamela, with rusty-red hair retreating from a freckly forehead.

Perched on his desk chair before his computer monitor, he brought up a file, and a few seconds later a faint chiming sound and a low purr signaled the arrival of a printout. Mort stood up, collected it from the printer, and handed it to Bettina with a bow.

She glanced over it and raised her eyes. "Lots of things to look forward to," she commented, adding a flirtatious wink and a shiver of excitement. "I'm sure we'll all be happy to put the old year behind us. Such a shame, the murder—and to have it get all tangled up with the auction."

Mort shook his head, managing to retain his affable mien while looking appropriately serious. "These things happen," he said. "Even in nice towns like Arborville."

"The auction was such a good idea too, and got such support from the community. I hope we can do it again next year." Bettina mustered a hopeful smile.

"I do too." Mort returned the smile, a wide-mouthed smile that made the skin around his pale eyes crinkle.

"So much enthusiastic bidding! And that big

rush at the end, with people so excited to claim the items they'd won . . ."

Mort nodded. "Maybe next time we'll allow more time between the end of the auction and the beginning of the tree-lighting ceremony."

"Experience is the best teacher, as my Wilfred would say." Mort continued to nod and Bettina nodded too, synchronizing her nods with his. Then, off-handedly, as if the answer wasn't really important, she murmured, "I know the police are going by the fact that Laurel Lewis had the winning bid for the . . . uh . . . but it seems like if things were confusing . . ."

Mort stopped nodding. "I know what you mean," he said, "and no, I certainly didn't see who claimed it. But you expect people to be honest. We announced the winning bidders. Other people bid on that scarf. Carys Walnutt bid on that scarf. But I can't imagine somebody who bid less would show up at the end, thrust some money at the volunteers, and grab something they hadn't rightfully won."

"No," Bettina agreed. "That's hard to imagine. Especially in a nice town like Arborville."

"What do you think?" Bettina asked Pamela as they left the library and began to advance across the parking lot toward where Bettina's faithful Toyota waited. The snowy expanse of the park was visible in the background.

"I think we should have lunch at Hyler's," Pamela responded.

Bettina stopped walking. "I don't think I could,"

she said in a small voice. "It's right next to where . . . where . . ." Her gloved hands fumbled the air as if to capture the right words.

"The crime-scene tape is down." Pamela gestured toward the mouth of the passageway between the brick buildings that housed Hyler's on one side and the hair salon on the other. "If everybody avoids Hyler's because it's next to what was once a crime scene, Hyler's will go out of business." She bent down to make eye contact with Bettina. "You wouldn't want that to happen, would you?"

"I'd miss the Reuben sandwiches," Bettina admitted. "But I won't walk through that passageway. We're going to have to go around the long way."

Hyler's oversized menus were the luncheonette's trademark, listing so many dining possibilities that one could eat at Hyler's every day for several weeks with no repeat, but Bettina scarcely looked at hers.

"Now I've got Reubens on the brain," she said, "and that's what I'm going to have, with a vanilla shake." She set the menu aside.

They were seated in one of the Naugahyde-upholstered booths along the restaurant's side walls. The booths were premium spots, more private and more comfortable than the wooden tables and chairs that crowded the middle of the floor. Today, however, most of the tables were empty, and the booths as well—though it was peak lunch hour.

The server, a middle-aged woman who had

worked at Hyler's as long as Pamela had lived in Arborville, approached. She was as cheerful as always, though the cheer seemed forced without the usual backdrop of laughter and chatter.

"I'll have the same," Pamela said after Bettina had placed her order. They watched the server retreat and then Bettina leaned across the table.

"Did we learn anything useful?" she asked. "I was trying to get him to talk without being obvious about what we wanted to know." She had shed her down coat, which now hung from a hook at the edge of the booth, to reveal a cozy wool turtleneck in a Christmasy shade of dark green that set off her scarlet hair to great advantage.

"Mort Quigley didn't see who claimed the scarf," Pamela said, "and the process of people claiming their auction prizes was rushed and confusing. I don't think there's a way we can know whether Laurel is telling the truth or lying."

"I believe her though"—Bettina nodded vigorously and the carefully waved tendrils of her coiffure vibrated—"despite the possible motive involving the writers' group."

The server appeared at the end of the booth with two vanilla milkshakes in tall, frosty glasses, crowned with froth. As soon as hers had been deposited on her paper place mat, Bettina pulled it closer and bent toward the straw.

Pamela pulled her milkshake closer too, but before sampling it, she said, "I guess we're assuming that if the scarf was the murder weapon then the person who claimed it has to be the murderer."

Bettina looked up. The tip of her straw now

bore the bright imprint of her lipstick. "That seems to be Clayborn's approach. How else would the scarf end up at the murder scene?"

"Think for a minute!" Pamela raised a finger as if calling attention to a lecture in the offing. As a mother she'd tried to resist lecturing Penny, but every once in a while the impulse to illuminate became too much to bear.

"I'm thinking." With furrowed brow and pursed lips, Bettina twisted her mobile features into a caricature of deep thought.

"The victim could have been wearing the scarf!" Pamela's triumphant shout would have turned heads at neighboring tables, except that the tables were unoccupied.

"Of course! Of course!" Bettina beamed across the table. "And didn't Mort say that Carys Walnutt also bid on the scarf?"

Pamela cut in. "And things were confusing with people rushing to pay for what they'd won and grab their prizes."

Bettina began talking almost before Pamela had stopped. "And based on what people have said about Carys, she seems like the kind of person who might grab what she wanted, whether fairly or not."

Then in unison, both said, "And then she was murdered with that very scarf!"

"Ironic," Pamela added.

The server was approaching, bearing the Reubens on oval platters garnished with pickle spears and paper cups of coleslaw. They were silent then, except for enthusiastic thank-yous, until the platters had been deposited and the server had turned away.

Pamela had not yet even tasted her milkshake. After a long sip that delivered a rich draft of creamy vanilla-ness, she commented, "If Carys was wearing the scarf, the killer could be anyone at all, totally unconnected with the auction."

"Like her sister?" Bettina's hand, holding a fork that bore a toasty morsel of Reuben sandwich trailing a strand of melted cheese, halted halfway to her mouth.

"She has an alibi. Remember?"

"I'm glad we ate there," Bettina said after they had returned to her car and settled into their seats. "I'd hate to think of Hyler's going out of business."

She twisted her key in the ignition, the car grumbled to life, and she focused for the next few minutes on backing up and maneuvering out of the parking lot. But as she waited to make the turn onto Arborville Avenue, she glanced at Pamela and inquired, "Have you decided what you're going to wear to my party tomorrow night?"

"Not really." Pamela shrugged. "It's not a formal occasion, is it?"

Bettina had been about to take advantage of a lull in the traffic flow but she stomped down hard on the brake instead. "Hello!" she said, swiveling to face Pamela. "It's a Christmas Eve party and you're bringing your handsome boyfriend, Brian Delano."

"He's seen me in jeans." Pamela bit her lip to suppress a teasing smile.

"Oh, for heaven's sake!" Bettina stepped on the gas, gave the steering wheel a violent twist, and the car lurched into a turn.

"I'll wear something nice. I promise," Pamela assured her. Bettina eased off on the gas.

"I don't understand why you two aren't spending Christmas Day together," Bettina commented as they cruised along Arborville Avenue. "With the Arborville children and the Boston children doing Christmas with the in-laws this year, Wilfred and I are happy that we're going to have you and Penny—but Brian would be more than welcome too."

"He's going to be with his parents in Kringleka-mack," Pamela said. "We've been over this before."

"And he can't take you? And Penny, of course." Bettina sounded as indignant as if she herself was the excluded guest.

"Things aren't at that stage yet," Pamela said. "It kind of . . . means something when a man takes a woman home for the holidays." She turned to Bettina. "Doesn't it?" she asked, her throat suddenly tight as she remembered that long-ago Christmas with her husband (then her husband-to-be) and his parents.

Bettina didn't notice the change in her voice. She shrugged. "Well, at least you have someone in your life now. That's an improvement over before. And I know Wilfred will enjoy chatting with Brian tomorrow night."

Pamela swallowed a few times. She didn't mind the fact that Brian Delano wasn't ready to present her to his parents. She wasn't ready to be presented and perhaps would never be. He was smart and interesting and—yes—handsome, and having *someone* in her life was a great deal better than being solitary, especially since the prospect of her daughter graduating and being out on her own loomed so close.

Bettina's voice interrupted, seeming to arrive from far away, so deep had Pamela been in her musings.

"You're home." Bettina leaned over. "Hello?"

"Oh! Yes!" Pamela shook her head as if to rearrange her thoughts. "Thank you. And I'll bring dessert on Christmas."

"Wilfred Jr. and I are picking up that trunk at Marlyn's tomorrow," Bettina said as Pamela reached for the door handle. "Want to come along?"

Pamela stared for a moment, still not quite back in the present. "Why?"

"Why not?"

It was early afternoon, with plenty of time to fit in the two chores that awaited: finishing the evaluation of "Spy-Craft" and wrapping a few more gifts. The gifts were for Penny, and ideally the wrapping would be done when Penny wasn't around—she was out at the moment, but the "Spy-Craft" evaluation and the two evaluations Pamela had already completed were due back by five p.m.

She hadn't finished her read-through of "Spy-Craft," and even the first few pages had been a time-consuming slog, so she climbed the stairs to her office, removed Catrina from her keyboard, and pushed the button that would bring her computer to life. She enjoyed the process of wrapping gifts, and an hour or so spent with festive holiday paper and rolls of colorful ribbon would be fitting reward for finishing the *Fiber Craft* assignments.

But ten minutes later she closed the Word file for "Spy-Craft: The Knitting Spies of World War II," opened the file she had titled "Evaluations," and wrote *"Spy-Craft: The Knitting Spies of World War II" is not only unpublishable, it is unreadable. I suggest that the author find another line of work or at least plan never to submit to* Fiber Craft *again.*

She skimmed the evaluations she had written for the sericulture article and the prayer rug article, decided they sounded fine, and saved and closed the file. After composing a brief cover message, she attached the "Evaluations" file and was on the point of clicking Send when her finger halted on the mouse. A vision of Laurel Lewis's face rose before her.

Could Laurel really have murdered Carys Walnutt to rid the universe of the person who had crushed her dreams of being a writer? A cruel critique could do things to a person—hollow them out in a way. Pamela was never sure whether her boss shared her evaluations with authors or merely took Pamela's advice into account and sent out bland acceptances or rejections. But what if she relayed Pamela's words verbatim? No one, no matter how horrible a writer, deserved to be crushed.

She opened "Evaluations," deleted what she had written, and substituted, *The author clearly is well-informed on this fascinating topic but the style might be better suited to a different sort of publication.*

Chapter Seven

The figure visible through the lace curtain was definitely Bettina, but the vehicle waiting at the curb was unfamiliar.

"It's Wilfred Jr.'s Subaru," Bettina explained Saturday morning as the door swung open. "There's plenty of room in the back for that trunk."

Pamela slipped into her coat, called goodbye to Penny, and stepped out onto the porch.

Wilfred Jr. was a younger and thinner version of his genial father. On this chilly morning his hair, thick and sandy like Wilfred's had been in his youth, was hidden by a stocking cap, and he was bundled in a puffy down jacket. He climbed out of the car and opened the back door as Pamela and Bettina approached.

"I'll play the chauffeur," he said as he gestured for them both to climb in the back.

The drive to the garden apartments was brief,

just up to the corner of Orchard Street and then seven or eight blocks along Arborville Avenue. As they neared their destination, they passed the rec center and, across the way, the traffic island with the noble pine tree that Arborville decorated every year for Christmas. The lush boughs decked with oversize iridescent balls, tinsel garlands, and winking lights, illuminated even during the day, were as beautiful a sight as in years past. But now the tree and the lighting ceremony were all tangled up with the auction that had provided the scarf that had strangled Carys Walnutt and led to the arrest of Laurel Lewis. Pamela sighed and looked away.

"We're here," Wilfred Jr. announced a few minutes later.

No one answered when they tapped at the door of the apartment that had been Carys's. Through the uncurtained windows, they could glimpse sealed boxes and bulging garbage bags, as well as the richly decorated trunk with its swirling peonies.

"It looks like she's got everything packed up," Bettina said. "I'll just step down to number twelve and fetch her."

Bettina was back in a minute, trailed by Marlyn tiptoeing along the chilly path in slippers and with a jacket draped over her shoulders.

"Yes," Marlyn was saying, "all my work is done. On Monday a charity group is coming to collect the boxes, and the garbage bags are going to the curb for the trash pickup. So the landlord should have time to do what he needs to do."

"No rest for the wicked," Bettina replied. In response to Marlyn's startled "What?" Bettina explained, "It's something my husband says."

Marlyn nodded in acknowledgment when Bettina introduced Wilfred Jr. and inserted a key into the apartment door's lock.

"The trunk *is* a beautiful thing," she said as they stepped inside. "I'm glad it's finding a home. I had to squeeze a whole houseful of stuff into an apartment after my divorce, and I barely have room to turn around."

It seemed too cumbersome to be managed by one person, even a sturdy young man, but luckily it had handles on the ends, wrought in the same ornate style as the latch. Pamela seized one handle and Wilfred Jr. seized the other and together they hefted it and began to edge toward the open door.

As they proceeded down the sidewalk, Pamela heard Bettina say, "I wonder what will happen if the police discover Laurel Lewis didn't kill Carys. I suppose they'll be asking around in this complex again, looking for people who might have had a grudge against your sister . . ."

Distracted, Pamela faltered for a moment, listening. Bettina had a trick of phrasing statements in a way that made people respond to them as if they were questions.

"Are you doing okay?" Wilfred Jr. was as solicitous as his kindly father.

"Fine, fine," Pamela said. "It's not really that heavy."

A few minutes later, the trunk had been safely stowed in the Subaru's hatchback and Bettina was making her way down the concrete path that led to the sidewalk. Just then the St. Willibrod's chimes began to sound from across the street, so Pamela had to hold off asking Bettina the question she was longing to ask as she counted eleven of the reverberating bongs.

"We were here longer than I thought," she observed as the last reverberations died away.

"Less than an hour." Wilfred Jr. checked his watch. "It's only ten. The chimes must be off, probably still on daylight savings time."

But Pamela was focused on Bettina now and barely heard him. "So—did you get anything out of her about people who might have had grudges?"

Bettina shook her head. "She's very loyal, despite what Carys did to her. I wish we had run into that Fran—she was sure happy to talk."

Pamela had not been serious about wearing jeans to the party. Standing in front of her closet she had hesitated between the elegant black sheath that had been a gift from Bettina and the ruby-red tunic she had knit for herself from a curious pattern involving long sleeves but bare shoulders. She had finally settled on the tunic, given its Christmas-appropriate color—even though she had worn it on several Christmas-related occasions in past years—and she had paired it with slim black slacks and her black pumps.

"Very festive," Brian said approvingly as he stepped across the threshold carrying a colorfully wrapped bottle and a small box tied with a red bow. "Merry Christmas." He leaned forward to give her a quick kiss, almost platonic, and handed her the box.

Brian Delano taught photography at Wendel-staff College. She'd met him there when her car battery died in the Wendelstaff parking lot while she was attending a fashion show. He was eminently suitable, as Bettina never tired of pointing out, and handsome, with dark good looks and a wolfish air that was tempered by a sweet smile.

Pamela offered him a box in return, larger than the one he'd handed her, and flat. "You can open it now," she said. "It's Christmas Eve."

"You first." He smiled.

She perched on the entry chair and untied the ribbon. Inside the box, cushioned on a bed of cotton, was a pair of earrings, gold and silver wires twisted into dramatic spirals.

"Beautiful!" Pamela exclaimed.

"I thought they'd look nice when you wear your hair up," Brian said, obviously pleased at her reaction.

"Your turn." Pamela nodded toward the box she'd given him, vacated the chair, and reached out to relieve him of the bottle he carried.

With both hands now free, he peeled off the wrappings and in a moment was holding up a small framed picture.

"It looks like the Manhattan skyline." He studied the picture more closely. "A pen and ink sketch. Very nice." He thought for a minute and then tilted his head to study her. "You remembered!" He laughed.

"You always take the upper level of the bridge

when we go into the city," Pamela said, "and you always comment on how much you like the view."

A wedding-china platter waited on the entry's small table. Under a protective film of plastic wrap, slices of poppy-seed cake were arranged in careful rows. There was no one to call goodbye to since Penny had left an hour earlier for a party organized by a college friend who lived in a nearby town. They set their gifts to each other on the table, Brian helped Pamela into her coat, and they headed across the street, Pamela carrying the platter and stepping carefully in her pumps.

Ice crystals speckled the asphalt, reflecting light from the street lamp. The night was clear and cold, and overhead tiny stars pinpricked the dark sky.

"Welcome, welcome, welcome!" Bettina greeted them, silhouetted against the brightness of her cheerful living room. The strains of "We Three Kings" drifted from within. She accepted the platter and stepped back to let them enter. When Wilfred appeared at her side, Brian presented him with the colorfully wrapped bottle.

Wilfred drew Brian aside with a hearty inquiry about his recent doings as Bettina set off for the kitchen bearing the platter. "I'm glad you wore the red tunic," she said, turning to speak over her shoulder to Pamela, who was following her, "though maybe it's time for you to think about acquiring a new Christmas outfit."

Bettina herself was in red as well, a red velvet fit-and-flare dress with a wide neckline and three-quarter-length sleeves. She had accessorized it with black suede pumps and a triple strand of pearls.

"You're the first ones here," she said somewhat unnecessarily as they passed through the empty dining room. In preparation for the guests, however, the table had been pushed against the wall, spread with a lacy cloth, and laden with delights ranging from a tempting cheese ball to fancifully garnished mini-sandwiches. Bettina's huge cut-glass punch bowl sat waiting for Wilfred to concoct the spicy wassail that was his holiday tradition.

"I invited all the Knit and Nibblers," Bettina went on, "but Karen and her husband have a family event." No sooner had she spoken than the doorbell chimed. From the kitchen they could hear the door open and then voices mingling as Wilfred greeted a wave of people arriving in a sudden rush. Bettina set the platter on the high counter that separated the cooking area of the kitchen from the eating area, where it joined a tray of carefully decorated sugar cookies and a plate of brownies. On the stove a large pot of cider simmered on a burner turned low. The nutmeg and cinnamon that Wilfred had added perfumed the kitchen.

When they returned to the living room, Wilfred was just helping Roland and Melanie divest themselves of their coats as Nell and Harold stepped over the threshold behind them. Brian had already been drawn into conversation with Holly and her husband, Desmond, and Bettina's Arborville friend, Marlene Pepper, was chatting with Wilfred Jr. and his wife, Maxie.

"Who's for wassail?" Wilfred surveyed the group, which even without the addition of spirits was brimming with holiday cheer. He himself was in fine form, with his red and green plaid wool shirt and a beaming smile that made his ruddy cheeks resemble apples.

"Me . . . me . . . me," came a chorus of voices.

He retreated toward the kitchen, followed by Bettina and most of the guests. Pamela always looked forward to Wilfred's wassail, but she didn't mind waiting a bit and, anyway, the doorbell had just chimed again.

Pamela greeted two couples she didn't know but whose female halves she recognized as friends of Bettina's, and before she could close the door voices called "Merry Christmas" from the front walk and more arrivals stepped onto the porch. Bettina reappeared and joined in the greetings. Coats were removed, guests were urged to join Wilfred in the dining room, and Bettina whisked the coats upstairs.

More and more people arrived and Bettina darted back and forth and up and down the stairs. When, after a bit, it seemed that the flow of new arrivals had ceased, Bettina returned to Pamela's side bearing two cut-glass cups containing wassail. She handed one to Pamela and looked around, saying, "I brought one for that handsome boyfriend of yours."

Brian, however, had supplied himself with his own wassail and was standing near the fireplace, where bright flames danced atop crisscrossed logs, deep in conversation with Roland.

"I'll drink it myself," Bettina said, and raised the cup in a toast. Pamela raised hers and took a sip. Wilfred's wassail, she knew, was hard cider spiced with his own special blend of spices and enhanced with a goodly dollop of brandy. It was warm in the mouth, with a nose-tingling hint of alcohol vapor and a lingering suggestion of nutmeg.

They stood in companionable silence for a bit as the sounds of laughter and conversation echoed around them, all with a backdrop of carols, as "Good King Wenceslas" gave way to "The Holly and the Ivy," and "The Holly and the Ivy" yielded to "Greensleeves."

"It's going well," Bettina commented. "Don't you think?" She surveyed the crowded room, where people dressed in their holiday finery mingled, some nibbling from small plates, others sipping from cups of wassail or glasses of wine or beer.

"Oh, very!" Pamela agreed. The wassail had eased the shyness she sometimes felt in crowds, and when Marlene Pepper detached herself from the group she had been chatting with and joined Pamela and Bettina, Pamela was happy to hold up her end of the conversation.

Marlene's topic was, blessedly, not the recent murder but rather the Arborville Players and their upcoming production of *Twelfth Night*, for which she had been on the costume committee. Pamela smiled and nodded, adding a comment here and there. More people joined them, Marlene departed, Brian replaced Bettina, Maxie stopped by to say how much she liked the trunk, and Melanie DeCamp accosted Maxie to compliment her hairstyle. With the carols and the chatter and the wassail Pamela found that she was enjoying herself.

Their whole group migrated to the dining room where they browsed along the buffet table. Ready to be spread on crackers, the cheese ball's rich cheddar-orange interior beckoned, along with a colorful paté featuring layers of red, green, yellow, and white vegetables. The mini-sandwiches, open-faced, included smoked salmon, thin-sliced roast beef, shrimp salad, herring, and prosciutto. Meat-balls on toothpicks filled a platter next to a tray of bite-sized onion tarts. Bright red cherry tomatoes shared a plate with cucumber spears and baby car-rots.

Once their plates were full, Pamela and Brian stepped off to the side to sample the buffet's bounty. Pamela started with a mini-sandwich, smoked salmon layered on pumpernickel and garnished with a sprig of dill, and moved on to a cracker heaped with the cheddar-mayonnaise blend, en-hanced with cayenne, from the cheese ball.

"I'll have to ask Wilfred for his meatball recipe," Brian commented after he'd deposited an empty toothpick onto his plate. "Plenty of garlic and just spicy enough."

They alternated eating and chatting, mostly about the food and Wilfred's kitchen prowess. After several minutes Bettina detached herself from a group that included Marlene Pepper and Nell and Harold Bascomb, swung by the buffet for more meatballs and mini-sandwiches, and wound up where Pamela and Brian were standing near the arch that led to the living room.

"Please have more," she urged, and then, wink-ing at Brian, added, "We're so glad you could come! What's Christmas without friends? And any friend of Pamela's is a friend of ours." For good measure, she reached out with her free hand and squeezed his arm.

Brian responded with a smile and said, "I'll take you up on that—especially these meatballs." He turned to Pamela. "Can I get you a second helping of anything?"

"I'm fine." Pamela shook her head, and she and Bettina watched as Brian made his way toward the buffet table.

"So handsome!" Bettina sighed. "He's really a keeper."

Brian did look handsome in slim, dark slacks, a dark turtleneck, and a dark tweedy jacket. As he neared the buffet table, he stopped to talk to Wilfred, who was trading a full platter of meatballs for one with only two remaining. In the buzz of conversation and with a particularly lively rendition of "Little Drummer Boy" coming from the stereo, it wasn't possible to make out what they were saying, but Pamela suspected Brian was making good on his resolve to ask Wilfred for his meatball recipe.

But her attention was drawn then to Holly Perkins. "Everything is just perfect!" Holly exclaimed with a smile that displayed her perfect teeth and activated her dimple. She had pulled her abundant waves, brunette streaked with violet tonight, into a loose up-do, with face-framing tendrils that enhanced her striking looks. Bold silver earrings that resembled Christmas tree ornaments dangled from her earlobes.

She shifted her bright gaze from Bettina to Pamela. "And what a sweetheart your boyfriend is—and so handsome."

Pamela wasn't sure how much credit she could take for Brian's appearance, so thanks didn't seem in order. Perhaps a smile would do, and the smile she offered in return was genuine, not the social smile she mustered on occasions that demanded smiles, whether heartfelt or not.

"I'm having such a good time that I've almost forgotten about the—" Holly looked around. "You know . . . the sad thing."

Pamela had almost forgotten too. She supposed that was the point of holidays like Christmas. Life was full of sad things, but celebrations provided a distraction that eased the mind.

"The police have solved it, I guess, so hopefully we'll soon hear no more." Holly raised a hand with crossed fingers, displaying a sparkly manicure that echoed the violet streaks in her hair. "But I don't think I'll ever forget that a scarf I knit became a murder weapon." She shivered. "It almost makes me feel like I'm guilty too."

Bettina reached out a comforting hand. "You had no way of knowing what use it would be put to. You're not guilty at all." She shook her head. "And I don't believe Laurel Lewis is guilty either."

"Who did it then?"

"Other people had motives." Bettina smiled a secret smile.

Holly's eyes opened wide and her lips parted as she inhaled deeply. "I did hear something . . ." She looked around again. "I know Nell is here and I know how much she disapproves of gossip, but . . ." She edged closer to Bettina.

Pamela herself did not like gossip—but in the

service of solving a crime? Well, that was something else.

"At the salon," Holly said, "a lot of our customers are from Arborville and of course the murder has been on everybody's mind and we've had
quite a rush with people wanting to look nice for
all their Christmas activities. Today was just crazy.
Anyway"—she paused and looked around—"Carys
talked her sister Marlyn into divorcing her husband."

"We heard that too," Bettina said. "And then
Marlyn asked him to come back but he wouldn't
come back."

"He's back now!" Holly announced, then hastily
covered her mouth as if aware that she'd spoken
too loud, given the topic.

"Since when?" Pamela whispered. She'd just
caught sight of Nell drawing near.

Holly shrugged. "Not sure." The next moment
she turned to greet Nell, who had edged between
her and Pamela.

Nell's ecological concerns had prevented her
from adding to her wardrobe for several decades,
but she looked festive in an Indian-inspired tunic
fashioned from rose-colored velour. Delicate fili-
gree earrings set with small diamonds complemented her soft white hair.

The topic of conversation shifted instantly, to
Bettina and Wilfred's plan to host the Boston children over the long New Year's weekend and Nell
and Harold's impending visit from their oldest son
and his family.

Pamela smiled and nodded but her thoughts

were elsewhere. How long had Marlyn's ex-husband been back in town—and why had he returned?

Suddenly the crowd was in motion, as conversational groupings dissolved and people backed up to create a pathway between the kitchen and the buffet table. Melanie DeCamp picked up an empty tray and headed toward the kitchen doorway, and Marlene Pepper followed with the meatball platter, still bearing one meatball with its toothpick at a rakish angle.

The seductive aroma of brewing coffee began to drift through the doorway.

"It looks like Wilfred has enough help," Bettina observed as Holly and Desmond joined in to help clear the buffet table. Soon poppy-seed cake, cookies, and brownies took their places on the lacy cloth, along with mugs and cups and saucers from Bettina's sage-green pottery set.

"I don't have enough of just the mugs or cups and saucers," Bettina explained, "but at least they're all the same color. And I think Wilfred's washing the little plates so he can put them out again."

As if on cue, Holly stepped through the doorway with a stack of plates, Desmond followed with another, and after a few more trips to supply cream and sugar and napkins, the table was almost ready for people to help themselves. The final touch was Wilfred's arrival bearing a large silvery urn with a spigot on the front.

"Please help yourselves," he urged, "and Nell, I think you're the only tea drinker. A cup of tea is coming right up."

Sipping coffee and handling a plate of goodies

at the same time required a place to perch, and several people migrated to the living room after serving themselves at the buffet. Bettina's attention was claimed by Marlene Pepper and one of her friends, who wanted to make sure that the *Advocate* planned to cover an upcoming coat drive sponsored by the women's club. Pamela and Brian found themselves sitting side by side on the bottom step of the stairs that led to the Frasers' second floor.

"I think I should have a party," Brian said. "Wilfred has inspired me." He turned to Pamela. "Would you come?"

"Of course!"

He set his coffee cup down, balanced his plate on his knees, and snuggled an arm around Pamela's shoulders. "Merry Christmas," he whispered.

"Merry Christmas," she responded and turned for a kiss.

Her poppy-seed cake, she was pleased to note, held its own against the other dessert offerings, though the brownies were so intense they were nearly fudge and the cookies were melt-in-the-mouth buttery—and adorable as well. She had chosen a Santa cookie, with white beard, black boots, and a red suit complete with silver buttons.

After a bit, the party began to wind down, and Pamela and Brian had to abandon their perch at the bottom of the stairs as Wilfred and Bettina made trips up and down to fetch coats. Pausing en route to hand an eye-catching fake fur to Holly, Bettina leaned close to Pamela and said, "Don't leave until everybody else is gone." Pamela nodded.

Soon everybody else *was* gone, clusters of people trooping out into the winter darkness as calls of "Thank you" overlapped with "Merry Christmas" in a reverberating chorus.

"So—" Bettina pulled Pamela aside while Wilfred and Brian continued toward the door. "We have to find out how long Marlyn's husband has been back in town."

"We do," Pamela agreed, "and—"

But just then Brian turned and offered his arm. "Shall we be off?" he said as Wilfred swung the door back and a chilly gust of wind entered.

"We'll talk tomorrow," Pamela whispered.

Chapter Eight

The cats were enjoying this interesting variation in the household's morning routine—though they'd suspected that something unusual was afoot several days ago when the cat climber was relocated to accommodate a full-sized spruce tree. Now Precious watched from the top platform of the climber as Catrina and Ginger capered about batting balls of crumpled wrapping paper here and there and leaping for the strands of ribbon that Penny dangled over their heads.

The tree lights made the carefully placed ornaments, with their faded vintage charm, gleam, and from the stereo came the strains of "Silent Night." The Patersons' Christmas rituals included bringing out a collection of holiday LPs that had belonged to Pamela's grandparents.

"Just two presents left," Pamela said. "One for you and one for me."

"You go first." Penny offered a box wrapped in mistletoe-patterned paper to Pamela, who was sitting near her on the carpet.

"Okay," Pamela said, "but here's yours." She handed over a smaller box, wrapped in the same paper. Then she slipped the ribbon from the box Penny had given her and peeled off the wrapping.

"Ohh!" she sighed as she lifted the lid and set it aside. Cushioned on a bed of tissue was a decorative porcelain plate. She picked it up.

"It's your zodiac sign." Penny smiled. "Aquarius, the water-bearer. I found it at my favorite thrift store near the campus. It's Royal Doulton—they probably did one for each of the twelve signs, but it was such a coincidence that the only one the store had was this one."

The design on the plate showed two young girls in Victorian pinafores carrying a large pail, presumably of water, between them. A garland of violets and lily of the valley occupied the space between the central image and the plate's scalloped edge.

"I never paid much attention to astrology," Pamela said, "but I love this plate. Thank you!"

"You're an air sign," Penny said. "Intelligent and independent."

"Well!" Pamela laughed. She nestled the plate back into its bed of tissue. "Now you open yours."

Inside the small box for Penny were the golden earrings Pamela had bought when she and Bettina visited the craft shop in Timberley. Penny slipped off the ribbon and offered it to Ginger, who had been pawing at a low-hanging ornament. She stripped the paper away, opened the box, and re-moved the square of cotton that hid the contents.

"Beautiful!" she exclaimed, lifting one of the earrings, which dangled from her fingers as if it was a real leaf stirred by a slight breeze.

"They're cast from molds made from actual leaves," Pamela said. "A local craftsperson makes them. I'm not sure what kind of leaves she uses though."

The earring was a long teardrop shape, quite elegant. Penny picked up its mate with her other hand and held both earrings up to her ears. The effect was glamorous despite the fact that the ensemble they accessorized was a fleecy pink robe over flannel pajamas.

"Thank you!" Penny tucked them back into their box and replaced the cotton and the lid. Then she climbed to her feet and added, "There are actually three more presents. But not for us."

She hurried up the stairs and returned with a large ziplock bag. From it she extracted three small parcels swathed in brown paper and loosely tied with string. Even before she stooped to toss the parcels on the floor, all three cats were on high alert—even Precious, who usually affected a blasé attitude toward even the most interesting phenomena.

Catrina immediately pounced on one of the parcels, while Ginger circled the one that landed nearest to her, jabbing it with a paw as her tail twitched spasmodically back and forth. Precious made a flying leap from the top platform of the cat climber and landed on the third parcel.

"I didn't do a very fancy wrapping job," Penny said. She sat down next to Catrina and nudged the string loose from the parcel Catrina had chosen. The brown paper peeled away to reveal a not-very-realistic mouse sewn from blue-checked fabric. The tail was a length of blue yarn.

"Catnip," Penny explained, though she didn't have to. The cats were occasionally treated to catnip, and each time the spectacle was the same: ecstatic writhing, belly up, as paws juggled the catnip-containing object, rubbing it against cheeks and throat and chest as tongues flicked out for a lick whenever it neared the mouth.

Catrina seized the mouse and carried it into the dining room, perhaps aware of how undignified her actions were but unable to help herself. Ginger had no such compunctions. She fell on her mouse once it was unwrapped, gripped it with all four paws, and rolled onto her back, bending her head forward to rub her nose against it. Precious was more refined, but even she seemed trans-ported by her gift, cuddling it as small squeaks emerged from her throat.

Leaving the cats to enjoy their catnip, Pamela and Penny went upstairs to get dressed.

Pamela was eager to confer with Bettina about the interesting new development Holly had re-vealed—the reappearance of Marlyn's ex-husband—and she suspected Bettina was eager to discuss it too. That evening's dinner would be a festive occa-sion, hardly an appropriate setting for sleuthing. Besides, Penny would be there, and Pamela and Bettina had insisted to Penny that they considered Carys's murder an issue best left to the police.

Dressed and back downstairs, Pamela busied herself in the kitchen for a few minutes, until she heard Penny's feet descending the stairs. She lacked Bettina's acting skills, to the point that even telling a lie was difficult for her. But the ruse she devised was simple. She opened the refrigerator and took out butter. Then she rearranged a few items, while making as much noise as she could, and closed the refrigerator door with a thud. Leaving the butter out to soften, she stepped through the entry to speak to Penny, who was sitting on the sofa watching the cats as they slept off their ecstasies.

"I need an extra egg," she said. "I have four for the cake, but I forgot that the filling needs an egg white."

Penny looked up, mildly interested.

"So I'm going to run over to Bettina's for a minute."

"Sure." Penny went back to watching the cats.

The Frasers' living room was in the same state as Pamela's, with crumpled wrapping paper and tangles of ribbon strewn over the carpet. Punkin the cat was playing with a plush ball weighted in such a way that it rolled in unexpected directions, batting it here and there under and around the tree.

Bettina was dressed for the morning in dark green leggings and a tunic-length red sweater whose front featured an elaborate Christmas tree decorated with multicolored spangles.

"So"—she led Pamela to the sofa—"what do you think about this returning husband story?"

"Whether he could be the one who killed Carys?"

Bettina nodded.

"Carys was killed last Monday night," Pamela said. "We talked to Marlyn on Thursday and again yesterday morning. Wouldn't she have mentioned that he was back?"

"I'd think so." Bettina nodded again. "He must have shown up in Arborville yesterday after we collected the trunk. News certainly travels fast through the gossip grapevine."

"What if he came back sooner though . . ." Pamela paused, distracted. Woofus the shelter dog had peeked around the corner from the dining room and then retreated.

"He's nervous." Bettina's brightly painted lips formed a sympathetic smile. "The party last night unsettled him, so it's probably for the best that the Arborville grandchildren are with their other grandparents today, though I do miss them." She shifted her gaze to Pamela. "Anyway, you were saying . . . ?"

"Suppose Marlyn's ex-husband had decided he wanted to reconcile but feared it would be impossible unless he removed the ongoing negative influence of Carys. So he came back unannounced, stayed at a hotel somewhere, stalked Carys for a bit, and killed her Monday night."

Bettina clapped her hands. "That works—and Carys was wearing the murder weapon."

Pamela nodded. "So, Marlyn's ex-husband strangles Carys and then waits several days to contact Marlyn in order not to pounce right after she has the trauma of losing her sister—"

"Though she didn't seem very sad about Carys's death," Bettina interjected.

"—and he shows up yesterday like he just flew in from wherever he'd been sailing—surely not near here in this weather."

"That all really makes sense," Bettina said. "And I'm glad because there's no other suspect. We've eliminated Marlyn because she has an alibi, and we're convinced—or at least I am—that Laurel isn't the kind of person who'd kill someone, writers' group notwithstanding."

Pamela nodded and stood up. "Penny's going to be wondering where I am . . . and"—she raised a hand with her index finger extended—"I almost forgot. I need to take back an egg, for the cake tonight."

"Ok-a-ay . . ." Bettina drew out the word and added a puzzled smile.

"That was my excuse to Penny to run over here," Pamela explained.

"And she believed you?" Bettina laughed. "Doesn't she know you're too organized to run out of ingredients?" Bettina turned toward the arch that led to the dining room and the kitchen beyond. "I'll be right back."

"Just one thing about our theory," Bettina said after she had handed over the egg. "It's all based on something Holly thinks she overheard at the hair salon. We don't know for sure that the ex-husband is really back." She continued on toward the door, twisted the knob, and pulled the door open. But before Pamela could step through it, she spoke again.

"Does the dessert you're making involve chocolate?" she inquired, joining her hands in a prayer-like gesture.

"Wait and see," Pamela responded. "Wait and see."

Back at home, Pamela returned to the kitchen, where she set about making the dessert that would complement the Frasers' Christmas menu. First she grated all the rind off an orange and juiced the orange. Then she mixed flour, cornstarch, salt, and baking powder in a small bowl and set the bowl aside. She creamed butter and sugar together and added egg yolks, orange rind, and orange juice. The dry ingredients were combined with the moist ingredients, and beaten egg whites were folded in. Soon the cake—for it was to be a cake—went into the oven and Pamela returned to the living room to knit and enjoy the tree and the Christmas music.

The dessert did involve chocolate, a rich chocolate buttercream frosting—and the filling to be spread between the layers did require an egg white, though it was primarily composed of powdered sugar and whipped cream. When the cake had finished baking and the layers had cooled, Pamela resumed her kitchen duties, making and applying frosting and filling. With plenty of time to spare, the cake was ready to be carried across the street.

Chapter Nine

Pamela carried the cake and Penny carried a tote bag containing the gifts for the Frasers. Stepping carefully, because unexpected patches of ice lurked after days of melting and nights of refreezing, they made their way across the street. Bettina greeted them at the door and ushered them into a living room fragrant with the aroma of roasting ham, accented with a spicy hint of Christmas pine. As Penny set the tote bag with the gifts under the tree, Pamela handed the platter containing the cake to Bettina and was rewarded with a happy sigh and the murmured word, *chocolate*. Both Pamela and Penny slipped off their coats.

Though the occasion was a small—very small—dinner party involving only comfortable old friends, Penny had pulled from her closet a glamorous dress she'd found on a thrifting expedition the previous summer. Fashioned from dark blue lace, it featured long sleeves and a neckline that skimmed the collarbone in front but swooped to a surprisingly deep V in back. And she had pinned up her dark curls to better display the dangling gold earrings that Pamela had given her that morning.

"Well, Miss Penny!" Bettina exclaimed. "Aren't you the fashionista! So glamorous! And Pamela— the red tunic sweater. I do enjoy seeing you in that. You've certainly gotten a lot of use out of it."

Pamela smiled. So she wasn't a clothes horse. The tunic was perfectly serviceable and quite festive.

"Too bad it's only us old folks tonight," Bettina went on, talking to Penny again. "No handsome young men for you to charm."

Penny laughed and, thankfully, seemed unembarrassed. Bettina was right though, about Penny looking glamorous. Surely there was a boyfriend up there in Boston—or home now, wherever he lived, for the holidays. Penny hadn't said anything . . . but hadn't Pamela just explained to Bettina the other day that introducing a romantic interest to one's parents was a significant step, a step that meant something serious was going on? And she wasn't ready for that for Penny . . . yet.

"I'll just take this divine-looking cake to the kitchen," Bettina said, "and you two come right along. We're going to have champagne."

Bettina herself was looking quite the fashionista in a red and green print wrap dress that hugged her waist and hips, green suede pumps, and a necklace and earrings of glittery green stones.

Wilfred was bent over the counter in the cooking area of the kitchen when they entered, but he straightened up and swiveled around to greet them with a hearty "Merry Christmas!" Lined up on the high counter were four champagne flutes and a pewter ice bucket from which protruded the telltale wire-bound cork of a champagne bottle. Next to the ice bucket was a small wooden dish of mixed nuts.

"I'll do the honors," he added. Facing them over the counter, he plucked the champagne bottle from the ice bucket, swathed it in a dish towel, and removed the wire cage that confined the cork. Careful to tilt the bottle so the cork wouldn't find a human target, he twisted. The cork came free with a satisfying pop and a puff of vapor, and he quickly tipped the bottle over one of the champagne flutes.

Bettina had set the cake, in all its chocolaty glory, on the high counter. She gestured toward the nut dish.

"I didn't think we needed much to nibble on," she said, "because Wilfred has such a fancy meal in store for us. But please help yourselves."

Meanwhile Wilfred was handing around champagne, to Pamela first and then Penny and then Bettina, and finally pouring a glass for himself.

"To the season!" he proclaimed, holding his champagne aloft. The delicate glass caught the light. Strands of bubbles like tiny beads rose through the pale liquid and vanished when they reached the surface.

"To the season," Pamela responded and took a nose-tickling sip.

They remained standing at the counter, sipping and chatting, with Wilfred chiming in as he worked, washing spinach, mashing potatoes, and slicing radishes and fennel. After a bit, the rest of the champagne was divided among the flutes to provide a few last swallows.

"I think we are just about ready," Wilfred announced as he straightened up from checking the contents of the oven. The oven door had been open for only the tiniest moment, but the aroma that wafted forth had given an intense preview of the honey-glazed ham—caramelized sweetness with a hint of smoke layered over the rich char of roasting pork.

"We're starting with soup," Bettina said. "You two go ahead and I'll bring bowls. And Pamela, please light the candles. The wine is already open—it's breathing."

Bettina's holiday table was set with a deep burgundy cloth, burgundy napkins, and her sage-green plates. Sleek wineglasses of Swedish crystal awaited the bottle of pinot noir at the ready in a pewter wine coaster. The candleholders were pewter as well, simple and modern in shape. A small flower arrangement in the middle of the table was composed of miniature white poinsettias.

After Pamela lit the candles, she and Penny took their usual seats on either side of the table. The head was reserved for Wilfred, with Bettina facing him at the other end.

"And . . . here we come," Bettina sang from the kitchen doorway. She entered carrying a bowl in each hand, and Wilfred followed, bearing two bowls as well.

"It's cream of pumpkin," Bettina explained as she set a shallow bowl in front of Pamela. The color and texture of the contents evoked melted orange sherbet, but the aroma promised a hearty flavor and hinted at an unidentifiable spice. As if reading Pamela's mind, Bettina added, "There's coriander in it."

Once all four bowls had been delivered and everyone was seated, Wilfred raised his soup spoon, and with a jovial "Bon appétit!" invited the others to join him in sampling his creation.

The soup was rich and mouth-filling, smooth but with a fragrant spiciness that enlivened the blandness of the pumpkin. No one spoke for a few minutes, content with wordless hums of pleasure.

"Very, very successful," Bettina pronounced at last, as her spoon pursued the last few driblets of soup around the bottom of her bowl.

"Yes, very!" Pamela's and Penny's voices overlapped.

Bettina and Wilfred whisked the empty bowls away, and Bettina took her seat again. When Wilfred returned, he was carrying a platter. The platter was large, but barely large enough for its contents—a plump and splendid ham, its glistening rind seared a deep golden brown and its spiral-cut surface a rosy pink. With a satisfied sigh, he lowered the platter to the table and set off for the kitchen once again.

"Let me help!" Penny started to rise.

Pamela, who was closer to the kitchen, jumped to her feet, saying, "Yes, please let us do something."

"It's all taken care of." Wilfred paused en route and waved them back into their chairs.

"He loves doing this," Bettina whispered. "It's like a performance for him."

Subsequent trips brought a pillowy drift of mashed potatoes in an oval bowl, accompanied by a large pat of butter on a small plate, and a dish of creamed spinach. After a happy bustle of passing plates to receive slices of ham, people helped themselves to mashed potatoes, butter to melt in golden pools atop the potatoes, and spinach. Wilfred's repeated "Bon appétit!" was the signal to lift knives and forks.

First there was silence, but for the click of utensils against pottery. Then Bettina led the way with a contented purr and a blissful expression involving closed eyes and a closed-mouthed smile. Pamela and Penny added their own appreciative sounds.

When Bettina spoke, it was to say, "You've outdone yourself!"

"Dear wife, dear friends—it was my pleasure." Wilfred's beaming countenance attested to his sincerity.

The conversation then progressed from the success of the meal to more tangential matters: the model fort Wilfred had built in his basement workshop as a Christmas gift for Wilfred Jr.'s sons, and the challenge of finding appropriate gifts for the Boston grand*child*. ("We're forbidden to refer to her as a *girl*," Bettina reminded them.)

"I could build something," Wilfred suggested. "Not a dollhouse, but maybe a puppet theater."

"When she gets a little older." Bettina nodded. Morgan Fraser had just turned two.

"Books?" Penny suggested.

"Oh, books. Yes." Bettina nodded again. "Suitble books, not girly books. No sleeping princesses bused by handsome princes. Greta made that lear."

Bettina looked so downcast that Pamela leapt in b change the subject. "I was so happy to hear that Maxie liked the trunk," she exclaimed.

"Some people appreciate pretty things," Bettina esponded, still glum.

"How about second helpings!" Wilfred took his urn at cheering Bettina up. "Or shall I serve the alad?"

In the end it was agreed that justice had been one to the ham and its accompaniments, particu-rly given that fennel salad was waiting in the vings, to be followed by Pamela's cake.

The fennel salad, prettily arranged on individ-al plates, was a refreshing contrast to the rich lishes that had come before. Wilfred had cut the ennel bulbs vertically to create slices that resem-led small hands with delicate pale green fingers. Ie had added thin rounds of radish, white but immed with bright red skin. He had garnished he fennel and radishes with sugared walnuts and resh-grated Parmesan and finished each salad vith olive oil and balsamic vinegar.

"Coffee and cake in the living room?" Bettina nquired after setting down her fork with a pleased igh.

"I'll serve it." Pamela rose, and the small group ollowed her into the kitchen, each person carry-ng a salad plate.

Salad plates were stacked on the counter near

the sink and fresh plates were produced for th
cake. Wilfred set water boiling for coffee whil
Bettina arranged a paper filter in the filter cone o
her carafe and spooned in a goodly portion of th
Guatemalan coffee she favored. Provided with
suitable knife, Pamela cut a careful slice of cak
and transferred it to a plate.

She was delighted to see that the effect was ju
what she had hoped. The cake itself, flavored wit
the fresh orange juice and grated rind, was a del
cate pale orange color, fine textured and mois
The chocolate buttercream frosting cut smoothl
without sticking to the knife, and the deep choco
laty color contrasted nicely with the cake itsel
The extra touch was the filling between the layers—
not more chocolate, but a pale and fluffy vanill
cream.

Chapter Ten

Settled around the coffee table some minutes later, with cake and fragrant cups of coffee before them, Christmas carols coming from the stereo, and the Christmas tree lights lending a warm glow to the far corner of the room, the Frasers and the Patersons smiled at one another in contentment.

Bettina was the first to taste the cake and comment, observing that the cake was perfect and the combination of chocolate and oranges seemed to fit the season.

"It does," Wilfred said. "Oranges were a special Christmas treat up here when I was very young. My grandfather had retired to Florida and shipped us a big box of them every December."

Penny, however, had ceased to smile. "I know about the egg, Mom," she exclaimed suddenly. "I forgot, until we started eating the cake."

Momentarily puzzled, Pamela wrinkled her nose. "What egg?" she inquired.

"The egg you claimed you had to borrow from Bettina because you were all out. When I opened the refrigerator later I saw half a dozen of them." Penny shifted her gaze from Pamela to Bettina and back to Pamela. Her youthful glow made her attempted sternness more comical than fearsome.

Pamela gazed back, unsure what to say, so Penny continued.

"You two are up to something and that's why you're sneaking around."

"She's turning into a detective." Bettina laughed delightedly.

"It's not funny!" Penny returned her fork to her plate with a *clunk*. "It's dangerous."

Sensing that a change of subject was in order, Wilfred turned to Pamela. "As one cook to another," he said, "your cake is a masterpiece. Tell me about the filling."

Pamela was happy for the excuse to avoid Penny's intense gaze. She turned to Wilfred and described the simple recipe behind the vanilla cream. Meanwhile Bettina deployed her charm and soon had Penny talking happily about her plans for the rest of her break from school.

The time passed pleasantly enough then, until the plates were empty but for golden crumbs and traces of chocolate, and the cups contained only dregs of coffee.

"I think there might be a few gifts left under the tree," Wilfred said with a teasing smile. He rose and started gathering the plates, silverware, and cups and saucers. Pamela joined him and this time he didn't urge her back into her seat.

"I know you and Bettina don't accept Clayborn's conclusion that Laurel Lewis killed Carys Walnutt," he whispered after they were safely out of earshot.

"Bettina's concerned." Pamela set cups and saucers on the counter near the sink. "She really likes Laurel and can't believe she'd do something like that."

"Perhaps she didn't." Wilfred added plates and two more cups and saucers. "But who did?"

Pamela resisted the temptation to explain the role Carys had in the breakup of Marlyn's marriage and why it was interesting that the ex-husband was back in Arborville. It was Christmas and there were gifts to be opened.

Pamela and Wilfred returned to the living room to find an array of colorfully wrapped boxes waiting on the coffee table.

"For you"—Penny offered Wilfred a rectangular box whose paper featured leaping reindeer—"and you." The box for Bettina was similar in shape and size but the wrapping featured holly with bright berries.

"From the gift shop at Paul Revere's house," Penny explained as Wilfred peeled away ribbon and paper to reveal a book about Paul Revere. "I know how much you like history."

"I do." Wilfred nodded.

Bettina meanwhile was oohing and aahing over a box of note cards decorated with eighteenth-century illustrations of flowers. "The Gardner museum has a gift shop too," Penny said with a pleased smile.

The gifts from Pamela were greeted with equal enthusiasm—carved wood items from a craft show *Fiber Craft* had been involved in: a wooden paperweight depicting a robin for Wilfred and a wooden bowl in the shape of a heart for Bettina.

"And now you two have to open yours." Bettina leaned forward, picked up a large rectangular box, and handed it to Penny. Wilfred handed a similar box to Pamela.

Once the paper—chorusing angels in improbable bright pink ensembles—had been removed, it was clear from the boxes that both gifts had come from the fanciest store at the mall. Inside Penny's box was a silky robe in shades of indigo and ruby.

"Beautiful," Penny sighed. "Too beautiful to even wear."

"But I hope you *will* wear it," Bettina said, "and for many years. I still have the robe I bought for my honeymoon."

"Thank you." Penny folded the robe back up and laid it reverently in its box. "And I'll always remember who gave it to me."

"And you, Miss Pamela"—Bettina's lips curved up in a teasing half smile—"I hope you'll wear your gift—though I do like the red tunic sweater."

Pamela folded tissue paper back to reveal . . . *something* . . . made of black and silver brocade. She lifted the *something* from the box and saw that it was a jacket, a short jacket, not too fitted, with large silver buttons that buttoned up the front to a chic cowl-shaped collar.

"It's your new holiday party top," Bettina said, smiling. "Just in time for New Year's Eve with your handsome boyfriend."

"Oh, Bettina . . ." Pamela sighed. "You are really hopeless." As Bettina's smile began to falter, she added, "But the jacket is gorgeous, and I love you—and Wilfred—for giving it to me, and I'll wear it on New Year's Eve, I promise."

"Try it on," Bettina urged, leaning forward. "And take the tunic off first so you don't have six inches of red sweater sticking out down below."

Pamela stood up holding the jacket and ducked into the dining room. A few moments later, she returned wearing the jacket. Bettina jumped up and joined her.

"It's fine with the black pants you have on," she said, after leaning close to adjust the collar.

"Thank you!" Pamela hugged her, holding on a bit longer than she usually did and bending toward Bettina's ear. "Fran would know if Marlyn's husband is really back," she whispered. "We have to talk to her tomorrow. I'll call you in the morning."

Chapter Eleven

Pamela's boss seemed never to rest. Apparently she had been hard at work over the holiday weekend, because on Monday morning an email from Celine Bramley popped into Pamela's inbox the moment she roused her computer to life. The stylized paperclip opposite the sender's name suggested that the email brought work, in the form of attachments.

Celine Bramley's email messages usually consisted of terse instructions to evaluate or copyedit and return by such and such a deadline. This morning's message was longer.

The ideas in "Spy-Craft: The Knitting Spies of World War II" are clumsily expressed, Pamela's boss had written, **and I don't think any publication at all would want it in its current form. But a summer issue with a patriotic theme is taking shape and "Spy-Craft" would fit in so nicely. Please do what you can**

to make it readable. I'm attaching two other articles
to be copyedited for the same issue. Summer is a
ways away but you might as well do this work now
(and return it by the end of the week) because next
week I'm sending you two books to review.

Pamela groaned. The thought of once again
wading through the murky prose of "Spy-Craft"
did not appeal, especially this early in the morning. She closed her email, swiveled her chair
around, and picked up the phone.

"Is this a good time?" she asked when Bettina
answered.

"I can't wait," Bettina said.

"I'll tell Penny I'm going for a walk. Meet me at
the corner in your car. She might be watching to
see if I'm telling the truth."

Downstairs, Pamela stepped over Catrina, who
was napping in the sunny spot on the entry carpet,
and took her down coat from the closet. Peeking
through the kitchen doorway, she greeted Penny,
still in pajamas and robe and lingering over the
Register.

"I'm running out to the Co-Op for butter," she
said.

Penny looked up, her lips shaping a suspicious
zigzag. "We have butter," she observed, "lots of
butter."

"It's for poppy-seed cake." Pamela smiled. "I
want to serve it to Knit and Nibble tomorrow night
and send a loaf back to Boston with you."

"Whatever." Penny raised her eyebrows, shrugged
and returned to the *Register,* clearly not convinced
of the errand's legitimacy.

Bettina's faithful Toyota slowed down and pulled

over as Pamela neared the corner. She climbed in, Bettina made the turn onto Arborville Avenue, and they were on their way.

The journey took less than ten minutes, and soon Bettina had parked in front of St. Willibrod's and they had climbed out of the car. As they paused at the curb waiting for a break in the traffic, they were startled by the reverberating bongs of the church chimes.

"Those certainly are loud when you're hearing them up close," Bettina commented, raising her gloved hands to her ears. The purple leather gloves and olive-green beret joined the pumpkin-colored coat to create a colorful contrast to the week-old snow on the church lawn behind them.

Pamela was listening to the chimes too, absent-mindedly counting the bongs. Eleven—but it was only ten a.m. The chimes were off by an hour though. Wilfred Jr. had pointed that out on Saturday when they picked up the trunk.

But if they were off by an hour, it meant that Marlyn's alibi, based on Fran's statement that she heard the chimes . . . might not be an alibi after all.

Bettina had stepped away from the curb and was waiting for one last car to pass before launching herself across the street.

"Bettina!" Pamela shouted, reaching out to grab her friend's arm.

Bettina spun around, her eyes and mouth wide. "What? What is it?"

"The chimes! They're not . . ." Pamela took a deep breath. "We have to ask Fran how long

Marlyn was actually shoveling snow on the night Carys was killed."

As they crossed the street, Pamela explained what she'd just realized about the chimes and Marlyn's alibi. "That's the main thing," she said. "If Marlyn has no alibi then the husband might be irrelevant."

Bettina took the lead when they reached Fran's doorstep, raising a purple-gloved hand to push the bell. Fran answered her door in bathrobe and slippers, carrying a cup of coffee, her gray curls still in disarray from sleep.

"Good morning, ladies," she said, puzzled but cordial.

"We're so sorry to bother you ..." Bettina smiled an apologetic smile. "But we were ... we were ..."

We were what? Pamela felt herself wince as Fran's expression became more puzzled. What would she herself think if two people she barely knew showed up at her door while she was still in her robe and slippers?

Bettina pushed her coat sleeve up and the cuff of her glove down to expose her watch. "Oh, good!" she exclaimed. "It really is only ten. The chimes ..."

Fran laughed and slapped her thigh. "Oh, the chimes! That happens every year. They're off by an hour, still on daylight savings time. They're not real, you know—just a recording on a timer, and the church secretary forgets to reset them. It used to drive Carys crazy."

The front door of the neighboring apartment,

Marlyn's apartment, opened and Marlyn stepped out to scoop up the *Register*, snug in its plastic wrapper. Fran edged over her own threshold to greet her neighbor.

"And how are you, my dear?" she inquired with a suggestive laugh. "Busy night?"

"None of your business," Marlyn replied, but her tone was light and a giggle accompanied her words. She backed up and closed the door behind her.

"*She* had a nice Christmas present." Fran's eyes crinkled with delight and her smile brought a flush to her pleasant features. "Hubby is back!"

"He is?" Pamela and Bettina spoke in unison.

"Yup!" Fran nodded. "All is forgiven. He flew in from Bermuda. Showed up around noon on Saturday, came straight from the airport, unannounced, in an Uber. But Marlyn was thrilled."

"What good news!" Bettina clapped her hands. "She's such a lovely person."

"Lovely!" Fran nodded again. "I'll miss her as a neighbor—I suppose they'll want a house like they had before. But I'm very happy for her." She paused, then focused her gaze on Bettina. "Now what was it you wanted to ask me?"

"Ask you . . ." Bettina studied her bootie-clad feet for a moment. "Oh, yes. Have you been getting the *Advocate* regularly? Sometimes our delivery people aren't as conscientious as they should be."

"I guess Laurel really did it." They had been silent on the drive along Arborville Avenue, but after she made the turn onto Orchard Street, Bettina spoke.

"I guess so," Pamela agreed.

Penny was gone when Pamela got home—and a good thing too, she realized, because she had forgotten that her purported errand involved butter. A note on the kitchen table advised that Penny was at her friend Lorie's and they would probably take the bus into the city.

Pamela climbed the stairs to her office, settled into her desk chair, let her mouse explore its mouse pad until her monitor woke from its nap, and opened the files attached to the email from her boss. The two articles that had accompanied "Spy-Craft" looked fascinating, and she was tempted to tackle them first.

One—"Old Glory, Glorious Again"—was about the challenges of restoring antique flags, and the other—"From Germany, with Love"—was about American soldiers sending salvaged German parachutes made of silk home to their girlfriends for sewing projects when silk was at a premium during World War II. But there was no way of knowing how long it would take to wrestle "Spy-Craft" into readable form, so she resolved to tackle that annoying project first.

She changed "splinting hairs" to "splitting hairs" and "viscous rumors" to "vicious rumors." In the next paragraph, she made danger rear its ugly head rather than its ugly visage and sighed over "While seemingly enjoying the view from an upstairs window, the knitting needles were in fact recording vital intelligence to be passed on to the Resistance."

"Knitting needles cannot enjoy a view," she muttered to herself as she inserted "the women wielding" after the comma.

But a phrase she came upon further down the page, "a case of mistaken indemnity," elicited more than a sigh and a mutter.

"A case of mistaken indemnity." She said it aloud once to herself, and then she repeated it to Ginger, who had looked up from her nap on the floor near the radiator. "A case of mistaken identity—of course. *Of course!*"

But instead of making that correction in the manuscript, Pamela swiveled her chair around, jumped up, and ran for the stairs. In the entry, she grabbed her coat, her purse, and her keys. Normally she'd walk such a short distance, but there was no time to waste.

Five minutes later she pulled into the library parking lot and scanned the spaces that faced the wide field. Yes, there was a spot, a designated spot, but it was empty at the moment—curiously, considering the holiday weekend was over.

She circled around to the lot's exit and set off for Laurel Lewis's townhouse near Arborville's border with Meadowside.

Thankfully, traffic was light on Arborville Avenue, and Pamela had no trouble finding a visitor spot in the parking area. She hurried along the sidewalk past the first cluster of townhouses, and the second, until she recognized Laurel's unit by the attractive balsam and berry wreath on the front door.

She wasn't sure whether her shortness of breath and thumping heart were due to her rapid pace or apprehension about what she might soon encounter, but she tried to ignore them as she bounded up the few steps that led to the door. She inhaled deeply and aimed a finger at the doorbell. From within came a faint echo-y chime but no sound of feet hastening to respond.

She rang again. An echo-y chime, then silence, but only for an instant. Now a voice squealed, "Help!"

Pamela reached for the doorknob and gave it an experimental twist. It turned easily with a faint click as the latch retracted. She pushed the door open cautiously and only a few inches, and peeked through the crack between door and doorframe.

She was looking at a man's back, a bulky man with rusty-red hair, leaning over a partially obscured figure sitting in Laurel Lewis's peach-colored armchair. The man's hands were not visible, but just past his right shoulder a woman's hand flailed hopelessly in the air. A woman's slipper-clad foot was splayed out near his knees.

"Help!" the woman was squealing. The voice was that of Laurel Lewis.

Pamela pushed the door open farther and stepped cautiously inside. The man was so intent on his task that he didn't realize he and Laurel were no longer alone.

Now Pamela became aware of another sound, a muted but urgent meowing sound coming from behind a closed door off to the left. She edged closer to the door, keeping her eyes on the bulky man. When she was within a few feet of that door, she reached over, twisted the doorknob, and gave the door a shove.

With an octave-scaling yowl more suited to a creature ten times its size, a calico cat sprang through the open door. It bounded toward the man and seemed to levitate, straddling his broad back. It then clambered onto the top of his head where the orange patches in its calico coat nearly matched the tones of the man's hair.

Hissing ferociously, it began to swat the man's left ear. He raised a hand in a vain attempt to fend off the attack.

Two more calico cats had slipped through the open door. At first merely curious, they soon joined in the assault. The smaller one dove for the man's left ankle, while the other scaled his right pants leg and leapt onto his shoulder. Crouching and snarling, it raised a paw to rake his cheek with unsheathed claws.

The man raised his right hand in an attempt to dislodge the cat, but it sank its teeth into his thumb. Cursing and muttering, he reeled backward with the smaller cat clinging to his ankle and the cat that had arrived first still perched on his head.

Once he was out of the way, Pamela got a clearer look at the peach armchair and its occupant, Laurel Lewis. She was staring straight ahead, her dark hair framing a face devoid of color but for her startling blue eyes. A strip of pale green cloth that looked like the belt of her robe was draped loosely around her neck.

"Mort Quigley," she mumbled, hardly moving her lips. "He tried to strangle me. But why?"

Pamela jumped out of the way as Mort Quigley careened across the carpet toward the sofa and the lamp table at its end. The table teetered as he grazed it, and the lamp tipped toward him, landing on his chest and scattering the cats. Except for the man sprawled on the carpet and the displaced lamp, the charming room looked just as it had the day Pamela and Bettina visited. The fourth cat, the white Persian, had even joined the calicos, which were now clustered around Laurel's feet.

Pamela had fumbled her phone out of her purse as soon as it became clear that Mort Quigley was no match for three cats bent on protecting their mistress. She touched the numerals that would summon the police, spoke into the phone, and then stepped quickly toward the peach armchair.

"Pamela," Laurel murmured in a quivering voice, "what a miracle that you arrived when you did." Pamela knelt at her side and took her hand.

Mort Quigley groaned and attempted to rise, but an irritated snarl from one of the calicos made him think better of the idea.

Pamela had not realized she was hungry, but by the time the police had come and gone, and Laurel had assured her she would be fine on her own, it was approaching two p.m. Now she was sitting at the scrubbed pine table in Bettina's comfortable kitchen, eating a bowl of Wilfred's five-alarm chili.

Bettina was sitting opposite her, watching closely for a sign that Pamela was ready to describe in more detail the adventure she had sketched out in a few breathless sentences when Bettina, surprised at the unexpected visit, greeted her at the door.

Intuiting her friend's curiosity, Pamela set down her spoon. "Mistaken identity," she said. "I was editing an article for the magazine and the author had written 'mistaken indemnity' but she really meant 'mistaken identity.' I realized that mistaken identity was the key to Carys's murder." She looked away from Bettina and focused on nothing in particular for a moment. "Though I suppose killing the wrong person could be sort of mistaken indemnity too."

"What?" Bettina pulled back with a puzzled frown.

"Mort Quigley really wanted to kill Laurel. He thought the person wearing the aqua scarf with the white snowflakes was Laurel because according to the bid sheet Laurel had the winning bid at the silent auction. He knew she was S. Claws because he'd seen her filling in her bid."

Bettina nodded. "But the person wearing the scarf was really Carys, because she claimed the scarf despite not having the winning bid."

"Right." Pamela nodded back. "And Carys was tall and so is Laurel, and with people bundled up and snow falling, one tall woman could look just like another."

"So far, so good," Bettina said. "I get the mistaken identity thing, but how did you figure out the killer was actually Mort Quigley?"

"Laurel told us that when she found the body in the passageway, she stumbled out to the parking lot and called to Mort Quigley, who was walking to his car. She didn't recognize him at first because he was facing the other way, but then he turned around." Pamela paused for breath. "Mort Quigley has his own special parking space, with a sign reserving it for him. If he had really been on his way to his car from the library entrance, he would have been facing the passageway. He had actually just strangled Carys and was walking away from the crime scene."

"Oh, my!" Bettina looked impressed. "That's very clever."

"There's more." Pamela raised her index finger. "Laurel said when he turned around he was shocked, as shocked as she was. But if he had nothing to do with the murder he wouldn't yet have had a reason to be shocked—he didn't know why she was calling to him." She shook the finger rhythmically to emphasize her point. "Since he was in fact the murderer and thought he had strangled Laurel, he was shocked to see her still alive."

"One more question." Bettina responded with a lifted finger of her own. "Why on earth did Mort Quigley want to kill Laurel?"

"He'd been embezzling from the library and that's why there was a shortfall," Pamela said.

"There was a shortfall? How did you know that?"

"Everybody knew," Pamela said, trying not to sound superior. "Nell even mentioned it at our last Knit and Nibble meeting."

"I must have been concentrating on my knitting." Bettina shrugged.

"Laurel was auditing the library's books. Remember—she told us that when we visited her. She was bound to realize something wasn't on the up-and-up, and she said she was planning to finish her work over the Christmas weekend. So I knew Mort Quigley would have to act fast if he was going to prevent his secret from coming out."

They were both startled by applause coming from the dining room. Then Wilfred stepped through the kitchen doorway, followed by Woofus.

"Back from our walk," Wilfred said, "just in time to learn that Mort Quigley is actually the killer. I presume he's in the hands of the police?"

"Definitely." Pamela smiled. "And Laurel is innocent, safe with her cats, which are hero cats—though that's another story."

Chapter Twelve

Speaking to Marcy Brewer, as well as a young woman from the local TV station, had been unavoidable. But at least they had left in time for Pamela to fit in a quick walk to the Co-Op for butter before it got too dark. Penny returned from her trip to the city, and over a dinner of ham and other Christmas leftovers, courtesy of Wilfred, Pamela mentioned offhandedly that the police had arrested Mort Quigley for the murder of Carys Walnutt.

Penny set down her fork, raised her brows, and stared silently at her mother. "And you didn't have anything to do with it?" she inquired after a while.

"The strangest thing." Pamela shrugged. "I happened to drop by Laurel Lewis's place right at the moment Mort Quigley was trying to strangle her. I called the police of course . . ."

Penny continued to stare. After a longer while,

she said, "*Mo-om!* Honestly, sometimes I don't know whether to laugh or to cry." At that she returned to her meal.

Now it was Tuesday evening and Roland De-Camp was just stepping over Pamela's threshold. Behind him, Karen, Holly, and Nell were hurrying through the light snow that had begun to fall only a short time before. Pamela greeted Roland and held the door open wide to welcome the remaining members of Knit and Nibble—Bettina had arrived early to lend a hand with preparations for the evening.

A fresh loaf of poppy-seed cake waited on the dining room table, along with cups and saucers and plates and napkins and silverware, all ready for the moment when Roland would consult his impressive watch and announce that break time had arrived.

"The snow is very welcome," Nell commented as she removed her ancient gray wool coat. "Last week's snowfall had gotten so dirty. Now everything will look fresh and white again."

Pamela reached for the coat, but Nell held on to it for a moment. "I hope you're all right," she said, staring into Pamela's eyes as intently as if eyes truly were the windows of the soul. "You put yourself in a lot of danger yesterday."

"I had no idea Laurel wasn't alone." Pamela tried to smile offhandedly, but Nell could be hard to fool.

"We'll talk no more about it," Nell declared and relinquished the coat. She turned to Holly and

Karen, who were lingering in the entry as they too slipped off their coats. "And that goes for both of you," she said. "Our little town's Christmas has been shadowed by a tragic event, not to mention what poor Laurel Lewis has been through, but now it's over."

"And we'll have a slushy mess, as always." Roland, en route to the living room, briefcase in hand, had apparently missed the quick exchange that took place after Nell's comment about the snow.

Bettina had already settled onto the sofa, and she beckoned Holly and Karen to join her there. Once they were seated, she presented Karen with the doll in the puffed-sleeve dress from the shop in Timberley.

"For your sweet little Lily," she explained, and Pamela held her breath waiting for Bettina to add that she was forbidden to buy such things for her own granddaughter.

But Bettina seemed happy just listening to Karen and Holly enthuse over the doll's embroidered face and yarn hair and general all-round cuteness. Pamela exhaled and steered Nell toward the comfortable armchair near the fireplace, Roland found a spot on the hassock at the other end of the hearth, and Pamela herself perched on the rummage-sale chair with the carved wooden back and needlepoint seat.

The opening of knitting bags and extracting of skeins and needles and pattern books was accompanied by a cheerful exchange of news about gifts given and received, and feasts prepared and eaten. Once it was clear that Christmas Day had lived up to everyone's expectations—and there was still the New Year's weekend to look forward to!—people turned their attention to their projects and the room fell silent.

Pamela resumed work on her in-progress sweater, happy that, with the ribbing completed, the part she was working on now required no counting or even thinking. The sweater's front, with the large cat worked in black against the tawny brown, would be much more challenging.

Lined up along the sofa, Karen, Holly, and Bettina were intent on their projects. Karen had started a new section of the pale pink cardigan for Lily, and Holly's lap was nearly covered with a swath of knitting that resembled a furry magenta pelt. Bettina was just finishing the body of her teddy bear. A rounded shape formed by strategic increasing and decreasing hung from her needles.

The silence continued for a time, interrupted only by murmured words and phrases—usually knitting directions spoken aloud by a knitter puzzling out a detail of a pattern. But after a bit, Bettina asked Karen about Lily's impressions of Christmas, and soon they were engaged in a lively conversation, with Bettina reminiscing about Christmases when her sons were young. Then Holly finished the section of her jacket she'd been working on, cast off, and crossed the room to crouch by the armchair where Nell was sitting. They chatted about Nell's teddy-bear project and the women's shelter where the bears would be delivered for the children in residence.

In fact, by the time Roland pushed back his starched shirt cuff to consult his impressive watch and announce that it was eight o'clock, the noise level had become such that he had to speak up quite forcefully to make his message heard.

Holly sprang to her feet as if she'd been poised to move as soon as she heard the announcement, and she reached the kitchen even before Pamela.

"You didn't really show up at Laurel's townhouse by accident, did you?" she whispered as Pamela seized the kettle and headed to the sink to fill it. For a minute the sound of running water made speaking pointless, and Pamela was grateful for a chance to ponder her answer. But by the time the kettle was full, Bettina had arrived and Holly had solicited *her* opinion about whether Pamela's appearance at the townhouse in time to prevent another murder had been more than a lucky coincidence.

"Of course it wasn't an accident!" Bettina declared. "Pamela figured the whole thing out and when she checked the library parking lot and saw that Mort Quigley's car was not in its spot, she knew exactly where he was."

As Pamela moved about the kitchen arranging the paper filter in the carafe's filter cone, grinding coffee, and measuring loose tea into the squat brown teapot, she smiled to herself, happy to let Bettina rehearse for Holly's benefit the reasoning process that had led her to conclude Laurel Lewis was not the killer and in fact was going to be Mort Quigley's next victim.

"Well," Holly said when Bettina had finished, "I'm still very sorry that the scarf I knit became a murder weapon, but at least the correct person has been arrested now."

The small kitchen had been gradually filling with the spicy aroma of fresh-brewed coffee, and the tea was steeping in the teapot. Bettina poured cream into the cut-glass cream pitcher, picked up the matching sugar bowl, and set out for the dining room.

"Coffee is coming right up," Pamela heard her announce. "And tea."

She reached for the carafe and gestured for Holly to take the teapot, but Holly hesitated. "Did you know *why* Mort Quigley wanted to kill Laurel?" she asked, her nose wrinkling and her pretty lips twisting into a quizzical knot. "Or was it just that everything pointed to him so obviously you thought he must have had *some* reason?"

Bettina peeked in from the dining room. "They're all wondering where the coffee is," she reported, giving Pamela a curious look. "And the tea."

Holly held up a hand, fingernails gleaming with bright green polish. "Wait," she whispered. "It's like the end of a mystery on TV. Pamela's just about to reveal the last puzzle piece." Pamela smiled. She'd let Bettina do most of the explaining, but Holly was such a rapt audience it would be fun to provide the final detail herself.

Nell, however, had appeared in the doorway. She edged past Bettina.

"The last puzzle piece?" Nell's expression blended suspicion with amusement as her eyes narrowed but her lips struggled to vanquish a smile. "You've been sleuthing again. I suspected as much and—"

"Time is a-wasting!" came a stern voice from the dining room. The voice belonged to Roland, who went on to add, "If we don't have our refreshments soon, we're going to have to just skip them—though I do enjoy your poppy-seed cake, Pamela. I have a knitting quota to reach tonight and I would like to get back to work, and I'm sure everyone else feels the same way."

Bettina edged back from the doorway and Pamela heard her say, "Oh, for heaven's sake, Roland. Lighten up. And speak for yourself."

"The tea is just ready!" Holly exclaimed. She darted toward the counter where the tea was steeping in the squat brown teapot. Teapot in hand, she whirled around and took Nell by the arm. As they approached the doorway leading to the dining room, they nearly collided with Karen.

"Did something happen?" Karen inquired in a small voice, after she had recovered her balance. "What was everyone doing in here? And what's wrong with Roland?"

"He needs to lighten up," Nell said.

Alone in the kitchen again, Pamela laughed. Then she picked up the carafe and joined the others in the dining room, where people were transferring slices of poppy-seed cake to wedding-china dessert plates and where the arrival of the coffee was greeted with enthusiasm.

In no time at all, they were settled back in their seats in the living room with their refreshments. Pamela wasn't sure whether people were eating and drinking more hastily than usual in deference to Roland's admonition or whether that was just her imagination. But soon Holly was collecting empty cups and plates dusted with crumbs, and everyone else was focused on their busy needles.

As nine p.m. drew near, knitters in mid-row

sped up, while others who had reached good stopping places began to tuck their work, their needles, and their skeins of yarn away.

Her work stowed, Holly looked up and suddenly said, "I wonder what will happen to the scarf I made for the auction now?"

"Police evidence. You won't get it back." Roland's voice was matter-of-fact and his lean face was serious. "It will doubtless be brought out in the courtroom when Mort Quigley goes to trial."

"I feel bad that Laurel didn't get the scarf she bid on." Holly's dramatic looks made her concern all the more moving. "I could make her another one. I have plenty of that aqua yarn left."

"Oh, my dear, I'm not sure that would be a good idea." Nell's words were discouraging, but her tone was sympathetic. "It might remind her of things she'd rather forget." Nell surveyed the group and added, "Things we all should forget." Her gaze lingered on Pamela. "No matter how proud we are of our detective work."

KNIT

Nell's Cozy Teddy Bear

This project is a little more complicated than the KNIT projects in the previous books have been, but it's great fun to do and the teddy bear would make a wonderful gift for a favorite child. Use yarn identified on the label as "Medium" and/or #4, and use size 8 needles—though size 7 or 9 is fine if that's what you have. The project takes about 150 yards of yarn.

If you're not already a knitter, watching a video is a great way to master the basics of knitting. Just search the internet for "How to knit" and you'll have your choice of tutorials that show the process clearly.

First make the separate parts.

Body
Cast on 15 stitches, using the "long tail" method. Casting on is often included in internet "How to knit" tutorials, or you can search specifically for "Casting on long tail method."

Knit 1 row increasing 1 stitch on every stitch so you end up with 30 stitches. To increase, use the "knit front back" technique. It's easy to find video demonstrations of this technique on the internet. Just search for "Knit front back."

Work 3 rows using the stockinette stitch, starting on a purl row. To create the stockinette stitch, you alternate rows of knitting and purling (or purling and knitting). Again, it's easier to understand "purl" by viewing a video, but essentially when you purl you're creating the backside of "knit." To knit, you insert the right-hand needle front to back through the loop of yarn on the left-hand needle. To purl, you insert the needle back to front.

Knit 1 row increasing 1 stitch on every other stitch so you end up with 45 stitches.

Work 6 inches using the stockinette stitch, starting and ending on a purl row.

Decrease by knitting 2 stitches together then knitting a regular stitch then knitting 2 stitches together then knitting a regular stitch, and so on, to end up with 30 stitches.

Purl 1 row.

Decrease by knitting every 2 stitches together for the whole row. Now you will have 15 stitches.

Purl 1 row.

Decrease by knitting every 3 stitches together for the whole row. Now you will have 5 stitches.

Cut the yarn leaving a tail of about a foot. Thread a yarn needle—a large needle with a large eye and a blunt end—with the tail, transfer the 5 stitches from the knitting needle to the yarn needle and pull the tail through the loops.

Head
Cast on 10 stitches, using the "long tail" method.

Knit 1 row increasing 1 stitch on each stitch so you

end up with 20 stitches. To increase, use the "knit front back" technique.

Work 3 rows using the stockinette stitch, starting on a purl row.

Knit 1 row increasing 1 stitch on each stitch again. Now you will have 40 stitches.

Work 3 inches using the stockinette stitch, starting and ending on a purl row.

Decrease by knitting every 2 stitches together for the whole row. Now you will have 20 stitches.

Work 3 rows using the stockinette stitch, starting on a purl row.

Decrease by knitting every 2 stitches together for the whole row. Now you will have 10 stitches.

Cut the yarn leaving a tail of about a foot. Thread a yarn needle with the tail, transfer the 10 stitches from the knitting needle to the yarn needle and pull the tail through the loops.

Arms (make 2)
Cast on 10 stitches, using the "long tail" method.

Knit 1 row.

Purl 1 row.

Knit 1 row increasing 1 stitch on every stitch so you end up with 20 stitches.

Proceed, using the stockinette stitch, until the arm is 3 inches long, starting and ending on a purl row.

Alternatively, you can count 13 rows instead of measuring. Since you want your arms to be exactly the same length, counting rows will guarantee that they match.

Knit 5 stitches, knit 2 stitches together, knit 6 stitches, knit 2 stitches together, knit 5 stitches.

Work the next 3 rows using the stockinette stitch.

Knit 4 stitches, knit 2 stitches together, knit 6 stitches, knit 2 stitches together, knit 4 stitches.

Work the next 3 rows using the stockinette stitch.

Knit 3 stitches, knit 2 stitches together, knit 6 stitches, knit 2 stitches together, knit 3 stitches.

Now you will have 14 stitches.

Work 2 more rows using the stockinette stitch and then cast off.

Legs (make 2)

Cast on 20 stitches, using the "long tail" method.

Knit 9 stitches, increase 1 stitch each on the next 2 stitches using the "knit front back" technique, knit 9 stitches.

Purl 10 stitches, increase 1 stitch each on the next 2 stitches using the "knit front back" technique, purl 10 stitches. Note: you will have to knit (rather than purl) the stitches you increase as there is no way I know of to do "knit front back" on a purl stitch. Be sure to transfer the yarn you are working with from the front to the back before doing the knit and to transfer it from the back to the front when you resume purling. Otherwise you will end up with extra, unwanted, loops on your needle.

Knit 11 stitches, increase 1 stitch each on the next 2 stitches using the "knit front back" technique, knit 11 stitches.

Purl 12 stitches, increase 1 stitch each on the next 2 stitches using the "knit front back" technique, purl 12 stitches. Now you will have 28 stitches.

Knit 1 row.

For the next 4 rows, decrease by knitting (or purling, on purl rows) the middle 4 stitches together in pairs. Now you will have 20 stitches again.

Proceed, using the stockinette stitch, until the leg is 4 inches long, starting and ending on a purl row. Alternatively, you can count 13 rows instead of measuring. Since you want your legs to be exactly the same length, counting rows will guarantee that they match.

Knit 5 stitches, knit 2 stitches together, knit 6 stitches, knit 2 stitches together, knit 5 stitches.

Work the next 3 rows using the stockinette stitch.

Knit 4 stitches, knit 2 stitches together, knit 6 stitches, knit 2 stitches together, knit 4 stitches.

Work the next 3 rows using the stockinette stitch.

Knit 3 stitches, knit 2 stitches together, knit 6 stitches, knit 2 stitches together, knit 3 stitches.

Now you will have 14 stitches.

Work 2 more rows using the stockinette stitch and
then cast off.

Ears (make 2)

Note: The ears are worked in the garter stitch
which means you don't switch between knitting
and purling.

Cast on 6 stitches.

Knit 1 row.

Knit 1, knit increasing 1 stitch, knit 2, knit increasing 1 stitch, knit 1. Now you will have 8 stitches.

Knit 5 rows.

Decrease by knitting every 2 stitches together for
the whole row to end up with 4 stitches.

Knit 1 row.

Cast off.

The end that you cast on will be sewn to the head.
Leave that tail long. Hide the other tail by thread-
ing a yarn needle with it and stitching in and out
with a whip stitch along the rim of the ear for half
an inch or so. Cut off the short tail that remains.

Muzzle
Note: The muzzle is worked in the garter stitch,
which means you don't switch between knitting
and purling.

Cast on 3 stitches.

Knit 1 row.

Knit 1 row increasing 1 stitch on every stitch so you end up with 6 stitches.

Knit 1 row.

Knit 1 row increasing 1 stitch on every stitch so you end up with 12 stitches.

Knit 3 rows.

Decrease by knitting every 2 stitches together for the whole row. Now you will have 6 stitches.

Knit 1 row.

Decrease by knitting every 2 stitches together for the whole row. Now you will have 3 stitches.

Cast off.

Now, assemble your bear.

Body: Pull tight on the yarn tail you ran through the loops and use the tail to sew the long edges of the body together, right sides facing in. It is helpful to pin first, to make sure you line the edges up evenly. There's a photo of this step on my website. You will end up with a small opening at the end of the body where you cast on. This will be the top of the body. Turn the body right side out. Stuff the body with fiberfill stuffing by inserting the stuffing a small amount at a time through the opening. There's a photo of this step on my website.

Head: Pull tight on the yarn tail you ran through

the loops and use the tail to sew the long edges of the head together as you did for the body. You will end up with a small opening at the end of the head where you cast on. This will be the bottom of the head. Turn the head right side out. Flatten the head into a bowl shape with the seam running down the back and position the ears on the fold about two inches apart at the top of the head. Sew the ears into place using the tails from when you cast on. Hide what remains of the tails by using the yarn needle to pull them through to the inside of the head and trim them to an inch or so.

Stuff the head with fiberfill. Position the muzzle on the face, anchor it with a few pins, and sew it on. When you have sewn nearly all the way around you can tuck a tiny bit of fiberfill inside if you wish. Hide the tail by taking a large stitch, pulling tight, and snipping the yarn, leaving half an inch or so of yarn buried inside the head.

You can use buttons for eyes—they must be shank type for ease in attaching. If the bear is for a child and you don't want detachable parts, you might want to simply embroider eyes.

Arms and legs: Right sides facing in, sew the bottoms and sides of the arms and legs together, using the tails from when you cast on and/or off if you wish. Cut the tails, leaving about an inch. Don't worry about hiding them because they will be inside when you turn the arms and legs right side out. The ends where you cast off should be left open. Turn the arms and legs right side out and stuff them with fiberfill.

Attach the arms and legs.

In attaching the arms and legs, make sure the body seam runs up the back of the bear and the arm and leg seams face the back of the bear. The open end of the arm or leg is the end that will be attached to the bear. Check the photos on my website for guidance in positioning and attaching the arms and legs. First anchor the arm or leg to the body at each end of the opening with one stitch and then go back and make smaller stitches all around. Hide each tail by taking a large stitch, pulling tight, and snipping the yarn, leaving half an inch or so of yarn buried inside.

Attach the head to the body.

The seam down the back of the head should line up with the seam down the back of the body. The openings on the body and the head are not the same size. Pick up stitches at the edge of the body opening and stitches a row or so in from the head opening. When you have stitched nearly all the way around, you can tuck in an extra bit of fiberfill to make sure the head doesn't flop over.

For a picture of Nell's Cozy Teddy Bear, as well as many in-progress photos, visit the Knit & Nibble Mysteries page at PeggyEhrhart.com. Click on the cover for *Christmas Scarf Murder* and scroll down on the page that opens.

NIBBLE

Pamela's Christmas Cake
(Orange-Flavored Yellow Cake with Vanilla Cream Filling and Chocolate Buttercream Frosting)

Christmas and oranges seem to go together, perhaps because oranges were one of the few fresh fruits available in the winter before we could get anything at any time flown in from who knows where—though oranges themselves were imported from sunnier climes. My husband, who grew up in Illinois, recalls that Christmas always brought a box of oranges from Florida, a gift from his grandfather who lived there in his retirement. I gave this reminiscence to Wilfred in *Death by Christmas Scarf*.

Ingredients
For the cake:
4 eggs, separated
1½ cups cake flour
½ cup cornstarch
½ teaspoon salt
4 teaspoons baking powder
8 oz. butter (two sticks), softened
1 cup sugar
½ cup orange juice—about the yield of one large
    orange
Grated orange rind from one large orange—1
    heaping tablespoon.

For the filling:
1 egg white

⅛ teaspoon salt
1 cup heavy (or whipping) cream
¼ cup powdered sugar
1 teaspoon vanilla

For the frosting:
1 cup butter, softened
½ cup unsweetened cocoa powder, sifted
4 cups powdered sugar
1 teaspoon vanilla
3 tablespoons heavy (or whipping) cream

Make the cake.

Beat the egg whites in a small bowl until stiff; set aside. Mix the flour, cornstarch, salt, and baking powder in a small bowl; set aside. Cream the butter, add the sugar a bit at a time, and beat until pale yellow. Add the egg yolks, orange juice and rind and continue beating. Add the dry ingredients and beat well. Using a rubber spatula, fold ⅓ of the egg whites into the mixture and blend, then fold in the rest of the egg whites and blend.

Divide the batter between two buttered and floured 9-inch round cake pans. Bake at 350 degrees for 25 to 35 minutes or until a wooden toothpick inserted in the middle comes out clean. Check after 25 minutes. Cool before proceeding with the rest of the recipe.

Make the filling.

Beat the egg white till foamy, add salt, beat until stiff. In a separate bowl beat the cream until it forms soft peaks, beat in sugar and vanilla. Fold the two mixtures together.

(If you are squeamish about a recipe that involves raw egg white, you can skip the filling and use some of the chocolate frosting between the layers instead. The frosting recipe makes plenty.)

Make the frosting.

This recipe makes a very generous amount of frosting.

Beat the butter and cocoa together in a large bowl. Beat in the vanilla and powdered sugar, about a cup at a time. Use a rubber spatula to scrape the mixture back to the bottom of the bowl if the mixer is flinging it around. Add the cream and continue beating. You can add more cream or more powdered sugar until the frosting reaches the spreadability you desire.

Assemble the cake.

Remove the layers from the baking pans. Center one layer on a plate large enough to accommodate it and spread the filling over the top. Add the second layer. Frost the whole cake with the chocolate frosting, starting at the top and working down the sides.

Because of the cream and raw egg white, store leftovers in the refrigerator, but the cake is tastier if it returns to room temperature before serving again.

For a picture of Pamela's Christmas Cake, as well as in-progress photos, visit the Knit & Nibble Mysteries page at PeggyEhrhart.com. Click on the cover for *Christmas Scarf Murder* and scroll down on the page that opens.

AN INVITATION TO
CATHOLIC
FAITH

exploring the basics

JOSEPH STOUTZENBERGER

TWENTY
THIRD 23rd
PUBLICATIONS
NEW LONDON, CT 06320
WWW.23RDPUBLICATIONS.COM

For Erin and Brendan, Flynn,
Cormac, and Thomas

~~~~~~~~~~~~ **IMPRIMATUR** ~~~~~~~~~~~~

In accordance with Canon 827, permission to publish
has been granted on April 30, 2013, by the Most Reverend
Edward M. Rice, Auxiliary Bishop, Archdiocese of
Saint Louis. Permission to publish is an indication
that nothing contrary to Church teaching is contained
in this work. It does not imply any endorsement of
the opinions expressed in the publication; nor is any
liability assumed by this permission.

COVER ART: Holy Spirit Window (2009) by Sophie D'Souza,
Ss Peter & Paul's Church, Northfields, London
www.sophiedsouzastainedglass.co.uk

Third printing 2015

TWENTY-THIRD PUBLICATIONS
A Division of Bayard
One Montauk Avenue, Suite 200
New London, CT 06320
(860) 437-3012 or (800) 321-0411
www.23rdpublications.com

ISBN: 978-1-58595-916-7
Library of Congress Control Number: 2013937867
Printed in the U.S.A.

CONTENTS

INTRODUCTION

IF YOU WERE TO GO SHOPPING IN A RELIGION SUPERMARKET, what would you find when you walked down the aisle labeled "Catholicism"? All Christians believe in God and Jesus, read the Bible, call for living a moral life based on Jesus, and even share many of the same spiritual practices. This book is an invitation to enter into a conversation about the unique features of Catholicism, about its rich traditions, and about how Catholics live and experience their faith. It attempts to give merely a taste of the richness that is Catholicism.

Any book on the Catholic faith must begin and end with Jesus. As the bumper sticker says about Jesus and Christmas, he's "the reason for the season." More importantly, Jesus is the reason for the church. Whatever faults its members may possess, the church as a body proclaims Christ. To be part of the church is to be a member of the "body of Christ." The church prides itself on being *we*, not *they* or *it*. Every spring much of a bishop's time is spent going around to parishes celebrating a ceremony for young Catholics called the sacrament of confirmation. What's the message of the sacrament? *You* are filled with the Holy Spirit; go out and be what you are—the church of Christ. For this reason, Catholics quietly run homeless shelters, hospitals, schools, and sports programs for kids. They try to figure out how to live their faith at home and work, in their schools and businesses. Catholic churches dot the landscape of most countries. Go to any trouble spot in the world and chances are Catholics are already there helping people in need. Throughout the world Catholic children learn prayers from their parents and teachers who want to pass on words and gestures that become part of the fabric of their lives—the Our Father, the Hail Mary, and the Sign of the Cross. A steady flow of Catholics comes to church services weekly and, at times, daily. Catholics from every continent contribute and put their own unique stamp on the faith, but all of them are united under one centralized authority, shared beliefs, and other clear signs of communion.

The book is designed to be a conversation starter. Chapters provide brief commentaries on key elements of Catholicism and have many features meant to foster reflection, response, and discussion.

Now, before beginning your reading, think about the following questions.

- Right now, what is your understanding of the essence of Catholicism?
- What are some things you already know about Catholic beliefs and practices?
- What more do you want to know?
- What difference does it make for you to learn more about and to talk more about the Catholic religion?

1 CATHOLIC FAITH: A DEEP AND WONDROUS JOURNEY

I know the plans I have for you, says the LORD,
plans for your welfare and not for harm,
to give you a future with hope.
Then when you call upon me and come and pray to me,
I will hear you.
When you search for me, you will find me;
if you seek me with all your heart,
I will let you find me, says the LORD.

JEREMIAH 29:11–14

Do You Want to Go Swimming?

AFTER HIS SERMON AT EASTER SUNDAY MASS, the priest went down to the first pew where two-year-old Cara rested in her mother's arms. Cara was about to be baptized. The priest said to her, "Now your time has come, Cara. We're just going to pour some water on your forehead. You don't mind water, do you? You like to go swimming, don't you?" Wanting to reassure her daughter, the mother said to Cara, "Do you want to go swimming?"

This exchange echoes what people interested in Catholicism must ask themselves about the community of believers called the Catholic Church: Do you want to go swimming? Do you want to take the plunge? The Catholic Church is a two-thousand-year-old sea of people and practices, beliefs and relationships. The waters can appear to be smooth and calm one moment, rough and murky the next. Sometimes while swimming the shore seems close at hand, bright and inviting. At other times it appears far away. Catholics find many people in the water with them inspiring—think of Mother Teresa. They are also likely to be puzzled about what some of the people are doing in the water at all. ("You used to be an organized crime hitman and still call yourself a Catholic?!") One thing is certain: in Catholicism, no one swims alone. We can go just about any place on earth and find pockets of Catholics who gather together to praise God, support one another, and try to figure out what it is God asks of them. We can look to a past peopled with an array of characters who lived out their Catholic faith in a variety of ways—sometimes rising to heroism in the face of great adversity. In particular, Catholicism sees itself as the link between all people and Jesus. For Catholics, Jesus represents the profound Christian mystery that, in him, *God swims with us!*

We might think of becoming Catholic as a decision people make. When we read about the first followers of Jesus in four books known as the gospels, we discover a different dynamic. *Jesus chooses them.* Jesus goes to where they are and invites them to join him in God's good work. While he invites them to join him in his mission, Jesus doesn't tell them to stop being fishermen or to cease being who they are. He welcomes them just as they are. Surely Jesus could have chosen a more suitable band of best friends to serve as his ambassadors than the bunch he gathers together. It's unlikely that any of them spoke more than conversational Aramaic, the language of the common people in the area known as Galilee. Most of them probably didn't know how to read or write, and if so only in a rudimentary fashion. None of them had a reputation for public speaking. If Peter and Thomas are any indication, they weren't even people of unwavering faith! Jesus wanted them as they were, with all their faults and failings. When they were bewildered by where all this would lead, he simply offered them the beguiling invitation, "Come and see."

....

O beauty ever ancient, ever new. Too late have I loved you.
I was outside and you were within me. And I never found you
until I found you within myself. ST. AUGUSTINE

The saying "Life is an adventure, not a destination" applies to the experience of faith as well.
- What would be alluring about being Catholic?
- What do you think someone receives by being Catholic?
- What do you think someone is committed to giving by being Catholic?

A Journey into Mystery
At its best what has Catholicism meant from the time of the apostles down to the present? Walk down a street past a Catholic church, especially an older one, and it is likely to evoke a sense of wonder and mystery greater than other structures you pass on the way. For Catholics, their faith operates in a similar fashion. It connects them to their roots—not just to their historical origins, but to the awesome mystery that lies within and behind the world they normally encounter. Catholic faith assures

them that they come from God, that God journeys with them as they make their way back to God, and that they go home together. Whether or not they experience much love in their lives, through faith Catholics sense a love that is deeper than any love they could ever imagine. Life can be confusing, troublesome, and disappointing; but faith assures Catholics that there is more meaning to their existence than they could possibly know. Even inexplicable suffering has meaning. The experience of Catholic faith, then, is a great mystery—just as life itself is. Catholics don't "have" faith; rather, they live in faith the way fish live in water. Faith connects each person to God, who may be invisible but who is nonetheless close at hand. It is more about who people are—their identity—than about what they believe. Catholic identity means identifying with Christ.

....

The LORD is gracious and merciful,
slow to anger and abounding in steadfast love.
The LORD is good to all,
and his compassion is over all that he has made. Psalm 145:8–9

Living the Faith ▪ For over fifty years, George has lived across the street from his church. During that time, whenever it snowed, George was one of the first people to go over and shovel the sidewalks in front of the church and school. He continues to do so even though he is now in his eighties. He has never sought, nor received, recognition for his good work, and yet hundreds of school children and parishioners have been graced with his little contribution to their welfare. George's Catholic faith has nourished him all during his life, including while spending months in a World War II prison camp. Taking care of the church across the street from his house is his little way of living his faith.

• Describe someone who models faith for you, even if unacknowledged and unnoticed.

The Heart, Head, Hands, and Soul of Catholic Faith

Faith is multi-dimensional; it involves a person's heart and mind, body and soul. In response to the gift of faith, Catholics commit themselves, as best they can, to work with Jesus in his dream of building on earth what he called the kingdom of God and look forward to its fulfillment in heaven. Becoming Catholic is both comforting and challenging. The first friends of Jesus knew both of these qualities when they joined him in the adventure of their lives. Mary Magdalene was a good friend who could only stand helplessly off to the side while he hung, suffering and dying, on the cross. A tax collector named Zacchaeus—taking money from fellow Jews to give to the hated Romans!—went to great trouble hoping merely to get a glimpse of Jesus. He received the gift of having Jesus join him in his home for dinner—much to the chagrin of the towns-people, who didn't understand why Jesus the Holy One would even give the time of day to a despised tax man!

When people become Catholic as adults, two parts of the ritual called baptism demonstrate the comfort and challenge of a life of faith. On the one hand, they are asked if they accept Jesus. On the other hand, they are asked if they reject the allure of Satan. Don't think of Satan as the stereotypical guy in the red outfit with a pointy tail and pitchfork. That figure is easy to reject. There are more commonplace demonic forces that challenge us. Can we share bread with people we don't like? Are we stirred to compassionate action when we encounter people who are homeless and appear dirty or suffer from an irritating form of mental illness? Do we accept responsibility for those who are too old and frail, or too young, to care for themselves—even when they are not family members? These are the types of challenges initiation into Catholic faith places before those who dare to take the plunge into baptismal waters. Satan tempts us to overlook them.

Come to me, all you that are weary and are carrying heavy burdens, and I will give you rest. MATTHEW 11:28

- What do you think are the comforts and challenges of being Catholic?

Heart: Faith as Basic Trust

What do we mean when we talk about "the Catholic faith"? It's not as if a priest or parish worker can hand you a book and say, "Read this and you'll know the Catholic faith." Faith is as much a matter of the heart as of the head. Saying "I believe" or "I agree" to a set of beliefs doesn't make someone Catholic. Underlying the reality of faith are experiences and commitments that cannot be reduced to words. (Isn't it equally true that when we say "I love you" to someone, no amount of words can capture what that phrase means?) Catholic faith doesn't mean "I know a lot about God." Catholic faith means that, despite any evidence to the contrary and through no merit of my own, I recognize that God loves me. How do I know this? Jesus. How do I know Jesus? The church. Such an experience of God in Jesus Christ is the basic meaning of Catholic faith.

> *God is not an idea, or a definition that we have committed to memory; he is a presence which we experience in our hearts.*
>
> **LOUIS EVELY**

As a matter of the heart, Catholic faith is an embodied faith. Along with picking up and reading the Bible, people should get a crucifix and spend time looking at it. Words can't capture the message of Jesus, in agony on the cross, giving his life blood for us. On the cross Jesus speaks to us heart to heart. If you were not familiar with Catholicism, something about it that you might find appealing, or that might make you uneasy, is its use of images. Many Catholics wear not only crosses but crucifixes. A crucifix displays the body of Jesus—sometimes dripping with blood. Statues of Mary with baby Jesus abound. Churches are likely to contain a statue of St. Joseph, complete with his carpenter's tools. Catholics have a whole host of other angels, saints, and images of Jesus that they can relate to in visible, bodily ways.

The heart of Catholic faith, then, is trusting in God through Jesus. It doesn't mean not having doubts or questions. It certainly doesn't mean always living up to the ideals we set for ourselves. It does mean that when times are rough we know we have a special companion. Jesus is one of us but also one with God; Jesus himself cried out to his Father in the midst of his own suffering. Becoming Catholic means wanting to allow Jesus into our life.

....

> *Listen! I am standing at the door, knocking;*
> *if you hear my voice and open the door, I will come in to you*
> *and eat with you, and you with me.* **REVELATION 3:20**

Basic Catholic Beliefs

Catholics share a set of beliefs about God, Jesus, the church, and the human condition. Church leaders, theologians, and everyday believers have spent a great deal of time exploring what the basic teachings of Catholicism mean—the "head" dimension of faith. In the year AD 325, Roman Emperor Constantine was upset over the arguments people were having about fundamental Christian beliefs. Because he didn't like the atmosphere of discord these disagreements were creating, he brought church leaders together at his summer palace in Nicea to hammer out a comprehensive statement of beliefs that all could agree on. What these bishops came up with, called the Creed of the Council of Nicea, or the Nicene Creed, is still recited at Catholic Masses today. More precisely, it is the Nicene-Constantinopolitan Creed, since a later council made additions to it. At Mass the congregation stands and recites the creed together. This seventeen-hundred-year-old statement sums up what Catholics believe about God, Jesus, the church, and the human condition. You can find the creed in the Mass booklets found in Catholic churches.

> *I believe; help my unbelief!*
>
> Mark 9:24

- Read and think about the Nicene Creed recited at Mass.
- Which statements in it do you find most appealing?
- Which statements do you find most baffling?

Hands: A Faith That Is Lived

A fundamental Catholic belief is that Jesus is both divine and human. Therefore, we don't just look up to see God; we also look around us. Jesus is God spending time with us. To be Catholic means spending time on the work that Jesus spent time on. If we read the gospels, we can get a sense of Jesus' main message. He healed, body and soul. He offered forgiveness. He was hospitable to all kinds of people, especially toward people often disdained by others. He shared meals with people whom polite society said he shouldn't eat with. Above all, he told us that God loves us and

> *All who have faith in Him must be sorry for their sins, be baptized in the Holy Spirit of God, live by the rules of love, and share the Bread together in love, to announce the good news to others until Jesus comes again.*
> **PART OF A CREED USED BY MASAI CATHOLICS OF EAST AFRICA**

that we are to love one another. Surely there's a message in the gospels about what someone might do to follow Jesus.

- Read through the Gospel according to Luke in the Bible. What do you notice Jesus being most passionate about?
- What core messages do you think Jesus tries to communicate?

Soul: Faith That Animates Us

Catholicism proclaims that there is a "more than," or "greater than," dimension to the human condition. The breath of life breathed into each of us by God doesn't end when our bodily organs cease to function. Our life is greater than our bodily existence. We could dissect our entire body and account for all the memories stored in our mind and still not capture all that we are. We need more than biology class, or psychology class, or even philosophy class, to learn about the totality of human existence. Imagine what human life would be without

the soul. An image from science-fiction movies comes to mind
in which human bodies are transformed into soulless crea-

> *Then the Lord
> God formed man
> from the dust of
> the ground, and
> breathed into
> his nostrils the
> breath of life; and
> the man became
> a living being.*
>
> **GENESIS 2:7**

tures. Without our souls faith would be
impossible. Through the grace of God
we actually share in divine life. We exist in communion with God. Catholic
faith requires this soulful, "the whole
is greater than the sum of its parts," dimension to human existence. Behind
our thoughts and deeds, our feelings
and relationships, is the soul that ani-
mates all that we are. It energizes us and

makes living in response to faith possible. To speak of the soul
is to humbly accept the awesome mystery that there's more to
us than we imagine. Catholic faith is faith in God and in God's
presence in the depth of our being.

- Soul refers to the spiritual principle within us. What
  experiences have you had of being in touch with this
  animating, energizing dimension of being human?

....

> *There are more things in heaven and earth, Horatio,*
> *Than are dreamt of in your philosophy.*
>
> **WILLIAM SHAKESPEARE (HAMLET, ACT 1, SCENE 5)**

Blessed Franz Jägerstätter—Faith in Adversity

Blessed Franz Jägerstätter—Faith in Adversity ▪ World War II provides us with
many examples of heroism. In 2007, for example,
the church beatified (a step toward sainthood)

an Austrian farmer from the time named Franz
Jägerstätter. An unassuming man, Franz and his
wife took their Catholic faith seriously. In addition
to running their farm, he also served as sacristan at
his parish church in his village of St. Radegund. The
couple had three young daughters. In 1943 Franz
was called up for active duty in the Nazi army. From
the beginning, he had opposed Hitler and Nazism.
He told of a vivid dream he had of a train filled
with people making its way toward destruction. He
understood that train to be Nazism.

He sought counsel from local church and secular
leaders. They told him that as a farmer he was in
no position to decide whether or not a war was
just; if called upon by the state, it was his duty to
serve in the army and obey orders. Franz, however,
could not reconcile his Catholic faith with Hitler's
agenda. He was convinced that active military
service for this purpose would be a sin. While in
jail, he heard of a priest who had been killed for
resisting the Nazis. It only strengthened his resolve.
During his military trial, he said that "he could not
be both a Nazi and a Catholic." For his "crimes"
against the state, he was beheaded in August 1943.
With his beatification, the church now recognizes
Jägerstätter as a martyr for the faith.

In many ways Jägerstätter's story exemplifies the
power of Catholic faith to change a person's life in a
profound way. His story could easily have been overlooked—what was one more execution at a time of

wholesale death? His protest against Nazism and the war didn't tip the scales even the slightest bit away from the Nazi agenda. And yet his wife and some of his fellow villagers kept his story alive. A bishop attending Vatican Council II in the early nineteen sixties told Franz's story, which influenced his fellow bishops to include strong statements in the council documents advocating personal responsibility and fidelity to conscience over blind obedience. Jägerstätter, then, was one of those seemingly insignificant people swimming in the sea of Catholicism. His response to his Catholic faith in a little village, apparently of little consequence to anyone other than his family, actually has had an impact on how we today understand what it means to be Catholic. Such connections get to the heart of Catholicism. In his last letter home from prison, Franz included a brief prayer. It's one that all Catholics can pray.

....

Heart of Jesus, heart of Mary, and my heart
be one heart bound for time and eternity.

ERNA PUTZ, ED., FRANZ JÄGERSTÄTTER:
LETTERS AND WRITINGS FROM PRISON

Let Us Pray
Jesus, Lord and Savior,
we thank you for sharing our journey with us.
Help us to be ever mindful of your presence
   and know you in heart, in mind, and in body.
Keep us always in your loving care.
Amen.

2 OUR THIRST FOR GOD: ENTERING INTO THE MYSTERY

We want to meet Him because He is God,
and we cannot live without God.
We want to meet Him because He is light,
and we cannot walk without light.
We want to meet Him because He is love,
and there is no joy without love.

Carlo Carretto, *The God Who Comes*

The Still, Small Voice

THE PROPHET ELIJAH IS ONE OF THE MOST PROMINENT FIGURES OF THE BIBLE. Chapter nineteen of the first book of Kings (1 Kings 19) tells about his search for God during a time when God seems to be particularly absent and the people of Israel are undergoing hard times. Elijah gets word from an angel to go up onto a mountain where he will hear from God. The first thing Elijah encounters there is a mighty wind. Since God is almighty, it makes sense that God would be manifest through tornado-force winds…But Elijah doesn't find God in the wind. Then an earthquake strikes. Even today, we call earthquakes "acts of God," as if God gets angry on occasion and displays that anger with a devastating show of power and destruction…But Elijah doesn't find God in the earthquake.

Then fire strikes the mountain. Once again, God elects not to be made known in such a forceful and expected way. Finally, God does come to Elijah, in "a sound of sheer silence." That particular phrase has also been translated as "a still, small voice," or merely "a gentle breeze."

We can be grateful for this account of Elijah's encounter with God. It mirrors the way most of us experience God. We are more likely to find subtle hints of God's presence than clear and definitive encounters with the divine. To the question "Where is God?" a popular old American catechism answered, "God is everywhere." We can go along our way, seemingly out of touch with God, because we don't have any earthquake experiences of God's presence. We can easily miss God in the silences of our life. Many medieval legends tell of knights who go in search of Jesus or the Holy Grail, only to find that the holy was back home but overlooked. We might have moments when we are overwhelmed with the wonder of God, such as at the birth of a child. However, the Bible tells us that every child remains an image of God throughout his or her life and into eternity. When we bump up against other people in our day-to-day activities, we can easily miss the sacredness they embody.

....

What are these people, His People, looking for in Him?
What characteristics do they expect when they see Him
*   for the first time?*
Power, glory, blinding light, triumph.
What happens?
Weakness, smallness, obscurity, anonymity.
    CARLO CARRETTO, *THE GOD WHO COMES*

- Tell the story of an instance when you experienced God present in your life in little, subtle ways.

St. Thérèse of Lisieux—The Little Flower

Here's the story of a French girl who experienced God intensely and became one of the most popular Catholic saints of all time. The young woman who came to be known as the Little Flower only lived to the age of twenty-four, from 1873 to 1897. She was not a long-ago saint; if she had lived a normal lifespan she would only have died fifty or sixty years ago. She lived during a time when many European intellectuals were turning toward atheism and looking to science, not religion, for answers. Her autobiography, *The Story of a Soul,* describes her understanding of faith and her simple, but profound "little way," her prescription for how to live the faith.

Thérèse was the youngest of a family of nine; five daughters survived to adulthood. One of Thérèse's sisters became a Carmelite nun when Thérèse was just a child. Carmelites are cloistered nuns who live an austere life in a monastery, with regular periods of formal prayer throughout the day. They maintain silence most of the time so that their entire focus can be on their relationship with Jesus. Thérèse herself entered the Carmelite monastery at the age of fifteen.

Considering that Thérèse lived secluded in a monastery from age fifteen till her death at age

twenty-four, we can say that she did very little to
warrant our attention. And that's the entire point of
her message. She proposes a spirituality of "the little
way." She suggests "scattering flowers" in the little
daily contacts we have—a smile to a stranger, acts
of kindness that go unnoticed, sending a note to a
friend just to say hello. Thérèse gives an example of
her own struggle to live the little way. She mentions
that she found the clicking sounds made by an older sister who sat behind her during evening chapel
to be particularly irritating. Her immediate impulse
was to try to ignore it, which didn't work. Next, she
thought to tell the nun to stop making the noise;
but that would surely upset the older sister, who
couldn't help it. Thérèse decided to incorporate
the sound into her prayer and to "offer this concert
to Jesus." No wonder she became one of the most
popular saints of all times! Hers was a spirituality
that all of us can—and must—practice.

Thérèse was not blind to the attacks on faith
in God swirling around Europe at the time. She
describes her own faith in what appears to be child-
like simplicity. At first it sounds naïve and overly
sentimental. In fact, her understanding actually
gets to the heart of faith. Because of the profound
impact of her writings, she is proclaimed a "doctor
of the church"—one of only four women to be so
honored. The church gives this title to people who
have been particularly inspiring through their intel-
lect and their writings. Thérèse mentions feeling at

times like a plaything of Jesus who has been discarded and left alone in a closet, which only increases her desire to be with him. She describes an image of Mary Magdalene coming to the tomb of Christ. Mary must get down on her knees to look into the darkness of the empty tomb to realize Christ has risen. Thérèse took from this incident that looking into the darkness is the way to come to the light. She needed to realize her "littleness" if Jesus was to carry her in his arms. Thérèse in fact once wrote a play for the sisters about how God in Jesus "stoops down" to be with us.

Thérèse's spirituality reminds us that Jesus is there for us even when we feel abandoned by him. And we don't need to do great things to live the Christian life. Perhaps the little things are the most important anyway.

....

My dear Mother, you can see that I am a very little soul and that I can offer God only very little things.

ST. THÉRÉSE OF LISIEUX, IN HER AUTOBIOGRAPHY *STORY OF A SOUL*

Living the Faith ■ Betty rarely leaves her hometown, which means she practically never sees her cousins in Milwaukee. And yet every holiday, including Easter and St. Valentine's Day, she sends them a card telling them how much she loves them.

She always includes the latest snapshots of her kids and, lately, her grandkids. When she can she also sends a little gift. Now that she's in a nursing home, her children ask their mother if they can get her anything. Betty never requests anything for herself. Instead, she asks for an assortment of cards and stamps so that she can continue to send out her little messages of love. Betty always had great devotion to St. Thérèse and her little way. For Betty, this is her way of doing the "little things" that Thérèse reminds us are signs of God's grace.

Logical Arguments for God

During the height of the Middle Ages an Italian Dominican friar named Thomas Aquinas discovered that the ancient Greek philosopher Aristotle offered logical arguments about why it is reasonable to posit the existence of God. Aquinas realized that we don't need to set aside reason when making a case for God's existence. He came up with what he called five "proofs" for the existence of God. He didn't mean that term in the modern scientific sense. He meant that belief in God is more reasonable, more logical, than the opposition position. We would need a philosophy course to understand the reasoning underlying Aquinas's way of addressing the question of God, but here's a generalized description of the type of thinking Aristotelian philosophers applied to it.

> To one who has faith, no explanation is necessary. To one without faith, no explanation is possible.
>
> St. Thomas Aquinas

Argument from motion. Everything in the universe is moved by something or someone else. However, there exists an "unmoved mover" behind all the movement and change happening in the universe. That's what we mean by God.

Argument from causation. We're here because of our parents. Our table and chairs, the very house we live in, exist because they were created by someone. We are left with two choices. Either the chain of causation has gone on forever or there was a beginning to it all. The more logical position is that there is a first cause or an "uncaused cause"—God.

Argument from necessity. Beings exist but can dissolve into nonexistence. Doesn't it follow, however, that ultimately there is "being" rather than nothingness? Pure being, without limitation and not dependent on anything else, is God.

Argument from perfection. While there are degrees to the things around us—bigger or smaller, better or worse—it follows that in the end there is perfection: God.

Argument from design. The intricacy we see around us and in the universe might be the result of pure chance. But its infinitely sophisticated design does suggest intelligence behind it all.

Using logic and reason to help us understand God has its place in theology. However, the great mystics know that there is too much of God for our minds to grasp. With them, we humbly say "Ah!" to the great mystery of God.

- Which arguments for God's existence are compelling for you?

....

Question the beauty of the earth, question the beauty of the sea, question the beauty of the air, amply spread around everywhere. Who made these beautiful changeable things, if not one who is beautiful and unchangeable?

St. Augustine, Easter Sermon c. AD 411

The Denial of God

Beginning about two hundred years ago, a number of European thinkers began proposing what had previously been unimaginable for most people—God does not exist.

What types of arguments did they put forth to dismiss God? For someone like Sigmund Freud, the father of modern psychology, God is merely a projection. The thought of being alone in the universe is so frightening that we project that there is a "father figure" who looks after us, just as children need parents to look after them. We humans created God; God didn't create us. The German philosopher Friedrich Nietzsche claims that we will never be free until we realize that we're on our own, responsible for our own existence. We're not adults until we venture out on our own without God as a crutch. Karl Marx sees religion itself as a drug—"the opium of the people"—that kept workers from fighting against the horrible conditions they experienced in nineteenth-century factories. By believing that reward comes only after we die, people aren't motivated to make the most of this life for themselves. People need to discard promises of life after death and belief in a God who makes everything right in the end.

Another argument for the denial of God is the reality of human suffering: how can a loving God allow such things as the Holocaust under the Nazis? An all-powerful God would never stand for such atrocities. The pervasive reality of suffering and evil leads to the conclusion that God does not exist.

- Does belief in God take away our freedom, or is the opposite true? Explain.
- Does belief in life after death result in people not working to better this world?
- An experience of suffering strengthens faith in God for some people, while for others it destroys it. Among people you know, what effect has suffering had on their view of God?

....

You, O eternal Trinity, are a deep sea, into which the more I enter the more I find, and the more I find the more I seek.

ST. CATHERINE OF SIENA

Dr. Takashi Nagai: One Catholic's Response to Suffering ■ Catholicism doesn't sugarcoat pain and suffering. If anything, Catholicism emphasizes that life is a valley of tears. A Catholic who witnessed suffering firsthand was Dr. Takashi Nagai. He was a doctor in Nagasaki, Japan, who survived the 1945 atomic bomb attack on his city until his death from leukemia in 1951 at the age of forty-three. After the bombing, he spent the remainder of his life contemplating this event and placing it in

the context of his Catholic faith. He was struck by
the confluence of coincidences that resulted in the
destruction of Nagasaki. His city was not initially
the intended target. The bombers were to target
a Mitsubishi munitions plant, but the only thing
jutting out from the clouds that day was the spire of
the Catholic cathedral in the city. The bomb crew
used the church spire for their target. At the time
Nagasaki was the center of Japanese Catholicism.
Catholics in Japan were already familiar with
suffering. For hundreds of years they experienced
persecution at the hands of other Japanese who
viewed Catholicism as "foreign" and an affront to
the homeland. When the bomb exploded, students
at a Catholic girls' school next to the cathedral were
praying their daily psalms. When Dr. Nagai made
it home, he discovered his wife's body reduced to
ashes. Next to her body he found her rosary beads.
In all, 8,000 Catholics died instantly that day.
Others, like Dr. Nagai, found themselves sickened
from radiation and died early deaths.

Dr. Nagai wrote a memoir of the bombing,
which became a bestseller in Japan. He spent the
remainder of his days in a hut he called his hermitage. He named it *nyoko-do*, which means "Love your
neighbor as yourself." In his writings and speeches,
Dr. Nagai created controversy by suggesting that it
was appropriate that a heavily Catholic city should
be the one that was destroyed. He saw the cross as
central to Catholicism. Jesus admonishes his follow-

ers to take up their cross, as he himself did. We can't expect our experience to be different from that of Jesus; only through suffering do we come to new life. Dr. Nagai's insights don't explain suffering; Catholicism doesn't provide answers to it. However, Catholic faith does suggest a response to suffering. For one thing, Catholics place their hope and trust in Jesus who underwent suffering and death himself on the way to triumph over them. Secondly, realizing the suffering we can inflict on others, a Catholic response is to do all that we can to avoid causing pain and to help others in their suffering. A message Dr. Nagai took away from the Nagasaki catastrophe: Love your neighbor as yourself.

....

To you do we cry, poor banished children of Eve!
To you do we send up our sighs, mourning and weeping
    in this vale of tears!

FROM THE TRADITIONAL CATHOLIC PRAYER "HAIL HOLY QUEEN"

Atheists Today

The existence of God can't be reduced to logical arguments, one way or the other. It's important to make some distinctions. Belief in God may be *non-rational*—that is, not capable of being proven by the scientific method or any other reasoning process. The term *irrational* is another matter. It implies that faith and reason are contradictory. They are in fact two different ways of seeking the truth, two different ways of interpreting our experience. They can be different without being contradictory. And from the time of the early church the dominant strain of

Catholic thought proposes that *faith and reason need each other*; the one keeps the other in balance. Reason makes us skeptical when someone is selling on eBay a piece of toast that has the outline of Christ's face burnt into it. Faith reminds us that we should nonetheless be open to signals of divine presence around us. In our education for life, we need both science class and religion class. Without *faith*, we could miss the ultimate mystery that surrounds us. We need to use our *reasoning* to try to make sense of it.

- What conflicts between "faith" and "reason" have you experienced in your life?
- What are some ways that you could balance faith and reason in your life?

....

God is closer to us than water is to a fish.
ST. CATHERINE OF SIENA

St. Paul—Apostle to the Gentiles ▪ Even though he was not one of the original twelve apostles chosen by Jesus, St. Paul was perhaps the most influential apostle in the first few decades of the church. Jesus and his first followers lived in a predominantly Greco-Roman world. Politically, it was under the control of Rome. Culturally, it was more Greek and had been since the time of Alexander the Great a few centuries before Jesus. Paul was not like the other apostles. They were mostly country peasants, like Jesus himself. They came from small villages by the Sea of Galilee. Jesus' hometown of Nazareth was a tiny, insignificant village in a nearby hillside. People who lived there were immersed in their Jewish heritage; but at the same time they were surrounded by a larger world, which was predominantly Greco-Roman.

> *Ever since the creation of the world his eternal power and divine nature, invisible though they are, have been understood and seen through the things he has made.*
>
> **ROMANS 1:20**

Paul was a Jew—a Pharisee to be precise, meaning, in part, that he was well educated in Jewish law. Paul was also a Roman citizen. Being a citizen of Rome didn't mean that you necessarily lived in the city; rather, it meant that you were granted the privileges of a citizen. Most people living in Rome were not citizens. Only an elite group possessed citizenship. Paul's hometown, Tarsus, was a Roman town in what today is Turkey. He was a Jew living in a city that was overwhelmingly non-Jewish. This combination made Paul uniquely qualified to take the message of Jesus and translate it into language that non-Jews could appreciate.

The best educated among the Gentiles (non-Jews) in the areas along the eastern shores of the Mediterranean Sea relied heavily on "reason" as the way to truth. Paul was the one early Christian who could "talk the talk" with thoughtful non-Jews. Much of the Acts of the Apostles, which chronicles

the life of the early church, centers on the travels of
Paul. He even made his way to Athens, the city in
Greece that had been home to Plato and Aristotle,
the greatest of Greek philosophers. Chapter seventeen of Acts describes Paul's discussions with
Athenians who were open to new ideas. Paul recognized that the people of Athens were religious; there
were statues, temples, and monuments to the gods
everywhere. Paul pointed out that all people seek
God in their own way. For Paul we human beings
are "hard-wired" to search for and find God. Paul put
it this way: God made all people "so that they would
search for God and perhaps grope for him and find
him—though indeed he is not far from each one of
us" (Acts 17:27). Paul explained to them that God
"not far from each one of us" can be found in the
person of Christ, divine but also human, raised from
the dead and living for all time and eternity.

• What most prompted you to seek and find God?

....

Gentiles have become fellow heirs, members of the same body,
and sharers in the promise in Christ Jesus through the gospel.

Ephesians 3:6

Let Us Pray

O God, grant me the grace to know and delight in
the wonder and mystery of you—Father, Son, and Holy Spirit.
Amen.

3 THE BIBLE: A LOVE LETTER FROM GOD

Now Jesus did many other signs in the presence of his disciples, which are not written in this book. But these are written so that you may come to believe that Jesus is the Messiah, the Son of God, and that through believing you may have life in his name. JOHN 20:30–31

IN HIS VERY FIRST ENCYCLICAL (A GENERAL LETTER FROM THE POPE TO THE CHURCH AND TO THE WORLD), Pope Benedict XVI reminded us that the Bible is a love story (*Deus Caritas Est,* #17.) The Bible tells the story of the love relationship between God and a band of poor, landless nomads who, with God's help, become a people—God's people. Like all intense love relationships, the one between God and God's people is at times contentious. In fact, the name of this people—Israel—means "one who wrestles with God," based on a story about Jacob who wrestles through the night with a stranger whom he recognizes as a messenger from God (Genesis 32:28). For Christians the love story reaches its climax, its fulfillment, in the person of Jesus and specifically in his torturous death and in the new kind of life that was his glorious resurrection. From there the story extends beyond the people of Israel and is available to all people. Anyone can now pick up a Bible and read this love letter from God to us.

There are so many questions we can ask of this intriguing collection of writings that Christians consider the word of God. Who wrote it? When and where was it written? What does it mean to call it "the word of God"? Even though more has been written about the Bible than about any other book, reading the Bible still raises many questions for us. Did God really destroy the whole world except for the inhabitants of one large boat? Why don't the gospels give us more information about the early years of Jesus, or what he looked like? Questions such as these are about the Bible and its makeup, not about what it means for a believing Christian. We raise these types of questions not to diminish the power and the glory of the book but to understand better what it says to us.

- How might the Bible be relevant today?

The Makeup of the Bible
If you pick up a Bible, what do we find in it? The Bible consists of two major divisions—the Old Testament (sacred writings belonging to the Jewish community prior to Jesus) and the New Testament (sacred writings centered on Jesus belonging to first-century Christian communities). The word "testament" is used for the important concept "covenant," meaning an agreement—in this case, between God and God's people. The Bible begins with the creation of the world and ends with a mysterious book about the end of time as we know it. Some Christians consider these accounts to be factual descriptions of our beginning and our end, which is not the Catholic take

on them. In between these two books are a variety of types of writing composed over a thousand-year period.

Jews call their Bible TANAKH or the Torah, although the latter term refers more precisely to only the first five books. Christians call these writings the Old Testament. In addition, Catholics accept seven more Old Testament writings than Protestants do. That's because between two hundred and one hundred years before Jesus, some Jewish scholars in Egypt translated their sacred writings from Hebrew into Greek and included an additional seven books that Jews in Israel at the time did not include. Christians accepted these seven books coming out of the Greek tradition as Scripture up until the Protestant Reformation of the sixteenth century. Early Protestants, who began a "back to the Bible" movement, felt that the "original" Old Testament was the Hebrew Bible without these seven later writings. Either way, the great majority of the writings in the Jewish Bible, or the Old Testament, are accepted as Scripture by Jews and all Christians. All Christians now recognize the same twenty-seven books of the New Testament as sacred Scripture.

If you pick up a Bible for the first time, you will notice that each "book" (Genesis, Exodus, and so forth) is also divided into what are called chapters and verses. It wasn't until 1227 that the Bible was divided into chapters and 1555 when a man known as Stephanus divided the chapters into verses. If you see a reference to a Bible verse, it will be listed as, for instance, Genesis 3:4. That means that the passage is the fourth verse of the third chapter of Genesis.

The Bible as the Word of God
The Bible was written between 900 BC to AD 100. Some sto-

ries in the Old Testament are older than that and were passed down as part of the oral tradition of the Israelites. Are the various

> *With all wisdom and insight [God] has made known to us the mystery of his will.*
>
> EPHESIANS 1:8–9

ous writings of the Bible a product of their time and place? Clearly, yes they are. Biblical writings reflect the awareness and perspective of their authors. But isn't God their author; isn't the Bible the word of God? Catholic teaching says that Scripture is the word of God *through* the words of human authors. It was revealed by God, meaning that God inspired its authors. Christians believe that all we need to know for our salvation can be found in the Bible. It is a gift from God and contains God's message for us. Even though the Bible is the revealed word of God, it reflects the circumstances, time, and place of its human authors.

The Bible is the product of a particular community that over time grew and developed in its awareness. While Jesus never rejects any teachings in the Old Testament, he gives his own interpretation of it. Early on the Christian community did reject some practices called for in the Old Testament, such as requiring circumcision as a sign of the covenant.

- How has your understanding of God changed over time?

Interpreting the Bible

For the past two hundred years, scholars have subjected the Bible to study and analysis using the many tools of modern science and critical inquiry. Beginning about one hundred years ago, archaeologists scoured the lands mentioned in the

Bible to see whether there was evidence that events actually happened the way the Bible describes them. Experts in ancient languages perused the literature of various cultures to discover whether biblical writers possibly borrowed from them.

Is this type of scrutiny mistreating the sacred nature of Scripture? In 1943 Pope Pius XII welcomed the use of modern techniques to help us understand Scripture better. These approaches, however, are not viewed kindly by all Christians. Fundamentalist Christians believe that the Bible should be understood solely as a literal, historically precise account of events despite what might have been the intention of the human author. If the Bible says that the world was created in seven days, then the world was created in seven days—regardless of what modern science tells us. The Catholic approach to Scripture is not a fundamentalist or literalist one. Catholicism doesn't dismiss the literal sense of Scripture, but it also recognizes that the original authors used a variety of types of writing and were not always describing "the facts." During the early centuries of Christianity great Christian thinkers believed that the words, images, and stories in the Bible have layers of meaning. Along with the literal level of meaning there are also spiritual, symbolic meanings. The story of the prophet Jonah being swallowed up by a big fish, only to come out alive after three days, is a symbolic reference to Jesus' three days in the tomb before he is raised from the dead. The lamb's blood that protects the Hebrew slaves from the death of their firstborn sons in Egypt is a precursor to Christ's bloody sacrifice on the cross. We need to develop a sense of symbolism and a realization that a text can have layers of meaning if we are to understand the message of the Bible.

At Vatican Council II, the gathering of church leaders that took place in the early 1960s, the council fathers pointed out that we gain insight into the meaning of Scripture through contemplation and study. Scholars give us a better understanding of the meaning of Scripture (*Dei Verbum*, #12). They can help us understand literary forms as well as historical and social contexts of the Bible. While scientific study of Scripture is important, we need to realize that the Bible is not just any other book or object of investigation. At the Eucharist, Scripture is not just read, it is proclaimed—"The word of the Lord." Catholics don't just read the Scriptures; they pray them. We approach Scripture seeking to find out what God has to say to us.

- Scripture scholars engage in *exegesis*, a Greek word that means "to draw out." What might you do to "draw out" the meaning of a passage during your own Bible reading?
- How could you "pray" the Scriptures rather than simply read them?

Living the Faith ▪ Some parishioners want to spend more time contemplating the Scripture readings they hear at Sunday liturgy. They gather at the parish center an hour before the first Mass to talk about the week's readings. They take turns leading the discussion and simply try to figure out how the messages from Scripture can apply to their own lives. Before liturgy begins, they gather with their family and friends for the formal service.

The word is very near to you; it is in your mouth and in your heart for you to observe. DEUTERONOMY 30:14

Is the Bible a "Catholic" Book?

Since the Reformation, Protestants have emphasized Bible reading. Until fairly recently, other Christians questioned whether the Catholic Church was indeed a "Bible church." Following the Reformation, Catholic leaders did caution against reading Scripture apart from the church community. The fear was that Protestants read the Bible and interpreted it for themselves, and look where it got them—outside of the one, true church! During the past century, the Bible has been restored to its rightful place as the bedrock of Catholic faith along with "Tradition"—the long history of Spirit-filled interpretation and application of Scripture within the church. Nothing that the church does or says can be separated from the word of God found in Scripture.

- What ways do you see Scripture incorporated into Catholic life and practices?

FAQs: Catholics and the Bible

1. Are Catholics "biblical literalists"?
No. Catholicism recognizes that not everything in the Bible is historically factual, nor was it intended to be understood as such. Some stories use figurative language. Catholicism distinguishes between what is written down in a story from the truth expressed in it. Also, not every account of events described in the Bible is merely figurative.

2. Is there an original copy of the Bible stored away somewhere?
No. The oldest complete copies we have are from hundreds of

years after Jesus. Older fragments affirm that the Bible as we have it is generally true to what existed much earlier. In other words, copyists worked diligently to stay true to the writings handed down to them.

3. Do Catholics read the same Bible as other Christians?

Basically, yes. The New Testament is the same for all Christian groups. Catholics include seven writings as part of the Old Testament that Protestants and Jews exclude. To understand why, read about the Septuagint—a translation of the Jewish Bible into Greek completed around 132 BC.

Genesis and the Beginnings of the Covenant

The first book of the Bible is Genesis, which begins with grand stories of God's creation and humanity's disobedience. Genesis then gives an account of the interaction between God and someone who probably actually existed some thirty-five hundred years ago or so—Abraham. In the story of Abraham we are introduced to a God who enters into a covenant with his people: "you shall be my people, and I will be your God" (Ezekiel 36:28). "Covenant," meaning contract or agreement, becomes a key concept throughout the Bible. God makes a promise to Abraham, and God is not one to break a promise. God promises Abraham that he will have many descendants and will possess the land. In case anyone

> *Now the LORD said to Abram, "Go from your country and your kindred and your father's house to the land that I will show you.*
>
> *I will make of you a great nation, and I will bless you, and make your name great."*
>
> GENESIS 12:1–2

doubts the power of God, Abraham is ninety-nine and his wife Sarah is ninety when God tells him they'll have a son! Also, God is promising Abraham possession of a land where he is, at the time, a foreigner, just passing through.

The Bible is primarily a story of God's interaction with his people. On their part, the people constantly fall short of what God asks of them, and they go through many difficult times. The refrain throughout the Bible is that God is faithful to his promises. Often a prophetic pronouncement or a psalm's lyrics begins or ends with the words "Be not afraid" or "Do not fear." That phrase resonates throughout the Old Testament, and it continues in the New Testament. In the gospels Jesus himself says similar words nearly twenty times.

Do not fear, for I am with you,
do not be afraid, for I am your God; I will strengthen you,
I will help you, I will uphold you with my victorious right hand.

ISAIAH 41:10

Peace I leave with you; my peace I give to you.
Do not let your hearts be troubled,
and do not let them be afraid.

JOHN 14:27

- How might you apply the biblical message "Be not afraid" to your own life?
- How can Scripture help in this regard?
- How might Catholic faith help?

Exodus—From Slavery to Freedom
The pivotal event in the Old Testament is the story of the

Exodus, which has shaped Jewish identity ever since and helped Christians understand the meaning of Jesus' death and resurrection. It tells of an oppressed

> *I have observed the misery of my people who are in Egypt; I have heard their cry on account of their taskmasters. Indeed, I know their sufferings, and I have come down to deliver them from the Egyptians, and to bring them up out of that land to a good and broad land, a land flowing with milk and honey*
>
> Exodus 3:7-8

and enslaved people set free by God and led by God through a wilderness to a wonderful paradise. The Exodus theme is one that speaks to all of us. Who doesn't long to rise out of slavery, in whatever form, and to be set free? Who doesn't hold out hope for a good and bountiful world where people can live in peace and prosper? Christians readily relate the Exodus experience of the Hebrew slaves to Jesus' journey from death to new life.

The book of Exodus is a good place to ask a question that can be asked of all of the Old Testament: Is the story true? If *truth* means did it happen the way it is described in the book, then the Exodus story comes up short. Instead, it represents an exaggeration of a kernel of historical facts. The story does, however, give a true accounting of the faith experience of a group of people in the twelfth century BC. Egyptian chronicles speak of some "Hebrews" whose slave labor helped build Egypt's greatest cities. However, apart from the Bible itself, no ancient record mentions plagues, wholesale release of a large number of slaves, or the mass slaughter of a pharaoh's army. History does support that lowly Hebrews grew in strength during the eleventh and tenth centuries, gaining control over Palestine. The main message of the story—its "truth"—is that the transformation from oppression to freedom, power, and a sense of self-worth was the work of God. The way to remain free and prosperous was to stay faithful to God. This same dynamic applies to other sections of Scripture in that the authors of the Bible looked for the hand of God at work in the events of their lives. During hard times they held out hope that God had not abandoned them. When good things came their way, they knew to thank God for them. When they forgot God or disobeyed his commands, prophets rose up to call them back to being faithful to God.

- How would you describe the theme of Exodus?
- How might you apply the Exodus story to your own life and to situations that exist in the world today?
- What are some forms of "slavery" that you experience in your life?
     How might Catholic faith help someone be set free?

The Prophets—Live the Way of the Lord

A prophet is one who speaks for God; the Hebrew word for prophet, *nabi*, means both spokesperson and "one who is called." After almost two hundred years in the new land, the Israelites changed their loose federation of twelve tribes ruled by judges into a full-fledged monarchy like the other nations surrounding them. Under their kings David and Solomon, the Israelites actually become a nation to be reckoned with.

> *and what does the Lord require of you but to do justice, and to love kindness, and to walk humbly with your God?*
>
> **MICAH 6:8**

The problems they face are familiar to us today: oftentimes with power come corruption, complacency, self-aggrandizement, ingratitude, and injustice. Kings were to rule according to the Mosaic law. When they chose to do otherwise, injustices resulted. Prophets rose up to call God's people back to living justly. These prophets were chosen by God, often against their will, to remind people of their covenant. God remained faithful to his promises, even though many of the people go astray. A large portion of the Bible is taken up with these prophetic voices calling people to get back on track.

For the prophets, fidelity to God is not measured by animal sacrifices; after all, the pagan neighbors of the Israelites also sacrificed bulls and other animals to their gods. God wants the rich to share their wealth with the poor; God wants widows and orphans cared for, strangers welcomed, and people who have come upon hard times restored to stable living conditions. The people seem to have put their trust in everything else but God—wealth, military might, and other gods. The prophets plead with them to return to God, to hold fast to God's covenant with them. Nonetheless, God reminds the people of his steadfast love for them:

....

Yet it was I who taught Ephraim [a tribe of Israel] to walk,
I took them up in my arms;
but they did not know that I healed them.
I led them with cords of human kindness, with bands of love.
I was to them like those who lift infants to their cheeks.
I bent down to them and fed them.   (**Hosea 11:3–4**)

- Who are the prophets and the voices for justice in our day?
- When did you experience God as "like those who lift infants to their cheeks"? Did you ever have such an experience of God?

Psalms and Wisdom Literature—
Praising and Pondering God

The Bible contains a song book—150 psalms. Like many song collections, the psalms express a variety of emotions. One psalm praises God for the works of creation; another calls for God's vengeance on perpetrators of injustice. One psalm offers comfort ("The Lord is my shepherd, I shall not want" [Psalm 23]); another pleads for God's help in dark times ("Let my tongue cling to the roof of my mouth if I do not remember you" [Psalm 137]). At every moment of the day, groups of Catholics are chanting the psalms somewhere in the world.

> *O sing to the LORD*
> *a new song,*
> *for he has done*
> *marvelous things.*
> PSALM 98:1

The Bible also contains a number of books labeled "wisdom literature." Here you'll find proverbs and much practical wisdom, such as the reminder from Ecclesiastes that "For everything there is a season...A time to be born, and a time to die" (3:1, 12). The book of Job and the love poem known as "The Song of Songs" also fall into the category of wisdom literature.

- Read and pray over the following psalms: 8, 23, 88, 139, 146. What do you see as the message of each one?
- Have you ever felt the need for songs such as these in your own life? What does each psalm say to you?
- If you want a greater challenge, read through the book of Job. What do you understand its main message to be?

Happy are those who find wisdom,
and those who get understanding,

for her income is better than silver,
and her revenue better than gold.

PROVERBS 3:13–14

King David—A Charismatic and Colorful King

A fascinating figure from the Old Testament is the ancestor of
Jesus known as King David. (Find his story in 1 and 2 Samuel.)
He's the youngest son of a man named Jesse from Bethlehem.
When the prophet Samuel goes to Jesse's house to anoint the
future king of Israel, he asks to see Jesse's sons. Jesse proudly
parades seven sons before Samuel, each one strong and handsome. But God tells Samuel that none of these is the chosen
one. Samuel asks Jesse if he has no other sons, and Jesse replies
that there is only his youngest, David, who is out taking care of
the sheep. Sure enough, this overlooked and least likely candi-
date is the one God has selected to be king.

David goes on to have a colorful career. Even as a youngster
he exhibits courage and cunning, slaying the mighty Goliath
with a stone from his slingshot. He is known as a musician,
calming King Saul with his songs even though Saul is jealous and afraid of David's popular appeal. The psalms are associated with David; perhaps he even wrote some of them.
As king, David brings the Ark of the Covenant, which contained the tablets of the Ten Commandments, to his capital
city, Jerusalem. He is so excited when the Ark enters the city
that he strips down to his loincloth and dances through the
streets—much to the chagrin of his more proper wife.

David also has his flaws and performs a deed as shocking
as the scandals we read about in the tabloids. He notices the
beautiful Bathsheba bathing; and, although she is married to

one of his generals, he sleeps with her. Fearing she is pregnant, David tries to get her husband home and in the marital bed so that he'll think that he's the father. The general will have none of it—he's too loyal to King David! So David sees to it that this faithful general is killed in battle and takes Bathsheba for his wife. Later David repents of his misdeeds, and never loses favor with God. In fact, God promises David that kingship will continue to reside in the House of David. Christians hail Jesus as son of David and fulfillment of God's promise to him.

- What message do you take away from the stories of King David?
- Jesus had more than one interesting and "questionable" ancestor. What does that say to you about Jesus? Do you know of any colorful ancestors in your own family tree?

Let us pray
God of our ancestors, you gave us your word in the Bible so that we may come to know more fully your Word made flesh, Jesus. May we find inspiration and guidance in the stories and teachings of Scripture, ever mindful that it tells of your love for us in Christ Jesus. Amen.

4 GOSPELS: GOOD NEWS OF JESUS CHRIST

We declare to you what we have seen and heard so that you also may have fellowship with us; and truly our fellowship is with the Father and with his Son Jesus Christ. We are writing these things so that our joy may be complete. 1 JOHN 1:3–4

HAVE YOU EVER GOTTEN GOOD NEWS—something so marvelous that you smiled from inside out and couldn't wait to share it? That was the experience of the very first people who came to be known as Christians. When the message of the gospel is grasped, it's also the experience of Christians today. The word "gospel" means good news. We get the term from the Gospel according to Mark, which begins with the simple but life-transforming words: "The beginning of the good news of Jesus Christ, the Son of God" (Mark 1:1).

To be precise, the good news is not the four books known as the gospels. The good news is Jesus himself, his message and the salvation brought about by his death and resurrection. The four gospels tell us about Jesus. For this reason Catholics believe that they deserve our veneration and attention. At liturgy, Catholics pray that the gospel message penetrates their minds and hearts and that it informs all that they do.

Do not be afraid; for see—I am bringing you good news
of great joy for all the people. LUKE 2:10

- What were some of the most joyful experiences you have had in your life?
- What do you think is the most joyful part of the gospel message?

How Did the Gospels Come to Be?

The four gospels come into existence through a three-stage process. Jesus' friends didn't want anything they had seen and heard to get lost or forgotten, and they wanted to share what they experienced with others in the hope that they too would believe and join the Jesus group. Second, people shared by word of mouth what eyewitnesses told them. This is known as "oral tradition." Finally, writers decided to put together in narrative form what they thought were the key stories of and about Jesus—what he had said and done, and what happened to him based on the stories circulating within the community of believers at the time. That's what the gospels are, the third stage in a process of communicating the message of Jesus. First, there were eyewitnesses telling of their experiences; then, these stories circulated in the community of believers;

"Are you the one who is to come, or are we to wait for another?" Jesus answered them, "Go and tell John what you hear and see: the blind receive their sight, the lame walk, the lepers are cleansed, the deaf hear, the dead are raised, and the poor have good news brought to them."

MATTHEW 11:3–5

finally, there were the four written gospels that we can read ourselves. Mark's gospel is the first to use this narrative format; Matthew and Luke used what he had written along with other sources to compile their own narrative of Jesus' life. John's gospel is different from the other three but still uses the gospel narrative form.

The gospels as we have them are generally believed to have been composed between 67 and 90 AD or so. If Jesus died around the year 30, then the formal gospels were written forty to seventy years later. Each gospel writer was addressing the needs of his particular community. Although Luke and Matthew tell stories of the birth of Jesus, we know only that he is well into adulthood when he leaves his quiet life as a laborer and begins preaching his message of salvation in the little villages around the Sea of Galilee. The Catholic Church recognizes that each narrative gospel offers a slightly different portrait of Jesus but that these four wonderful stories of this unique person, who was human but also divine, contain the message for our salvation.

Now I would remind you, brothers and sisters, of the good news that I proclaimed to you...that Christ died for our sins in accordance with the scriptures, and that he was buried, and that he was raised on the third day in accordance with the scriptures, and that he appeared to Cephas [Peter], then to the twelve. Then he appeared to more than five hundred brothers and sisters at one time, most of whom are still alive, though some have died. 1 CORINTHIANS 15:1, 3–6

- Read through the four gospels. What impressions do you get of Jesus?

The Gospel according to Mark:
Jesus, the Wonder Worker and Suffering Messiah

In the Gospel according to Mark Jesus is constantly involved in a flurry of activity. The gospel writer doesn't spend much time explaining Jesus; after all, even back then actions spoke louder than words. What's interesting here is that Jesus doesn't want too much to be made of the miracles he performed. He's concerned that his friends won't get the heart of his message if they focus on his amazing gifts of healing, driving out demons, and forgiving sins. A few times in this gospel Jesus performs miracles and then says to his apostles not to tell anyone about it. For Mark, the heart of Jesus' message is when he is on the cross. Jesus is abandoned by his friends and followers, except for a group of women who look

> *But so that you may know that the Son of Man has authority on earth to forgive sins—he said to the paralytic—"I say to you, stand up, take your mat and go to your home." And he stood up, and immediately took the mat and went out before all of them; so that they were all amazed and glorified God, saying, "We have never seen anything like this!"*
>
> **MARK 2:10–12**

from afar at Jesus dying in agony. Before he dies, Jesus cries out that he has even been abandoned by God: "My God, my God, why have you forsaken me?" (Mark 15:34). Then when Jesus breathes his last breath, a Roman soldier standing guard proclaims, "Truly this man was God's Son" (Mark 15:39).

That's the gospel for Mark in a nutshell. Jesus' total giving of himself in pain and suffering and abandonment, and finally in death itself, is the clearest possible statement about God's love for us. Certainly his miracles indicate that God is present in Jesus. Clearly his words are the words of eternal life. But it is this ultimate act of self-emptying that is the message. When some women come to anoint his body after the Sabbath, they discover that he is not there; he is raised and no longer resides among the dead.

....

Later [Jesus] appeared to the eleven…And he said to them, "Go into all the world and proclaim the good news to the whole creation…" **MARK 16:14, 15**

• Mark gives us the most human portrayal of Jesus. Read the account of Jesus' arrest and crucifixion, at least Mark 15:33–39. How does this account illustrate Jesus' very human response to what was happening?

The Gospel according to Matthew:
Jesus, Teacher and Messiah

Matthew's gospel is called the first gospel and is always printed first in the Bible because, even though Mark's was written earlier, the early church thought Matthew's was more complete and more usable in liturgies. The gospel includes a genealogy of Jesus, tracing his lineage back to the great Hebrew patriarch Abraham. By doing so, the author of the gospel is identifying Jesus as a direct descendant of great figures of the Old Testament. The gospel also has the bulk of the teachings of Jesus collected into five main sermons, the first of which is the famous "Sermon on the Mount." The author of the gospel has an agenda in mind: Jesus fulfills the promises made to Abraham, David, and the prophets. Jesus is the "new Moses." The heart of the Hebrew Scriptures is found in the first five books, the Torah. The heart of the teachings of Jesus is found in his five sermons. Moses went up onto a mountain to receive the law, including the Ten Commandments. Jesus goes up a mountain to give his commentary on the law. (Six times in the Sermon on the Mount Jesus says, "You have heard it said, but I say to you...") Matthew emphasizes that Jesus is the fulfillment of Jewish expectations, the Messiah or the one anointed to fulfill God's promise to his people. Messiah means "anointed one" or, in Greek, "Christos," from which the English "Christ" is derived. The gospel also emphasizes Jesus as the teacher. He is called "rabbi" or teacher most frequently in this gospel.

> *Now when Jesus came into the district of Caesarea Philippi, he asked his disciples, "Who do people say that the Son of Man is?" And they said, "Some say John the Baptist, but others Elijah, and still others Jeremiah or one of the prophets." He said to them, "But who do you say that I am?" Simon Peter answered, "You are the Messiah, the Son of the Living God."*
>
> **MATTHEW 16:13–16**

....

Do not think that I have come to abolish the law or the prophets; I have come not to abolish but to fulfill. **MATTHEW 5:17**

- Matthew's gospel contains what are sometimes called "hard sayings"—teachings that seem difficult and even extreme. Read Matthew 5:38–48. Which statements in the passage would you say go against conventional perspectives? Are these "hard sayings" for you?
- Read Matthew 25:31–46. How might you apply its message to today?

Modern Model of the Beatitudes—Notre Dame Sister Dorothy Stang (1931-2005)

■ Sister Dorothy Stang spent over half of her life far from her birthplace in Ohio. She dedicated her life to working with impoverished people living in the rainforests of Brazil, even becoming a Brazilian citizen in the process. The major problem she encountered in her work was deforestation. Wealthy loggers and ranchers bought up huge parcels of rainforest with the intention of leveling the majestic trees and wildlife, with no regard for the impact on the forest or on the people living in the area. Sr. Dorothy helped local people organize so that they would have a voice in decisions about the land, and with them she constantly petitioned government representatives to ensure that laws and rights were not overlooked.

All this made Sr. Dorothy very unpopular with loggers and ranchers. First, they tried to despoil her name by claiming she was a rabble rouser interfering with their right to do whatever they wanted with their private property. She then received death threats and knew that her life was in danger. Finally, when two hired gunmen accosted her, she knew that this moment could be her last. A friend who witnessed her killing reported that she took out her Bible and began reading aloud the beatitudes. Sr. Dorothy died clutching the book that inspired her life, the gospels of Jesus Christ.

• From what you have read so far, what story or passage in Scripture would you turn to in times of crisis?

In his 2009 encyclical on justice, Pope Benedict XVI highlighted the connection between concern for the environment and concern for those who are poor:

....

The environment is God's gift to everyone, and in our use of it we have a responsibility towards the poor, towards future generations and towards humanity as a whole.

CARITAS IN VERITATE (CHARITY IN TRUTH), #48.

The Gospel according to Luke:
Jesus, the Compassion of God

Luke's gospel also contains a genealogy. It traces Jesus' origins all the way back to Adam himself! In this gospel Jesus is the "new Adam"—the new human person and a model of creation as God intended. Jesus' message is good news meant for all people, Jews and non-Jews alike. Actually, the gospel writer emphasizes that Jesus and his message are good news in particular for those who are poor and oppressed or simply overlooked in society. Jesus is a model of Christian compassion. Even Jesus' mother, Mary, speaks up for the lowly and the outcasts in this gospel. She praises God because "he has brought down the powerful from their thrones, and lifted up the lowly; he has filled the hungry with good things, and sent the rich away empty" (Luke 1:52–53).

Some of the most endearing of Jesus' parables are found in Luke: the good Samaritan, the prodigal son, and the lost sheep. These parables once again emphasize that Jesus is particularly concerned about those who are lost and hurting in society. The

'Good Shepherd leaves the ninety-nine sheep to search for that one who is lost. Even on the cross Jesus extends words of welcome and forgiveness to a thief crucified beside him. Could the first one to enter God's kingdom be a convicted criminal? That would be perfectly consistent with the message of Luke's gospel.

> *"The Spirit of the Lord is upon me, because he has anointed me*
>
> *to bring good news to the poor.*
>
> *He has sent me to proclaim release to the captives*
>
> *and recovery of sight to the blind,*
>
> *to proclaim the year of the Lord's favor."*
> **LUKE 4:18–19**

Luke's gospel has a second part to it: the Acts of the Apostles. Acts is set apart from the gospel in the Bible, but it is written by the same author and continues the story for us. In the gospel, Jesus is the Spirit-filled Son of God. In Acts, the Spirit resides in the followers of Jesus who carry on his work, the church. Chapter 2 of Acts describes the transformation of the followers of Jesus into a community committed to carrying on his message. We celebrate that event as Pentecost, when the Holy Spirit inspires Peter to proclaim with courage and confidence, "This Jesus God raised up, and of that all of us are witnesses" (Acts 2:32). In Acts, we read about how the gospel message is spread far and wide. Accompanied by wondrous deeds and despite hardships, the fledgling community of Jesus' followers becomes a place of refuge for people in need of hope and support.

....

> *By the tender mercy of our God,*
> *the dawn from on high will break upon us,*
> *to give light to those who sit in darkness*
> *and in the shadow of death,*
> *to guide our feet into the way of peace.* **LUKE 1:78–79**

- Read Luke 1:46–55, Mary's Song of Praise. What themes do you find expressed in it? How are they similar to the themes of Luke's gospel discussed above?
- Read one of the parables in Luke, such as the parable of the great dinner (14:15–24) or the prodigal son (15:11–32). Describe the story from the perspective of each of its characters.

Living the Faith ■ Some parishioners in up-state New York wanted to live the gospel message beyond what they heard on Sunday mornings. They discovered a need in their community for food and clothing among families who are poor. They now gather together Tuesday evenings at the parish center, where they collect and organize food and clothing. On Saturday mornings they return to the center to distribute these goods to the community. Before they begin their work, they read from the gospels and pray over them.

- What expressions of compassionate action are you aware of in your own community?

The Gospel according to John: The Word Made Flesh
Matthew, Mark, and Luke are called the synoptic gospels (meaning "at one glance") because they are so similar. We can place these three gospels side by side and see how they reflect a common tradition. John's gospel is different. It begins not

with the birth of Jesus or even with his public life. Instead, it begins with a reflection on Jesus as Word of God made flesh. Jesus is with God and enters into time to be with us. The gospel writer never lets us forget that Jesus is a divine presence.

> *In the beginning was the Word, and the Word was with God, and the Word was God.... And the Word became flesh and lived among us.*
>
> John 1:1, 14

Even during his trial and execution Jesus is portrayed not so much as suffering or questioning his fate but as completely aware of the sacrifice he has chosen to make.

Scholars call the first half of John's gospel the "book of signs" because it is shaped around seven miracles or "signs" as John calls them. Through these signs John indicates who Jesus is and what he is doing. Jesus begins explanations of these signs with the words, "I am..." When his Jewish audience would hear those words, they would likely think about God's words to Moses from the burning bush: Tell Pharaoh that "I am" (in Hebrew, "YHWH" or "Yahweh") sends you. Jesus uses symbolic images to explain himself: He is the true vine, the bread of life, living water, the light of the world. Sometimes a listener can't quite grasp the meaning of the imagery because it has different levels of meaning. For example, when a Pharisee named Nicodemus is told by Jesus that he must be born again, he tries to imagine how he could re-enter his mother's womb. Nicodemus understands what Jesus says only on a material level and misses Jesus' spiritual meaning.

Scholars call the second half of John's gospel "the book of glory" because it describes Jesus' journey to the cross and resurrection through which he is glorified. In it Jesus speaks at length to his disciples, telling them of the difficulties they will encounter but encouraging them not to lose faith. In the end all will be well, but for now: "This is my commandment, that you love one another as I have loved you" (John 15:12). Jesus provides one model of what his love for them is like when he gets down on his knees and washes their feet. If Christians are to follow Jesus, what are they called upon to do? Share meals together and wash each other's feet!

- Which symbolic image of Jesus in John's gospel most appeals to you? Why?
- Read John chapters 14-15. How would you apply its message to your own life?

Let us pray
We give thanks to you, our Father,
for the life and knowledge you have imparted to us
through Jesus your Son;
glory be yours forever. Amen.
TEACHING OF THE TWELVE APOSTLES (THE DIDACHE)
[LATE FIRST-/EARLY SECOND-CENTURY CHRISTIAN WRITING]

5 JESUS: OUR LIFE AND OUR LIGHT

For God so loved the world that he gave his only Son,
so that everyone who believes in him
may not perish but may have eternal life.

JOHN 3:16

The Meaning of Christ's Birth

At Christmas time, preachers often tell the story of a man who refuses to join his family for midnight Mass. He rejects the very idea of Christmas, that God would be present in a helpless child. He stays home alone, gazing out his picture window into the cold night. He notices some birds nestling by the window, shivering. Some birds even fly into the glass, seeking the light and warmth inside. A number of times he goes outside to try to direct them to where they would be safe. Each time his presence frightens them, and they fly off into the darkness. "Is there nothing I can do to reassure the birds that I am a friend and not a foe?" he wonders. "Is there no way to convince them that I care for them?" He then realizes—"if only I could become one of them, then I could reach them. If only I could become like them…" With that, the man falls to his knees. He finally understands the awesome mystery of Christmas. Jesus is Emmanuel, God-with-us. Jesus is God become human for us. (See Matthew 1:23.)

Those of us who accept Jesus as the human face of God may scoff at this man's narrow-mindedness before his Christmas Eve revelation. But, in fact, isn't his initial position the more reasonable one? God is God; human beings are human beings. Anyone who looks around at the messiness of the human condition couldn't possibly expect the Perfect One to enter into it. In the case of Jesus, that notion becomes even more absurd. Jesus is born poor and powerless, away from home and decent living quarters, if the account in Luke's gospel is accurate. He grows up in out-of-the-way Nazareth, a tiny village in the Galilean hill country. No outsider would go there on purpose, and no one would expect to come across a boy in a Nazareth carpenter shop who is savior of the world! Except for a fateful trip to Jerusalem, Jesus never travels far. His active life of preaching spanned perhaps three years of involvement, mostly with people who live within a day's walk of his home. He dies young, a "troublemaker" condemned to die a painful and publicly humiliating death. His story gives special meaning to the saying "God works in mysterious ways."

- What do you think would be lacking from the world if Jesus had never existed?

Teachings about Jesus

The Incarnation: Breaking the Bonds That Separate Us from God
Christians believe that Jesus is both divine and human. This "both-and" identity of Jesus is what Christians call the mystery of the Incarnation—God is "incarnated," enfleshed, in

and through him. The Incarnation is a mystery in the sense that it is a truth we hold on faith but which evades complete understanding since no explanation can exhaust its meaning. It's easy to slip into looking at Jesus as only human or only divine. For instance, we might imagine the child Jesus knowing full well all that is to happen to him, as if he has no choice in the matter and knows what the future holds. He simply "goes through the motions" of being human. However, the Scriptures tell us that Jesus "emptied himself of his divinity" by becoming one of us, fully and completely human. Strike him and he feels pain. When he hears of the death of a friend, he weeps. He doesn't want to drink from the cup of suffering that awaits him any more than the rest of us would. Christ's divinity is found in and through his humanity, not in spite of it. In Christ Jesus, God is embracing humanity in a most profound and total way. The separation between us humans and God is overcome through the Word made flesh. If Jesus is not fully divine and fully human, our restoration to God would not be complete. Jesus is the shining light of divinity that shares in our humanity. No wonder Catholics celebrate Christmas with such joy and mark the season with gift-giving, despite the crass materialism now often associated with it. The birth of Christ is God's great gift.

> *"Look, the virgin shall conceive and bear a son,*
> *and they shall name him Emmanuel,"*
> *which means,*
> *"God is with us."*
>
> MATTHEW 1:23

....

With the incarnation, the all-powerful
One becomes the little, powerless one. JEAN VANIER

- What are some ways that people could celebrate Christmas that would help bring out its true meaning?

The Paschal Mystery: Suffering, Death, and Resurrection

In most languages the feast of the Resurrection is called by some variation of the Greek "Pasch," referring to the Jewish Passover. ("Easter" refers to a pre-Christian goddess associated with springtime and was applied by English speakers to the feast of the Resurrection.) The Passover/Exodus story tells of a journey from slavery to freedom. The paschal mystery tells of Jesus' journey from suffering and death to new life over the three-day period that Catholics celebrate in a series of rituals during the

> *Thus it is written, that the Messiah is to suffer and to rise from the dead on the third day, and that repentance and forgiveness of sins is to be proclaimed in his name to all nations, beginning from Jerusalem.*
>
> **Luke 24:46–47**

Easter Triduum ("three days") from Holy Thursday evening to Easter Sunday. Each gospel describes the arrest, imprisonment, torture, and horrible death that Jesus underwent. Everyone at the time would have known the gruesome nature of crucifixion and what leads up to it. Our savior is chained to prison walls, stripped and beaten to the point of death, and publicly humiliated as he carries his cross through the crowded streets of Jerusalem. He hangs on the cross suffering excruciating pain in public view, mocked by strangers, and abandoned by all but a handful of his companions. St. Paul admits that Christ's crucifixion is a "stumbling block" for Jews and "foolishness" to Gentiles (1 Corinthians 1:23). It takes some doing to make any sense of such senselessness.

Catholic tradition insists that we must not gloss over the horror of Jesus' crucifixion. All Christianity hinges on one core message: the death of Jesus is not the end of the story. Just as springtime thaw follows winter's chill, so Jesus is raised from the dead. Two sources of evidence are given in the gospels for the resurrection: the empty tomb and the appearances of Jesus to his friends. In one gospel account, the apostles Peter and John rush to the tomb when they hear from some women that it's empty. What could have happened? Did soldiers remove the body? Or perhaps the promises Jesus had made to them actually did come true! The gospels go on to tell stories of Jesus appearing to apostles and friends—enough times that a fledgling group of them speak with certainty that they had indeed encountered him raised from the dead. They don't realize who he is at first. Mary Magdalene, one of his closest friends, mistakes Jesus for a gardener. Who could believe such a wondrous event?

Having Christian faith means to bend down with Mary Magdalene and to peer into the tomb of Jesus, only to find it empty (John 20:11–12). It means to break bread with a stranger and in so doing to discover Christ (Luke 24:30–31). It even means to doubt and be taken by surprise, with the apostle Thomas, that such a wonderful event could have taken place (John 20:25–28). With every encounter, the risen Christ says, "Be not afraid," and "Peace be with you." Resurrection is central to Christian faith. It is not only about Jesus. His experience opened the gates for all of us. The Christian life is one lived in the hope of resurrection.

- How might the symbolism associated with the Easter Triduum speak to your own life?

Easter Triduum

HOLY THURSDAY—The Last Supper, agony in the garden, Jesus' arrest and imprisonment

GOOD FRIDAY—Torture, carrying of the cross, crucifixion and death of Jesus

HOLY SATURDAY—Jesus in the tomb; a time of waiting, anticipation, and hope

EASTER SUNDAY—Jesus raised from the dead; celebration begins with Easter Vigil Saturday night

Teachings of Jesus: The Reign of God

In the synoptic gospels (Matthew, Mark, and Luke), the central theme of Jesus' teaching is the kingdom or reign of God. Matthew uses the term—either as "kingdom of God" or "kingdom of heaven"—over fifty times. Even though it is central to his message, its exact meaning evades us. Part of Jesus' message about the kingdom is that God intends the world to be one way, but that how things are at the time do not measure up. The Roman rulers take the world's riches for themselves; if people followed the rule of God then the goods of the earth would be shared, especially with those most in need. Some Jewish leaders view themselves as the righteous ones, lording it over the ritually unclean who do thankless dirty work while living on the margins of society. God's reign

> *Jesus went throughout Galilee, teaching in their synagogues and proclaiming the good news of the kingdom and curing every disease and every sickness among the people.*
>
> MATTHEW 4:23

has a special place for the downtrodden, the little ones, those who suffer and weep. (See the beatitudes, Matthew 5:3–12 and Luke 6:20–22.) The people who attend the great feast of the kingdom come from "the streets and lanes of the towns…the poor, the crippled, the blind, and the lame" (Luke 14:21).

Jesus knows how elusive the kingdom is. He speaks of it most often in indirect, symbolic ways. It is a treasure hidden in a field, leaven added to bread that causes it to rise, a tiny mustard seed that grows into a big bush, a net gathering fish, and seeds of wheat planted among the weeds. The teachings of Jesus describe ways that people can participate in God's reign. Love your enemies…Do not judge others…Forgive, and you will be forgiven…Give, and you will be given…Use your talents wisely…Feed the hungry…Seek God's help, and you will receive it…Love your neighbor as yourself.

> He said to them, "When you pray, say:
> Father, hallowed be your name.
> Your kingdom come. LUKE 11:2

- What image for God's kingdom is most meaningful for you? Why?
- What image would you use for the kingdom of God? Why?

Jean Vanier—Founder of the L'Arche Community

If Jesus envisioned the reign of God as a place where the "little ones" would have a home, then L'Arche communities are embodiments of that vision. Over one hundred and thirty L'Arche communities in thirty-four countries exist today. They were begun by Jean Vanier, born in Canada in 1928. As a young man Vanier served in the navy and then spent years studying in Paris. After spending time at a French institution for men with disabilities, in 1964 he decided to purchase a house where he and people with various disabilities could live together. Soon others joined him, and he named the house "L'Arche," after Noah's Ark.

Vanier did not envision his communities as places where people without disabilities would help those with disabilities. Rather, he wanted an environment where people would live together, share lives together, and give and receive as each one could. He wanted to create a spirit of family, a home, where the gifts of all people could be shared and appreciated. One story illustrates the spirit of L'Arche. Once while Vanier was chatting with a visitor in his office, a young man with Down syndrome named Jean Claude entered the room. Jean Claude came in smiling and excitedly shook Vanier's hand. Introduced to the visitor, he also shook his hand with delight and laughter. After Jean Claude left, the visitor shook his head and said, "It's so sad… children like that."

When recounting that story, Vanier points out that the man visiting him that day totally missed what should have been obvious, that Jean Claude was not sad at all. In fact, he was very happy; and his joy and enthusiasm for life are contagious if we would allow them to be. Vanier also reminds us that all of us have our strengths and weaknesses, and that at different periods in life they may be more or less pronounced; we are all "differently abled." Perhaps recognizing our needs is a starting point for entering the kingdom of God Jesus speaks of.

Life flowing from one to another is a strange and wonderful thing—and sharing weaknesses and needs calls us together into a common humanity. JEAN VANIER

Jesus and Parables

Jesus is a storyteller. Sometimes we think that he told stories to simplify a message, the way a parent or teacher might tell

> He began to teach them many things in parables...
>
> MARK 4:2

a small child a story. "Don't waste food" and "Share with others" often come through more vividly in stories than in direct statements. However, when we look at the parables of Jesus with fresh eyes, we discover that they don't convey simple messages at all. They are a far cry from the common-sense wisdom of popular proverbs such as "A penny saved is a penny earned," or familiar moral tales such as the one about ants who work all summer, storing up food, while a grasshopper fiddles the summer away. Come winter, the sensible ants enjoy their bounty while the grasshopper, hungry and homeless, shivers away in the cold. The message: Hard work pays off; playing around doesn't.

The parables of Jesus are more likely to confound his listeners than offer "sensible" messages. In one of his most famous parables Jesus tells of a man going from Jerusalem to Jericho. He relates the story in response to the question "who is my neighbor?" Jesus is talking to a gathering of his fellow Jews. Presumably his audience is to identify themselves with the traveler. Thieves fall upon the man, rob him, and leave him beaten by the side of the road. A Jewish priest and a law teacher pass by, but neither one stops to help. A Samaritan passes by, stops to help the man, and then goes way beyond common courtesy in seeing that he is cared for. We are used to putting together "good" and "Samaritan," but that is not the connection those hearing this parable would have made. For centuries most Jews had hated Samaritans and called them "dogs." Samaritans were from a region north of Judea who had split off from Judea, often married non-Jews, and had their own religious practices that Jews saw as a desecration of their own. To Jesus' listeners, then, the story must have been very unsettling. Does Jesus mean that we are to look upon hated foreigners or members of different religions as our neighbors? Are we to expect help from unexpected sources? Are "the good" not so good after all, and "the bad" not so bad? Jesus' listeners must have been startled by what Jesus' story implied.

Other gospel parables seem to confirm that Jesus wants to overturn commonly held perceptions. A landowner has two sons. One takes his inheritance and spends it carelessly. The other son stays home and helps his father. If you were a parent, which son would you prefer? Read about the prodigal son and his brother in Luke 15:11–32 to see the strange message that Jesus draws out of the story. Another gospel lesson shares this spirit of overturning commonly held perceptions. Jesus contrasts a Pharisee, an admired member of Jewish society, with a tax collector, who belongs to a group universally hated by fellow Jews. Surprisingly, the tax collector is the one described as the favored one of God.

Jesus himself, his message and his life story, is a "parable" that also overturns commonly held expectations. He didn't even represent what most Jews expected from their messiah. Why would anyone accept that he was God's son? If anyone in the empire was the "son of God" it was the emperor himself. We have images from just before this time depicting the great Caesar Augustus bearing the title "Son of God." It's not a stretch to think of the great emperor of all the land as God's son. And yet in Mark's gospel when Jesus breathes his last breath a Roman soldier declares, "Truly this man was God's Son!" (Mark 15:39). The soldier should know better than to make such a foolish comment. A true son of God is not supposed to end his days the way Jesus did—on a cross. And common sense tells us that death marks the end of life, not a doorway to life everlasting. Both in his stories and in his very life and death Jesus overturns commonly held assumptions about wealth, power, goodness, and true happiness.

....

I speak in parables, so that "looking they may not perceive, and listening they may not understand." LUKE 8:10

- Read a few of the following parables from Luke's gospel: the rich fool (12:13–21), the barren fig tree (13:6–9), the mustard seed (13:18–19), the great feast (14:16–24), the lost coin (15:8–10). What surprising message does each one contain?
- Did you ever have an experience that turned out to be an unexpected blessing? Tell the story.

Living the Faith ▪ Nowadays, many young parents center much of their lives around their children. This was not always the case. At the time of Jesus, children were held in low status—to be seen and not heard, of secondary concern to the "important" matters of the adult world. Jesus directly overturns this view of children. One day he admonishes some overzealous disciples who want to shield him from some children and proclaims that we all need to become like little children if we are to enter God's kingdom. Today, Catholic parishes offer a variety of programs and services, from schools to special "children's Masses," that reflect Jesus' care and concern for children.

Let the little children come to me, and do not stop them; for it is to such as these that the kingdom of God belongs.

LUKE 18:16

- What are some ways children can be made greater participants in the church?

The Questions of Jesus

A few years ago, Jesuit Father John Dear wrote a book titled *The Questions of Jesus*. In it he points out that in the gospels, Jesus is asked 183 questions. He directly answers only three of them. Jesus is more likely to respond to a question with another question, or a story, or a baffling comment. In all, Jesus himself asks 307 questions in the four gospels.

We tend to see Jesus as the one with the answers. As he went about his ministry, he is actually more often the one with the questions. He leaves us with hard questions, not easy answers. In the foreword to the John Dear book, Father Richard Rohr suggests what Jesus is doing through his constant questioning: "Jesus' questions are to reposition you, make you own your unconscious biases, break you out of your dualistic mind, challenge your image of God or the world, or present new creative possibilities" (*The Questions of Jesus*).

> *When Jesus turned and saw them following, he said to them,* "What are you looking for?"
> JOHN 1:38

Before we can come to understand Jesus, we need to undergo what is often a difficult and painful process of letting go. We tend to have many false assumptions that need to be questioned. Jesus says that the key to happiness is giving ourselves to others when we would much rather receive. Jesus points us toward identifying with the overlooked poor rather than the rich and famous. Jesus' constant questioning opens up a crack in our protective armor and allows light to shine through.

- What questions have created an opening in your consciousness, allowing light to shine through?
- What questions do you sense Jesus is asking you right now?

Let Us Pray
Lord, by your cross and resurrection you have set us free.
You are the savior of the world.

6 CHURCH: ABODE OF THE SPIRIT

Once you were not a people,
but now you are God's people.

1 PETER 2:10

DURING CHRISTIANITY'S FIRST THREE CENTURIES MEMBERS OF THE CHURCH WERE SOMETIMES SUBJECTED TO PERSECUTION. A story is told of a deacon named Lawrence who was accosted by a Roman official. The official had heard rumors that the church possessed great wealth, and he wanted a part of it. Lawrence told him to return in three days, and he would bring the wealth of the church to him. The official thought, three days! Surely this church has great wealth if it takes that long to gather it. Three days later Lawrence showed up with beggars, people who are blind or diseased, and other undesirables from the streets. He told the official that these are the wealth of the church. Enraged, the official had Lawrence burned slowly over an open fire. Whether this incident actually happened or not, it provides an accurate understanding of what the church is called to be. Jesus gathered a ragtag community around him, and the church has been a community of his friends and followers ever since.

The earliest days of the church are chronicled in the New Testament book called "The Acts of the Apostles." In that book Christians refer to themselves as followers of "the Way." With a sense of Jesus' presence among them and inspired by the Spirit, followers of the Way took on a radically new lifestyle. For instance, they "had all things in common; they would sell their possessions and goods and distribute the proceeds to all, as any had need" (Acts 2:44–45). Praising God and breaking bread together were regular practices. Joining this community was a life-transforming experience. Its members obviously caught the eye of people who met them, and generally people liked what they saw so that their number grew steadily. No doubt, followers of the Way were known at least as much for what they did as for what they believed. Today, Catholics realize that they are members of a pilgrim church, people still on the Way.

If you think you have to be perfect to join this group, you need to read some church history. The church is home to saints *and* sinners. In fact, most of us have both our saintly and our sinful moments. Even the pope goes to confession. The church gets its holiness from Christ. One image for the church is "bride of Christ"—that's how closely connected the church is to the Holy One. The church and its members strive to stay united to Jesus and his vision; otherwise it would violate its very reason for being. And as strange as it may seem, Jesus needs the church. The church is the "body of Christ" dedicated to carrying out his mission on earth. Whatever their limitations, Jesus calls all women and men to join him in transforming the world into the way God intended it to be. That's how the church works.

....

It is above all the "poor" to whom Jesus speaks in his preaching and actions. The crowds of the sick and the outcasts who follow him and seek him out find in his words and actions a revelation of the great value of their lives and of how their hope of salvation is well-founded.

POPE JOHN PAUL II, *THE GOSPEL OF LIFE*, #32.

- The American spirit tends to emphasize the individual. The Catholic spirit emphasizes community—not "me and God" but "we and God." Can spiritual life ever be divorced from community?

The Holy Spirit and the Church

Christianity holds what at first appears to be a baffling conception of God as a Holy Trinity—Father, Son, and Holy Spirit. The church always proclaimed that there is one God, a belief Christians share with Jews and Muslims. Early in its history, however, debates arose among Christians in particular about the relationship between Jesus and God. Church leaders realized that, although Jesus and the Father are distinct, they are of one substance. But the Bible, Old and New Testaments, also makes reference to the Spirit of God. How does that notion fit into a true understanding of God? The

> *When the Spirit of truth comes, he will guide you into all the truth.*
>
> **JOHN 16:13**

Bible story that most clearly describes the role of the Spirit is the story of Pentecost told in chapter two of the Acts of the Apostles. The Jewish festival of Pentecost occurs fifty days after Passover and would have brought many people to Jerusalem to celebrate it. Ten days earlier, Jesus had ascended into heaven, so the fol-

lowers of Jesus now had to face the world without his bodily
presence among them. The apostles and a number of women, including Jesus' mother, gathered together in a room in Jerusalem.
Suddenly a burst of wind swept through the room, "tongues of
fire" appeared over their heads, and "all of them were filled with
the Holy Spirit" (Acts 2:1–4). The first effect of the Spirit was that
they could speak in ways that their fellow Jews from other lands
could understand them in their own language. Peter gave a rousing speech to the crowd, which again was understood by people
who spoke different languages. Many of those gathered were "cut
to the heart" by Peter's words, and about three thousand were
baptized that very day.

In the Acts of the Apostles the Pentecost experience shows
the followers of Jesus that Christ is not absent from them. He
remains present in and among them through the Spirit. This
recognition of God as Holy Spirit—an active, vibrant presence
in their midst—completes the Christian understanding of
God. Identifying God as Father emphasizes the creative, all-
embracing power of God. Recognizing Jesus as Son of God
allows us to realize the extent of God's love—in Jesus, divine
power merges with our human frailty. The Holy Spirit extends
the Christ event into our very being. St. Paul reminds us, "Do
you not know that your body is a temple of the Holy Spirit
within you?" (1 Corinthians 6:19). An ancient Celtic prayer
known as "St. Patrick's Breastplate" captures something of this
sense of our union with Christ in the Spirit:

> Christ with me, Christ before me, Christ behind me,
> Christ within me, Christ beneath me, Christ above me,
> Christ at my right, Christ at my left.

....

The Spirit dwells in the Church and in the hearts of the faithful,
as in a temple. VATICAN COUNCIL II,
"DOGMATIC CONSTITUTION ON THE CHURCH," #4.

The Mystery of the Holy Trinity

Christians use words with special theological meanings when describing God. They understand God to be the Holy Trinity, made up of three persons. "Person" is a word with a Latin root that translates the Greek *prosopon*, meaning "mask." In Greek drama, characters wore masks, but not to hide their identity. Masks were merely something characters spoke through. Their real identity was revealed through the words they spoke and the relationship they had with other characters. Similarly, God is made up of three persons who together in relationship share the same essence; they are of one substance. The one divine essence can be distinguished as Father, Son, and Spirit, each with a unique role as Creator, Savior, and Sanctifier. Again, to understand the Trinity it is necessary to realize that words like "person," "essence," and "substance" have particular philosophical and theological meanings when applied to God. If you have already read the Nicene Creed you encountered the term "consubstantial" to describe the relationship between God the Son and God the Father. Christian theology uses the term "person" to indicate that the one God is made up of three persons who are distinct centers of being and activity in loving relationship with one another. The Trinitarian reality of God reveals that God's very nature is love.

- St. Patrick famously used a shamrock to illustrate the Trinity to the Irish people. What are some words and images that might help people understand the mystery of the Holy Trinity—Father, Son, and Holy Spirit?

- What difference does it make to understand God as Father, Son, and Holy Spirit?

Living the Faith ■ A welcome event on college campuses is spring break. After months of hitting the books, writing papers, and taking exams, students have a chance to take it easy for a week. Florida beaches or the warm weather resorts in Mexico or the Caribbean Islands are the destinations of those who can afford it. But many Catholic colleges and universities sponsor programs called "alternative spring break." Leading up to the break, students hold bake sales and raffles to raise money to go someplace where they can actually do some good rather than just get some good time in the sun! Who are these young people heading off to Ecuador to spend a few days learning about victims of leprosy or to Haiti to help repair a damaged school? They are the church.

> *We not only believe in the Church but at the same time we are the Church.*
>
> POPE JOHN PAUL II

Father,
may your Spirit fill the life of each of us,
may your Spirit fill our hearts,
may our community overflow with love,

may prophets arise, may dreams grow,
may mercy spring forth,
may your Spirit flow throughout the world.
THE SANT'EGIDIO BOOK OF PRAYER

Mary, Mother of the Church

Mary, a young girl in a small village, becomes pregnant. She is betrothed but not yet married. Joseph, her betrothed, knows that the child is not his. According to custom, for this transgression she should have been returned to her family in disgrace as damaged goods. But an angel assures Joseph of the divine nature of her being with child. Joseph marries Mary and names the child Yeshua or Jehoshua (in Greek, "Jesus"), which means "God saves." By saying "let it be according to your word," Mary becomes mother of our savior. She is the first one to recognize Jesus as the Christ, the first one to bear him

> *The angel said to her, "Do not be afraid, Mary, for you have found favor with God. And now, you will conceive in your womb and bear a son, and you will name him Jesus…" Then Mary said, "Here am I, the servant of the Lord; let it be with me according to your word."*
>
> LUKE 1:30–31, 38

within herself. As Mother of Christ she also becomes Mother of the church since those who make up the church are the body of Christ. She bears Christ and gives birth to him, as all Christians are called to do. To join the church is to sign up to be a "Christ-bearer." New church members are "Christened" through baptism. At the moment of their baptism till the moment of their death, Christians pray with Mary the words she says in response to her invitation to bear Christ: "Let it be with me according to your word" (Luke 1:38).

When the bishops of Vatican Council II wanted to describe the unique role of Mary in the story of salvation, they decided to tell about her in the document on the church. They recognized Mary as the "first Christian," a type or image of the church itself, and a model for all Christians. The Blessed Mother lived the intimacy with Christ directly that all Christians experience indirectly. The church is united to Christ as Mary is united to him through her motherhood.

Catholicism Has Always Accorded Mary Great Honor

Anyone familiar with Catholicism knows that Mary is accorded great honor throughout its history. Beginning with the Reformation, some Christians questioned this emphasis. Isn't Christianity all about Jesus, not his mother? Catholicism counters that *to honor his mother is to honor Jesus.* A popular subject for medieval painting was the Madonna (the Blessed Mother) and child. Often Mary is pointing at her infant son in case we miss where our focus should be. When Catholics pray the prayer called the "Hail Mary," they acknowledge that Mary is full of grace because "the Lord is with you."

Realizing that the union between Mary and her child remains for all eternity, Catholics humbly pray that Mary will intercede for them—especially at the hour of their death when they meet the Son face to face. They find a basis for this form of intercession in the Bible itself. In John's gospel Jesus performs his first miracle at his mother's bidding. The two of them are at a wedding, and the bridal party runs out of wine. Mary knows her son. She says simply, "They have no wine." Jesus seems to protest what she is implying—you have the power to help them, my son, so do it! Mary tells the stewards, "Do whatever he tells you." Jesus saves the day by transforming some water set aside for washing into fine wine. Even Mary's gentle prodding brings a response from her son, giving rise to a popular traditional saying among Catholics: "To Jesus through Mary."

- How could Catholics model their life after Mary?

....

My soul magnifies the Lord,
and my spirit rejoices in God my Savior.
MARY'S SONG, "THE MAGNIFICAT," LUKE 1:46–47

The Visible Structure of the Church

The most thorough modern theological statement about the nature of the church is the "Dogmatic Constitution on the Church" written and approved by Vatican Council II in 1964. The document calls the church "the People of God." It points out the important role played by the pope and bishops in the universal church, but all members of the church have their role to play: "each part contributes

> *We are not on earth as museum-keepers, but to cultivate a flourishing garden of life and to prepare for a glorious future.*
>
> **BLESSED POPE JOHN XXIII**

its own gifts to the other parts and to the whole church" (# 13). Four "marks" identify the church: one, holy, catholic, and apostolic. The church is one: We could meet up with Catholics from any continent and there would be a basic unity of beliefs and practices. The church is holy: It gets its holiness from Jesus, who as Son of God is all holy. The church is catholic: The word "catholic" means universal. We find Catholic communities across the globe; it is not identified with only one nation or culture. And the church is apostolic: Apostle means "one who is sent" to spread the message and carry on the work. Catholic bishops today trace their origins back to the apostles themselves, and all church members seek to live an apostolic life. These four marks are included in the creed recited by Catholics at Mass.

The Catholic Church is a visible and tangible reality. It is known as the "mystical body of Christ," but like any body it requires the workings of all of its parts. The pope has his role to play, but so does the auto mechanic near your home. If your car breaks down, you might actually consider it more of a blessing to have the mechanic drive by than the pope! Catholics might like the makeup of the church to be different in any number of ways. They might wish that the pastor's homilies were not so boring or that crying babies would not always end up in the pew with them while they're devoutly trying to pray. But the church is not an imaginary body; it is made up of real people, from the pope on down.

- St. Paul gives us an extended meditation on the members of the body of Christ in the first of his two letters to Christians in Corinth, 1 Corinthians 12:12–31. How does this analogy apply to the church today?
- The pope is head of the universal Catholic Church. What value is there to having one identifiable leader of the church?

For just as the body is one and has many members,
and all the members of the body, though many, are one body,
so it is with Christ. **1 CORINTHIANS 12:12**

The Communion of Saints: We're All in This Together

One of the blessings of Catholicism is its veneration of the saints. The New Testament does identify members of the Christian community as "saints," but for some Christians, attention given to the saints comes close to being idolatry—we should venerate Christ and him alone. Saints model what giving oneself over to Christ is like in concrete, specific ways. There is a three-stage process by which the church officially recognizes saints, but that was not always the case. Early saints were the subject of popular devotion without a formal process of "canonization." Even in modern times some Catholics acclaim certain people "saints" before the church makes that official designation. Mother Teresa of Calcutta and Pope John Paul II come to mind.

We can trace something of a history of the saints. For the first three centuries of Christian history, the saintly ideal was the martyr. The word means "witness," and Jesus did commission his disciples to be witnesses throughout the world (Acts 1:8). Before Emperor Constantine made Christianity legal in 313, Christians were potential objects of persecution. Christians who underwent extreme persecution and death were understandably revered by their fellow Christians. The second-century writer Tertullian proclaimed that "the blood of the mar-

> *The really great saints of history don't ask for imitation. Their way was unique and cannot be repeated. But they invite us into their lives and offer a hospitable place for our own search. Some turn us off and make us feel uneasy; others even irritate us, but among the many great spiritual men and women of history we may find a few, or maybe just one or two, who speak the language of our heart.*
>
> HENRI NOUWEN,
> REACHING OUT

tyrs is the seed of the church." Christianity might have died out if people like Stephen, the first martyr, most of the apostles, and a great number of women and men after them had not braved torture and death for the faith. Accounts of martyrdom abounded in the fledgling Christian communities. Two young women martyrs from Carthage, North Africa, were saints Perpetua and Felicity. Both women were newly baptized when they were arrested. Perpetua, a noblewoman, had recently given birth, and Felicity, her servant, was pregnant. Both had reasons to live, and both were offered a way out. Deny Christ and they could live. Neither did, and they ended up in the local arena to be mauled and devoured by lions for the entertainment of their non-Christian neighbors. For whatever reason, the lions steered clear of the two women, and a soldier was dispatched to go out and slit their throats to end their lives. You may hear the names of Perpetua and Felicity during one of the eucharistic prayers used at Mass.

As Christianity became more and more accepted and powerful, some Christians still wanted to give themselves completely to Christ. A famous model for this practice was an Egyptian whom we know as St. Anthony of Egypt. Late in the third century he came across the challenging statement from Jesus, "If you wish to be perfect, go, sell your possessions, and give the money to the poor" (Matthew 19:21). Anthony took the passage to heart. He headed out into the desert away from society and from all creature comforts, living his days in a cave. Over time other people wanted to imitate him and came to him for guidance. He helped them set up a way of living alone but communally—what we today would call a monastery. Anthony himself went farther into the desert, living this time in an abandoned fort. By the Middle Ages, living in monasteries was a popular choice for many Christians drawn to the spiritual life. Both women and men lived this way, and monasteries can still be found throughout the Catholic world.

One of the most popular saints is the Italian St. Francis of Assisi, born Giovanni di Bernardone. He lived at a time when there were new opportunities for members of the middle class to make money. Francis's father was a wealthy cloth merchant who loved the French styles and hence nicknamed his son Francesco—we might say "Frenchy." After being injured in a battle—physically and perhaps psychologically as well—Francis turned his life around. He renounced the flamboyant lifestyle he was accustomed to and looked for ways to give himself to Christ. He decided to embrace "Lady Poverty," returning to his father even the clothes he was wearing and putting on a beggar's robe. Francis didn't want to live in a monastery; it seemed too comfortable to him. Instead of living apart from society, he decided to live within society and to be totally dependent on the charity of others. Thus, Francis and, in Spain, St. Dominic began what are known as "mendicant" religious orders. Mendicant means "beggar." Franciscans and Dominicans remain two of the most influential religious orders in the church today.

The sixteenth century in Europe, time of the Reformation, marked another change in how Christians chose to lead a spiritual life. It was a time of nation building for Europeans and the discovery of new lands far from their shores. People recognized that many needs cried out to be met: education, care for the poor, health care, and missionary work among non-Christians. St. Ignatius of Loyola, another soldier who turned his life around after being injured in battle, began the Society of Jesus (Jesuits), known for their high-quality schools and dedication to missionary work. St. Angela de Merici gathered together a group of women to educate girls that grew into the Ursuline order of sisters. In France, Sts. Vincent de Paul and Louise de Marillac started programs to help poor people, the homeless, and prisoners. They essentially began what we today would call social services or social work. Another Frenchman, St. John Baptist de la Salle, formed a group of men to educate poor boys. St. Camillus de Lellis dedicated his life to caring for the sick and is recognized as patron saint of nurses. Communities of men or women who joined together for particular types of work are known as "religious orders." If you see "S.J." after a man's name, that means that he belongs to the Society of Jesus. "O.F.M." means "Order of Friars Minor"—one of a number of groups who look to St. Francis of Assisi as their founder. "R.S.M." refers to a community of religious women known as Mercy Sisters, or the Religious Sisters of Mercy. There are many such religious groups of men and women who usually take vows of poverty, chastity, and obedience and live in some form of community life in addition to engaging in a particular type of ministry. Some orders are ancient—Benedictines and Augustinians, for instance. Others have only recently begun, such as Mother Teresa of Calcutta's Sisters of Charity.

Who are the models of sainthood today? One answer is: time will tell. Traditional expressions of holiness are still available to Catholics. Mother Teresa of Calcutta's religious order of sisters follows fairly closely a traditional pattern of religious life that is thriving worldwide. Young men still enter seminaries to be ordained priests, and religious women still carry on God's work throughout the world. However, people are experimenting with new forms of spiritual life as well. The Catholic Worker Movement in the United States is a small but significant contributor to Catholic life. A number of communities and organizations offer ways for lay people to express their spirituality—the Community of Sant'Egidio being one example. Begun after Vatican Council II, it was made up of young Italian Catholics who wanted to dedicate their lives inspired by Jesus and by Francis of Assisi. Married couples also are seeking to make their vocation to family life more overtly spiritual. And Catholicism has a special day, November first, known as "All Saints Day." It's a day when all of us can celebrate our universal call to saintliness, however we choose to live it out.

- Who are models of saintliness that exist today?
- What kinds of saints do we need more of today?

....

The unique role of laypeople is to sanctify the world...the gospel is most urgently needed in the building up of the faith in our families, at work, and in our neighborhoods, and in the transformation of society.
CHARLES J. CHAPUT, O.F.M. CAP., *LIVING THE CATHOLIC FAITH*

Patron Saints

Name a profession, a disease, or a country, and Catholics probably have a patron saint for it. In an earlier era a "patron" was someone with greater power who could be called upon for help. For Catholics, patron saints can inspire us and serve as intercessors before God. St. Michael the Archangel is patron saint of police, St. Florian the patron saint of fire fighters. St. Nicholas, of course, is patron saint of children, among other things. A story is told of the good bishop Nicholas anonymously tossing a bag of coins to hungry children as he passed by. There's even a patron saint for television—St. Clare of Assisi, who was bedridden one day but saw the Mass on her bedroom wall as if she were actually there. A few years ago the Vatican solicited suggestions for a patron saint of the Internet. It settled on a seventh-century Spanish bishop, St. Isidore of Seville, to be the Internet's patron saint. Why? Near the end of his life this great scholar wrote a book titled "Etymologies" in which he laid out a survey of the knowledge of his day in a clear and comprehensive style. His overview of knowledge, with the scope of the sources he used in creating it, became a mainstay of learning into the fifteen century. In other words, he was a storehouse of knowledge—just as the Internet is today.

- What do you see as a benefit of the Catholic practice of naming patron saints?
- Your patron saint is the saint whose name you share. Since patron saints intercede and serve as models for us, your patron saint is also one whose style of spirituality speaks to you. Who are your patron saints?

Story of a Saint? ▪ Jacques Fesch (French, 1930-1957) was not your ideal Catholic. He was quite the playboy as a youth, fathering a child by a woman whom he later married, only to father a son by another woman soon afterwards. His father was a banker and so had some money. Jacques was not interested in working and instead asked his father for money to buy a boat. His father refused, and Jacques attempted to rob a money changer. A police officer came upon Jacques at the crime scene.

Jacques shot and killed the policeman—a father who had young children. Jacques was arrested minutes later. During his trial and his first year in prison, Jacques remained unrepentant of the wrong he had done and the pain he had caused. Then one night he had a conversion. He felt Jesus present in his cell as if he were actually there. He began to express remorse for his crime and for the suffering he had caused his family, wife, and children. He spent another three years in prison and kept a journal that describes deep levels of spirituality. He was guillotined in 1957 at the age of 27.

In 1993 the cardinal archbishop of Paris proposed that Jacques Fesch be considered for beginning steps toward official recognition of sainthood. The archbishop believed that Fesch's story would help prisoners who struggled with coming to repentance and redemption. In 2009 Pope Benedict XVI met with Fesch's sister to hear about her brother's conversion and to receive a copy of the journal he had kept in prison. Some people, however, are angry that Fesch is even being considered for sainthood. After all, he killed an innocent police officer in cold blood. Should someone who committed such a heinous crime be seen as a saint? He wouldn't be the first prisoner faced with the death penalty who "found God." On the other hand, there is the constant refrain of Jesus in the gospels, "your sins are forgiven," and Jesus' acceptance of the conversion of the criminal crucified beside him.

- Find out more about Jacques Fesch on the Internet.
  Would you vote for his canonization?

Let Us Pray
Lord, make me an instrument of your peace:
where there is hatred, let me sow love;
where there is injury, pardon;
where there is doubt, faith;
where there is despair, hope;
where there is darkness, light;
where there is sadness, joy.
O Divine Master,
grant that I may not so much seek to be consoled as to console,
to be understood as to understand,
to be loved as to love.
For it is in giving that we receive,
it is in pardoning that we are pardoned,
and it is in dying that we are born to eternal life. Amen.
Prayer attributed to St. Francis of Assisi

7 A SACRAMENTAL WORLDVIEW: RECOGNIZING GOD'S PRESENCE

The people who walked in darkness have seen a great light;
those who lived in a land of deep darkness—
on them light has shined.

ISAIAH 9:2

HAVE YOU EVER TRAVELED TO IRELAND? If you have, you might have noticed something that Americans aren't accustomed to. During certain times of the year, twilight can begin before 7:00 PM and continue past 10:00 PM. Thus, the Irish live a sizeable portion of their lives in this in-between time. Twilight is a time of mystery—not quite light and not quite darkness, a time of crossing over between two worlds. Perhaps the prolonged twilight nurtures the Irish talent for storytelling. It also helps shape Irish spirituality.

Celtic spirituality talks about "thin places"—places where the borderline between heaven and earth is not so thick, and times when the veil separating us from God is lifted ever so much. It's like a sacred twilight zone. To go to a thin place is to step onto holy ground and to enter sacred time. Time spent in a thin place refreshes our spirit and renews our faith that we are indeed connected to something greater than we normally are aware of. To experience a thin place we need to pay attention and to listen. We could be in the midst of one and not even notice. Birth and death are thin places, or should be recognized as such. Surely God is present whenever someone enters or leaves this life. A couple committing themselves in marriage is also a thin place.

Sacraments are like thin places. They are ceremonies that are rich in meaning and by which God's grace comes to us. Each sacrament celebrates the saving mystery of Christ in its own way. Sacraments celebrate births and deaths, marriages and entering adulthood. The beginning of the eucharistic liturgy invites us to enter into a thin place: "Brothers and sisters, let us acknowledge our sins, and so prepare ourselves to celebrate the sacred mysteries." In other words, set aside all that separates us from God and his grace. We are entering into a sacred mystery now where we can encounter Christ. Every sacrament is a window through which the light of Christ can shine into our darkness. More accurately, every sacrament is a doorway through which Christ comes into our lives.

- Describe the three holiest places you know. What makes them holy for you?
- What was your experience in these holy places? How did it change your life?

....

The mystery will be as intrusive in us
as we by listening allow.

John McNamee, "Prayer Walk"

Developing a Sacramental Vision

Sacraments reflect a Catholic worldview. One way to express this worldview is to say, "Do you see the people and the world around you? God is like that." In other words, God communicates to us *through* the stuff of the earth, not divorced from it. To the eye alive, matter is not a distraction from God but a revelation of God. God reaches out to us in sensuous, material ways—a water bath, dabs of oil on our body, bread shared and eaten, rings exchanged. Words accompany the rituals, but it's the material objects and actions that speak more forcefully. The Catholic view is that all reality rightly understood is sacramental. God permeates the world and our very souls.

> *Ever since the creation of the world his eternal power and divine nature, invisible though they are, have been understood and seen through the things he has made.*
>
> ROMANS 1:20

The sacramental perspective flows from the notion of God as Holy Trinity. God is not distant but is close at hand. God the Father wants to communicate to us so much that he sent his Son. Father and Son desire so much to be with us everywhere and always that they sent the Spirit. That's why we can look around us and within us and see God there. The world is sacramental, filled with thin places, if we but look with the eyes of faith.

How can we develop this sacramental vision? For one thing, we need to appreciate how symbols and rituals work. "Symbolic thinking" recognizes that there are multiple layers of meaning in what we do and in what we see around us. A kiss means more than what the physical act entails. That's why when Judas betrays Jesus with a kiss it is particularly offensive. A kiss means love or at least care for another, a gesture of peace. Early Christians applied this symbolic consciousness to Scripture itself. They realized that every biblical story contains depths of meaning not readiliy apparent.

If we are to appreciate sacraments, we need to apply this same spirit of probing Scripture for deeper meaning to the things of nature and the gestures we perform. For instance, the ritual for ordaining a priest involves a bishop laying hands on the newly ordained person's head. Of itself, that gesture doesn't seem to be particularly powerful or meaningful. Why is this action different in the context of ordination? A bishop is ordained when two bishops before him place their hands on his head. Those bishops were ordained in similar fashion, in a continuous chain going back to the apostles. Jesus healed and blessed people with laying on of hands—power going out from him to them. Even before the time of Jesus, laying on of hands marked the transfer of power and blessing from one person to another. Psalm 139, verse 5, describes God laying hands on the psalmist's head. The New Testament also has many references to blessing, healing, and transferring of the Spirit through laying on of hands.

Sacraments make use of objects and actions that have layers of meaning. Water, for instance, means both life and death. Imagine coming upon a pool of water in the desert [life] and then being swept away by a wave in the ocean [death]. The church didn't invent the symbols and rituals in its sacraments, as if they entailed a secret password or handshake. Typically, the actions and objects involved in the sacraments have meaning by their very nature. At least on their basic level, bread and wine don't need to be explained, nor does placing a ring on another's finger. The act of people gathering together for liturgy doesn't need explaining either. Joining others in prayer and worship has a meaning by its very nature. In the sacraments, natural, familiar symbols and rituals are transformed into sacred signs of God's presence through Christ.

- What are some ways that you might further develop a sacramental view of the world and other people?
- Describe some symbols and rituals that are meaningful for you.
- What religious symbols speak most powerfully to you?

....

A Christian life is a sacramental life, it is not a life lived only in the mind, only in the soul; through the bodies of men and women Christ toils and endures and rejoices and loves and dies.

Caryll Houselander

Jesus, the Primary Sacrament

Catholics are used to thinking of sacraments as referring to "the seven sacraments" which we'll look at in the next chapter. They can miss the broader context in which the seven have their meaning. One reason Catholics have a history of separating the seven sacraments from the rest of their spiritual life is that many Protestants early on rejected elements of the theology behind them. A traditional Catholic definition of sacrament is that it is an outward sign instituted by Christ to give grace. Protestants emphasized inner conversion rather than external rituals, which rules out oral confession of sins to a priest

> *What was visible in Christ has now passed over into the sacraments of the Church.*
>
> **Pope St. Leo the Great**

and, for some, infant baptism. If a sacrament is an outward (visible, tangible) sign of God's presence, then the primary sacrament is not a what at all but a who—Jesus. God's grace finds its perfect expression in Jesus; that's the mystery of the Incarnation. In turn, Christ acts through the sacraments. The sacraments themselves are meaningless apart from Jesus. The traditional definition of a sacrament includes the phrase "instituted by Christ." Jesus was a healer; there are sacraments of healing. Jesus transformed people into his body, the church; there are sacraments of initiation. Jesus served others; there are sacraments of vocation through which people can serve their communities.

Catholic sacramental theology addresses the question, how do we meet the living God? For Christians, the answer is, first and foremost, Jesus. Catholics don't separate Jesus from creation. The universe and all that it contains manifest the glory of God. We can't appreciate the Catholic sacramental vision unless we have a sense of reverence and awe for the goods of creation. That's why the following questions represent a false dichotomy: "Why do I have to go to church? Can't I worship God on the beach or walking in the woods?" From a sacramental perspective, of course we can discover God all around us. If we don't find Christ in the woods or on the beach, then we have separated him from the very world he entered into to transform. The seven sacraments, however, are graced moments that flow from the mission of the church given by Christ. They link us directly to his saving act of dying and rising to new life. They are for each one of us personally but also situate Catholics in the community of Jesus. There are many ways to encounter Christ. The church has identified seven that guarantee that God's presence (grace) will be there and be effective for salvation.

- How do you reconcile Jesus as sacrament with the sacramental nature of creation?
- What connections do you see between Jesus as primary sacrament with the seven sacraments?

....

The world is charged with the grandeur of God.
GERARD MANLEY HOPKINS

The Church as Sacrament

Jesus is the sacrament of God; the church is the sacrament of Jesus. The people who make up the church are an outward sign (visible, tangible) of Christ present to us. Getting away from the hustle and bustle of busy lives can be refreshing and rejuvenating. Hopefully, such experiences increase our capacity to appreciate how we are Christ to one another at work, at school, in church, even in shopping malls.

Thomas Merton, our most famous American monk, entered a Trappist monastery in the late forties and lived there until his death in the nineteen sixties. Trappists live a life of silence, regular prayer, and communal work apart from contact with the "outside world." Merton was also a prolific writer

> *...the church, in Christ, is in the nature of sacrament— a sign and instrument, that is, of communion with God and of unity among all men.*
>
> **VATICAN COUNCIL II, "DOGMATIC CONSTITUTION ON THE CHURCH," #1.**

who captured people's imagination with his honest and vivid descriptions of his spiritual struggles and insights. He tells of an incident when he went into Louisville, Kentucky, for a doctor's appointment. Standing on a street corner, he suddenly had an intense experience that he was connected to all the people who passed by. He realized that part of his motivation for entering the monastery was to get away from the world. He knew on this day that this was an impossible and in fact an un-Christian task. We are all connected to one another. His time in the monastery actually intensified his realization of the oneness we share. From his solitary hermitage Merton kept up with events in the world and produced thoughtful and influential writings on peace, social justice, other religions, and other pressing issues of his day. In a sense, the sacraments are like our time in a monastery. They are not "holy times" with no connection to the rest of our lives. Sacraments remind us of the holiness of all time. If the church is sacrament, then it follows that its members are sacramental. What an awesome responsibility people take on when they join the church! For Catholics this means that we accept that others come to know Christ through us; we are channels of grace and the peace of Christ. Our neighbors may never meet the pope, or a bishop, or even a priest, but they meet us. We are called upon to be sacrament to them. Other people are also sacrament to us, outward signs giving grace.

- What are some ways the church and its members are sacraments?
- What are some ways you might deepen your appreciation for other people as sacramental?

Faith in Action ■ Miguel enjoyed singing, so when he was approached by some choir mem-

bers he joined them in the parish choir. Since
his wife, Katie, usually accompanied him to Mass
when he sang, she decided to get involved as
well. At first, she volunteered to be a lector. Then
her pastor asked if she would like to be a eucharistic minister. Once she overcame her initial
nervousness, Katie couldn't believe how much
she enjoyed giving Communion to her fellow
parishioners. Never had she felt so connected to
Christ and Christ's presence in the motley array
of people with whom she shared Eucharist. She
beheld them and the sacred bread with a reverence that she had never experienced before. At
first, friends and neighbors, who made a point
of getting in her line, smiled and nodded at her.
Neighborhood children beamed at the opportunity to receive Communion from the mother of
one of their friends. On occasion, Katie would
take Communion to members of the parish who
couldn't attend Mass. These brief visits became
one of the highlights of her week. She had
thought that distributing Communion would be
a way for her to give to the church. She soon came
to realize that she was the one receiving.

• Ask someone who is involved in a church ministry
  to describe what the experience is like.

*Only the Holy Spirit is capable of building the church with
such badly hewn stones as ourselves!* CARLO CARRETTO

Sacramentals—The Richness of Catholic Spirituality

Besides the official sacraments, Catholics have available to them a vast array of prayers, devotions, sacred actions and gestures, and holy objects that can serve as a blessing to them. Sacred objects are called "sacramentals"—a term that connects them to the sacraments but also distinguishes them from the sacraments. Sacramentals offer opportunities for Catholics to engage in devotional practices apart from the sacraments themselves. Sacramentals include crucifixes and medals, blessed rosary beads, candles, palms blessed on Palm Sunday, and ashes on Ash Wednesday. In every case a sacramental is not mere ornament. Rather, it provides an opportunity to excite the mind to the contemplation of the divine.

> *There is scarcely any proper use of material things which cannot thus be directed toward the sanctification of men and the praise of God.*
>
> **Vatican Council II, "The Constitution on the Divine Liturgy," #61**

The simple act of entering a church can involve a series of sacramentals—blessing oneself with holy water, lighting a candle, and saying a prayer before a statue, for instance. Medals and what are popularly known as "holy cards"—bearing an image of Jesus, Mary, or a saint with a prayer on the back and small enough to fit into a wallet—are sacramentals. Different cultural groups have special prayers and devotions that may include sacramentals. If you travel to Mexico City you might notice young men on their knees making their way to the basilica that houses the image of Our Lady of Guadalupe. Or an Italian church might sponsor a procession in which a statue of the Blessed Mother is carried through the neighborhood. Some Catholic parishes hold novenas, nine days of special prayers and liturgies, related to a particular saint or concern. Stations of the Cross during Lent and crowning a statue of Mary in May are regular practices in most American parishes.

Sacraments and sacramentals display sensitivity to our makeup as bodily creatures. We communicate more nonverbally than through the words we use. Every study done on communication supports this assertion. Good health-care workers know the importance of nonverbals, as do parents and childcare workers. The Council of Trent, convened soon after the Reformation, explained the reasoning behind the Catholic use of sacraments and sacramentals: "Without external helps he (the human person) cannot easily be raised to the meditation of divine things" (Session XXII, chapter 5). Jesus is not just a spoken word; he is a material, bodily word—Word made flesh. God continues to speak to us in material, bodily ways through sacraments and sacramentals.

- Name and describe some sacramentals with which you are familiar.
- Which sacramentals speak most powerfully to you?
- Do you or would you have a holy object such as a crucifix, statue of the Blessed Mother, or rosary beads displayed prominently in your home? Why or why not?

....

God made the world for the delight of human beings—if only we could see His goodness everywhere. His concern for us. His awareness of our needs: the phone call we've waited for, the ride we are offered, the letter in the mail, just the little things.

BLESSED MOTHER TERESA OF CALCUTTA

***Blessed Pier Giorgio Frassati—Man of the
Eight Beatitudes*** ▪ The Catholic Church
depends on the enthusiasm and vitality of young
people, and it continues to be blessed with young
women and men who bring joy and spontaneity
to the work of Christ. Pope John Paul II especially
appreciated young people, and he initiated "World
Youth Day" to celebrate them and to celebrate with
them. The old pope sitting intently watching young
people performing break dancing is one of the
classic images from his papacy. No doubt Pope John
Paul was particularly pleased to pronounce Pier
Giorgio Frassati "blessed" in 1990.

Pier Giorgio only lived to the age of twenty-four,
from 1901 to 1925. His father ran a newspaper in
Turin, Italy, and from an early age Pier Giorgio dem-
onstrated the zest for living and generosity of spirit
that marked his entire short life. Once, when he was
a child, a man and his son showed up at his family's
home begging for food. Pier Giorgio noticed that
the boy had no shoes, so he spontaneously took off
his own and gave them to him. In college he was
an average student academically. Perhaps that was
partially because he gave so much of his time and
energy to other things. He was acutely sensitive to
the plight of the poor people whom he met during
this troublesome time in Italy between two world
wars. Asked why he gave so much of his time to
helping those who were poor, he said simply that,

"Christ comes to me each morning in the Eucharist. I return the favor by visiting him each night in the poor." He saw much wisdom in the modern Catholic social teaching put forth especially in Pope Leo XIII's 1891 encyclical on labor. He constantly gave whatever he had—even the coat off his back—to those in need, but he also realized that more needed to be done. He said, "Charity is not enough: we need social reform." He was active in many organizations seeking such change.

Pier Giorgio enjoyed friends and nature as much as caring for needy people; everything for him was cause for joy. He was an avid mountain climber, completing forty-nine serious climbs. He remarked, "With every passing day, I fall madly in love with the mountains." Even while making his way up a mountain he paid attention to the needs of others. Friends of his noted that he was known to say, "Let's take a break; my feet hurt," not because he was tired or sore but because he knew other climbers were and he didn't want them to be embarrassed about slowing down the group. Unfortunately, Pier Giorgio became seriously ill—probably because of the close contact he had with so many sick people. Even while dying, he thought not of himself but of the people he was helping out. He painstakingly scribbled out instructions about who needed help that he knew. At the ceremony when he was declared "blessed," a step toward sainthood, Pope John Paul II proudly named Pier Giorgio "man of the eight beatitudes." Today he is an inspiration to young Catholics throughout the world.

Let Us Pray

Praise the Lord from the earth... Mountains and all hills, fruit trees and all cedars! Wild animals and all cattle, creeping things and flying birds!...
Young men and women alike,
old and young together!...
Let everything that breathes praise the Lord!
Amen.

PSALM 148:7, 9-10, 12; PSALM 150:6

8 THE SEVEN SACRAMENTS: FULLNESS OF GRACE

God chose to take created reality and raise it to the level
of a sacrament so that through it the very love of God could
touch us. Bishop Donald W. Wuerl, *The Catholic Way*

THERE ARE SEVEN DAYS OF THE WEEK, SEVEN DAYS OF CREATION, AND SEVEN SACRAMENTS. Catholic tradition lists seven gifts of the Holy Spirit and seven deadly sins. Jesus told his disciples to forgive others "seventy times seven" times. The use of this number is no accident. Like other dimensions of Scripture and spirituality, numbers have deeper meanings. Since it combines four (the four corners of the earth) and three (the heavens), seven represents the fullness of heaven and earth.

The seven sacraments provide the fullness of grace. Grace is God's presence in our life. We may not even be aware of how God is present through the sacraments. That's okay. God takes the initiative. We receive and participate in God's work, as do a lot of people through whom God touches us. Sacraments are not isolated events; they are community rituals. Each one is connected to the larger church community. Even that most private of sacraments, reconciliation, has a communal dimension. And each sacrament is part of a larger, ongoing process of conversion. While each sacrament celebrates a particular transformation, conversion itself is a process that takes a lifetime. God is present in our lives in different ways during different times in our life. Sacraments celebrate and bring about the grace of those events. We can divide the seven sacraments into the three sacraments of initiation, the two sacraments of healing, and the sacraments of service.

SACRAMENTS OF INITIATION

....

*Sacraments are the most visible sign of our participation
in and identification with the Church.*
BISHOP DONALD W. WUERL, *THE CATHOLIC WAY*

We know from the Pentecost story that from the church's beginning water baptism was used to initiate new members into the Christian community. In the story, the account of a large-group baptism is followed by a description of the Christians sharing a communal meal. The Catholic Church today continues this process in the sacraments of initiation, beginning with baptism and culminating in full participation in the Eucharist. For adults, this movement from baptism, through confirmation, to Eucharist happens in one ceremony—usually at the Easter vigil. When infants are baptized, their first Communion is delayed until around the age of seven and confirmation often even later. In Eastern Catholic and Eastern Orthodox churches, infants receive baptism, confirmation, and Communion (in the form of consecrated wine) in one ceremony. Whether or not the three sacraments of initiation are experienced at the same time or separately, they are organically connected. We can look at each one separately as long as we realize that together they celebrate the conversion experience Jesus offers his friends and are part of initiation into his family, the church.

Baptism: Our Welcome into a Community of Life

When we arrive at a friend's house for dinner after a long journey, we're probably invited to wash up first to refresh and renew ourselves. Baptism represents coming home after being a stranger in a strange land. In the Genesis story, Adam came into existence in a garden paradise. He, and by extension all humanity, went astray, becoming estranged from God. Jesus, the "new Adam," restores humanity to its rightful home, reunited with God. The new life received at baptism is restoration of the original blessing bestowed on humanity by God. The central ritual action of the sacrament of baptism is immersion in a bath of water or at least pouring water onto a person's head. Even when the person being baptized is a newborn, the pouring of water or immersion is a moment in a process. Much has taken place leading up to this event; and the event itself represents a faith commitment on the part of the person, family and friends, and the local Christian community, as well as the universal church itself. That commitment on everyone's part doesn't end when the water dries.

> *Do you not know that all of us who have been baptized into Christ Jesus were baptized into his death? Therefore we have been buried with him by baptism into death, so that, just as Christ was raised from the dead by the glory of the Father, so we too might walk in newness of life.*
>
> **ROMANS 6:3–4**

At first, baptism was as simple as going down to a nearby stream and being dunked in the water while the words "I baptize you in the name of the Father and of the Son and of the Holy Spirit" were said. These are the words that Jesus, at the end of Matthew's gospel, told his disciples to say (28:19). Soon baptism became more formal. Preparation for baptism was a long process, perhaps as much as a few years. During this preparation time candidates known as "catechumens" had a sponsor who guided them in their journey through the initiation process. The last, intense period of preparation was the lenten season of forty days of prayer and fasting before Easter when baptisms typically took place. The rite of initiation, consisting of baptism, confirmation, and participation in the Eucharist for the first time, took place at the Easter vigil. In addition to water, the baptismal ceremony used oil, candles, and a new garment to signify the great transformation taking place. If you attend the vigil services on the evening before Easter Sunday you will notice that they are filled with references to water and light, two symbols central to baptism. You might also witness the exciting event of new members being initiated into the church.

For a long time baptism involved total immersion in a pool of water, three steps down and three steps up to represent the Holy Trinity. Candidates stripped naked; they were baptized, doused with oil, and then clothed in a new white garment. They were now ready to participate in the Eucharist. We can only imagine what it must have been like when people seeking to join the Christian community had to wait years before they could join in the eucharistic celebration and partake of Communion. The sense of entering into new life must have been intense and palpable. Today the Rite of Christian

Initiation of Adults (RCIA) is used for the initiation of adults into the Catholic community. It is modeled after the initiation rite practiced in the early church. In time most adults in Christian lands had already been baptized, so practically the only ones still needing baptism were infants. Even today we think of baptism as a celebration primarily for infants. In fact, until the late 1960s the words of the baptism ritual were addressed to infants as if they were adults. That's one reason why godparents were so important; they spoke for the child. After Vatican Council II two distinct ceremonies for initiation into the church were established. There is now a ritual specifically for infants and another for adults. Initiation of adults is really not one rite but a process that culminates in baptism, confirmation, and First Eucharist, and continues with additional assistance and instruction even after initiation.

By God's gift, through water and the Holy Spirit, we are reborn to everlasting life. In his goodness, may he continue to pour out his blessings upon these sons and daughters of his. May he make them always, wherever they may be, faithful members of his holy people. RITE OF BAPTISM

Baptism and Original Sin

We may think of sin as referring either to actions that people do or to actions they should do but don't. Catholicism talks about another kind of sinfulness. Building on the Adam and Eve story in the Bible, Catholicism refers to humanity's alienation from God and longing for wholeness as our shared "fallen state." Adam and Eve fell from grace; all human beings long for a restoration of grace or life with God. Original Sin refers to a state of being, a deprivation. In that sense it is the reverse side of

the Good News of Jesus. None of us is immune from this capacity to misuse our freedom. Even the great St. Paul admits: "For
I do not do the good I want, but the evil I do not want is what
I do. Now if I do what I do not want, it is no longer I that do
it, but sin that dwells within me" (Romans 7:19–20). God gave
us human beings the great gift of freedom, and too often we've
made a mess of it. We are needy creatures who long for salvation, and as limited creatures we can't get there on our own.
Original Sin describes a weakness in our nature, a wound that
we carry within us that needs healing, a deprivation that longs
to be set right, and an inclination or tendency to oppose God's
will with our own misguided choices. The good news is that
the troubles and any misdirected inclinations that come with
being human pale in comparison with the promise of Christ,
who faced them head-on and conquered them. Sin, original or
otherwise, is no match for Christ. That's the dynamic of baptism and Original Sin. Baptism celebrates the victory of Christ
over the seemingly invincible tyranny of evil, and that victory
is manifest whenever people show care and compassion for one
another as Jesus called upon everyone to do.

- Read the section on Original Sin in the *Catechism of
  the Catholic Church* (#396–412). What do you think
  Catholic teaching about Original Sin says about our
  human condition and the role of Christ in it?

Confirmation: Strengthened by the Holy Spirit
In the western church, as Christian communities grew beyond
major cities, bishops permitted priests to represent them in
celebrating baptisms. However, bishops reserved the right to

"confirm" the initiation at a later date. Over time this led to a separate sacrament focused on the reception of the Holy Spirit. Of course, in one sense baptism already confers the blessing of the Spirit. St. Paul makes this point in 1 Corinthians 12:13: "For in the one Spirit we were all baptized into one body—Jews and Greeks, slaves or free."

Confirmation came to be associated with taking one's place as an adult member of the church. In other words, being Christian involves doing more than the minimum. Confirmation marks the time when members of the community commit themselves to being instruments of the Holy Spirit in doing God's work. The words of the ceremony speak of becoming "witnesses" and "active members of the church." The rite of the sacrament mentions seven specific gifts of the Holy Spirit that can assist Christians in carrying out this task: "Give them the spirit of wisdom and understanding, the spirit of right judgment and courage, the spirit of knowledge and reverence. Fill them with the spirit of wonder and awe in your presence."

Confirmation incorporates two rituals used in other sacraments as well: laying on of hands and anointing with oil. The laying on of hands represents calling down the Holy Spirit. Anointing with oil represents the dual significance of strengthening, such as a soldier preparing for battle, and being sealed with the gift of the Holy Spirit. Again, every sacrament invokes the power of the Holy Spirit; but here the Spirit is called upon to be the helper and guide of those being confirmed. As they seek to live the Christian life, they'll need all the help they can get.

- With confirmation, Catholics commit themselves to witness for the faith. What are some ways that could be done today?

- Which gift or gifts of the Holy Spirit would you most want to cultivate in yourself? Why?

Living the Faith ■ Young Catholics who are candidates for confirmation perform some service and pursue greater knowledge of the faith. They might also be interviewed by a priest or parish minister to explain why they want to receive the sacrament. For most of these young people, this is a time for them to commit themselves to the church they have been part of since infancy, and they welcome this opportunity to give back. Confirmation is a gateway into a maturing, other-centered Catholic faith.

- What would you recommend incorporating into a program accompanying confirmation to bring out its meaning most effectively?

Eucharist: Remembering Christ's Sacrifice

Every eucharistic celebration is a remembrance of the Last Supper, the meal Jesus shared with his friends the night before he died. During the meal Jesus did something that apparently was common in the Passover meal of the time—he blessed and broke bread, then passed it around for all to eat; he blessed wine and passed it around for all to drink. Jesus added two dimensions to the ritual. For one thing, he said, "This is my body; this is my blood" over the bread and wine. Second, he said, "Do this in memory of me." Every celebration of the

Eucharist looks back to the Last Supper, lest we forget the great gift that Jesus gave us that night. The word "eucharist" means thanksgiving. The Greek word for remembrance—anamnesis—is the opposite of amnesia—"forgetting." Imagine if Christians forgot the great sacrifice of Jesus who gave his body and blood on the cross! In the Eucharist, remembering is re-membering, re-embodying. Every eucharistic celebration is rightly called the holy sacrifice of the Mass. Giving thanks through breaking and shar-

> *By the mystery of this water and wine*
>
> *may we come to share in the divinity of Christ,*
>
> *who humbled himself to share in our humanity.*
>
> **FROM THE PREPARATION OF THE GIFTS AT MASS**

ing the bread of communion and drinking from the cup makes the sacrifice that Jesus made on the cross a present reality. Jesus gave his life for us on the cross; he gives his body and blood to us in the bread and wine and the celebration of the Eucharist. In the words of the Catechism, "To receive communion is to receive Christ himself who has offered himself for us" (#1382).

What do Catholics understand is going on at the Eucharist? For one thing they recognize that Christ is present in multiple ways with every eucharistic liturgy. Christ is present in the gathering of the people; after all, they're the body of Christ. Christ is present in the proclamation of the gospel; that's why people respectfully stand during it. Christ is present in the person of the presider, who leads the body of Christ in worship. And Christ is present in the consecrated bread and wine. Catholics differ from some other Christian groups in their understanding of Christ's presence in the bread and wine. The term "transubstantiation" has been used since the Middle Ages to describe the Catholic understanding of the transformation that happens to the bread and wine at Mass. Medieval philosophy observed that all persons and things are made up of appearances and substance. During the liturgy the substance (what something is in itself) of the bread and wine changes but the appearances remain the same. In other words, if we were to place a Communion wafer under a microscope before and after its consecration, its physical makeup would be exactly the same. However, it would be *substantially* different.

Participation in the Eucharist, then, is the centerpiece of the Christian life for Catholics. It connects us to the past—Jesus and the apostles at the Last Supper. It is a present reality, communion with Christ and the Christian community. It is also a foretaste of the future "heavenly banquet" when we will be united fully with Christ.

> *We must find the Lord not only in the table of the Eucharist, but in the table of the world around us. If we do not see Jesus in the table of the world, we will really not find Jesus in the table of the Eucharist; if we do indeed find Jesus in the table of the Eucharist, we should leave the Eucharistic celebration with eyes of faith that allows us to find Jesus throughout the table of the world.*
> **KENAN B. OSBORNE, OFM**

The Eucharist and Social Justice

A major area of concern for Catholics is the connection between the Eucharist and living the Christian life. Every sacrament is meant to be lived; it's not just the ritual itself. Since the Eucharist provides spiritual nourishment, a natural question is: How does the sacrament inspire us to act when so many people lack even the physical nourishment they need? The Eucharist and social justice go hand in hand. Inspired by the Eucharist, people who have bread look for ways to make "a place at the table" for those who lack bread.

....

> *The Lord gives himself to us in bodily form. That is why we*
> *must likewise respond to him bodily. That means above all that*
> *the Eucharist must reach out beyond the limits of the Church*
> *itself in the manifold forms of service to men and to the world.*
> **JOSEPH CARDINAL RATZINGER,** *GOD IS NEAR*

- Like all the sacraments, the Eucharist is meant to influence how we live when we step out of the doors of the church. What are some ways that people could "live the Eucharist"?

The Two Sections of the Liturgy—Light and Nourishment
The Mass has two parts to it—the Liturgy of the Word and the Liturgy of the Eucharist. The first part centers on Scripture and concludes with a homily on two or three Scripture readings, and then the proclamation of the creed and the community's prayers for the church and world. The second part celebrates a sacred meal and centers on the breaking of the bread and the sharing of the cup. In this way, with each eucharistic celebration we receive light (wisdom from Scripture) and nourishment (from the sacred meal).

SACRAMENTS OF HEALING

Reconciliation: Return to the Father and the Church
If baptism is the sacrament of "welcome," then reconciliation is the sacrament of "welcome back." The gospel story that serves as an inspiration for this sacrament is the prodigal son parable

found in Luke 15. In the story, a son leaves home and leads a
wasteful life spending the inheritance his father had given him.

> *Return to me with
> all your heart…
> Return to the Lord,
> your God,*
>
> *for he is gracious
> and merciful,*
>
> *slow to anger,
> and abounding
> in steadfast love.*
>
> Joel 2:12–13

When he reaches rock bottom, he
decides to chance going home and
asking if his father would take him
in as a servant. Little did he know or
expect that every day his father had
been going out to a hillside hoping
for his wayward son's return. Seeing
his son in the distance, the father
rushes out with open arms to greet
him. He displays no hint of anger or
"I told you so," only unconditional rejoicing that his son has
returned.

The early church soon discovered that there were "backslid-
ers" who did not live up to the ideals of the Christian community but who wanted to remain in or return to it. Over time a
formal process for reconciliation with the community became
standard. It was used exclusively for the most serious of offens-
es, behaviors that clearly indicated that someone was outside
the good graces of the community. In many ways it resembled
a re-initiation. Penitents were publicly identifiable. Only a
bishop could oversee the ceremony that would readmit them
as members in good standing, and only after they had spent
a long time demonstrating sorrow for their wrongdoing. The
opportunity to rejoin the community was available only once.

Then, around the sixth century a new practice began that
shaped what came to be known as "confession." Before they
became Christian, the Irish people were great warriors—men
and women alike. When they became Christian, many of these
Irish warriors gave themselves equally intensely to living their

Christian faith. Many became monks or nuns and lived very austere lives. One practice they used to help them in their spiritual discipline was to report their sins and failings to the head of the monastery, who would suggest a penance to do to make amends and overcome the problem. People outside monasteries began to want the same opportunity to confess their sins, to be directed in performing appropriate penances, and to receive assurance from a holy monk that their sins were forgiven. Irish monks introduced this practice to the rest of Europe, giving people a personal experience of God's forgiveness. Since priests—men—heard confessions, screens were provided for women so that neither priest confessors nor women confessing would be embarrassed or hesitant to speak of any manner of sin.

At times this practice emphasized judgment and even condemnation more than forgiveness and welcome home. Changes introduced after Vatican Council II sought to balance out the experience of the sacrament. While the sacrament maintains its personal character through private confession of sins, current practice emphasizes that there is always a communal dimension to it as well. Sometimes parishes hold communal penance services accompanied by opportunities for private confession. The sacrament is also more closely linked to Scripture, in particular to the message of forgiveness that Jesus repeats over and over again. Even the name of the sacrament underwent a change. Use of the word "reconciliation" emphasizes the "welcome back" message more than the terms "confession" or even "penance" do. Each of these terms actually refers to a step in the process of accepting God's forgiveness and being restored to grace.

In the sacrament, confession of sins is not a counseling session. Some priests may be good counselors, but that's not the purpose of confession. In confession we acknowledge our wrongdoing and our desire to overcome anything on our part that separates us from God. As a sacrament it is a time to worship the all-merciful God and to thank God for mercy and forgiveness. The priest in confession represents Christ and the church; the sacrament is an outward sign of Christ's message, "Be not afraid. Your sins are forgiven."

- How might the experience of being forgiven by God affect a person's life?
- How would you answer those who say that "I confess my sins directly to God. I don't need to tell them to a priest"?

....

One of the greatest challenges of the spiritual life is to receive God's forgiveness. There is something in us humans that keeps us clinging to our sins and prevents us from letting God erase our past and offer us a completely new beginning...Receiving forgiveness requires a total willingness to let God be God and do all the healing, restoring, and renewing. **Henri J. M. Nouwen**

Anointing of the Sick: Care for Those in Need

Even a casual reading of the gospels reveals that Jesus was a healer. Compassion for those who are sick was a hallmark of his character. According to the Acts of the Apostles, both St. Peter and St. Paul were also blessed with an ability to heal. The letter of St. James indicates that praying over the sick and anointing them with oil were practiced from the beginning of the Christian community. Today the sacrament is not limited to anointing. The rite refers to "anointing and pastoral care of the sick." The church has rites for combining anointing with the sacrament of reconciliation or with receiving Communion and even with confirmation. Some parishes hold communal healing services and include prayers for the sick during Sunday liturgy. In other words, the church takes seriously that care for the sick is an essential component of carrying on the work of Jesus.

> *Are any among you sick? They should call for the elders of the church and have them pray over them, anointing them with oil in the name of the Lord.*
>
> **JAMES 5:14**

Before Vatican Council II the sacrament was called "Extreme Unction," referring to anointing with blessed oils, or "the Last Rites." These designations suggested that the focus of the sacrament was preparation for death rather than healing. Since Vatican II the sacrament reflects more Jesus' ministry of healing. Prayer and anointing by a priest offer great comfort to the dying. For Catholics the sacrament of healing helps them die "healed." That is, it places their dying in the context of Christ's own death and resurrection, which they celebrated in their baptism and in every Mass they attended.

- How can prayer, the sacraments, anointing, the message of Jesus, and other elements of the church's ministry of healing help those who are sick?

SACRAMENTS AT THE SERVICE OF COMMUNION

Marriage: A Covenant of Love

The concept that the Israelites used to describe their relationship with their God was "covenant." It meant contract or agreement, but applied to their relationship with God, it also included a sense of intimacy and mutuality. (See Isaiah 54:5, Jeremiah 31:32, and Hosea 2:19.) In a sense the Israelites were "married" to their God, just as later Christians referred to the church as the bride of Christ. Catholicism recognizes marriage as a similar covenant. It too involves love, mutual give and take, creativity, and commitment. For the Roman Catholic Church marriage has a distinction among the sacraments in that the official ministers are the couple themselves. The priest is the official witness of the church.

> *Keep them faithful in marriage and let them be living examples of Christian life.*
>
> *Give them the strength which comes from the gospel*
>
> *so that they may be witnesses of Christ to others.*
> **FROM THE RITE OF MARRIAGE**

People don't need the church to tell them that marriage is a special event. People were getting married well before the church became involved in overseeing the ceremony, and now couples around the world get married every day without the benefit of the church. Why marry in a church service? Although love and lifelong commitment are holy apart from the church, Catholics connect all that is important in their lives to Christ. The church designates marriage to be a sacrament because it is clearly a pivotal way that people experience God in their lives. Marriage never involves two people alone. Marriage in the church reminds everyone that more people are involved in making this commitment work than the couple themselves. They have been deeply blessed to be where they are—in love and ready to commit themselves to each other for life and to the possibility of offspring. Their commitment to each other is sacred. Catholics humbly recognize that this gift they have received comes from God. A Catholic wedding places all that has led up to the ceremony and all that will come of it in the context of God's ongoing love for us in Christ Jesus, and our participation in that love. Vatican Council II called the family the "domestic church." Parents sitting down with their children to go over homework, husbands and wives doing what they can to make life better for each other, and both sacrificing for their children—this is essential, sacramental work of the church that receives little recognition or fanfare. And marriage provides a "home base" from which families can be involved in the broader community as well.

What Are Annulments?

Catholicism views marriage as a lifelong commitment, mirroring the eternal relationship that Christ has with the church. However, divorce has become commonplace in recent years. The church grants annulments. An annulment is not a divorce. Rather, it is a determination that there was an impediment from before the marriage was ever entered into that makes the marriage agreement null and void in the eyes of the church. The marriage is legal in civil law, but it was not a valid sacrament. Since the late sixties, the church began to apply a much broader understanding of what constitutes entering into a marriage freely. The emotional or psychological maturity of one of the partners may have been so undeveloped that he or she could not have been capable of making a true commitment to married life. The annulment process is subject to the official rules of the church called Canon Law and therefore involves a process similar to a civil court case for and against granting an annulment. Work on each case requires a number of people, such as canon lawyers and secretaries, to handle

the paperwork—similar to a civil court hearing. For this reason couples seeking an annulment are usually charged a fee
to cover these expenses. Dioceses also have available funds to
help with the cost for those who can't afford them. The church
makes very clear that granting an annulment in no way affects
the legitimacy of the children born of the couple.

- What does the concept "covenant" add to an
  understanding of marriage?
- What examples of family as "domestic church" have
  you seen?

St. Gianna Beretta Molla: Woman of Principle
Lists of saints contain many names
of priests and nuns, people who heroically lived
a celibate life for Christ, and even those who
shunned life's pleasures. Even though marriage is
a sacrament, few saints are recognized for being
married, raising a family, and making a go of it "in
the world." In 2004 Pope John Paul II broke that
mold when he canonized Gianna Beretta Molla. St.
Gianna lived during the middle part of the twen-
tieth century, from 1922 to 1962. Born in Brazil,
she married and lived in Italy where she and her
husband had four children. She also was a medical doctor—a pediatrician and surgeon. So not
only was St. Gianna a wife and mother, she was a
professional woman working outside the home as
well—seeking the same kind of balance between

work and home that so many married people strive to achieve today. She considered both her work as a pediatrician and her marriage to be her "mission" in life. She dedicated herself wholeheartedly to creating a Christian family and engaged in Catholic Action programs to help in particular young people. Gianna also enjoyed the niceties of life such as fine clothes, travel, and opera. (After all, she lived in Italy!) She also played piano and painted, and enjoyed sports such as tennis, skiing, and mountain climbing.

Gianna faced a crisis late in 1961 when she was two months pregnant with her fourth child. Doctors discovered a fibrous tumor on her uterus and suggested that the best course of action would be to terminate the pregnancy. Gianna's response was: "If you must decide between me and the child, do not hesitate: Choose the child—I insist on it. Save the baby." She elected to have an alternative procedure performed that did not harm her baby, and she recovered sufficiently to give birth to a daughter in 1962. Although the surgery performed earlier was successful, complications set in after she gave birth. She died within months.

Saints are recognized for their holiness, but it is also significant how they lived out their holiness. St. Gianna exemplifies a life lived by many modern Catholics who seek to balance the many challenges that come with married life. She didn't shun the finer things of life; art, beauty, and culture properly understood are gifts from God. She lived her holiness both through her career and through her dedication to her family, especially to her unborn child. And when faced with a crisis, she acted on her principles and her faith. Although she died at the young age of thirty-nine, she provides a model for the saintliness that can be found through the sacrament of marriage.

Holy Orders: Imaging the Priesthood of Christ

The second sacrament of service to the community is holy orders. For Catholics, Jesus is actually the one high priest, and all baptized members of the church share in that priesthood. However, three specific types of priestly service are singled out in the sacrament of holy orders. The root meaning of these three orders tells us something of their role: overseers (bishops), elders (presbyters or priests), and assistants (deacons). Early in Christian history overseers led their communities in prayer and worship and organized the services required for those in need. They were assisted in their work by deacons. At the same time elders shared in governance of their communities, in presiding at liturgical services, and in caring for the needs of community members. This structure of leadership and service continues in the Catholic Church in the form of the three holy orders of bishop, priest, and deacon.

> *It is true that God had made his entire people a royal priesthood in Christ.*
>
> *But our High Priest, Jesus Christ, also chose some of his followers*
>
> *to carry out publicly in the church a priestly ministry in his name.*
>
> FROM *RITE OF ORDINATION TO THE PRIESTHOOD*

Today parish priests spend much of their time presiding at daily Mass and at Sunday liturgies. They are also called upon to preside at marriage and funeral services and offer people their support. Parish priests usually are on call all the time in case someone in the parish becomes sick and requests the sacrament of the sick. Deacons or priests can preside over baptisms and weddings; only priests can hear confessions and preside at Mass. In addition to caring for the spiritual needs of their parishioners, priests are also administrators in their parishes.

In addition to priests who serve a particular geographical location known as a diocese, priests can also be members of one of the many religious communities found in the church. Communities of priests, brothers (non-ordained men), and sisters or nuns commit themselves to particular kinds of work, such as education or health care and usually take vows of poverty, chastity, and obedience.

For Catholics priests stand out not only for what they do but for what they represent. Priesthood is a sacrament, meaning that priests are one more "outward sign" of God's care for us. Priests are visible reminders of Jesus' sacrificial love. They are men who have been called by God and the church to dedicate their lives to serving their communities. All Catholics are part of a priesthood of service and all Catholics participate in prayer and liturgy, but priests take on special roles in prayer and service. For that reason, regardless of his flaws or shortcomings, for Catholics a priest represents Christ. In a sense, priesthood is so important to Catholics because the sacraments are essential to their life with God. Priests are sacramental embodiments of the priesthood of Jesus and the shared priesthood of all Catholics.

St. John Vianney—A Priesthood of Service ▪

When Pope Benedict XVI decided to dedicate 2009
to 2010 as "the year for priests," he chose the feast
of St. John Vianney to begin it. Why this particular
saint? Often the person who must work hardest to
achieve the goal prizes it the most.

Jean Marie Baptiste Vianney was born into a
small farming community in France in 1786. To
read his life is to read about a man flawed in many
ways. He entered the seminary but struggled with
his studies; he especially found Latin difficult to
master. He held some views about sin and the devil
that by today's standards seem strange. Because of
his poor academic achievement, he was expelled
from the seminary. Vianney still wanted to become
a priest, and his local parish priest worked with him
on his Latin enough that the bishop accepted him
for ordination at the age of thirty and then sent him
to a small village named Ars in an out-of-the-way
part of the diocese. The village church had a mere
twenty rows of seats, plenty to accommodate the
local population, and the people in the area had a
reputation for being rough.

Vianney soon won over his parishioners. His
homilies were simple but clear and to the point. For
instance, regarding prayer, he said, "The soul should
move toward prayer the way a fish should move
toward water; they are both a purely natural state."
He especially became popular as a confessor. People
reported that he seemed to know the condition of

their soul before they even spoke to him in the con-
fessional. At times he spent up to eighteen hours a
day hearing confessions. Soon his reputation spread,
and people came from all around to stand in line
for hours to go to confession to the humble "Curé
of Ars." So many people came that near the end of
his life France built a train line to Ars just to accommodate them. The French people revered him so
much that he received the nation's Legion of Honor
award. Vianney also built an orphanage for girls
across from the church to provide shelter and education for young girls during the time following the
Napoleonic wars. Surprisingly, this man who barely
made it to ordination and served his priesthood in
a seemingly God-forsaken remote village is the only
parish priest ever canonized a saint.

- How would you explain the sacramental nature of
  priesthood to non-Catholics?
- What do you think are the greatest challenges and
  rewards of being a deacon, priest, or bishop?

Let us pray
Good and gracious God, we give you thanks
for the many ways you communicate your love to us.
May your gift of the sacraments
   continue to keep us close to you
through Christ our Lord. Amen.

9 OUR MORAL LIFE: LIVING IN RESPONSE TO JESUS

Beloved,
let us love one another,
because love is from God...

1 JOHN 4:7

A Story of Two Brothers

TWO BROTHERS OWNED ADJACENT FARMS. One brother was single, and the other was married with four children. One season, because of a drought, the grain harvest was going to be poor. The unmarried brother thought, "My brother needs grain more than I do; he has more mouths to feed." The married brother thought, "My brother needs grain more than I do; he has no one else to take care of him." That night, in secret, each brother loaded up a cart with grain to take to the other brother's barn. They met each other halfway and immediately realized what the other was doing. They hugged each other, and on that spot they built an altar to worship God.

This folk tale from the Jewish tradition illustrates an insight that the people of Israel discovered early in their history—namely, *our relationship with God cannot be separated from care for other people.* The Ten Commandments that come out of this tradition list rules of conduct for the proper worship of God and for how to treat our neighbor. The Jewish spirit of generosity and care for others did not die with Christianity. If anything, Christianity expanded it. Jesus said, not only are you to love your sisters and brothers but you are to love your enemies as well (Matthew 5:44). Don't just take care of your kinfolk; look to the needs even of strangers who are struggling.

A Morality of Response

The starting point of the Christian life is not what we do or even what we are supposed to do but rather *what God does for us*. The underlying dynamic of Christian morality is this: Jesus' dying on the cross reveals the extent of God's love for us; now what

> *I give you a new commandment, that you love one another. Just as I have loved you, you also should love one another.*
> **JOHN 13:34**

are we going to do about it? In other words, Christian morality represents a response to love; out of our experience of that love we naturally seek to love as Jesus loved us. If we think of morality as a set of rules disconnected from this source, then we miss the heart of Christian morality. Rules alone can't capture teachings of Jesus such as: "if anyone wants to sue you and take your coat, give your cloak as well; and if anyone forces you to go one mile, go also the second mile" (Matthew 5:40–41). That command goes beyond the requirements of laws. We go the extra mile not because the law requires it but because love inspires it.

Christian history gives us many examples of people who responded to God's love for them by actively loving others. Dorothy Day [1897-1980], co-founder of the Catholic Worker Movement in the United States, spent her early adult years involved in radical groups advocating social change. One day she left a socialist cell meeting where a few people were discussing the plight of the poor. As she walked through a poor neighborhood in New York City, she passed a Catholic church. Poor people began streaming out of it. She realized that most people who are poor weren't attending socialist cell meetings; they were going to church. She began to look into Catholic teaching, especially Catholic social teaching, and realized that it provided much guidance for how we should live our lives if we are truly concerned about improving society and helping those who are poor.

St. Peter Claver [1581-1654] left his native Spain to work in the Spanish colonies of Latin America. When he arrived in Cartagena, Colombia, he was appalled at the conditions of the African slaves being brought and sold there. He realized that he could not eliminate the slave trade, but he determined to help these people shackled in chains, physically and psychologically worn down, and frightened at what awaited them in this strange land. As soon as they arrived in port, Claver took food to the slaves and cared for their needs as best he could. He stood up for slaves when he saw them mistreated. He welcomed Africans in his church, even though it cost him the support of slave owners and other Spanish settlers. Over three hundred thousand Africans chose to be baptized by this man who showed them compassion in the midst of their hardships.

Dorothy Day and Peter Claver are just two examples of Catholics who saw injustice and harm being done to people. In response to Jesus' gift of love they walked with him down the difficult path of love. Like many others, they are exemplars of what living the Christian moral life means.

- What difference does it make if we approach morality as response to God's love rather than as obligation?
- What circumstances in our world today cry out for a Christian moral response?
- What opportunities to live the Christian moral life present themselves to you?

....

If I speak in the tongues of mortals and of angels, but do not have love, I am a noisy gong or a clanging cymbal. And if I have prophetic powers and understand all mysteries and all knowledge, and if I have all faith, so as to remove mountains, but do not have love, I am nothing. 1 CORINTHIANS 13:1–2

Compassion: Hallmark of the Christian Moral Life

Living the Christian moral life means working with Jesus to transform the world into the best it can be. The Catholic perspective is not a "Christ against culture" one. Rather, Christ calls us to become engaged with the world around us for good. Human beings should use all of their creative forces to serve those most in need. The world is in God's hands, but God works through our hands. All areas of human endeavor should come into play when addressing problems. Scientists have their role to play, as do politicians, business leaders, construction workers, entertainers, and those in the media. All of us have multiple ways

> *Catholics are meant to be a reflection of Christ's presence in the world, preaching the gospel, spreading the kingdom of God, building up the community of the faithful, and then reaching out to those who are most in need.*
>
> CHARLES J. CHAPUT, O.F.M. CAP., *LIVING THE CATHOLIC FAITH*

to contribute to building up God's kingdom and thus to live the moral life.

....

You are the salt of the earth. You are the light of the world.

Matthew 5:13, 14

- Who are some of the people you are responsible for?
- What are some ways that you live out the Christian call to live responsibly?

Three Foundations of Catholic Morality: Scripture, Natural Law, and Tradition

Catholicism has a rich tradition of addressing moral problems. From the earliest letters of St. Paul down to the latest papal encyclicals, the church has been a strong and vocal advocate for morality and justice. What do Catholic leaders look to when making pronouncements about what's right and wrong? Catholicism looks to three sources upon which it bases its moral teachings. When you hear about or read about where the church stands on various moral issues, look for references to these foundations.

Scripture—God's Word as Moral Guidance

The primary source of Catholic moral teaching is, of course, Scripture—in particular the life and teachings of Jesus. In the gospels Jesus addresses moral issues most often in stories and in short, one-line statements. His very life models what the moral life should be. However, Jesus is not a systematic moral teacher. He doesn't address every moral problem or explore every application of his teachings such as his two great commandments to love God and your neighbor as yourself. He advocates following the "golden rule" that other traditions also express: "do to others as you would have them do to you" (Matthew 7:12). He is silent on many of the issues that we face today, such as genetic engineering, climate change, and private property rights versus the common good. Catholic moral teaching, therefore, combines Scripture with two other sources of moral truth.

....

You shall love the Lord your God with all your heart, and with all your soul, and with all your strength, and with all your mind; and your neighbor as yourself. LUKE 10:27

Natural Law—Using Reason to Determine Moral Principles

As the Christian community moved away from its Jewish moorings and into the Greco-Roman world, it relied more and more on the modes of thought prevalent in that world. By the time of Christ the great Greek philosophers had been addressing morality for centuries. The approach to morality formulated by Aristotle and others is known as Natural Law. The philosophers of old relied on one instrument as the gateway to truth, including moral truth—reason. With the help of reason, human beings can better understand the morality of their actions. What does reason investigate? It studies nature—specifically, in the case of morality, human nature. Certain behaviors flow from what it means to be human; other behaviors do not. People don't create morality; rather, they discover it within the natural order itself. Human nature is universally shared. Individual people differ, and each culture differs somewhat from all others; but underlying all humanity is this universally shared nature. Since human nature is common among all people, reason can identify universal moral norms ("laws") based on that nature. The traditional term for this approach to addressing moral issues is "natural law." "Law" here means rules or norms. According to natural law, moral behavior is human behavior. Thus, moral rules should be based on using reason to determine what is the human thing to do.

What might this process of moral reasoning look like in concrete terms? Here's an overly simplified application of it. Reason tells us that part of what it means to be human is the capacity to communicate, so communication is part of human nature. Truth-telling flows naturally from this dimension of our humanity; lying distorts communication and thus what it means to be human. A general moral norm is "Tell the truth," or stated negatively, "Don't lie." Moral norms derive from the very structure of our nature—our capacity to communicate, our sexuality, our need for nourishment and other basic necessities, our right to life, our dignity as human beings, and so forth. You might hear someone say that certain actions are wrong "by their very nature." Another way to state this idea is to say that an action is "intrinsically wrong" or "objectively disordered"—that is, it violates the natural order. That's the language of natural law; and, coupled with Scripture, church documents on ethical issues continue to resonate with this basis for moral reasoning.

Tradition—Wisdom of the Ages
Catholicism has always had great respect for reason. Scripture and reason—Jerusalem and Athens—go hand in hand. A third foundation in the pursuit of moral truth is Tradition. Tradition means that which is handed down. Spelled with a capital "T,"

it refers to the great collection of teachings produced within the church over the past two thousand years. Jesus told his apostles to teach in his name. Church leaders have taken and continue to take that responsibility seriously. A Latin word for the church's teaching authority today is *magisterium*, meaning "teacher." Catholics look to church leaders for guidance in understanding morality. For example, for hundreds of years now popes have issued special letters called "encyclicals" on a variety of topics; these often contain teaching on matters from justice and peace to care for the environment. Bishops, either individually or as a group, write pastoral letters. Since the late 1980s when it was written, the *Catechism of the Catholic Church* provides a summary of moral teachings based on the Ten Commandments. Thus, Catholic moral teaching is unique in that it is based on the interplay of Scripture, reason, and Tradition—think symbolically "Jerusalem, Athens, and Rome."

Applying Morality to Our Lives

Morality doesn't happen in a book or in a gathering of people discussing issues in isolation from the real world. Morality happens in our day-to-day encounters with other people and in the specific situations in which we find ourselves. Along with objective moral principles, it's important to remember that there is also a subjective dimension to morality. The Catholic tradition emphasizes that we don't exist merely as separate individuals. We exist as persons in communion with other persons and in communion with God. Recognizing the personal dimension of our life, especially our moral life, doesn't take away from the importance of Scripture, reason, and Tradition. Rather, these foundations for morality need to be applied to our here-and-now reality. Morality happens in Amazon rain-forests, in African countries threatened by expanding deserts, in the boardrooms of multinational corporations, at the border between the U.S. and Mexico, as well as in our homes, hospitals, and movie theatres. Every facet of our coexistence has moral implications.

- What contribution can each of the foundations of Catholic morality make to your moral decision making?
- How does each foundation build on and add to what the others provide?
- What acts do you believe are always and everywhere wrong, intrinsically immoral?
- Is there room for exceptions to any universal moral principles?

....

So rather than asking, "What would Jesus do?" we ought to ask, "How can we be as faithful in our obedience to God and in giving loving service to others in our day as Jesus did in his?"
RICHARD GULA, S.S., *MORAL DISCERNMENT*

Conscience—Making Moral Judgments

According to the Catechism, conscience refers to a judgment of reason that we make about moral decisions (#1778). If we read through the Catechism's discussion of conscience (#1776-1794), we can identify three dimensions to conscientious moral decision making. To begin with, conscience requires a basic awareness that there is right and wrong and that to be human means to be drawn to doing the good. To the degree that someone lacks such a basic awareness, that person can't be said to possess conscience. Many factors can diminish someone's ability to make judgments based on reason. Second, it refers to taking steps to inform, educate, and develop our capacity to know right from wrong. Here's where, for Catholics, Scripture, reason, and Tradition come into play. When it comes to conscientious decision making, "ignorance is not bliss." Finally, conscience means judgment, moral decision making itself. Thus, popular understandings of conscience

> *Man's dignity therefore requires him to act out of conscious and free choice, as moved and drawn in a personal way from within, and not by blind impulses in himself or by mere external constraint.*
>
> VATICAN COUNCIL II, "THE CHURCH IN THE MODERN WORLD," #17.

are inadequate. For some, conscience is that "little voice inside us"—Walt Disney's Jiminy Cricket. For others conscience comes into play after we do something; specifically, we suffer from a "guilty conscience" when we've done something we regret. Or we might simply think of conscience as the sum total of moral messages we have received during our upbringing—our "internalized parent." None of these ways of understanding conscience is adequate to describe the reasoned decision making that the church says moral decision making requires.

Especially in light of Vatican Council II, Catholic teaching is that people are called upon to act in accordance with a thoughtful and informed conscience—by definition, conscientious decision making is thoughtful decision making. The Council recognized that conscience is necessary for the dignity of the human person. Most bishops at the Council knew the affront to human dignity that was the totalitarian mindset found in fascism, Nazism, and communism. They had heard the excuses Nazi leaders made following World War II: "We are not responsible. We only did what we were told." The bishops advocated freedom and personal responsibility as hallmarks of human dignity and thus called upon people to develop and use their conscience.

St. Thomas More served as Chancellor of England during the turbulent reign of King Henry VIII. You may already know about King Henry and his many wives. It was the early sixteenth century, the period of the Reformation. King Henry was married to a Spanish noblewoman named Catherine of Aragon, who also happened to be the aunt of the Holy Roman Emperor at the time. King Henry desperately wanted a son; he believed that the sovereignty of England depended on it. Without a male heir England would appear vulnerable, or a nobleman from the continent could make a claim for the English crown, and England's independence would end. Henry lost faith that his wife Catherine would bear him a son, so he petitioned the pope to have his marriage to her annulled so that he could marry his mistress, Anne Boleyn. The pope refused to grant Henry the annulment. Henry then declared himself head of the church in England and granted himself the annulment. He also required that all of his leading subjects sign an oath recognizing him as head of the English church.

That's when Thomas More came face to face with the dictates of his conscience. Thomas believed that the pope was head of the universal church, including in England. This belief placed him in a precarious position. Most of the other leading men of England, including cardinals and bishops, signed the Oath of Supremacy. Thomas enjoyed life and his freedom; he had a wife and children. He was also known as a man of wisdom and integrity. If he didn't sign the oath, it called into question its legitimacy. Thomas realized that his life was in danger. Perhaps the right thing to do in the circumstances would have been to sign the oath even though he disagreed with it. No doubt other prominent men of the time did. He was imprisoned but still refused to sign. He was placed on trial, but even threatened with the death penalty he declared that in conscience he could not sign the oath proclaiming the king head of the church. For remaining true to his conscience—placing his understanding of God's law above all other concerns—Thomas was beheaded.

Conscience is an important concept in Catholic moral teaching. Should people always follow their conscience? Ponder that question even for a few moments and a whole host of other questions arise. Not everyone is as noble as Thomas More. Do we really want all people to do what they think is right? Conscience is a judgment of reason, but isn't reasoning swayed by a person's upbringing and culture, so that people's consciences tend to differ from culture to culture? Actually, at times conscience means going against what the surrounding culture views as right and wrong. Obviously, conscience doesn't mean simply doing what "feels" right. In the case of Thomas More we discover that in difficult situations it frequently doesn't mean doing what we want to do. If we are following our conscience we recognize the moral quality of our actions, and we are obliged to follow faithfully what we know to be just and right. (See the Catechism, #1778.)

- What does "follow your conscience" mean?
- Do you think that people should follow their conscience when making moral decisions?
- Is there a viable alternative to following conscience as a basic moral principle?

- What cautions and clarifications would you include when advocating that people should follow their conscience?

Catholic Teaching on Sin

Catholic moral teaching includes the notion of sin. The Catechism begins its definition of sin with the words: "Sin is an offense against reason, truth, and right conscience" (#1849).

> Then Peter came and said to him, "Lord, if another member of the church sins against me, how often should I forgive? As many as seven times?" Jesus said to him, "Not seven times, but, I tell you, seventy-seven times."
>
> MATTHEW 18:21–22

Scripture uses a number of terms to describe sin, including one that means "to miss the mark." Sin is an aberration, a violation of our human dignity and right relationship with God and others. It is a conscious and free choice to do wrong and to go against God's will. While Protestants generally speak of our overall human sinfulness, Catholics also speak of specific sins. One reason why Catholics emphasize individual sins is the practice of personal confession. Accompanying the historical popularity of confession, books were written for priest-confessors to help them identify the seriousness of sins and appropriate penances for people who commit them. Catholic teaching distinguishes the most serious (mortal or deadly) sins and less serious (venial) sins. Underlying the practice of confession and the focus on sinful behavior is the belief that the human condition is essentially good and the church serves as an instrument of Christ by which people can be restored to sharing in the divine life with Christ.

The dynamic of the sacrament of reconciliation places sin in the context of Christ's message of salvation and forgiveness. As part of the sacrament Catholics spend time in an examination of conscience. Then, of course, the sacrament makes no sense unless they experience real sorrow for any harm they have done themselves or others. Then they lay their sins before God in confession, seeking forgiveness and the grace to reject all sin in the future.

- How can we balance recognition of sin with Christ's message of forgiveness and redemption?

Modern Catholic Social Teaching

Catholic moral teaching doesn't just provide guidance for personal behavior. It also addresses society in general and the structures of society, such as its social and economic systems. Jesus was concerned about helping people who were hurting. Modern Catholic social teaching recognizes that people are hurting not just because of the actions of individuals but also because of the way the institutions of a society operate. The current world economic system relies on people working for wages that barely provide for their family's needs. Even in our country the quality of education children receive depends largely on where they are born and on the wealth of their parents. Children who

> *Action on behalf of justice and participation in the transformation of the world fully appear to us as a constitutive dimension of the preaching of the Gospel, or, in other words, of the church's mission for the redemption of the human race and its liberation from every oppressive situation.*
>
> 1971 WORLD SYNOD OF CATHOLIC BISHOPS, *JUSTICE IN THE WORLD*, #6.

are poorly nourished don't learn as well as well-fed children. School systems that rely on outdated textbooks don't measure up to those schools with the latest facilities. Inadequate health-care and work opportunities diminish the ability of people to survive and thrive. For over one hundred years popes and bishops have spoken about "social sin" and "sinful social structures." For instance, Pope John Paul II addressed issues of social sin and social justice in his 1987 encyclical "On Social Concern."

Christianity has always called for helping people in need. However, one particular statement from a pope marks the beginning of modern Catholic social teaching. In 1891 Pope Leo XIII wrote an encyclical called *Rerum novarum*. In English it is known as "On the Condition of Labor." At the time conditions experienced by many workers were sinful. Factories hadn't been around that long, and abuses abounded. Child labor laws didn't exist. Workers had no rights. Owners determined who worked, how long they worked, and under what conditions they worked. In his encyclical Pope Leo pleaded that human dignity demanded greater concern for workers. Because of its forceful and insightful examination of an important contemporary problem, *Rerum novarum* is considered the beginning of modern Catholic social teaching. Since 1891 popes have regularly addressed new social problems, establishing a comprehensive core of Catholic teaching on justice.

- What are some ways that social systems (for example, economic, health-care, education, and criminal justice systems) can help or hurt people?
- What are some ways that Catholics can address "structures of sin"?

Living the Faith ■ For many years now Anne has brought her family to a church hall during Thanksgiving to help serve meals to people who are homeless or lack the means to provide a meal for themselves. She wants her children to know that giving thanks to God leads to giving to others.

....

Come, you that are blessed by my Father, inherit the kingdom
prepared for you from the foundation of the world;
for I was hungry and you gave me food,
I was thirsty and you gave me something to drink,
I was a stranger and you welcomed me,
I was naked and you gave me clothing,
I was sick and you took care of me,
I was in prison and you visited me.
MATTHEW 25:34–36

Sister Ignatia Gavin, C.S.A.—the Angel of Alcoholics Anonymous ■ Most Americans know someone who has struggled with alcoholism. Most Americans also know A.A., Alcoholics Anonymous, the most successful program for addressing the problem. A.A. meetings are now held in church halls and community centers in practically every community of the U.S. The strong scent of coffee and the clatter of folding chairs serve as the backdrop for these meetings where alcoholics commit themselves to helping one another keep sober one day at a time. What many people don't know is that A.A. has only been around for about seventy-five years. One of the people instrumental in the early development of A.A. was a nun from Ohio named Sr. Ignatia Gavin.

When Sr. Ignatia joined the Sisters of Charity of St. Augustine she initially pursued her passion for music through performing and teaching. In mid-life she experienced a physical and emotional breakdown. She gave up her music and became the admissions director at St. Thomas Hospital in Akron. It was there, in the mid-1930s, that Sr. Ignatia became what all of us are called to be—a wounded healer. Sr. Ignatia got into hospital work because she herself was wounded. Despite her own setbacks, or perhaps because of them, she was a person who had great empathy for people struggling with their own failings. One doctor on the hospital staff, Dr. Bob Smith, struggled with alcoholism. At the time alcoholism was not considered a disease but a moral failure. This left alcoholics to fight their problem alone and in the shadows while also dealing with the added burden of shame and guilt. Hospital policy was that beds should not be given to alcoholics but only to people who were truly sick.

As admissions director, Sr. Ignatia was determined to work with Dr. Bob to get alcoholics into the hospital to start them on the road to sobriety. However, she had to work around those in charge of the hospital who didn't want care for alcoholics to interfere with the work of the staff and take up the limited space. Sr. Ignatia came up with creative ways to get around hospital policies so that she could get alcoholics into treatment. Eventually, she turned a little-used section of the hospital into a separate wing strictly for alcoholics. There the focus was on alcoholics supporting and helping each other— again, the wounded healer model. It also opened onto the balcony of the hospital chapel where Sr. Ignatia encouraged the alcoholics to seek God's help rather than carrying the burden alone. Meanwhile, Dr. Bob Smith and a New York stockbroker, Bill Wilson, also an alcoholic, created the famous twelve-step program that has been associated with A.A. ever since. Sr. Ignatia oversaw the fledgling A.A. program at St. Thomas Hospital and then later in Cleveland. She helped initiate three guiding principles of A.A.—"trust God, clean house, help others." For her pioneering work in the care and treatment of alcoholics, Sr. Ignatia is known as "the angel of A.A."

- Give examples of how being a "wounded healer" serves as a model for living the Christian moral life.

Let Us Pray
Good and gracious God, fill us with wisdom to know your will and courage to live it. Guide us in the way of compassion, hospitality, and justice. And place a blanket of love over all that we do. Amen.

10 PRAYER AND SPIRITUALITY: KEEPING CLOSE TO GOD

From one ancestor he made all nations…so that they would search for God and perhaps grope for him and find him—though indeed he is not far from each one of us. For in him we live and move and have our being. ACTS 17:26–28

ELIZABETH MARSHALL THOMAS HAS A FASCINATING STORY TO TELL. In the early 1950s, as a teenager, she set off with her American family to Africa. Her father knew that there were people living in parts of Africa at the time who had never encountered anyone beyond their own tribe. We couldn't make such a fascinating journey today. To our knowledge, no such people—untainted and untouched by an outside world—exists. Elizabeth's father wanted to see for himself how these people lived and what they were like. He thought they would be something of a window into how most human beings lived before what we call "civilization" began. His daughter Elizabeth recorded her experiences and later wrote about them in her book *The Old Way: A Story of the First People.* She tells about a night when all members of the community she was living with spent the night dancing to drums around a blazing fire.

Some of the men entered a trance-like state and placed their hands on people to drive out the "star sickness" that causes mean-spiritedness and dissention in the community. They would scream out to the spirits to take away jealousy, danger, and death. Such all-night dances happened regularly among these "first people."

To be human is to pray. Scientists who study such matters today propose that we humans are hard-wired to experience ourselves as related to and part of a whole; in a sense, human wholeness includes holiness. As human beings, we grope for God. Indications are that our earliest ancestors had a sense of the sacred, that we humans are part of a larger, deeper reality and that we can be in touch with that reality. Through dance and drumming, ritual and art, they—or, more accurately, we human beings—sought a connection with a spiritual presence. Catholicism says that when we reach any degree of clarity in our God-seeking we discover that "in him we live and move and have our being." Catholicism has many practices aimed at helping us experience God's presence.

- According to the Catechism (#28), expressions of religion "are so universal that one may well call man a religious being." Are human beings universally religious creatures? How would you make a case for or against this statement?

Catholic Treasures, Old and New

Catholics have a treasure trove of prayers, styles of praying, and spiritual practices old and new. Catholic worship can include the ancient form of plainchant popularly known as "Gregorian

Chant," named after Pope St. Gregory the Great (d. 604). It also makes use of majestic hymns written over the course of centuries—for example, the Easter

> *Therefore every scribe who has been trained for the kingdom of heaven is like the master of a household who brings out of his treasure what is new and what is old.*
>
> Matthew 13:52

hymn traditionally known as the "Exsultet." More recently, composers of liturgical music have produced contemporary styles of music and music from various cultures for use in church services. Often these composers set to music passages from Scripture. For example, Catholics can now hear the comforting words of Jesus "And I will raise him up on the last day" sung in a contemporary style of music during funeral services. These modern hymns add greatly to the beauty and meaning of Catholic liturgical celebrations.

The sacraments are the heart of Catholic spirituality. However, many other practices help Catholics enrich their spiritual life. Some are for private use; most are intended for communal sharing. Formal prayers are linked to the great events in the life of Jesus, Mary, or the saints. Less formal prayers also connect us to the good news that is Jesus Christ. In this chapter we will look at some forms of prayer and spirituality that Catholics engage in to keep them close to Christ.

- What Catholic prayers and spiritual practices are you familiar with? Which ones appeal to you most right now? Why?
- What would you recommend for someone who is interested in developing a prayer life?

Prayer: An Intimate Conversation with a Friend

When asked, "Do you pray?" a majority of Americans today answer "yes." Most probably they mean that they take time out occasionally to ask God to help them or simply to be with them as they go about their business. Catholics also engage in such prayer. In fact, the great Spanish mystic St. Teresa of Avila says that prayer is an intimate conversation with a friend. When we're with a friend we don't always have to say words to be in conversation.

> *Prayer is essentially an attitude. We trust God, we believe in Him, we turn to Him. An attitude is something permanent. So how could prayer stop when we, as it were, stop praying? It would be as if your relationship with your parents existed only when you were in actual contact with them.*
> **SISTER WENDY BECKETT**

In that sense, Catholics don't "take time out" to pray. Rather, any prayer practice they engage in reminds them that their entire life is a "prayer."

- Do you pray? If so, when and where do you most often pray?
- What words do you find most beneficial to say in your praying?
- How are private prayer and communal prayer different, similar, and mutually enriching for you?

....

Praying is no easy matter. It demands a relationship in which you allow the other to enter into the very center of your person, allow him to speak there, allow him to touch the sensitive core of your being, and allow him to see so much that you would rather leave in darkness. **HENRI NOUWEN**

Sacred Time #1: Daily Prayer

Many Protestant churches have communion services once a month or so. The Eucharist is available to Catholics every day. Large numbers of the faithful don't attend daily Mass, but those who do so attest to the great value Catholics find in the Eucharist. It represents Christ among us in a visible, tangible way. Consecrated bread is kept in a special container, called a tabernacle, even when Mass is not being celebrated. A long-standing Catholic tradition is to spend time in the presence of the eucharistic bread in the tabernacle, if only for a few minutes. Before the fear of vandalism, Catholic churches remained open for the faithful so that they could stop in for a visit and pray at any time. Some parishes have special times when the eucharistic bread is placed in an ornate container called a monstrance so that it is visible to all. A monstrance is typically golden and circular, with rays jutting out to symbolize the healing light of the sun.

The official daily prayer of the church is the Liturgy of the Hours, also called the Divine Office. Seven times a day monks and nuns gather to chant psalms and listen to Scripture. Priests are to take time out from their day to pray and reflect on these psalms and readings. Lay Catholics are also encouraged to make use of these prayers of the church. By spending regular times in prayer each day Catholics are engaging in a type of conversation or exchange between themselves and God. They recall God's presence and respond to him in prayer. Because of the practices of daily Mass and the Liturgy of the Hours, throughout the world Catholics are unceasingly praising God and giving thanks for God's gift to us in Christ.

Another daily Catholic practice is a prayer called "The Angelus," recited three times a day to call to mind the

Incarnation. The Angelus apparently began in the early Middle Ages as a prayer to say when monasteries rang their evening bells. It was later expanded to three times a day by Franciscan friars. One theory is that St. Francis himself introduced the practice because he was impressed with the way Muslims pray five times a day. Many Catholics recite morning and evening prayers and grace (*gratia*, giving thanks) before meals as regular reminders of Christ's presence in their daily lives. If a Catholic prays upon rising, before going to bed, and then at mealtime, that would amount to five times a day.

- Why is it important to praise and give thanks to God?
- What are some ways you might incorporate prayer into your daily life?

Sacred Time #2: Sunday, Day of Thanksgiving

While Catholics can celebrate the Eucharist together every day, Sunday is a special time for weekly community worship. Don't think of Sunday as only the first day of the week. In the Christian story it is the "eighth day" of creation, the day following the Jewish Sabbath that marks the end of the biblical creation story. God created the world good. Then there was a fall from grace. The resurrection of Jesus on Easter Sunday marks a restoration of our broken union with God—a New Creation. Every Sunday celebrates this Easter event. Catholics praise, worship, and give thanks to God by participating in the Eucharist and enjoying a day of rest. Actually, Sunday rest is also worshiping God; taking time out to enjoy the day is a way to give thanks for God's good gifts

> *Remember the Sabbath day, and keep it holy.*
>
> **EXODUS 20:8**

to us. On Sunday we stop our "doing" and just "be." Sunday rest is not just physical. Whatever we do on Sunday, it is meant to be accompanied by a different mental and spiritual attitude. Sunday is a weekly reminder that, in the big picture, we live in God's time of Easter new life. For Catholics Sunday is a time to worship God and support fellow Catholics in the faith.

- How might the following activities add to or subtract from the spirit of Sunday: a picnic, gardening, sports, leisurely reading the Sunday paper, shopping, family meal?
- What would you recommend as ways to "keep holy the Sabbath"?

Living the Faith ■ Many Catholic families make sure that they enjoy a Sunday meal together and that the meal begins with prayer. They recognize that the food they eat and the companionship they share are an extension of Sunday Eucharist. Some families also include visiting relatives or shut-ins from the neighborhood as part of their Sunday ritual.

Sacred Time #3: The Liturgical Year
Does your mood change with the seasons? Do winter's cold and shortened days get you down? Is springtime invigorating? We live by the rhythms of the seasons. Even if we live in Florida or southern California, daylight is longer or shorter as the earth revolves. Since early in its history the church has

linked the great Christian themes to the seasons. If you attend Sunday Mass regularly, you can get a sense of the changes simply by observing the color of the vestments the presiding priest wears. The church year follows what is known as the liturgical calendar. It begins with Advent leading up to Christmas time, followed by Ordinary Time, Lent, the Easter season, and Ordinary Time again,

> *Within the cycle of a year, the Church unfolds the whole mystery of Christ...*
>
> VATICAN COUNCIL II, "CONSTITUTION ON THE SACRED LITURGY," #102.

until Advent begins the year anew. Each season has Sunday Scripture readings that reflect its spirit. Through Sunday liturgies, Catholics become familiar with each of the most important parts of the Old Testament, the gospels, and the rest of the New Testament.

The two great liturgical seasons of Christmas and Easter celebrate the Christian mysteries of Christ's Incarnation and his death and resurrection. At Christmas time we celebrate that Christ is among us. At Easter we celebrate his sacrifice leading to new life.

Fasting and Feasting Built into the liturgical year are periods for fasting and for feasting. Both practices acknowledge that our spiritual life cannot be separated from our bodily existence. Lent offers a time for giving up certain pleasures and for abstaining from eating for periods of time. Fasting is a spiritual as well as a physical practice, a form of prayer. In the Northern Hemisphere, Lent takes place during the closing days of winter leading up to spring and Easter. In olden days in Europe, this time of year commonly required fasting because food was in short supply. That reality didn't diminish the spiritual significance Lent had. Today Lent provides Catholics an opportunity to turn their attention toward God.

Jesus spent forty days fasting in a desert before embarking on his grueling public life. However, Jesus gained a reputation for his feasting rather than his fasting. John the Baptist was known for fasting and self-denial, not Jesus. There is a place for both built into the liturgical calendar. Lent is a time for fasting and restraint. The spirit of Advent is conversion, hope, and anticipation of the wonderful Christmas event that is coming. Christmas and Easter are times for sharing good meals and good times with family and friends.

- What do you think is the spirit underlying each of the liturgical seasons?
- What activities and prayers could help you enter into the spirit of each season?
- Would you like to see lenten practices of self-denial emphasized more or less in the church?

Private Prayer

Spiritual Reading. For Catholics, private prayer can mean quietly reciting the Our Father, Hail Mary, the rosary, or some other memorized prayer. Using your own words to pray was something Catholics tended to do on a personal level. Today Catholics are encouraged to practice a variety of private prayer forms. One type of prayer that has attracted many Catholics recently is called in Latin *lectio divina*, or "spiritual reading"—usually

> *The spiritual journey is a process of liberation, of unfolding, much like the petals of a flower in the light of the morning sun.*
>
> THOMAS RYAN

of Scripture. St. Ignatius Loyola, founder of the Jesuits in the sixteenth century, developed an approach to reading the gospels that involved trying to place oneself in the setting of a gospel story. He suggested imagining the dusty roads of ancient Israel and the reactions of people of the time to what Jesus said and did. In other words, *lectio divina* means spending time with Jesus, not just reading about him.

The Psalms. The psalms are the church's prayer book. They make up the heart of the Liturgy of the Hours and are sung or recited during the liturgy. Jesus himself was fond of quoting the psalms; some sayings of Jesus—such as his words on the cross—are actually passages from the psalms. The psalms reflect a variety of emotions and therefore can give expression to what we might be feeling during different prayer times. If Jesus knew certain lines from the psalms by heart, it certainly would also benefit us to have available phrases such as:

> "The LORD is my shepherd, I shall not want" (Psalm 23:1).

> "For it was you who formed my inward parts;
> you knit me together in my mother's womb.
> I praise you for I am fearfully and wonderfully made"
>   (Psalm 139:13–14).

The Rosary. One object popularly associated with Catholicism is rosary beads made up of five sets of ten beads strung together with a crucifix and three additional beads attached. The rosary incorporates three prayers that Catholics learn by heart—the Our Father, Hail Mary, and Glory Be. Each "decade" of the rosary (a set of ten Hail Marys) is also dedicated to a mystery in the life of Jesus or Mary—joyful, sorrowful, and glorious mysteries, and recently expanded to include what are called the five "luminous mysteries." Beads are used in many religious traditions. Hindus, Buddhists, and Muslims make use of them. They serve as a counting mechanism so that the person praying doesn't have to pay much attention to what she or he is doing. Early in the Middle Ages the rosary functioned as something of a "poor man's" psalter. There are 150 psalms. For those who can't read and don't have books available, 150 Hail Marys are recited during the course of three rosaries. That's why traditionally there were fifteen "mysteries," one to accompany each decade recited.

To appreciate the rosary, we need to think about what prayer is. Here's how St. Thérèse of Lisieux describes prayer: "For me, prayer is a surge of the heart; it is a simple look turned toward heaven, it is a cry of recognition and of love, embracing both trial and joy." Prayer for Thérèse is a surge, a turning, a cry, an embrace. Prayer happens in the "heart" rather than in the "head." It is an experience rather than a rational explanation of experience. Similarly, when a joke is funny it brings on a spontaneous "surge" of laughter. If we have to explain a joke, it's no longer funny. Any rational explanation of love also falls short of love itself. Saying the rosary doesn't require concentrating on the words said; it's more like background music. Catholics can be riding in a car or on a bus and say the rosary. It can be recited while preparing meals in the kitchen. Rosary beads on a bedside or dangling from a car's rearview mirror can help bring about a "simple look toward heaven" that is prayer.

....

Usually prayer is a question of groaning rather than speaking, tears rather than words. St. Augustine

Novenas and Litanies. Two Catholic practices that you may hear about are novenas and litanies. "Novena" derives from the Latin word for the number nine. There are prayer services that people can participate in over the course of nine days—either nine days in a row, one day a week for nine weeks, or the first Friday of every month for nine months. Novenas offer another form of concentrated prayer for Catholics. They remind us that prayer is communal and it requires perseverance. The spirit of a novena is similar to that of the disciples and Mary waiting for the Holy Spirit to come at Pentecost.

A litany refers to using a list during prayer, such as repeating "Lord, have mercy" and "Christ, have mercy" three times in a row at Mass. During baptisms and the Easter vigil, listen for a litany of saints. The leader of the service recites the names of saints and after each one the congregation responds with "Pray for us." Litanies listing the attributes of God or titles of Mary are also popular.

Litanies once again reflect the Catholic emphasis on images. Hearing the names of one saint after another conjures up images of the great communion of saints that Catholics see themselves as being part of. Hearing the Blessed Mother referred to as "Gate of heaven," "Health of the sick," "Comfort of the afflicted," and so forth in an ongoing succession of images helps Catholics appreciate Mary's role as our advocate before her son, Jesus.

Stations of the Cross. One of the ways you can identify a Catholic church is that it usually has images of the fourteen stations on its walls so that people can move around and stop and pray before each one. Each station highlights an incident during Jesus' journey to Calvary—his arrest, trial, torture, and death. Lent

is the usual time for meditating on the stations. They afford
Catholics an opportunity to connect to the horrible suffering
endured by Jesus. Some modern prayer books based on the
stations also connect them to the suffering that people endure
in our world today.

- What are some ways that you could incorporate any
  of the above Catholic prayer forms into your own
  prayer life?

Sr. Thea Bowman, F.S.P.A.—"Lord, let me live until I die." Bertha Bowman was

born in rural Mississippi in 1937. Although not
Catholic, her parents enrolled her in a Catholic
school. Bertha must have been impressed with the
sisters who taught her, for she was baptized at the
age of ten and then, to her family's surprise, at the
age of sixteen she entered the community of the
Franciscan Sisters of Perpetual Adoration, where
she took the name Sister Thea.

Sr. Thea continued her schooling as a nun in
LaCrosse, Wisconsin, a lone black woman in an
otherwise all-white religious order. She entered
into the style of prayer and spirituality commonly practiced in the American church of the
time. Traditionally, Irish spirituality dominated
American Catholicism. Most bishops and priests
were of Irish background—many came from
Ireland itself. This understated style of spirituality

was a far cry from what Sr. Thea knew growing up in Mississippi. While studying in Washington, DC, Sr. Thea again encountered the gospel music and spirituals, dancing and testifying commonly used during services in the black church. She was convinced that Catholicism and the spirituality dominant in black churches were perfectly compatible. She went on to receive a Ph.D. in English and taught in schools at all levels. Then the bishop of Jackson, Mississippi, asked her to be the consultant for intercultural affairs for the diocese. With that appointment Sr. Thea began a busy schedule of speaking before groups throughout the world. "Speaking" is not actually what she did. She would regularly interrupt her presentations and burst into song. She would tell stories and recite poems and get her audience to sing with her, standing and clapping their hands.

In 1989 Sr. Thea was invited to speak to a group of U.S. Catholic bishops. In her usual style, she coaxed the bishops to get up, clap their hands, and sing a freedom song. Although it took them out of their comfort zone, the bishops joined in and appreciated Sr. Thea's spirited approach to communicating the message of Jesus.

Sr. Thea faced another challenge when she was diagnosed with bone cancer. For years she continued her work despite her ongoing battle with cancer, giving presentations even when she was confined to a wheelchair. She was determined to live

life fully until she died. As in her other endeavors,
she succeeded at this with grace and joy.

- What spiritual practices from various cultures do you
  find meaningful for your own prayer life?
- Are there particular times and circumstances when
  different prayer forms are more meaningful for you?

Let Us Pray
Dear Lord,
we lift our hearts and minds to you.
When words fail us, we pray that you read our hearts.
When we get distracted, we pray that you accept our faltering
    attempts to praise you.
May all of our words be prayer,
our thoughts and deeds prayer, our lives prayer.
Amen.

11 CATHOLIC FAITH TODAY

I am continually with you;
*   you hold my right hand.*
You guide me with your counsel,
*   and afterwards you will receive me*
*   with honor.*

PSALM 73:23–24

AN AFRICAN FOLKTALE SPEAKS ABOUT AN EAGLE RAISED WITH CHICKENS, SO THAT IT BELIEVES ITSELF TO BE A CHICKEN, scouring the ground for bits of grain all day long. A naturalist comes along and reminds the farmer that the eagle should be soaring in the sky, not living earthbound like a chicken. The farmer says that the eagle has lived like a chicken for so long that it doesn't know how to fly. The naturalist takes the majestic bird to a mountaintop where she carefully and caringly introduces the eagle to a new way of being. After a few faltering attempts she holds the eagle high and off it flies into the sky, never to return to the life of a chicken. It has realized its true nature—it is eagle.

In a sense, Jesus is that naturalist. There's a spark of the divine within us, and Jesus caringly and lovingly wants to bring it to life. Jesus is different from the naturalist in the story in that in him God actually enters into our world of materiality and sensuality. The sacramental, incarnational perspective of Catholicism reminds us that we come to God through the stuff of the earth. The material, sensual world is God's creation; and as the saying goes, "God doesn't make junk." We don't come to God by trying to get around our earthiness; we only get there through it. Catholic faith doesn't remove us from the messiness of life but nudges us to see its connection to God in Christ Jesus. The "everydayness" of our lives is also holy. The mystery of Catholic faith is that through it all we can discover our true nature. Just as the eagle discovered its true nature that lay dormant, we are meant to share in divine nature. Catholics pray for this grace at every Mass: "By the mystery of this water and wine may we come to share in the divinity of Christ."

A Catholic's experience of faith, therefore, mingles with everything going on in our world. American society's fast pace, barrage of loud sounds, absence of complete darkness even at night, and ever-present screens affect people's prayer life and appreciation for liturgy. Wars and the state of the economy can't be separated from how people view God. Even the success or failure of favorite sports teams makes a difference in whether people are hopeful and energetic or depressed.

- How might Catholic faith affect people's perspective on "the messiness of life"?
- What recent events and developments have had an impact on your experience of Catholicism?

The "Both-And" Nature of Catholic Faith

Isn't Catholicism the same today as it always was? Yes and no.

The essence remains the same, but its expression and the challenges it faces reflect changing times and differing cultures. The Vatican has a website, and the pope has a twitter account. Some U.S. parishes now hold "get to know the faith" sessions at local bars rather than at church halls. Catholicism at its best engages in a constant interplay between the essence of the faith—the saving message of Jesus—and the challenges of the day. Personal faith is meant to be a living, dynamic experience as well. For that reason, the Catholic imagination has a "both-and" quality to it.

We strive for an ideal spiritual life, but we also need to laugh at ourselves to think that on our own we can achieve it or even believe that we can fully comprehend it. Thus, Catholicism blends together a healthy respect for soul and body,

> *The joys and the hopes, the griefs and the anxieties of the men of this age, especially those who are poor or in any way afflicted, these are the joys and hopes, the griefs and anxieties of the followers of Christ... Therefore, the council focuses its attention on the world of men, the whole human family along with the sum of those realities in the midst of which it lives.*
>
> VATICAN COUNCIL II, "PASTORAL CONSTITUTION ON THE CHURCH IN THE MODERN WORLD," #1–2.

the spiritual and the material. Mistreatment of our bodies is sinful, as is mistreatment of the earth. We see this concern for the physical in the set of "deadly sins" issued by the Vatican in 2008. One of the newly identified sins is: polluting the environment. (Reporting on this Vatican pronouncement at the time, one news journal began its account with the headline: "Recycle or go to Hell!") The earth and all creatures, including most especially ourselves, deserve utmost respect and care. Human beings are natural and supernatural, both at the same time.

Catholic spiritual life reflects this "both-and" quality as well. There's a place for "Catholic action"—go out there and change the world; make it a better place. However, action must flow from contemplation. "Contemplation" refers to a prayerful attitude that involves appreciating and experiencing the gift-edness of what is. Contemplation means the prayer of presence—simply being open to God's presence, which is always there but which we can miss if we're caught up in constant activity. Contemplation is receiving rather than giving, not doing rather than doing. There's a need for both action and contemplation in Catholic spirituality.

The interplay of rational thought and Catholic teaching also demonstrates a "both-and" approach in the pursuit of truth. A recent survey found that over forty percent of Americans don't believe in evolution. That's not the Catholic take on it. In the midst of debates about human origins that were taking place in 1996, Pope John Paul II noted that "there is no conflict between evolution and the doctrine of the faith" that God is our creator. He wasn't proposing something new here. Rather, he was simply reiterating the long-standing Catholic position that in the pursuit of truth Catholic beliefs and reason should go hand in hand.

- How do you tend to view the human condition—as "either-or" or as "both-and"? What difference does it make?
- Is Catholicism "environmentally friendly"? If so, how does Catholicism lead people to be conscientious caregivers of the earth?

***Blessed Frédéric Ozanam—Founder of the
Society of St. Vincent de Paul*** ■ Walk into an
old-fashioned Catholic church and you are likely to
find a holy water font and a container in which to
put money for those who are poor—a "poor box."
These two objects symbolize the "both-and" nature
of Catholic faith. Catholics bless themselves with
holy water to be reminded of their faith; their faith
is lived out by giving themselves for others. Here's
the story of someone who embodies these twin
dimensions of Catholic faith.

In the early 1800s intellectual life within France
was dominated by a spirit of skepticism, atheism,
and anti-Catholicism. The French Revolution saw
Catholicism as an instrument of enslavement, not
of freedom. A young man studying in Paris felt
otherwise. Frédéric Ozanam (1813-1853), had his
doubts about religion as well, but he came to see
Catholicism as the source of truth and as a means
to true freedom. Frédéric heard religion ridiculed
so often in his classes that he formed a history club
where a free exchange of ideas could be discussed
and debated. At one meeting in 1833 an oppo-
nent of religion criticized Frédéric and his fellow
Christians for being all talk and no action. They
were talking about faith while Paris was bursting at
the seams with downtrodden and desperate people.
Frédéric realized at once that this criticism was
valid. With some of his friends he began a charity
club to go along with his history club. Its members

went in pairs into the poor sections of Paris and did what they could to help the people there. By 1853 they were regularly visiting and helping a third of the poor of Paris. The club, in time named the St. Vincent de Paul Society, grew rapidly and soon spread to other European cities. Today it continues as a leading worldwide organization dedicated to helping people living in poverty.

Apart from his work with poor people, Frédéric was also a highly regarded scholar who taught literature at the Sorbonne in Paris and wrote seminal works on medieval poetry, especially Dante's great Italian and Catholic epic *Divine Comedy*. He received numerous academic awards for his scholarly work. The cause he is most famous for, care for the poor, was a full-time passion but a part-time occupation. He was married and had a daughter. He was a man of faith who also engaged in a rigid pursuit of truth. In true Catholic fashion, faith, intellectual curiosity, and service went hand in hand for Frédéric. In 1997 Pope John Paul II gave him the title "Blessed."

....

You [who are poor] are our masters, and we will be your servants. You are for us the sacred images of that God whom we do not see, and not knowing how to love Him otherwise shall we not love Him in your persons? **BLESSED FRÉDÉRIC OZANAM**

Catholic Faith and Religious Diversity

America is now a marketplace of religions. Although still predominantly a Protestant Christian nation, America has become very diverse religiously in the past fifty years. To a degree that didn't exist before, people today ask themselves, "What does it mean to be Catholic—or a member of any religion for that matter—in relation to other religions?"

A major turning point in Catholic attitudes toward other religions came with Vatican Council II in the mid-nineteen sixties. Before that time Catholics were cautioned against even entering a non-Catholic house of worship. Catholics who married non-Catholics were routinely denied marriage in the sanctuary of a church and might have a quick ceremony in the rectory instead. Certainly it would have been unacceptable for a Catholic to get married in, say, a Lutheran or a Methodist church. Then people who paid attention to the workings of the Vatican Council discovered that Protestant leaders attended the council sessions. They even had front-row seats to the proceed-

> *Does the Catholic Church teach that God wishes the salvation of all? Yes. Does the Catholic Church teach that salvation was made possible for the world through the cross of Jesus Christ? Yes. Does the Catholic Church believe that there is salvation for those who do not know Christ? Yes. Does the Catholic Church believe that salvation of those who do not know Christ is somehow made possible by Christ, whether or not those saved have ever heard of him? Yes.*
>
> GEORGE WEIGEL, *THE TRUTH OF CATHOLICISM*

ings, and Christians from every denomination seemed to get along. Afterwards, rules on Catholics and non-Catholics marrying loosened up. A Catholic might marry a Lutheran in a Lutheran church with a Catholic priest attending the service and adding a blessing. Catholic parishes joined other religious groups in various activities such as programs for needy people or inter-religious prayer services. Pope John Paul II made history by being the first pope ever to enter a Jewish synagogue and a Muslim mosque, and he gathered together world religious leaders to pray for peace in Assisi, Italy.

One of the documents that came out of the council was the "Declaration on the Relation of the Church to Non-Christian Religions." At the very beginning of this statement the council bishops point out that "One is the community of all peoples." They acknowledge that "mankind is being drawn closer together" today and that this is a good thing. All people are brothers and sisters made in God's image. Concerning other religions, the document says: "The Catholic Church rejects nothing that is true and holy in these religions. She regards with sincere reverence those ways of conduct and life, those precepts and teachings which, though differing in many aspects from the ones she holds and sets forth, nevertheless often reflect a ray of that Truth which enlightens all men" (#2).

How does the Catholic Church reconcile this openness toward and high regard for other religions with its belief in Jesus as savior of the world? About thirty years ago two scholars proposed distinctions to help explain possible outlooks on religious diversity. The terms are often used differently, and many scholars find them objectionable for a number of reasons. They do provide a vocabulary for addressing a challenging situation. Even Pope Benedict wrote about them before he became pope. Exclusivism means that my religion is the only true religion; no other religion possesses truth. Pluralism means that different religions while searching for truth express it in their own way. More than one religion can serve as an effective path to "salvation." This doesn't mean that every religion is "true" or that every belief or practice of a particular religion is good. Inclusivism from a Catholic perspective proposes that through Jesus we can come to know God who is love and who cares passionately for all people. Jesus is savior of the world and the means of salvation for all people, whether they are Catholic or not. In a sense, a Catholic inclusivist attitude toward other religions doesn't reject pluralism rightly understood. An expansive, inclusivist understanding of the people of God is expressed in Vatican Council II's "Dogmatic Constitution on the Church," *Lumen gentium*, #14–16. It says that the church of Christ is larger than and not exclusively identical with the Catholic Church. Catholics are directly connected to Christ through his church, but other people of good will are indirectly connected to Christ and his church. Members of other religions are "separated brothers and sisters," but brothers and sisters nonetheless.

- What do you think would be Jesus' attitude toward members of other religions today?
- How might someone hold onto proclaiming the truth of Jesus and Catholicism while not denigrating other religions out of hand?

Faith in Action ▪ In 2003 a group of Chicago high school students from Jewish, Christian, and Muslim backgrounds gathered together to tell their stories. In 1998 Eboo Patel, a young Muslim who had come to appreciate his own religion after working with the local Catholic Worker house, and other young people formed the Interfaith Youth Core

(IFYC) with support from the Catholic archdiocese and other Chicago leaders. The group sponsored the event because it believed that story sharing was the best way to begin to understand and appreciate oneself and others. Patel knew of what he called "religious totalitarians" with narrow-minded visions who tell young people stories to enlist them in carrying out acts of violence against others—using "religion" to support terror, for instance. The IFYC wanted to use young people's own life stories to move them away from an understanding of "Truth" that saw others as the enemy. When the young people heard one another's stories about what it is like to grow up in their particular tradition, they both appreciated their differences and also recognized their common humanity.

- What have you been taught about the relationship of Catholicism to other religions?
- What has been your experience of religious diversity? What challenges and opportunities have you faced in relation to these experiences?
- What do you see as specific ways to foster the respect for diversity advocated by the Catholic Church in recent decades?
- *American Grace*, a 2010 book on religion in America, observed that Americans tend to be very religious but also very tolerant of other religions. The authors cite what they call the "Aunt Susie Principle." Most Americans have a family member, a helpful neighbor,

or a friendly coworker who is of another religion. Because of their personal encounters with the goodness of people from other religions—"Aunt Susies"—they respect those religions. Who has been an "Aunt Susie" for you? How did that person help you appreciate that other religion?

"Spiritual" but not "Religious"?

A popular sentiment today is that many people consider themselves to be "spiritual" but don't want to be associated with any one religion. Many books are available to guide people in this kind of go-it-alone spirituality. There seems to be a spiritual hunger among many people but a reluctance to commit to an organization such as the Catholic Church that has both its dark and light sides. Far from denigrating this spiritual hunger, many church statements over the past fifty years see it as a seed that can blossom into belief in Jesus and joining the Catholic Church. For instance, in 2009 the Vatican newspaper praised the television show "The Simpsons" for its insightful portrayal of "modern people's indifference toward and great need for the sacred." Perhaps Homer Simpson's missteps and cries for help mask an actual longing for God; he wants to believe.

An ancient image for the church is that of a ship filled with pilgrim people, building on the symbolism of Noah and the ark and Jesus on the Sea of Galilee with his disciples in the storm. We hear of people today, even very young people, who sail around the globe alone in their boat—a great individual triumph. However, they're the exception; and even they have a large support system making their safe journey possible. The modern spirit praises individualism and independence but

My Lord God, I have no idea where I am going. I do not see the road ahead of me. I cannot know for certain where it will end. Nor do I really know myself, and the fact that I think I am following your will does not mean that I am actually doing so. But I believe that my desire to please you does in fact please you. And I hope that I have that desire in all that I am doing. I hope that I will never do anything apart from that desire.

And I know that if I do this you will lead me by the right hand though I may know nothing about it. Therefore will I trust you always though I may seem to be lost and in the shadow of death. I will not fear, for you are ever with me, and you will never leave me to face my perils alone.

Thomas Merton

pays a heavy price for that pursuit. Aren't we by nature communal and interdependent? That reality is not a curse or a failure. Even modern businesses, while they may tout the value of competition, actually rely more on cooperation for success. Catholic faith longs to be shared, and the Catholic Church is a very large ship. Some passengers we may not care for, but that's the nature of community. (Aren't there even members of our own family who make us groan when we hear they're joining us for Thanksgiving dinner?) And if we try to go it alone, we may miss the beauty of Jesus who is "the stone that was rejected by you, the builders; it has become the cornerstone" (Acts 4:11).

• Do you think the world would be better or worse off if people no longer believed in Jesus?
• Do you think the world today would be better or worse off without Christianity?
• Do you think the world would be better or worse off without the Catholic Church?
• What can a community do that individuals can't?

What Difference Does Faith Make?

Rich is a good man. He does his work as a school counselor conscientiously. He checks in regularly on some elderly neighbors who need help. He is involved in organizations that benefit his local community. There are a number of causes that he donates money to. He keeps up to date on world affairs. He was raised Catholic but doesn't see the point of it. He believes: "Of course we should help people out when we can and lead a good life. Why do we have to bring Jesus and religion into it? I do what I do as a human being. I don't see that Catholicism adds anything to it."

- How would you respond to Rich?

Joining the Mission

Belonging to the Catholic Church involves joining people on a mission. If it seems daunting to think that each of us has a mission, for Catholics the "mission" is really joining in the work of Jesus.

Faith itself is a gift, and any good that people do is the hand of God working through them. Over twenty-five percent of health care worldwide is provided under the auspices of the Catholic Church. Church-affiliated agencies provide a large share of social services to Americans in need. Catholic Relief Services has a reputation for providing quality help in the world's trouble spots. The Catholic Campaign for Human Development assists poor people to be self-sufficient. Catholic schools always make service to the community part of their mission and of the experience of their students.

According to Catholicism, everyone has a mission, and everyone is an essential link in the chain that binds all people together. The challenge of living a Catholic life today is to determine how best to walk in the footsteps of Jesus. Catholic consciousness develops over a lifetime. If we were to see someone whose car has broken down by the side of the road, many different thoughts and images might immediately come to mind. We may think of earlier experiences we've had being in a similar situation. We might think of a movie we saw that depicted just such an event. If we're Catholic, we would also have the Good Samaritan story in our mind nudging us to respond in a certain way. Catholics hear stories, share experiences, engage in practices, learn "rules of the road," memorize prayers and songs, reflect on symbols, and participate in rituals that shape their consciousness.

> God has created me to do Him some definite service. He has committed some work to me which He has not committed to another. I have a mission—I may never know it in this life, but I shall be told it in the next. I have a part in a great work; I am a link in a chain, a bond of connection between persons. I shall do good, I shall do His works; I shall be an instrument of peace.
>
> JOHN HENRY
> CARDINAL NEWMAN

They bring their Catholic consciousness to bear as they go about the mission of living their lives in creative and compassionate ways.

- Whether or not you are Catholic, what do you see as your mission in life?
- How might Catholic faith help people understand and carry out their mission?
- What do you see as the principal "rules of the road" laid out by Jesus and his church?

Catholic Faith Is Larger Than Oneself

In his book *Almost Catholic*, Jon M. Sweeney says that the first step on the way to being Catholic is "to acknowledge that our faith is larger than ourselves." Catholic faith is a matter of belonging that then is expressed in a set of core doctrines and practices; it's finding a home and then trying to figure out what to do from that home base. Just as we belong to our family, so being Catholic means experiencing oneself as part of the family of Jesus. Considering that Catholics proclaim Jesus as the savior of the world, that family is quite large. Jesus is good news, and Catholic faith means graciously accepting that good news and sharing it with others.

The beginning of this book told about a two-year-old girl about to be baptized being asked, "Do you want to go swimming?" She was being asked to join in something greater than herself. If Catholic faith is all that Jesus promised, then she will come to know God's love for her. That love is a gift. Faith too is a gift, as is hope. Everything about Catholicism is meant to nurture these gifts. If this book described any aspect of Catholic faith as not pointing ultimately to the message of God's love, then it has misrepresented the faith. In the end, Catholic faith recognizes that nothing "in all creation will be able to separate us from the love of God in Christ Jesus our Lord" (Romans 8:39).

- What might people get from Catholicism that they can't get from anywhere else?
- Tell the story of a reaction you had to one concept, person, or passage as you read about Catholic faith.
- Tell the story of how a previous understanding you had about Catholicism was either reinforced or

changed during your study of Catholic faith.

- What questions about Catholicism are left unanswered for you?
- What more would you like to know about Catholicism?

Let us pray

Risen Jesus, fill me with the joy of your Resurrection. Surround me with the radiant light of your glory. Transform all the areas of my life that are in need of your healing touch. Like Mary of Magdala, let me hear you whisper my name. Like the disciples on the road to Emmaus, help me to know you in the breaking of the bread, the holy Eucharist. With Thomas, let me touch you and cry, "My Lord and my God." Risen Jesus, cover me with the radiance of your love. Let me be your messenger of peace, joy, and love to all I meet. Amen.

FROM *CATHOLIC PRAYERS AND DEVOTIONS*